The Boy Who Could Swim

This is the first novel by the author. He has served as president of an NGO, worked for the UN Refugee Agency in Afghanistan, Sudan, North Macedonia, and Switzerland; Danish Refugee Council; EU in Georgia; UNICEF; and WaterAid. He roamed the globe as an independent journalist focusing on writing, photography, and documentary film. The two latter earned him awards. www.adam-jacobi.com

In the process of researching the book *The Boy Who Could Swim* the author spent seventeen days in an Iranian security prison charged with spying; witnessed a warlord in Afghanistan attack his neighbour— another warlord; had to be evacuated after a Taliban attack killed several colleagues and travelled and interviewed migrants on the move. The author's story is pale though in comparison to that of *The Boy Who Could Swim* and the many displaced children out there right now—alone and on the move.

Adam Jacobi Møller

The Boy Who Could Swim

Dedicated to the millions of Yakup's and Mariam's around the world.

Thank you to everyone around the world who has not only been a part of this journey, but made it so memorable.

In Athens—Penny and the Danish Institute as well as the many Afghans and local homeless people who made time to speak with me, especially Jacup and Hassan.

In Istanbul—Nu, Isil, and the Syrian refugees I met.

In Iran—Hasan 'the carpet maker' from Mashad as well as the hospitable Iranians and the less hospitable ones, who, if nothing else, forced me to think.

In Denmark—my parents, family, and friends who believed in me and stood by my side from afar, even when I was in peril.

In France—the hopeful and the desperate in the 'Jungle' of Calais, most notably Phillippe as well as agent AG, Pelé, and Sam Gamwise.

In Belgium—Noel and family for being there—always.

In North Macedonia; the thousands and thousands of refugees and migrants I met who had crossed the border from Greece during the late summer and autumn of 2015 as well as my colleagues in UNHCR, UNICEF, and the many NGOs and civil societies who assisted the mass flow of people in need.

In Afghanistan—friends and colleagues who gave me insight, not least of which included the fantastic Afghans I met in all aspects of life and who called Kabul, Jalalabad, Mashar-i-Sharif, and of course, Bamiyan 'home'. One day, my friends, one day.

Lakambini Sitoy who provided valuable editorial help at the early stages and Kate Papenberg who offered her advice and editorial skills towards the end.

Rubbing elbows with each of you has helped shape me and this book. Most of all Karen, Hugo and Oskar—my gems and wisest teachers.

England
France
Italy
Greece
Turkey

Iran
Afghanistan

Part I

Afghanistan

1

BAMIYAN

Sixteen hundred years ago a young monk lived in the Bamiyan Valley in the Central Highlands of Afghanistan. One day, towards the end of his daily meditation, he scratched his head and looked at the dusty, brown cliff face towering above him, feeling as though something was amiss. Many days passed and towards the end of each one, that same feeling entered his mind. He was frustrated. The missing piece was a disturbance; the peace he sought through meditation eluded him.

One day when the sun was about to set, a shadow fell on the cliff face in a way that made him smile and bow his head in awe. There it was—the missing piece. He visualised two enormous statues carved into the cliff. The brown and red rock would make a perfect frame for two giant Buddha statues that would spread peace and tranquillity over the Bamiyan Valley, touching lives around the world. Invigorated by his idea he ran to the elders in the village, his red and yellow robes trailing behind him. Short of breath and none too serenely, he stammered out the words of his vision.

At first, the elders dismissed him. But stubborn as he was, he slowly but surely managed to muster support for his grand idea. In the years that followed, two captivating Buddha statues slowly took shape, until one day they rose nearly 50 meters high on the brown and red cliff face.

On the day the sculptures were finally realised, the young monk, who was by now an old monk, sat cross-legged on a hill opposite the two great statues of the Buddhas and smiled. As he meditated, he found serenity and tranquillity at last. He was happy and felt blessed that the world was now enriched with this holy source of peace.

Little could the ageing monk have known that these two, seemingly indestructible sources of bliss would fall, blown to pieces, at the feet of a group of bearded men and young boys some sixteen centuries in the future. It would come to pass, then, that the mere existence of the statues was a crime against their deity. It took them roughly five days of disorganised demolition to flatten the two idols, which had stood carved into the Bamiyan cliff faces for generations. Now, the statues were but scattered rubble lying broken at the foot of the cliff wall.

This was the story Grandma Amaya told her grandson, Yakup. Maybe it was not completely true, but for him, it was enough, for it was here, below and above the two empty spaces where the Buddhas had stood, that Yakup had played as a little boy. He never really understood how a couple of rocks carved into the wall could pose a threat to God, when, according to the local Mullah, A.J., God was in charge of the whole world and universe; an omnipotent being. And so, he did not question the bearded men as they knew more than he did about such things.

Yakup's family was headed by his mother. It hadn't always been like that; now it was. She struggled with making ends meet for him and his two younger sisters. Every morning his mother bought vegetables on credit from a farmer to sell at the market and Yakup often helped her. She had to pay most of her earnings to the farmer the following morning. This hadn't always been the case either.

When Yakup's father was around, the farmer hadn't demanded so much. But it was the only job she had ever known and the only way to feed her children. She had lost two children already—Yakup's two brothers. The older boy had died before Yakup was born. His mother rarely talked about him. From the bits and pieces Yakup picked up, he imagined that his older brother had been the pride of the family. Yakup both admired and resented this mysterious older brother. He admired him for being strong and loved by his mother, but resented him for those same reasons.

His other brother had died at birth. Yakup had a grim suspicion that his mother preferred those dead brothers to him; that she was blaming him for the loss of her two other sons.

When Yakup was done helping his mother in the morning, he rushed to school. He used to attend class under a tree. One tree sheltered an entire group of children and their teacher—the whole class. Now the school was a brown clay house with long wooden benches and small ramshackle tables. There were about 30 boys in the class, which had moved from under the tree to under a roof. There was Rafi, who could run faster than the others. The twins, Zabi and Zamir, who always wrestled each other and anyone else who wanted to, but only lost to each other. Then there was Haroon, the top student who came from an influential family. Farhad had a poet's heart and impressed the girls, and the teacher, by reciting verses he had memorised. And then there was Rashid. He was a few years older and was bigger than the rest of the boys. His two friends, Dani and Osman, always followed him around and spread fear among the rest of the class.

The teacher had studied in Kabul, lived in Pakistan and worked in Iran. He was a clever man. Yakup enjoyed how, in class, his own mind got busy and drifted into maths, literature, physics, languages, and his favourite subject, history.

After school, Yakup would walk home along the winding dirt roads. He lived, together with his family, in one of the many caves that now marked the hills around where the Buddha sculptures used to be. The afternoon hours, before his mother returned from the market, were the most precious of the day. His two sisters, younger than he, were usually at home then.

Nooren, or Noor as most people called her, was the older of the two. Noor was the quiet type. She helped their mother with the daily chores, to the extent that sometimes she seemed more of an adult taking care of her mother than the other way around.

Zahra was the youngest. To the envy of Noor, the boys kept an eye out for Zahra and for good reason. While Noor was not unpretty, Zahra had an aura that pulled most people towards her— boys in particular. But Zahra did not eye the boys back. She preferred to outdo them at brain games or outrun them in races.

Grandma Amaya had always been there. She didn't know how old she was exactly, but she could tell stories from her childhood when Emir

Amanullah Khan had declared independence from British influence as well as from time spent under the reign of Zahir Shah, the King of Afghanistan.

Yakup and his sisters knew no greater indulgence than to listen to her stories. He imagined her as a child with the soft skin of a young girl, playing in an Afghanistan so different from the one he knew. Today her wrinkled skin proved to be more of a history than any of the rewritten tests in his books at school. It was a history of hardship, having been forged by equal parts scorching summer sun and freezing winter winds.

Around that same time of day, when the sun painted the Bamiyan Valley in orange and pink, Yakup's mother returned home. She brought back picked-over vegetables that none of the customers had found worthy of their money—black, speckled carrots and potatoes, mushy onions.

"Come! Help me with dinner," Noor said to Zahra.

"Noor jan, I have to study. It is important for my future," Zahra said as she cocked her head and bit the tip of her pencil. She frowned, her eyes brightening as she began scribbling in the tattered notebook she held in her lap.

"What is important for your future, is that you learn how to cook what little we have and avoid burning the naan. No man will marry you if you cannot fix him a satisfying meal," Noor said. She rearranged the steaming black pot, heavy with layers of soot, on the crackling fire and poured a bit of water over the vegetables.

"When I have an education, I can get a job. I don't need a husband. They just expect you to give them children and to cook and clean," Zahra said. She stopped scribbling in her little notepad and cupped her chin in her hand as great thoughts materialised in her mind.

"An education does not put food in your belly," Noor said.

"An education can give me a job. I want to be in control of my own life and not depend on some stupid, ignorant man." She turned her back on Noor and continued her scribbling.

"I am sure Maman will think differently, especially when I tell her that you do not want to cook," Noor said. The threat of telling their mother was usually enough for Zahra to put her notepad aside. It was hard to say if Zahra was really a bad cook, or if she did her worst out of spite. The consequence was that Noor was the master chef and Zahra her recalcitrant assistant.

After dinner their mother did a few chores and then either fell asleep or simply sat at the entrance of their cave home, staring up at the night sky. None of them knew what went on inside her head during these late evening moments.

Grandma Amaya would often take the children aside and ask, "Noor, tell me, did you pay attention in class today?"

Zahra and Yakup always tried to keep grandma Amaya's post-dinner questions to a minimum; not because they did not want to answer her, but rather, they knew that if it was one of those nights when grandma Amaya felt so inclined, she would tell them a story from the old days. Sometimes these tales were about her own life; other times, they were about Afghanistan.

"I paid as much attention as was expected of me," Noor would say, combing out her long dark hair.

"Remember, Noor jan, that a good man does not only want someone who can take care of him, but also someone whom he can talk to," grandma Amaya said.

"Maman only went to school for a few years. Was Baba not a good man, Grandma Amaya?" Noor would retort, with the comb moving rhythmically through her hair.

"Of course, he was—one of the best," grandma Amaya said. "But life has a funny way of changing with the passage of time. Throughout time a society shifts and changes, and with it so too do the expectations of the people living in it. More girls go to school these days It is expected that you have some knowledge, that you can calculate small sums, and most important, Noor jan, that you can think for yourself. You never know how long a man may last in this country."

Grandma Amaya would look toward her daughter-in-law sitting cross-legged at the mouth of the cave, the flames from the fireplace sent shadows dancing around her. Yakup's mother gazed into the darkening sky, as though she were far away. The neighbouring caves began to appear one by one, like stars in the night sky, as the evening's fires burned bright, each with their own stories.

"I came second in the spelling test in school today. Only that 'know-it-all' Neelab, beat me," Zahra interrupted. Grandma Amaya turned her gaze towards her granddaughter and smiled. "I think, I will do better next time, but all this cooking is stealing valuable time from my studies," Zahra said, sending a baleful look in Noor's direction. Her older sister had put the comb down and was looking at her nails, ragged from the constant housework.

"Zahra, if you do not give some of your time to the house chores, then Noor and Yakup will not have time for their homework. Education is important for all of you," Grandma Amaya said.

"But if Noor really wants to cook and I really want to study, why do we have to make sacrifices for what the other does not value, Grandma?" Zahra asked. Noor looked up from her nail-styling efforts and nodded approval.

"The Russians did what they wanted. The Mujahideen and warlords did what they wanted. The Taliban did what they wanted. What if everyone did what they wanted?" Grandma Amaya asked. There was silence for a while.

"Do you understand that we have to respect each other? That there are different needs and wants? We cannot all get what we want," she continued.

"I just want a man," Noor said, looking into the waning glow thrown off by the embers of the dying fire.

"One day you will find a man, but make sure he is the right one for you," Grandma Amaya said. "If you give the wrong man your little finger, he will devour the whole of you. This is not a place where women have much control over their own lives."

Noor filled their cups with chai. Steam floated from the four cups towards the rocky ceiling of the cave. She placed one cup at the cave entrance next to her distracted mother.

And while Grandma Amaya told her grandchildren the story of how their grandfather had married her, Maman sat, motionless, staring up at the night and contemplated her own, dark past.

2

FATHER

He remembers how his father's beard tickled him when he held him in the air and tossed him around and made him laugh so much that he almost threw up. He remembers how all three siblings tackled their father in an attempt to wrestle him to the ground, but always ended up being tickled until tears streamed down their cheeks. He remembers Baba's friendly eyes and how a sparkle came into them every time he looked at Maman. He remembers, too, how his mother giggled like a little girl whenever Baba teased her and held her in his arms. He remembers how his mother was someone else back then. He remembers how it was before it all changed.

Yakup's father was a Hazara like most others in Bamiyan and able to trace his heritage back to the steppes of Mongolia. He was also a farmer and worked for a landowner in the valley. He didn't make much money, but not many of the men did. That was how it was. He was a hard worker and respected by his colleagues. His father before him was a farmer and so was his father before him.

Sometimes, after school, Yakup went to the fields to meet his father on the way home and carry his tools or his bag for him. Men greeted them on their walk home. He thought his father knew everyone and that everyone knew him.

It was a late autumn afternoon and the Bamiyan Valley was orange with dust glimmering in the sun. The fields were being harvested and around the boy and his father were bundles of hay neatly packed and prepared to be stacked in the warehouse. After the Taliban were unseated from power, many foreigners came with ideas and money. Most left soon after with broken ideas and empty pockets.

"Afghanistan is changing, Yakup jan. If the government and the foreigners live up to their promises, then we might see more development, even here, in Hazarajat, our ancestral," Baba said.

A tired donkey pulled a wagon past them, wheels groaning under the heavy load.

"Son, if you study and do well, you can get a job much better than that fated to you as a farmer," Baba continued. Yakup pondered this. The Hindu Kush and Koh-i-Baba Mountain ranges stretched into the distance, the limits of Yakup's world.

"But you're a farmer, Baba. Is there something wrong with farming?" Yakup asked and looked up at his father's weather-beaten face. The man smiled and looked down. A rough hand tousled the young boy's brown hair.

"There is nothing wrong with farming. If you have enough land, farming can be a very good business and many people can make a living from what they sow. We are beholden to landowners, though, Yakup jan, which makes us vulnerable to a failed harvest. We could lose everything to a cousin first in line for a job, an accident or an illness. This would have terrible outcomes for us." The yellow cornfields, still waiting to be harvested, danced like waves in the wind and hissed like snakes ready to do battle with the scythe.

"If you and your sisters become educated and get jobs, you can perhaps offer yourself and your families better lives and more security," his father said.

"I feel secure," Yakup said.

"That makes me happy." But Yakup could see that his father did not look happy. Two dogs were growling and fighting over a bone by the side of the gravel road.

"Your two brothers would have been alive today if I had been wealthy enough to afford to call a doctor for them," his father lamented, looking away. It could have been the wind blowing dust obscuring his vision, but Yakup was almost certain that he saw tears springing forth in Baba's eyes. It was the first time he had ever seen his father cry, and so he took the man's hand in his and held it. It made him feel like a big boy, and a sudden sympathy for his dead brothers swept through him. He felt proud and happy to be there for his father. If his brothers were alive, he wouldn't have been. The thought made him shudder and the feeling of pride quickly subsided to that of cold guilt.

3

WATER

As it was the weekend, the family intended to go to the Band-e-Amir lakes for a picnic. The drive was long so they had to get up early. Autumn was still warm, though the days were getting shorter. This would be the last picnic at the lakes this year. Earlier that summer Yakup's father had taught him how to swim, and as the end of the season was approaching, he had become a decent swimmer.

For Yakup, these moments with his father were pristine, as he relished the uninterrupted time they got to spend together, free from worry and worldly care.

"Don't forget to pack the naan and the lamb kebab," Maman said to Noor.

"They're already in the bag together with the tomatoes, salad, lemons, peppers, onions and juice," Noor replied.

"Good girl," Maman said as she gently touched her daughter's neck.

"Where is Zarha?" she asked, looking around.

"She is with Baba fastening the bundle with the blankets and spare clothes," Yakup said.

"Everything is under control, Nooreen jan," Grandma Amaya said and put a hand on Yakup's shoulder.

Yakup's father had arranged a lift with one of his friends. It was a three-to-four-hour drive depending on traffic, accidents, weather and chai stops. The road was good this morning. It hadn't rained for a while and not a cloud was visible in the pale morning sky. The tarmac soon turned into a gravel road that took them deeper into the valley, leaving the cave and the empty cliff that had once housed the Buddhas behind them.

As usual, they played games in the car, sang songs, and once in a while, Grandma Amaya would tell a story. The car moved along the curved road, past soft honey-coloured hills, continuing upward through the passes of rugged mountains until it would finally reach the lakes. The three lakes appeared as tiered pools of turquoise water, one below the other and the next.

As soon as the car came to a halt, Yakup and Zahra rushed out to find a spot among the many picnic camps. They zigzagged their way through the juicy smell of roasted meat, the cries and laughter of children, the men in their loose shalwar kameez, who drank tea and smoked and the chatting and laughing women in their veils and burqas. Swan paddle boats, crowded with teenage boys and fathers with their children, dotted the lake. On the other side of the shore was a small mosque and a little shed near the water for women to cool themselves in the lake. The women entered in their veils and burqas, dipped themselves away from the curious gaze of the men, and returned to the shore refreshed and hidden away still under the cover of their garments. Yakup's mother and Grandma Amaya never went to the women's shed.

"If those women want to submit themselves to the silly rules imposed by long-bearded men with turbans, they are welcome, but I will not," Grandma Amaya said and frowned.

"Why do they have to go into that ugly little cage, grandma?" Zahra asked. She was barefoot and still too young to wear a veil or burqa. She sat on the blanket next to Noor, who wore the veil with no complaints, and grandma Amaya, who had decided that she could not be bothered too much with either of these two, considering her age.

"Some people believe that it is disrespectful to God if women show their hair, and curse me, any part of their body," Grandma Amaya said, and shook her head in visible dismay, allowing her hair to fall loose in the breeze. Zahra looked at her feet.

"Why did God give us hair and body then?" Zahra asked. Grandma Amaya lifted her skirt with a bit of a smug smile and revealed her ageing legs, replete with their varicose veins.

"Dear girl, I don't think that it was God's intention, but some people who believe they have a special status to convey God's intention, pretend that men are above women, and they use God as a reason, an excuse," she said.

"Don't give the girl ideas," Maman snapped. "She is rebellious enough as it is. It will only bring her trouble."

"The children have to know what is up and down in life," grandma Amaya said. "But your Maman jan has a point. In a male-dominated world, we women have to be careful not to step on the wrong toes. Even a light but wrong step can make you stumble and fall, Zahra jan."

At this point, Baba joined them. He had been drinking chai with a group of men he knew. "What a beautiful sight that meets a simple farmer on this wonderful day. Would the lovely children, the esteemed grandmother and the beautiful lady that I'm lucky enough to call my wife, allow this humble farmer to join?" Yakup's father said. They all laughed.

"Before I eat, I believe a good swim is in place. Who will join me?" he asked as he looked around, undressing all the while. Yakup immediately got up and followed his lead. Yakup's mother stayed put and so did Noor. Grandma Amaya looked at Zahra, who looked at her bare feet.

"I'm coming!" Grandma Amaya yelled. "Zahra, can you help an old woman into the water?" Zahra looked up and smiled. Their mother was about to say something, but before she had a chance to intervene, their father grabbed Zahra and lifted her high in the air.

"Of course, my sweet little daughter should not be left here on the shore. Come Grandma Amaya; Zahra and I will help you," Baba said, while their mother conceded the battle with a vague smile. Noor stayed with her and helped prepare the food.

Grandma Amaya and little Zahra stayed in the shallow part. Yakup and his father played with them for a while, splashing the water and lifting Zahra high in the air before letting her go in a mix of fear and laughter. When they had had enough the men prepared for their swim.

Throughout the summer they had built up a routine that grew longer each time. Yakup couldn't keep up or swim as far as his father in the beginning, but as the summer grew shorter, he swam farther and farther.

"I feel strong today, son. Are you up for a long one?" his father asked while stretching sinewy arms. "It may be the last swim of the season, so we might as well use all our energy before the end of summer—no reason to hold back." He looked at Yakup with a challenging frown, blinked, and dove into the turquoise water. His wet body surfaced a few meters away. His back glimmered in the sun. Then his arms attacked the surface of the water while his legs worked up and down, generating a contrail of white foam. Yakup followed ready to prove to baba that he was worth three sons.

It felt good. Yakup sliced through the cool water. His arms and legs worked independently of his mind. Air coursed in and out of his lungs at every third stroke. He didn't have to count any more, as he had in the beginning. His thoughts escaped him and travelled across hills and mountains. He crossed deserts, seas and cities in faraway places he didn't know. He moved like clockwork: tick-tock, tick-tock, tick-tock; air, strokes; tick-tock. And then he felt a hand on his leg.

"Son, that is how far I can go… I'm impressed!" His father panted, glistening with water and smiling in approval at Yakup, who himself was panting from the effort. His father dipped his head in the water and gave his son a hug. Yakup felt like bursting with pride. Tears poured from his eyes, but the water gave him cover and if his father noticed, then he did not show it.

"Come. Let's return to shore." Yakup followed him, dizzy from the physical effort. The sun remained high in the sky and bathed them in heat and light.

"Isn't that Rashid?" Yakup's father pointed at a boy who sat alone on the shore. Yakup looked up and confirmed that, indeed, it was Rashid, his bullying classmate.

"Do you want to go and say hello?" Yakup's father asked. Rashid did not look happy and Yakup did not want to spoil the moment.

"Maybe another time. He looks busy."

"Fine," his father said and started off towards the women who had finished preparing lunch. Yakup turned and peered through the reeds at the lake shore where Rashid was sitting with a group of young men smoking and talking under a tree. Their voices travelled on the wind.

"Rashid, what are you doing? Do you think the chai makes itself?" one of them chided.

Rashid reluctantly got up.

"My little brother thought he came here to be with the men. Rashid, you are just a boy. Well, a big one I must say," Rashid's brother said and drew the outlines of a fat belly in the air. The rest of the group burst out laughing. As Rashid passed with the kettle, his brother grabbed his flank and tugged at his flesh. The kettle fell to the ground, spilling the chai.

"You clumsy fool! If you cannot hold onto a kettle just because someone pulls you a little, how do you think you would do in a fight? If you drop your weapon, you die." Rashid's brother yelled.

"Feel this," he said squeezing Rashid's flank. "This brother of mine has enough flesh to feed a family for a whole winter." Rashid yelped and wriggled to escape his brother's torture. But behind him was the water and in front, the others were laughing. When he realised that there was nowhere to go, he stopped struggling.

"Let us see this mighty belly that you have grown." Rashid's eyes flickered as he searched for escape or sympathy. He found none.

"Come now, little brother. Or do you prefer it the hard way?" His bother made a move to get up. Rashid flinched and took off his kameez shirt. It fell to the ground. "Brother. What are you hiding behind that skin?"

"Maybe he has stored a goat in there," one of the others chimed in.

"Or all the baker's bread," another said. Rashid stared at his feet, his face red.

"I think I know what it is," a third one said. "He has taken all the candy the foreign soldiers are trying to buy our hearts and minds with. I guess all they got was one fat kid. Or maybe that's the foreigner's strategy—to fatten up the children of Afghanistan so they can no longer fight." The older boys roared with laughter.

"Look at me," his brother said, and stood up. He dropped his shirt, revealing a muscular physique. He moved closer to Rashid and tightened his upper arm. "Now feel this, brother, and tell me what it is." Rashid lifted his hand and reached out to touch his brother's flexed bicep. The older boy grabbed Rashid's soft upper arm with a quick move and stared into his eyes. "You are my brother! Even though we don't have the same mother, you bring dishonour to our family, understand? You are fat and stupid. The kids in your class are younger than you, yet they are doing better." He slapped Rashid's fat belly with his palm.

"What do you think our father would say if he was still alive? He died for our country, fighting for our future. We have to stay strong and fight for our future. You cannot do that if you are fat and stupid. Do you understand?"

Rashid nodded trying to suppress hot, wet tears.

"Are you crying?" his brother yelled into Rashid's face. His hand moved quickly, leaving five red finger marks where the slap had impacted.

"Now cover your fat belly, make us some tea and get out of the way." He threw Rashid's kameez in his face and sat down. Rashid walked out of the circle and sat down with his head resting on his hands and knees, a subordinate animal suffering at the hands of its master.

From behind the reeds, Yakup edged away, but the noise alerted the injured animal. Their eyes locked and Yakup saw a sort of begging request in Rashid's. He looked away and started off, but could not help glancing back at Rashid. By now, however, there was no longer any plea in the eyes of the animal. Yakup could sense the unspoken threat—a carnivore threatening its prey. He turned and hurried back to his family.

"Ah, there you are," his father said as Yakup reached their blanket, the food spread over it and ready to eat.

"Did you go and see Rashid after all?" the man asked with a smile. Yakup nodded.

"Good. That kid has had a difficult time. No father, the only son of his mother, and brothers who believe that fighting is the only way forward. He needs friends. I'm proud of you, Yakup jan." Noor handed Yakup a plate with food, but he had lost his appetite.

4

BROKEN

Every spring the nomadic Kuchi people cross parts of the Central Highlands of Afghanistan with their flocks of animals in search of pastures to graze freely. If this does not come to pass, then the animals die and the lifeblood of the Kuchis disappears. The lives of these nomadic tribes depend on seasonal migration. They travel with their flocks of sheep, goats, camels and donkeys. They camp with their tents and often keep to themselves so as to be left in peace.

Every year the Hazara farmers in the Central Highlands lose vast quantities of crops—land destroyed and water resources depleted—when the Kuchis pass through the steppes. The animals eat the crops and drink the water. The lifeblood of the highland farmers disappears.

This struggle has been so for a long time and brings with it arm-to-arm combat, pitting nomad against farmer year after year. All able men must join the battle—a sort of moral obligation for boys and men of a certain age.

"Why do you have to take up arms?" Yakup's mother asked Baba. "You have a family to take care of. What will become of us if you don't…" she let her question linger, unasked.

"I will come back… like I do every year," Baba assured her as he wrapped the mother of his children in a warm embrace. But she collected herself and brushed him off.

"It is stupid! The land and crops are not even yours! These people are just using you. They… they send you and the other poor men and boys to the front with old rifles to protect *their* land, while they sit and sip chai in comfort and await the results in the safety of their remote shelters." Her entire body shook, reflecting both fury and fear.

"If the crops are destroyed there's no work for me. I am a man. I must protect my family. If that means protecting another man's land so be it." He walked back and forth in the confines of the cave.

"I am a good worker. For that I'm respected. But if I do not take part in the fighting, that respect will evaporate and the landowner will hire another worker to take my place," Yakup's father said with frustration.

"Why can't all these foreigners do something? What if the landowners took these problems to the United Nations or the foreign soldiers with all their expensive equipment? Perhaps, then, you could borrow their modern war machines to do battle?" she pleaded.

"If these foreigners were serious about helping us, why do you think that, after all these years in our country, it is *we*, us, who still fight in the south, the east, the north and the west for our land? Why are we living in a cave? Why do our children, the elderly and the weak die come winter? Why are they leaving without fixing the problem they came to solve? No, this is *our* country. And no matter how many foreigners with expensive machinery and promises come to our land, we will be the ones left with it, and we have to deal with those problems left unresolved along with the new ones they create," he said.

"You have to promise me to come back. I don't know how to live without you," she admitted.

"I promise," he said and held her for a while in the small cave. The centre of their universe. Their home.

Grandma Amaya sat with Zahra, Noor and Yakup near the fireplace. She had scooped them all into the folds of her soft, black dress and they allowed themselves to be comforted by her familiar scent and warm embrace.

Yakup wanted to be strong. But he was scared. For the first time, he saw his father as a fragile man, a farmer working for pennies to create wealth for others. He imagined his father wandering along the rough and merciless land, an old rusty rifle with a wooden handle on his shoulder, together with a group of boys and men that, like him, were supposed to provide for and protect their families. Proud, yes, but still fearful of the outcome.

Among his siblings in his grandmother's lap and with the glow of the fire on his face, Yakup saw death in the glaring eye of the sun. Shots ringing out. Men shouting. Fighters falling like lumps of meat.

When Yakup's father left to fight the nomads this time, it was really no different than any other year. The sun was growing stronger and the days longer. For Yakup and his sisters the absence of their father, and their mother's incessant worrying, stretched their days and evenings to breaking, but they still went to school, helped out at home, listened to grandma Amaya's stories and played on the hillside near the empty hollows where the Buddhas once stood.

One afternoon, a party of three men came wandering up the path towards their home. Yakup's mother was inside preparing food, Grandma Amaya and the girls were at the market and Yakup was sitting right outside the cave doing homework.

The three men approached him. Yakup recognised one of them as the landowner's foreman, who had once given Yakup a piece of candy. The two others had AK-47s hanging from their shoulders.

"Hello Yakup," the foreman said. "You have grown." He measured Yakup with a glance and pulled something from his pocket. "Here's some candy. Is your mother here?"

Yakup pointed to the interior of the cave with the hand not holding the sweet in its crisp paper wrapping.

"Do you mind fetching her?" he said, gazing towards the cave. Yakup got up and went in. His mother was chopping onions.

Her eyes were watering from the job. Yakup stood there and looked at her for a while, hoping that the men outside were but a fragment of his imagination. They hadn't told him why they had come. But deep down Yakup knew that it was not good news that they bore. He imagined how his mother would blame him. Yakup already carried the heavy burden of not being his brothers. Would a lost father now be added to that load? She looked up and wiped her wet eyes.

"What are you doing?" she asked. Yakup remained silent.

"Have you grown dumb, son?" She placed a tomato in her hand and started slicing it. When Yakup didn't move, she put it down and rose.

"What is wrong?" she asked and took her son's hand. He started to cry, and she took him in her arms.

"There, there, son, what is wrong with you? Did you hurt yourself?" She caressed Yakup's hair. He was reminded of a time he barely remembered any more; a time when he was still his mother's son. He had forgotten how her love was and he ravenously devoured every bit of it, fearing that she would soon forget to love him again.

When she finally read the apprehension on Yakup's face, her motherly instinct evaporated.

"Baba," Yakup said in a thick voice. His mother looked towards the door. Light poured into the dim cave. She remained still for a few seconds. The air grew instantly heavy and it was difficult for any of them to move. His mother slowly walked towards the entrance and outside to the foreman. Yakup stayed where he was for what felt like hours. When she came back inside, she looked at her son. Her veil covered all but her eyes.

The softness that moments before had made Yakup feel like a proper son, was gone from her eyes. Two burning and condemning mirrors were all that remained. It was as if the little love and optimism she had left were reserved now for his smaller sisters only. It was a trade-off of sorts: by directing her pain and sorrow at Yakup, she could create a small space in which to still love Noor and Zahra.

The spring continued into the summer like always. To most, it was not different from any other year. People grew older, couples got married, some had children and others, like Yakup, lost their fathers.

5

SEEKING

The time that followed was difficult. Yakup needed answers to questions that had none; questions that adults learned to accept, but that children, with their clarity and naivety, neither fully come to accept nor understand entirely. And so, Yakup queried anyone who would listen.

Mullah A.J. was old. People went to him for advice, asking, *how do I ensure a good harvest? Why is my cow only yielding half the milk it used to? Why is my baby crying? Will my son be a successful and rich man? Should my daughter marry the neighbour's oldest son?*

Yakup knew him from the Madrasah. For hours he and the other boys had to sit and recite the Quran. If a boy forgot to recite and instead thought about a recent cricket match, his football skills or how he would impress a girl by showing off his ability to throw stones, the punishment was often swift and fierce. Mullah A.J. could miraculously detect when a boy was mumbling gibberish and not verses from the holy book. In his white cloak, he silently drifted around the chanting boys. Only when he had passed the daydreaming boy, did his cane take flight, and with an accuracy built up by years of practice, reduce a boy's ear to a thin red line speckled by bright, red. In tears from the stinging pain, the boy then recited as if his life depended on it. Gone were the dreams of championing sports and impressing girls. Left was the humiliation and the knowledge that his ear would reveal that he had neglected the Quran, which might very well earn him more punishment when he got home. Mullah A.J.'s effective disciplinary methods never left a sinner without a permanent reminder of how he very, nearly grew estranged from the holy book.

Yakup had only felt the shame of the cane once. Since then, he learned to be wary of the elder and his cane. Yakup's father had enjoyed the doubtful honour of the Mullah's cane when he himself was a boy, which meant that when Yakup came home with a red ear, his father simply laughed it off as an unavoidable experience that all boys in Mullah A.J.'s Madrasah had to go through. His mother was more cautious and worried about how this might reflect on the family. Yakup himself only cared about the stinging pain.

Yakup was in fact not too bothered by religion, but he thought that maybe, just maybe, Mullah A.J. could help with answers to his questions. So, one day after school, Yakup stayed in the mosque and helped with the cleaning.

He had been particularly active and had proved his dedication by reciting the Arabic verses throughout the day.

"You did well today," Mullah A.J. said and smiled at Yakup. He had put the cane aside. "How are things at home?"

"We are moving on," Yakup said.

"Your father was a brave man. He is respected for his dedication to the struggle," he said. The end of his white cotton turban hung heavily across his shoulder and ended halfway down his chest. He wore a white shalwar kameez. The hem dragged along the floor as he walked. Perhaps it had fitted him better before the years began to lay heavily upon him, too. Fine black kohl lined his eyes, already opaque with cataracts. His beard, downy with flecks of black, competed only with the ends of his turban in length.

"He is a martyr, and as such, is in heaven with the other great men," the Mullah said. The mosque was empty but for the two of them.

Dust was playing in the rays of sun that cut through the windows, cutting and carving shapes of luminescence in the tiled floors.

"Why did he have to die?" Yakup asked. The Mullah looked at him through his yellowing eyes.

"We all have to die and leave our earthly lives. That is a consequence of life and how God decided it to be. Your father is in a better place now. He is happy there," Mullah A.J. said.

"How can he be happy without Maman and me and Zahra and Noor? He left us. We are mourning and in pain. He left us with no way to survive. Why would God do that to my father and to us?" The Mullah sat pensively and thought for a while.

"First remember this: God cannot be questioned, my son. All he does, he does with great purpose and your father, you and your family have a role to play. We are but men and cannot understand all God does. He is omnipotent," Mullah A.J. said.

"But you said my father is happy now?"

"Your father has moved beyond, and he understands why his sacrifice was necessary. He expects you to respect the will of God. He is happy because he has realised God's plan. You live on earth only a fragment of the totality of time, while the kingdom of God is eternal. Do you understand?" The Mullah said. Yakup felt he understood the meaning of the words, but not the rationale. The Mullah didn't give him any clear answers.

"Yes," Yakup said and told the old man that he had to go home and help his mother.

Deep in thought, Yakup walked along the narrow dirt path that crawled up the rocky walls behind the mosque. Lizards rushed under rocks and into the yellow grass with each and every step he took. His mind was not satisfied. No matter what the Mullah told Yakup, he knew that his father would not be happy knowing that his family was in pain. How could he be?

He did not walk straight home. Instead, he climbed the path to reach the peak above their home. This was where he found Grandma Amaya. She had not noticed her grandson treading up the path. Yakup stopped before he reached her. From up there, the family had a panoramic view of the valley. This was the sight the two lost Buddhas had once enjoyed for centuries—the Bamiyan Valley with the changing rock colours going from yellow, dark and red, to fields of yellow and green. The valley's inhabitants being born and dying all beneath their watchful eye. In the background, the Hindu Kush and Koh-i-Baba Mountain ranges stood with white peaks, forming a natural bowl of protection for the valley. To the east lay Kabul, and further, to the west, Herat.

Grandma Amaya was sitting in silence, the sun warming her. Her white hair hung loose and framed her furrowed face; it looked like the bark of an old tree. *How much longer was God allowing her to stay?* Yakup wondered.

"Come here my child," grandma Amaya said. As always, Yakup had underestimated her senses but was pleased to be invited to join her. He sat next to her, and for a while, stayed that way.

"Grandma Amaya, can I ask you something?"

"Of course! But I cannot promise you that I have an answer," she replied.

"Why did God take Baba away?"

"God did not take away your father. A gun did… A gun held by another man, trying to survive… We Afghans have been fighting for such a long time that we have forgotten what it means to not fight. Unfortunately, it is often the poor people, like us, who are sacrificed first. The men in power believe that we are dispensable and that they are more worthy of life as compared to us… So, no, God did not take your father— powerful men who have forgotten why we are here killed your father and they will continue to stand idly by while many more poor Afghans face slaughter," Grandma Amaya said as she took Yakup's hand with her crooked fingers and rough palms, squeezing reassurance into his.

"Mullah A.J. told me that God has a purpose with everything he does and that we are not meant to understand why he does it, but to just accept it because he knows everything," Yakup said. A lazy bee was trying to land on a lonely yellow flower that had grown in between two rocks. Its wings froze every time it tried to land on the fragile flower, which would kneel beneath the load until the bee, too wary to continue the exercise, departed, unfazed.

"Mullahs say a lot, but often very little. It is easy to answer a question if you can refer to a greater purpose. It can explain everything and at the same time not explain anything. I have known the old Mullah since he was a little boy," Grandma Amaya said. "In the beginning, he worked in one of the small villages. He was green and wanted to have an answer to everything. There was no doctor in the village and those who couldn't go to the nearest doctor would come for advice. There was a woman who had a sick infant. The child cried and cried and despite having no medical expertise, Mullah A.J. prescribed a drug that he thought could soothe the child and stop her from crying.

"He recommended the mother administer a small portion of the drug to the child every day until the baby recovered. The crying ceased, but unfortunately, the baby became addicted to the opium prescribed. Soon after, the child succumbed to her sickness in even more pain and misery due to the side effects of the Mullah's miracle cure. That baby was not the first nor the last to suffer at the hands of an ill-informed religious leader who thought he had the answer to everything. Mullah A.J.'s explanation to the mother of that first little victim was the same as he gave you."

Down in the valley, the horn of a truck wailed and reverberated throughout the canyon walls until it, too, died away.

"Religion is too easy an escape. It is a dangerous and powerful tool used by some people to obtain power, to suppress or abuse. We have to believe… and I do, but the dogmatic nature of religion does little good, especially in the hands of the wrong people.

"The Buddhas were created from religion and destroyed by it," she said, and looking at her grandson, continued, "This is what I think: you have to make up your own mind. Just remember this: there are many sheep that are only looking for the smallest hint of an opportunity to cry wolf, and in so doing, cull the herd. It is important that you are careful, then, when and where you question religion and God."

Yakup thought he knew what she meant—after all, it was not so long ago that their land had been under the control of the Taliban with women suppressed, music outlawed, and televisions, among other modern-day conveniences, declared anathema to only the strictest interpretation of Islam. Grandma Amaya, Mama jan, and girls like his sisters, were rendered subordinate to all men. Any deviation from these rules and regulations imposed by the men and boys in black turbans and long beards resulted in horrific consequences, some of which proved fatal.

"A mother should not live to see her children die. Too many mothers in this country have outlived their sons," grandma Amaya said, shaking her head. Clouds were gathering on the horizon, tumbling down and between the mountain peaks like an avalanche. "Your mother should not live to see another of her children die."

"I don't think she would be sad if it was me," Yakup said softly, dropping his head to where it fell between his knees.

"You do know that your mother loves you very much, Yakup jan? She may not show it often, but she has had a tough life. All the men she has known are gone—you are the only one that remains," Grandma Amaya explained still holding Yakup's hand in hers, her long, white hair hung as a thin cape around her shoulders.

"But she never shows it," Yakup countered and let go of his grandmother's hand. She pulled him towards her, buried him in a mix of her hair and clothes and kissed him on the top of his head.

"My child. Have no doubt. Your mother loves you. Trust your old grandmother on that." Her hair was getting wet where Yakup's cheek rested. He wanted to believe her.

6

DOGS OF WAR

The following day in school Yakup could not focus. Thoughts of who he was and what role he played in the lives of others kept surfacing and resurfacing. If the Mullah was right, then he should live his life according to the verses of the Quran, which, in reality, would not alter his destiny. The old Mullah A.J. did have a point, Yakup felt since there was the prospect of eternal happiness in the afterlife. Still, Yakup didn't really understand why, then, he had to suffer in this life.

His thoughts were interrupted by a penetrating voice.

"Yakup, do you have an answer?"

"Um?" he replied.

The teacher stood before him. Hands crossed behind his back.

"Maybe I should repeat the question or are you too busy with extra-curricular activities?" the teacher said.

Laughter broke out in the class.

"I'm sorry," Yakup said. More laughter. He turned and walked over to the small board covered with layers of scribbling that would never fully come clean. This did not matter in the grand scheme of things as there existed no chalk. The board remained merely out of principle more than anything else. "A gift from the people of Japan", a small sticker read. Apparently, the people had forgotten to include chalk and a sponge in which to clean the board.

"Now boys, be quiet. My question was, and still is, if you can tell me, what is the capital of Laos?"

"Yakup!" The teacher caught him in the doorway, as the class ended. "You seemed to be floating today. How is your family?"

"We're managing," Yakup replied.

"You are not the first of my students to lose a father, you know."
The teacher scratched his head. "Farhad lost his father some years ago…
And so did Rashid. I know that is of no consolation to you, but they have
managed to move on."

A mangy-looking dog was sniffing around in the doorway. Yakup
thought of that autumn day at Band-e-Amir, where he had seen Rashid.
If there was one thing he did not want, it was to move on the way Rashid
had.

"What do I have to move on to?"

"Your father's memory will always be with you and your family. In
a way, his spirit will be with you. You can choose to use that presence as
you like and pay it the respect it deserves. Physically he is in the past—
an entity that would only ever be temporary. He gave you life and
sustained you until now. But he also gave you many other tools to carry
with you into this next phase of your life. He moulded you for a period
and has set a course for your life."

The teacher stopped and looked over at the doorway, where the dog
now lay resting.

None of what he had said came as either a surprise or consolation.
Yakup just wanted to go home to the soothing company of Grandma
Amaya. He rustled his notepad and made to go.

"The path you chose in life will bear the mark of the people you pass
on your way," the teacher continued. He had clearly not finished. "But
you must choose who you are and what kind of person you want to be.
You will meet people with seedy motives throughout life who will want
to use you. These people will teach you important lessons," the teacher
said, pacing back and forth, raising the dust that covered the cracks of
the grey concrete floor. "The boy you are today is readily influenced by
people like me, the Mullah, your friends, and of course, your mother,
sisters, family, and not least of which includes the memory of your father.
It is your choice how you use the input from these people." The teacher
stopped walking and stared out through the small plastic window that sat,
recessed, deep into the wall. Next to it hung a faded map of the world.

"How do I know what path to choose?" Yakup asked, wondering
whether he had ever chosen to do anything in particular bearing in mind
that it could have a direct impact on his life. He remained standing,

listening to the teacher moralizing and babbling about hazy notions.

"I've known you for years. You are a good kid. If you work a little harder on your homework, I believe that you can go on to study and move on to accomplish great things. You have a knack for languages. There are good universities in Kabul. I have contacts that I can pull to get you in. But you must show me you want it for yourself. Maybe you can become a teacher or a translator."

In the doorway the mangy dog yawned, stretching its jaws as wide as possible, and then turned to gnaw viciously at a bald spot on its rump where fleas were trying to set up a colony.

"Why would I want that? Aren't I just a pawn? Do I even have a say in where this thing called life will take me? On the one hand, the Mullah is saying that God has a plan. That no one really knows the details of where he is meant to go, but nor should he care. Are we supposed to blindly trust God's master plan? I find it difficult to understand why this omnipotent manager of the master plan leaves us in complete oblivion to his intentions and outcomes. We are born, we live and we die with no answers. Just acceptance; that seems to be the mantra that the religious leaders lay upon us. They tell us that there is a purpose. Okay, fine. But what is that purpose then?" Yakup stopped. The teacher seemed a bit perplexed by this sudden outpouring, but before he could speak, Yakup continued: "If this is true, and my choices are not mine, but depend instead upon powerful people who influence my life. For example, by forcing my father into a conflict that ended up ripping him from the lives of my mother, sisters and me, then those very people could do the same to me. How long will it be before they knock on my door and ask me to follow in Baba's footsteps?"

Yakup suddenly realised that he was talking too much. This was what Grandma Amaya had advised against. Again, he made to leave.

The dog in the doorway had given up on the fleas and was now apathetically panting, pink tongue hanging heavily from his mouth.

"Yakup, life is given to us, and it is ours to live. We are born on different steps of the ladder. Some of us have to struggle to climb up and it can seem almost impossible to continue at times. But here we are. And we have to do our best with what little time is granted to us. Where life will take us does not so much depend on our choices. The only certainty is that we will die and that we do not know when this will happen. We must simply do our best while constantly living in the ever-present shadow of death."

The teacher pointed towards the doorway, where the dog was still panting. From time to time, it turned a tired head in the direction of a passing sound. "Look at that sad, old, mangy creature," the teacher said. "He doesn't have long to live. He has lost his fur; bugs feast on him and he is too weak to fight them off. He eats scraps of food he finds in the garbage."

The dog had placed his head between his paws. A fly was attacking the oozing mucus that sprang forth from the dog's eyes. "He wasn't always like that. As a pup, he lived in a small world with his mother and siblings, getting into fights, running after rodents and chasing butterflies. Children played with him and scratched his smooth belly. He sucked milk from his mother's teats and ate what was brought to him. He didn't have a care in the world." Yakup looked at the scrawny beast in the doorway, finding it difficult to imagine him as a pup.

"He grew older. He ran with a pack of other dogs, chasing passing cars and trying to scare lonely street vendors in the hope that they would drop a scrap of meat.

"In winter, they kept each other warm and on hot summer nights, they howled together. Some days he roamed in solitude sniffing at corners of other dogs' turfs while looking for bitches in heat. He often came to this school, where I fed him and scratched him behind his ears. There was no obvious pattern in his doings, and I don't know who else he might have gone to for comfort.

"He has, in essence, spent his entire life being dependent—going from one provider to the next. First, his mother and then his pack, and finally, on to people. These circumstances were not his own, but he capitalised on certain opportunities as well as others without consciously choosing to do so.

"Today he is old. His joints are sore, his breath is foul, he has cataracts and there's hardly a reaction when you call him. He doesn't even notice when you eat a juicy kebab just meters away from him. Still, on some days, his deteriorating senses catch something reminiscent of days past. A howl reaches his ears or a familiar scent catches his nose.

On these occasions, he briefly believes he is a young dog again, roaming the same streets he once did when he was always on the lookout for food and adventure. That is when his tail wags and he forgets about the fleas and the pain."

The teacher sat down and beckoned for the dog to come with a pat of his leg. It took a few calls for the animal to react, but when he did eventually climb to his feet the teacher rubbed his old friend behind the ears and the dog slowly closed his eyes with delight.

"What people and animals alike choose to do, then, is up to them. The framework in which we exist can change. And does so. We are living in a fluid time that we are capable of shaping. It is up to you to decide whether you want to live within the framework, apathetically accepting how it is shaped by others, or choose to take control and become a shaper yourself," the teacher said. Yakup looked at the dog and wondered if he himself was a 'shaper'.

"What are you?" Yakup asked. The teacher indicated to the dog with a final pat that it was time to leave so, the dog got up on his feet once more and made for the door. The teacher got up too. He put his papers in the drawer of the lone desk in the classroom. "School is over for today. You better get home, or your dear grandmother may grow worried. I have already kept you too long."

"But are you a shaper?" Yakup said.

"What do you think? Now, I have to be somewhere else," the teacher said, ushering the schoolboy towards the door, behind the dog. Yakup reluctantly took his notepad and stepped into his sandals, starting for home and his family. He felt confused. Who was he supposed to be? What was he supposed to become?

The afternoon was warm. Summer had come and Yakup missed his father.

Over the following months, the entire family tried to adapt to their new normal. It was as if Yakup's mother had somehow donned yet another layer of solitude and heartache that estranged her, further still, from her children. When she did break her silent mourning ritual it was to mainly complain or scold the children.

Sometimes the girls could reach her through this seemingly

impenetrable layer of suffering and find kindness, but Yakup was locked out. Money was short, meals smaller and less satisfying, and the picnics by the Band-e-Amir lakes ceased to exist. Yakup did his best to be a son, a brother and a man. He and the girls went to school. Summer and autumn passed. Winter was quickly upon them and all with Yakup's mother still stuck in her invisible capsule of sorrow and darkness.

Grandma Amaya was the pillar and as time passed, they did adapt.

7

THE DONKEY

Yakup walked along the path from the cave towards the school. Here and there a small chimney of dust whirled from the ground and danced until coming to a halt further down the valley. The rock formation with the old fortress, Shahr-e-Gholghola, 'the City of Screams,' stood to the east, riddled with land mines. Still further on, and at the entrance of the valley, remained remnants of Shahr-i-Zohak, or 'the Red City', which had once stood guard over Bamiyan, protecting it from hostile intruders. The valley stood as it had for hundreds of years. Time had brought new buildings here and there with a few paved roads so the vehicles could traverse the valley quickly, to the benefit of local traders and travellers.

On quiet days, at dusk and again at dawn, columns of smoke from the many wood-burning stoves gave off thin grey columns of smoke, which stood from the floor of the valley, contrasting the orange and pink rays of the sun. The fragrance of burning wood mingled with the vestiges of warm food and chai and seemed to spread from one small home to the next.

The valley was a peaceful and pleasant place on those days.

"Did you know that Farhad believes our school was built by someone who came from outside of Afghanistan?" Rashid said one day during a break between lessons. Farhad pretended not to pay attention. Dani and Osman laughed. "It is funny, of course, because I swear that I saw, with my own two eyes, men from the village building this school with their strong Afghan hands," Rashid said, patting the wall of the building. His eyelids drooped, one of them a bit lazy.

"Who paid the men that built the school and where did the material come from?" Farhad countered, without looking up from the Sufi poetry book he was reading. Rashid turned and walked up to Farhad. Dani and Osman trailed him

"Does the *poet* have more to say?" Rashid inquired. "Did he not see for himself those men from town putting up the structure, preparing the clay, adding the roof and cleaning the walls?" Farhad looked up at Rashid.

There was a flicker of fear that passed over his face, but his eyes remained stalwart in their opposition.

"One man can do a lot, but from time-to-time support is necessary in order to become who he is destined to become," Farhad said and looked from Dani to Osman who appeared as sentries on either side of Rashid.

"What do you mean?" Rashid hissed.

"The school was built with the hands of our fathers and brothers and with money from foreigners. We needed a school and they needed us to have a school. It is built by all of us. Even you Rashid," Farhad said with a smug smile.

In his calculating way, and knowing he had lost the argument, Rashid decided that it made no sense to take the discussion further and as he turned to leave said, "I know one person, who did not build the school: your father."

It was known among the boys at the school that Farhad's father had been missing for some time. Many said he was a 'rat,' having worked for the Taliban, and thus, was killed in retribution after they were defeated by the Americans and their allies; others said he was an informer and helped to defeat the Taliban. In the end, no one really knew.

A darkness came over Farhad's face. He leapt up and attacked Rashid. In an attempt to wrestle Rashid to the ground, Farhad clung to his opponent's back, who struggled to shake him off despite spinning and landing blows upon Farhad. But his thick arms could not catch hold of his attacker and it was only when Dani and Osman intervened that Farhad was freed and placed in front of the scrappy and sweating Rashid.

"You son of a dirty rat," Rashid shouted as he landed a fist deep into Farhad's belly. It left his opponent short of breath and stumbling toward the ground. Rashid wasted no time in dealing a swift kick to Farhad's back before the punishment was interrupted by the teacher calling them back to class. Yakup helped Farhad up and dusted off his shalwar kameez.

"That bastard! Just because he is bigger than us, he thinks he is allowed to do, and say, whatever he wants," Farhad panted.

"Maybe it is better to stay away from him," Yakup said feeling like a coward.

"We have to stand up to people like him. Otherwise, they take control," Farhad reasoned. He straightened his shirt and the two of them walked to class.

The teacher had returned to Afghanistan only after the Taliban were no longer in power. Like many others returning from abroad, he, too, had wanted to be a part of restoring his.

"Does anyone know what countries border Afghanistan?" the teacher asked. Haroon's hand shot into the air.

"Haroon."

"To the west is Iran and to the north is Uzbekistan and Tajikistan. China is east and Pakistan lies to both our south and east."

"Good. Can anyone tell me why we should concern ourselves with which countries form our boundaries?" A few hands sprang into the air. "Farhad?"

"Millions of Afghans have lived, and do live, in both Iran and Pakistan. We often complain about harassment from our neighbours, but they have given millions of Afghan refugees shelter, food and work for years and years," Farhad said before he was interrupted by Haroon.

"But they were also the cause of the wars that resulted in there being refugees in the first place," he retorted and turned to the teacher, who was standing with his hands crossed behind his back, which carried a black vest over his pale shalwar kameez.

"Is this true, and if so, how and why? Should we hate or love our neighbours?" the teacher asked. Hands took to the sky.

"Rashid?"

"The Taliban were Pashtuns and Kuchis. They killed our brothers. In Peshawar, they are still killing Hazara Afghans. These people are our enemies," Rashid said. He stared at Farhad, who, without fear, stared back. Haroon jumped in.

"Rashid is right, but he is also wrong. Pakistan also helped the Mujahideen defeat the Soviets. Without supplies from western countries and Pakistan, the Mujahideen would not have won."

The class fell silent. The teacher paced back and forth, kicking up dust mites, which danced in the light penetrating the small windows of the building. A dog barked outside and a breeze rattled the leaves littering the courtyard.

"The Soviet Union was a crumbling superpower when it left Afghanistan. Whether they would have left had there not been a strong, foreign intervention propping up the Mujahideen, one cannot say for sure. At the same time, we have to accept that not all who are interested in Afghanistan are interested in Afghans. We are a people who have fought wars with many enemies, including ourselves, unfortunately.

"After the Russians were driven back, our allies didn't follow up with assistance to improve the lives of everyday Afghans, which resulted in the lawless aftermath many of us bore witness to over the course of the last decade.

"In most of Afghanistan's cities and their connecting roads, anyone with a few men and Kalashnikovs could, and often would, demand bribes and payments and abuse men and women. Kidnapping and rape were normal. There was no established central power and the random and arbitrary attacks resulted in a fearful and gloomy atmosphere that shrouded Afghanistan in a dark cloud of its own design.

"The Mujahideen, who had once fought sidelong against the Russians, became each other's enemies and fought terribly despite numerous civilian casualties and the near destruction of all Kabul. They laid waste to the capital and when Hekmatyar, backed by the Inter-Services Intelligence, or ISI, Pakistan's strong and largely independent intelligence service, decided not to obey the peace and power-sharing agreement, "The Peshawar Accord" that the rest of the Mujahideen had agreed upon, the civil war entered an indescribable phase of destruction. Larger cities, including Kabul, Mazar-i-Sharif and Kandahar, became epicentres of battle, which, for once, left the countryside largely unto itself.

"The different factions changed sides depending on how the wind blew. Hazaras, Pashtuns, Tajiks and Uzbeks created and destroyed alliances as did the Sunnis and Shias. At the same time, proxy wars played out by foreign powers such as Iran and Saudi Arabia, Pakistan and other nations, both near and far who had geo-political interests. This mishmash of unholy alliances perpetuated a civil war that was equal parts ugly and brutal and ultimately weakened the entire country.

"In the fall of 1994, a group of young religious students from the areas surrounding Peshawar in Pakistan created their own following and declared a jihad to establish what they called the *true Islamic order*" out of the mess of warlords and small-time crooks who were destroying Afghanistan. These were the Taliban, and at first many believed that they were the saviours come to free them from the infighting of the Mujahideen.

"They had studied in the thousands at hard-line Islamic madrasah schools, which received sponsor dollars from Saudi Arabian donors or the government of Pakistan. In these extremely religious schools, would-be warriors were indoctrinated vis-à-vis a conservative interpretation of Islamic ideology. With military weaponry flowing freely from Pakistan's ISI, it didn't take this latest faction long to secure the southern city of Kandahar where the leader of the Taliban, the one-eyed Mullah Omar, entrenched himself and created a vortex of power.

"Soon the Taliban recruited thousands of men who quickly made headway into other cities such as Herat, Jalalabad and Kabul, where they executed Mohammed Najibullah, the Communist leader and former president, castrating him, tying him to a land cruiser and dragging him around the palace's compound. What remained of his corpse was eventually displayed on a traffic post for all to see and heed.

"It was a strong signal. By the end of 1996 the Taliban, who two years earlier only consisted of a few hundred young men, controlled over two-thirds of the country."

The teacher stopped by the window. He clasped his hands behind his back.

"For a brighter and better future, we must look beyond that time, but also take care not to forget our mistakes. This will not be easy. We need to work together and put tribal alliances and ethnic differences behind us. There is an old guard in power who will take advantage of our differences so as to ensure that they remain in power. Is that productive?

Is that how we prosper?"

Yakup couldn't help wondering how they, the 30 of them, could have any effect on a brighter future for their country when they could not even agree among themselves.

On his journey home Yakup passed the small field where they played football and cricket in the summer.

Yakup's favourite game was football, though most of the other boys preferred cricket as it was the game many refugees had adopted and brought back to Afghanistan after nearly three decades abroad. Yakup turned the corner and found the field barren, a sodden piece of bumpy land. The only living creature on the field was a lonely donkey. The grey animal didn't seem to notice the boy and if it did, it couldn't have cared less.

Yakup recalled a legendary football match one summer evening several years ago. There had been enough boys for two equally strong teams. Younger boys and girls were playing and watching the match. Yakup had played well and scored the victory goal for his team. Yakup stood in his own thoughts of long summer nights for a while, until someone called to him, startling him back to the present.

"Hey!" the voice said, causing him to spin around.

He turned and saw Rashid with his two buddies.

"Hi, Rashid," Yakup said and looked around to see if anyone else was there.

"Looking for someone to play with?" Rashid asked.

"I was just passing the field."

"There doesn't seem to be anyone else here," Rashid said and looked from side to side to emphasise his point. "There is the donkey. Do you want to play with the donkey, Yakup?" Rashid twisted his lips into a sardonic grin.

"Yeah, you wanna play with the donkey?" Osman repeated.

"Yeah," Dani said. They all three laughed.

"I don't think the donkey can play football," Yakup replied. The donkey hadn't moved. Yakup turned and made to leave.

"Wait a minute," Rashid said, cutting Yakup off. His facial hair was more than a shadow, covering his upper lip with a few long black hairs beginning to cover his chin.

He was almost an entire head taller than Yakup with a body bulging out of his tunic. A smell of sweat always surrounded him, even on cold winter days.

"I heard that donkeys are excellent sportsmen. Maybe we should test it out," Rashid said. He bent down and found a small stone. He picked it up, took aim, cocked his arm and hurled it towards the donkey. He missed.

"Good thing this is not a cricket match," Dani said.

Rashid turned and stared at him with a strangely mean look. Dani immediately realised his mistake.

"Well, if we… I mean… It's just a stupid donkey," he stuttered. Rashid bent down and picked up another stone. This time he hit the donkey on the flank. The animal flinched, indicating that something had disturbed its meditative mood. He picked up a bigger stone. Dani and Osman followed suit. The three stones hissed through the air. Two of them missed, but the third connected with the donkey's front leg, causing the animal to start, stamp and shake. The white of a bone peaked out but was quickly repainted in red by the blood that spread onto the grey.

"Nice shot, Dani," Rashid said with a smile. Dani blinked a few times

"Rashid! Leave the donkey alone. It has done nothing to harm you," Yakup cried.

"Why? You were the one looking for someone to play with. We are doing this to help you," Rashid said.

Another stone. Another bruising blow, this time to the animal's forehead.

The donkey shook its head and let out a plaintive groan. It didn't move.

"Stop it, Rashid," Yakup said and moved a step or two closer to the bigger boy and his pack of goons.

"The game hasn't even started yet!"

Rashid picked up a large rock, moved a bit closer and threw it at the stunned donkey. It hit the donkey's flank with a thump like a cricket bat hitting a lump of meat. The donkey flinched at the impact but stayed put. It was looking at the four boys, wondering what they were doing, and presumably, hoping that the sudden pains would stop.

"Rashid, maybe you should stop," Dani said.

"What? It's a donkey! Who cares? Whose side are you on anyway?" Rashid said.

That seemed to do it for Dani, though, he still looked unnerved by the entire sequence of events.

"You are hurting the animal. It is bleeding," Yakup said. He didn't know what else to say, but felt he had to say, or do, something.

"Just because others abuse you, doesn't mean that you can go and abuse innocent animals," he blurted out, catching Rashid's eye.

Yakup saw his words land harder than any punch he could have thrown. The two of them were suddenly back at the lake. For a moment it seemed that Rashid would back off.

But he didn't. He defiantly picked up another stone. Yakup ran towards the donkey with his arms pumping.

"Get away! Move! Run! Get out of here you stupid donkey!"

Yakup ran right up to the animal. It didn't seem to understand, or care, about the imminent threat of danger. Yakup gave it a good slap on the rump, but nothing happened. Instead, he felt a sharp pain on his right arm. First, he thought that the donkey had bitten him, but when another similar pain sprang forth from his lower back, he realised that he had become the target of Rashid's wrath.

Yakup turned and saw a stone heading straight for his face. He only managed to divert it by a few centimetres. He heard a small thump from behind him as the stone dug into the flank of the donkey.

"Stop it!" Yakup yelled.

Rashid and Osman were laughing. Dani was nowhere to be found.

"!" Yakup yelled again, but this time Rashid bent down and picked up another stone.

"Look! Now you two donkeys can go play together."

He threw two stones in quick succession. One of them missed, but the other hit Yakup's shin. The pain brought tears to his eyes. The only solution was to hide behind the donkey, which was what he did. He picked up a few stones and weighed them in his hand. They were a good size if defence became necessary. A few stones whizzed past the donkey and Yakup. And then nothing.

He waited, but still nothing. After a while he looked out from between the donkey's legs and saw Rashid and Osman walking away. He could hear their mumbling voices as they disappeared down the path.

"Stupid donkey… Crazy…"

As soon as they disappeared, Yakup came out from his make-shift fortress.

"Sorry, donkey," he said and stroked its back.

Flakes of coagulated blood remained in the donkey's fur. The animal's flank was bruised and there was a nasty bump just before a massive cut on its forehead. The animal's large eyes looked up at Yakup as if to ask why someone would do that to him. He felt bad for the donkey. Yakup looked at his own arm, then. There was a red mark. He could feel a little bump on his back and his shin was bruised. He left the wounded donkey and walked back to pick up his notebook lying in the dirt. Someone had stepped on it and ripped some pages out. Yakup dusted it off and started, once more, for home.

8

THE BEETLE

Zahra was sitting in front of the cave with a book between her crossed legs. She still didn't wear a veil around the cave, though, now she had to use it when she was in town. It didn't please her, but the potentially dire consequences forced her to wear it.

"Maman is home," she said, barely glancing up from her book.

"That is early," Yakup said.

"Something about an important mission from Kabul, so the hotels bought everything at the market. Picked each stall clean," she replied.

"How is her mood?" Yakup asked.

"As usual," Zahra said and shrugged her shoulders.

"Are they Americans? The 'cyborgs?" Zahra asked. The children called the foreign soldiers cyborgs because of their equipment. Sometimes it was impossible to see if there was a human behind the helmet, goggles, heavy armour, guns, grenades and radios. They might as well have been robots.

"I don't know," Yakup said. The cyborgs had become part of everyday life in Afghanistan.

"Well, there were lots of them today," Zahra said.

Yakup nodded. He didn't really care much. Everyone kept saying that the Americans were on their way out. The men in town had varying opinions on the consequences. There were those looking forward to the international forces leaving and expected a peaceful transition. Then there were those dreading the departure, expecting a decline in security with the renewed spike in violence and internal conflict, pulling the country deep into an abyss of violence. The latter marked a majority.

But Yakup was more focused on his own problems. He wasn't interested in cyborgs nor was he at all interested in pandering to his mother's ongoing depression.

Without saying more, he walked past Zahra, leaving her to her book, and went to sit on the little peak further up the hill. He checked the damage to his notebook. It was clear another was needed. Yakup recalled the sting of pity he had felt for Rashid that day by the lake. His sympathy had evaporated, replaced with a burning fury for the bullying, fat Rashid. *He deserved that humiliation*, Yakup thought.

Yakup wanted revenge but didn't know what to do. With a crazy mother, two younger sisters and an old grandmother, there was no help to be found at home. If he chose to fight, then Yakup would be at the mercy of the much bigger boy. He could see no proper solution to his quandary.

A beetle was pushing a ball of dirt and straw from side to side, sometimes tumbling around with it, but always with a purpose, it seemed. Yakup wished he knew what the purpose was. It was unfair that this tiny beetle had a purpose and he didn't. The shadow of his foot crawled threateningly close to the struggling beetle, completely covering it. Yakup didn't hear the person walking up the rocky path until she was standing right behind him. The moment his foot went down and flattened the beetle and its ball into a mishmash of dirt, straw and flakes of black beetle, Grandma Amaya's voice rang out: "Yakup!"

The boy jumped, embarrassed and hoping that she had not seen what he had just done.

"Grandma," he said and felt like throwing up.

"Zahra told me you were up here," grandma Amaya said, "Your mother came home from the market early today. It is good for her. She is working too much." She sat down next to her grandson and took his hand. "Tell me what is troubling you, Yakup jan," she said. Yakup hoped she would not judge him for the death of the beetle. She looked him in the eye. There was no condemnation, only a grandmother's concern.

Yakup lowered his head and told her about Rashid and how he had thrown rocks at the donkey, his punishment of Farhad, how they all loathed him and how none of the boys knew what to do to exact revenge for his bullying. He told her about that day by the lake and how he hoped Rashid's older brother would punish his chubbier sibling.

"It is not easy on Rashid," Grandma Amaya said once Yakup had stopped talking.

"What do you mean? He is the one harassing the rest of us. He is the evil, abusive, bigger boy. Me and Farhad, we have a difficult time because of Rashid," Yakup said.

It was the first time he felt a sting of anger toward Grandma Amaya. Why couldn't she see that he was the victim here? For a while neither said anything. The only sound was that of a helicopter's rotor blades somewhere in the valley.

"The executioner can be the victim. That doesn't mean that what he does is moral or correct," Grandma Amaya said. She put her hand on Yakup's leg. "Sometimes we do things without thinking of the consequences until it is too late. Our anger and fear turn to violence and are directed toward those weaker than ourselves."

Yakup could feel the small, squashed beetle under his sandal and the weight of guilt. He was no different than Rashid.

"Do you hate me?" he asked.

"Don't be silly, Yakup jan. You have a grandmother who will love you no matter what happens; you have two sisters who adore you and a mother who loves you in her own way, trust me. We are not put on this earth with all of the answers, nor can we be expected to do the right thing all the time. What Rashid is doing is wrong. Like you, and many other children, he is having a hard time growing up in a place where cultures clash. Rashid has brothers, who treat him as an outcast."

"I understand that it is difficult for him, but it doesn't make it easier for me or Farhad," Yakup said.

"Feelings are difficult to control and understand, but sometimes we must go deeper in order to understand their source. When you plant a seed and it doesn't grow, you don't blame the corn itself. Instead, you look into the root causes—fertiliser, soil, water, nourishment, pesticides, climate and so on. Now, when a person does something wrong, do you blame him? You must look at his circumstances and understand why he is driven to behave a certain way," Grandma Amaya said.

Until then, Yakup had seen himself as the worst-off person in the world, but coming to terms with what Grandma Amaya was telling him helped him understand that Rashid didn't just have to carry the sorrow of losing his father, but that he also had to live with his brothers who constantly tormented him and stole the whisper of a memory that was once his father. Rather than feeling anger towards Rashid, Yakup started to feel pity toward him.

"But Grandma Amaya, what can I do?"

"I'm not sure you can do much for Rashid. But you can do something for yourself," she paused, rearranging her dark veil. A few strands of white hair escaped on the afternoon breeze.

"Like what?"

"It is for you to choose."

"But I don't know what to choose. I don't even know, what it is that I can choose…"

"Your father wanted you to have an education and get a better job than he had. Your teacher has told me that he believes in your ability to get an education. I don't have to mention that I believe in you," she squeezed his arm and smiled.

"I guess that is an option. But then what? You have told me that people in power control us. What if they decide to send me into battle?" Yakup asked.

"We can speculate about what may or may not happen and take no action. But then, suddenly we find ourselves at the end of the path, realizing that we forgot to act, because we constantly weighed what might happen, paralyzed by indecision. If something does get in our way, we have to deal with it, but only then. If nothing else, at least we know, we tried and that we did our best. No one can take that away from us."

Yakup looked at his torn notepad and flipped a few pages.

"Your two sisters do not have the same opportunities as you do, Yakup jan. Noor is stuck on the idea of being someone's wife. Hopefully, she will be gifted to a good man. Zahra is focused on getting an education and taking care of herself. I trust she will, but as a woman in this country, she has a nearly impossible climb in front of her. She has chosen to deal with those battles when they arise. Your mother will need some assistance as she grows older and I will not be around for long."

Yakup slowly allowed this realization, that Grandma Amaya would not be around forever, to watch over him. He looked at her furrowed skin and felt an acute pain at the mere thought of losing her.

At that moment he decided that it was time to take control of his life.

He wanted to get an education and become a 'shaper' as his teacher had put it.

"Grandma Amaya, I want to do what father hoped for. Not just for him, but for me, Noor, Zahra, you and Maman." Yakup smiled at her and wanted to get up, but realised that his foot was still resting on the remains of the beetle. He hesitated.

Grandma Amaya sensed this and said, "I saw what you did. I did not, and do not, like it, but I understand. No more squashed beetles, understood?"

She stroked his hair. He felt the sting of conscience.

"No more squashed beetles," he ceremoniously repeated.

They got up and Yakup held his grandmother's arm as they picked their way to the cave in the dying light of the day.

9

SOLD

Yakup set out on his quest with great vigour and determination; education was the goal. He got up early and studied for an hour in the new light of the day. He helped his mother to the market. He focused and stopped daydreaming during class. As a consequence, his grades started to improve.

As Yakup's focus on studying began to produce more tangible results, he and the teacher engaged in discussions about opportunities within higher education. There were talks about Kabul University, though that was a few years away. Nonetheless, the prospect helped Yakup to focus on various subjects in school. He had a purpose and a goal.

While he concentrated his efforts on studying, the increasingly brutal Rashid stopped bullying him. The skinny Dani had distanced himself somewhat from Rashid until one day he was simply gone.

Yakup had taken up weekend work on behalf of the landowner for whom his father had worked. It wasn't what he wanted, but the dire situation at home necessitated it. The landowner could use an extra hand and Yakup knew the job.

The snow was melting. Rivulets of water crisscrossed the hillsides creating furrows where the snow and ice had receded from the thawing dirt. Stones and rocks emerged. A forgotten shoe, a broken bottle and the occasional stiff carcass of a dog that had slept under the heavy duvet of winter, slowly re-emerged, frozen in time. Soon, however, ravenous insects devoured the softening, rotting meat from the post-winter rot. The scent of new life, feeding on last year's thawing leftovers, marked the beginning of yet another season.

With new life, came also the promise of death. Mothers and wives with the steadiest of hands dropped plates or cups for no reason. Children were chastised by their parents for minor offences. Sisters cared more intensely for their teenage brothers. A feeling of restlessness engulfed the valley. Outsiders might have sensed a tension surrounding the locals, but it was too vague and latent to be tangible. The locals knew that the tension was caused by the coming of spring and the inevitable fighting season.

It was early morning and Yakup was reading near the only window in the cave with a schoolbook close to his face so as to catch the few rays of light that penetrated the panes of the murky glass. Noor, Zahra and Grandma Amaya were still asleep. The two girls shared a mattress. Grandma Amaya had her own. In the quiet early hours of the morning only Yakup and his mother were up.

"Yakup," his mother said.

"Mmhmm," he replied. They were having a theme on socialism in school. Yakup was studying South America trying to understand how the one real superpower and capitalist country of the world, allowed the rise of left-wing socialism in its backyard.

"Where is the small cup?" she asked.

"Mmm, sorry?"

"Open your ears. Have you seen the small brown cup I drink my chai from?"

"Your cup? No. Sorry." He returned to the book. The country of Cuba had caught his fancy. A few sparsely equipped freedom fighters had managed to remove a US-supported government, and most impressively, retain power.

"I talked to the landowner the other day. He told me that you're doing a good job," his mother said.

"Mmhmm." Not only had the small country kept power since the 1950s, but they had also averted an attempt by the US to stage a coup. Cuba had sustained itself during some of the strictest embargoes the world had ever seen until but a few years ago. These similarities with Afghanistan were not lost on him. If one small country had managed to survive a game waged between superpowers, albeit not without scars, then there was hope for Afghanistan yet.

"Ah, here it is." She unearthed the cup from beneath a pile of cutlery thrown haphazardly into a pot. Zahra moaned and turned over on her mattress. Yakup's mother poured steaming chai into her small brown cup as well as another for her son. This small gesture was one they had gotten used to.

His mother was still struggling with her own expectations for a life that left much to be desired. She lived in a cave that was moist in summer and cold in winter. Her husband was gone as were two out of five children. It was not how she wanted her life to unfold, but that was how it was.

Some nights she woke up screaming. Her nightmares pulled her out of her sleep and into the dark cave that ruthlessly shoved reality into her confused mind. Maybe the nightmares were better than reality and in the faint beam of a small flashlight that was the only light during the night, she couldn't even recognise her own children. Grandma Amaya soothed her, mumbling stories of summer and faraway places. The older woman stayed awake with her until she was calm and asleep.

"Thank you," Yakup said, smiling up at his mother.

She returned this gesture with one of her own, and though forced, marked the morning as a rare occasion indeed. Yakup placed the cup next to the window, but the hot chai fogged the glass pane, so, he moved the rugged tin cup to the floor and returned to his book.

"He also told me that he is expecting this season to be good," she said.

"Mmhmm, who?" Yakup asked distractedly.

"The landowner will take you on for more days. Or afternoons, if you still want to go to school for a while," she said in a matter-of-fact voice.

"I want to go to school," Yakup said finally looking up at her. "I want to go to school and then university. That's my goal."

"Well, the landowner pays you—the school does not. Who knows if you could even graduate let alone get a job? Working in farming is a family tradition. It would be a good idea to take the opportunity. And …" She hesitated before continuing, "we need the money to survive." She finished the chai in her cup and helped herself to more of the dark liquid, adding two heaping spoonsful of sugar.

"I want an education," Yakup repeated, dumbfounded.

She looked at him. The smile disappearing from her face.

"We all want something, but life is tough, and we have to make do with what we have. School is too expensive. You could be making money instead of wasting time studying for hours on end. This is not up for debate." She turned her back to him.

Her fragile body didn't match her adamant tone.

"The teacher has contacts at the university. He says he can help me get an education."

"If the teacher has contacts, why is he not there himself? You cannot trust him. He is working in a small school. Do you know he has no wife? What kind of man does not have a wife? How will he pay respect to his own family and forefathers if he doesn't have any children? No, he is not to be trusted."

The questions and accusations spewed out. *Was there a choice somewhere*, Yakup wondered, *or had she already made a final decision?*

"Dad wanted me to get an education," Yakup said and braced himself. She stopped with her back towards Yakup, a silhouette against the little kitchen space. The small brown cup shimmered in her hands. Leper hands that could flip a piece of naan in a hot pan without flinching or hold a tin cup of boiling chai. Then the cup fell to the ground and shattered. The sugary, brown liquid spread on the rocky floor. She slowly turned around, oblivious to the destruction at her feet.

"The landowner has made an offer. He wants you to take the place that was fated for you."

The shards of the cup lay scattered on the cave floor.

"I don't want to work as a farmer! I want an education. I want to have a job and support myself and my family. That includes Zahra, Noor, Grandma Amaya and you. Can't you understand that we can break away from *this*?" Yakup asked, making an exasperated movement with his hands.

The book sat, forgotten, on the windowpane. The boy was on his feet in outrage.

"There is nothing to discuss. It is decided—the landowner will give you the position and will expect you to observe all the responsibilities that go with such an offer," his mother said.

The girls and Grandma Amaya were awake. The smashing of the cup and the raised voices had yanked them into the unpleasant morning. They were still under their covers, Noor coughing, Zahra yawning, a cracking noise coming from Grandma Amaya as she stretched her old bones.

"And those obligations include participating in the seasonal spring fighting if he desires," she said with no change in tone. Yakup was stunned. Her statement was in stark contrast to the arguments she had put up the year before when Yakup's father told her that he had to go fighting.

"You hate me!" Yakup cried.

"I have to go to the market. No need to help me today," she said.

The broken cup lay on the floor. The confused boy stood by the windowpane. Forgotten were South America and Cuba and the struggle for socialism. Evaporated were the hopes for a brighter future.

The girls and Grandma Amaya slowly grew aware of the change in plans. They pleaded with Maman and tried to reason with her, even admonishing her for being selfish and bringing potentially greater harm to the family. None of it helped. The deal was done with the landowner and Yakup's mother had no intention of going back on her word.

From time-to-time Yakup felt his mother gazing at him. Sometimes he sensed a vicious smile on her lips, but he tried to brush it off as just a figment of his imagination.

Yakup continued to go to school, but his enthusiasm was gone. The realization that he would soon have to use a weapon and try to shoot people he had never met overshadowed any scholarly subject. Suddenly the letters in the books seemed utterly dead. School signified a shut door that could only be opened by those with a future.

Rashid came up to Yakup a few days later during a break in the lessons. He moved with confidence, swaying a bit. The teenage years were not kind to him. He looked like a distorted baby—an adult that had not quite broken free of infant fat. Thick, black eyebrows formed a bridge above his already too-thick nose.

"I hear you're fighting this year," he said with a smirk.

"Maybe," Yakup replied. The idea of fighting in the mountains with bullets whizzing past, blood spurting from friend and foe, muscle shorn from bone, made Rashid's bullying all but laughable. Was this what it felt like to step out of childhood and become a man—the realization that death was everywhere?

"I'm going as well," Rashid said, trying to sound casual. "I heard that the battle will be fierce this year," he continued.

Yakup sensed the bully momentarily reaching out to him and that perhaps he saw Yakup less as a pestilential schoolboy and more as a brother in arms.

Rashid's eyes flickered as he said, "I have been practising my aim with my brothers."

He pretended to point a non-existent rifle towards Farhad, sitting not far away under a tree and pretending to read a book. Rashid's lazy eyelid was barely open as he took aim. He pulled a trigger that didn't exist and shot Farhad.

"Well, I don't know if I'll go this year," Yakup said.

"That's not what I heard. I heard that your Maman has forced you to work and to fight," Rashid laughed in a condescending manner. "Here's a rumour I bet you haven't heard: they're putting you on the front line. Cannon fodder. I will be behind you with my brothers, so even if you do try to run you will be shot. It is just a question of by who." He aimed his imaginary rifle and pointed it at Yakup's forehead. He turned around and swaggered away. It was difficult not to despise him. Yakup wondered if he would have shot him back had he been holding a rifle then and there.

Farhad got up and walked over to Yakup.

"What was that about?"

"My mother has agreed with the landowner that I will work for him and am to fight in the spring. Rashid and his brothers are fighting as well. He told me to be cautious about crossfire," Yakup said.

Farhad's face contorted in disbelief. "What are you going to do?"

"I don't know. Fight, I guess," Yakup shrugged.

"You have no experience fighting. This is not like maths where if you make a mistake, you get a second chance. What if something happens?" Farhad asked.

"I'm a farmer now," Yakup said unconvincingly.

"A farmer!" Farhad looked straight at Yakup concerned, but without condescension. "Do you have any say in this at all?" Yakup shook his head, fearing his voice would crack if he spoke.

"There's only one option as I see it," Farhad said before continuing, "you have to leave Bamiyan. Go far away from here. People do that all the time."

The thought had crossed Yakup's mind, but he had brushed the idea off before it could materialise into action. Now that Farhad had said it out loud, however, the words crystallised into a sensible option.

"Where to go, though?" Yakup asked.

"Where do you want to go?"

They both smiled.

Yakup skipped the rest of school that day. He now had more important issues to attend to. As he hurried home, he found his old grandmother at the foot of the hill near the cave. She was sitting with a group of blue and black-clad women that Yakup had known forever.

As soon as she saw her grandson, she got up and nodded farewell to her friends. Grandma Amaya knew that Yakup did not pass her way in the early afternoon of a school day without coincidence.

They walked until they were out of earshot of the group.

"What is it, Yakup jan? What plans are you hatching? You do know you can tell me anything, right?" the old woman said.

"I know, grandma… I'm not sure what to do… and I want your advice."

Yakup worried that the old woman would take offence at his suggestion that she help him leave and quite possibly, never return or see her again.

"I'm listening, my child."

She looked worried as he began, "I want an education; I don't want to fight. I think I must go.

Grandma Amaya sighed deeply and nodded. "I think that may be an option."

They stopped under a leafless tree and each found a large rock to sit on. There was still a bit of snow on the northern side of the tree, but it wouldn't survive for long.

"You think… it's a good idea?" Yakup stammered.

"I have thought about it as well and I think we can get you out of here and set you up somewhere… better. It depends, of course, on what you were thinking. Where do you want to go?"

"I don't know… maybe Cuba." It was the only place Yakup could think of at that moment. Grandma Amaya let out a laugh.

"My dear child, that is a very good idea, but maybe you could choose a closer place to begin with. Um, perhaps Kabul would be easier?"

Yakup realised how stupid his suggestion was, but he was too heartened to feel embarrassed. One of grandma Amaya's strengths was that she did not chastise Yakup even when he'd been a fool. That was one of the reasons why he loved her so much.

"Kabul is easier," Yakup agreed, "and I have never been there."

"Good. Kabul it is then. We don't have long. Maybe a few days to make the appropriate arrangements. I will set you up with your cousin in Kabul. He is a bit careless and inattentive, but when ends meet, his heart is in the right place. He owes me for many years of trying to raise him."

She then moved to pull her grandson into a hug. Her familiar scent soothed him. Grandma Amaya was far more advanced in planning his escape than he had dared hope. Still, something bothered Yakup. Something that his grandmother could do nothing to mitigate—soon she would not be there for him any more.

10

FAREWELL

Yakup steadied himself as he began to prepare his escape from the only place he had ever known in favour of Kabul—an unknown monster of a city that he was ready to challenge yet feared to be devoured by.

His two sisters were the most difficult to say goodbye to. They had to keep his departure a secret to avoid questions from their mother and so they spent stolen afternoons together. Those short days with his sisters were a time of sadness, but also great joy.

The evening before his departure, Yakup packed a small bag with some clothes, pens and paper, an old faded birth certificate and a black and white shot of a young Grandma Amaya and Yakup's grandfather. The picture captured the two sitting on a bench in a lush garden wearing fine western-style clothes. Around them were a number of children. They looked happy in the tranquillity of that exact moment in time. One of the surrounding images in that photo was of his teenage father. In the picture, Baba had been the exact same age as his son who now held it. At last, he packed a crisp piece of paper from Grandma Amaya with an address in Kabul and a phone number for an uncle in England.

Yakup had difficulty sleeping in the darkness of the cave. Sleep was indifferent to his efforts to court it; it refused to embrace him. He felt a twinge of regret for leaving his family behind. In the humid darkness, he got up and paced the rock floor of the only place he had ever called home.

His fingers moved along the edges of the stone wall. He knew exactly where the wall twisted and turned, where the rock was soft and where its edgy stones stuck out as sharp as teeth. He breathed in the scent of 'home'. He stopped by his mother's bed, then, with her silhouette lying on the same side of the bed as it always had, and likely, always would as it left just enough space for, her deceased husband's space to go untouched. Her breath was almost inaudible. Yakup stood there in the darkness, making certain that she was asleep. He sat on the untouched part of the bed and thought that soon his mattress would have an empty spot and the cave would be deprived of any male inhabitants. The contour of his mother's face was visible in the darkness. Her black hair had strands of silver in it that refracted the darkness of the night.

He pushed aside a lock of hair from her face and kissed her forehead. His lips rested there longer than he meant to. Yakup's nostrils were between her parted hair, trying to imprint it her scent in his mind. As he pressed his lips toward her forehead, a faint sensation of happier days stole into his memory; Summer, lakes, picnics, smiles and laughter, and a mother that lifted a son and kissed him without condemnation or sorrow.

A vague moan pulled him back to the reality of the cave. His lips left his mother's forehead and her scent evaporated from his nostrils.

Yakup's bare feet stepped back onto the rugged, hard floor. Zahra had cuddled up to Noor. Both were sound asleep. He carefully sat down at the edge of his two younger sisters' mattress. "Take care of yourselves and mother. One day I will come back. I promise you that." he whispered.

He kissed each of them and then looked towards his grandmother. He was surprised to see her eyes blinking in the semi-darkness. She lifted her blanket and invited him to crawl in next to her as he had done so many times as a little boy suffering the shock of a nightmare. She whispered a song and caressed him to sleep one last time.

The following morning, Yakup was up and out before the crack of dawn. In the cave, all was still. His small bag was prepared and all he needed to do was to avoid convincing himself that he should stay. The path, descending down from the mouth of the cave to the valley floor, was dimly lit by a fading moon. A sliver of orange lay on the horizon. The darkness was not a problem, for he knew each step of the path that he had traversed a thousand times before. His mind struggled to process and retain all the practicalities of the coming journey. He kept a mental list of items and balanced that with the itinerary that lay before him. Focusing on these tasks held his emotions at bay. The practical part of his brain won and not once did he attempt to double back.

He walked along the rock face riddled with cave dwellings. He stopped by the empty spaces where the Buddhas had stood, to bid them a final goodbye, bowing deeply before turning away for good.

The valley was waking up. The crowing of a rooster alerted the other roosters, who did not want to appear as lesser cocks and chimed in with the growing chorus of dogs barking and donkeys and goats braying. Yes, the valley was alive again and bracing itself for another day.

"Wait!" a faint voice yelled from behind Yakup.

Someone was racing towards him. A child. It was Zahra.

"Zahra! What are you doing here?"

She did not slacken her pace until she was tackling Yakup. They fell to the ground, Zahra landing atop her brother.

"Don't," she said in between breaths. Her small fists pounding Yakup's chest.

"Stop, Zahra," he managed to say, before catching hold of her thundering fists.

"It's not fair," she sobbed.

"I know."

"Why do you have to go?"

"Zahra."

"But why?"

"You know why."

"No!"

"I will miss you too."

"No, you won't!"

"Don't be silly, Zahra. I will miss you more than anything."

"Are you sure?"

"Of course. I'm sure of it... and you have grandma Amaya, Noor and mom."

"But I want *you* to stay."

"I want to stay, too."

They got up. The first rays of sun licked the tops of the hills. "But you know I can't."

"I know," she said and started to cry. They hugged for a long time.

Two more people suddenly descended the path. Noor trailed by Grandma Amaya.

"Yakup," Noor stammered and embraced her brother and sister.

"My dear children," Grandma Amaya said and joined the crying and hugging club.

"I couldn't stop them," she said through tears.

"My brother can't leave me without saying goodbye," Zahra said in her small, but firm voice.

"Of course not, my dear, of course not," grandma Amaya said as they embraced one last time.

Yakup left them there that early spring morning on the narrow path.

11

KABUL

Grandma Amaya had paid a friend of a local driver to ferry Yakup, in the back of a truck full of sheep to Kabul.

"Are you the driver?" Yakup had asked the only person next to the sole truck on the desolate road at the agreed-to meeting point.

"Are you the boy going to Kabul?" the driver had replied.

"Yes.

"You can sit in the back. I'm having a couple of others join me so the seats are taken."

"Ok!"

"Do you want your bag up front?" he asked.

Yakup hesitated before the driver continued, "It's up to you, boy, but I'm warning you—it can get messy back there."

Yakup gave him the bag, but only after stuffing a few things in his pockets.

The road was marred by potholes and each time the driver steered the truck through one, it tested the shocks and fenders with a terrible cry. The sheep did not seem to pay much attention to their fellow passenger.

At first, the stench of acrid sheep faeces caused Yakup to gasp for breath as his stomach churned. But once the drive commenced, the chilled morning air created a turbine of sorts that allowed him to, if anything, remain conscious. The constant blast of cold mountain air, however, soon saw Yakup shivering with cold and longing for the foul sheep smell. He managed to find a corner, and in the lee of one of the sheep, stay somewhat warm.

The day before his departure, Grandma Amaya had handed Yakup a small roll of afghani notes for his journey and first days in Kabul.

It was evening when the truck finally jolted to a halt. A flat tire had prolonged the ride by a couple of hours and the bad traffic along the access road to Kabul had kept the engine in first gear for what felt like hundreds of kilometres.

The driver appeared at the back of the truck.

"This is your stop."

"Thanks," Yakup said. His skin was covered in a layer of dust. The animals had defecated and urinated everywhere and their faeces had dried into flakes amid a slick of urine and filth. Yakup's pants had soaked up much of the muck from the truck bed with the cloth clinging uncomfortably to his legs. Yakup remembered how the smell had made his eyes water when he had first entered the truck and that now, he, too, radiated that same smell. His whole being yearned for a bath.

"How are the animals doing?" the driver said. He scratched his head and looked slightly nervous.

"All right, I think. Most of them in any case," Yakup said. He pulled himself up by the iron bar and jumped down from the truck. They had stopped at a marketplace on the outskirts of the city.

"What a smell," the driver said and pushed his white pakol to the back of his head.

"The sheep pissed and shat. I think one of them slipped in its own piss and broke a leg," Yakup said. He didn't mention that he had pulled his pants down along the way and delivered a contribution to the existing waste.

"It happens. Most of them are destined to be slaughtered so a broken limb or two shouldn't affect the price." The driver remained standing, looking worried.

"Do you think you can tell me where my cousin lives?"

Yakup handed the driver the small slip of paper with his grandmother's writing. He looked at the note, scratched his butt and let out a small burp.

"Hmmm," he said and turned around.

"Wait! Don't leave!" Yakup said.

The driver yelled to a seller at a chai stand and gestured with his arm for him to approach the back of the truck. The seller hurried towards them.

"Give me and the boy two cups of chai and afterwards you can give him directions." The driver's face was shiny with perspiration after a day of driving without a wash. His white pakol, now stained yellow with dried sweat, made his already greasy hair appear still darker.

He pulled a bag of nuts from the pocket of the grey vest that he wore over his tunic and offered Yakup some. He opened his sticky hand and the driver poured a small pile into it. The nuts were pocket-warm and had a faint hint of urine and sheep to them, but Yakup's neglected stomach didn't mind. The sweet, black tea did its best to cleanse his lungs from the dirt his body had absorbed throughout the day.

"Can you tell me where I can find this place?" Yakup passed the note to the seller.

"If you tell me what those letters say," the man replied.

"It's my cousin's place. In Darul Aman," Yakup said.

"Darul Aman. It is out there," he pointed. "Well, you want to pass Kabul Zoo. There you turn onto the big road and continue. On your right, you'll pass the Russian Embassy. Then soon you'll see the destroyed Darul Aman Palace. I don't know the area well. Ask someone there," he said.

A customer ordered a cup of tea. It occupied the man for a while. The moon was peeping above the rugged hills that looked so different from the mountains in Bamiyan. It cast a silver glint to the city.

"It's getting late," the seller said. "This city isn't kind to newcomers in the dark of the night. Too much poverty out there," he smiled and winked.

"Maybe I'll wait until tomorrow then," said Yakup. "Thank you."

"A pleasure to help a small sparrow in the forest." The vendor laughed and pulled his wagon towards a group of newly arrived travellers who were surely better for business than Yakup. The truck driver had his head and hands deep in the engine.

"Can I help with something?" Yakup asked.

"Hmm… this bucket of bolts is still holding together all right, but that's only because I treat her better than any of the other old complaining ladies in my life—my wives, my sisters" He slammed the hood shut and patted it. His arms were greasy up to the elbows where his shirtsleeves had been rolled up. He wiped his arms and blackened hands on a cloth, but his nails stayed rimmed with black. They probably always bore that faint, dark imprint of grease and petrol. He gave Yakup a knowing smile.

"Hardware, engines, tyres—now that is something I know about. Animals? Not at all. I don't like them. Simple yet complex. If they die, they are dead. An engine on the other hand can die and be resurrected over and over again. We can switch off its life support and just as easily turn a small key that will magically bring it back to life. Amazing, huh?" His eyes were glimmering. He threw the cloth onto the seat.

"I tell you what. If you want to help, you can take care of the animals. If you agree, I'll get some food and you can sleep under the truck?"

Yakup agreed and spent the next hour cleaning out the truck bed amid bleating sheep, pushing them aside and shovelling their excrement out onto the road. He gave the animals water and some hay. He then found a cold-water tap where he washed as much as possible from his arm and legs before changing into his only other pair of pants.

Tired, almost clean, and pleased that he had survived his first day on the road, Yakup settled under the truck with the pile of rice pilau that the driver had left for him. The night was clear, the noises different. He was not used to the passing cars and the sound of a city nor to sleeping under a truck full of sheep. But the day had taken its toll and the exhausted boy soon fell asleep with a full belly and a bit of rice on his chest.

"You cheap scoundrel! Bandit!" Yakup woke up to the braying of sheep and loud voices next to the truck.

"You are a day late! I lost business. A wedding. That customer was an influential man." Yakup could see two pairs of shoes. One of them a pair of dusty leather sandals; the other a set of blue plastic flip-flops.

"It's not my fault that the roads are littered with potholes and that the government has not expanded the access roads. More cars on worse roads. What did you expect?" the flip-flops said, one foot scratching the other.

"I can expect problems with my business partners because you didn't get my goods here on time. That's what I can expect," leather sandals retorted. The big toes wiggled up and down.

Yakup decided that there was no reason for him to stay, so, he wrapped up the remaining rice pilau and shoved the small parcel into his bag, emptied his painful bladder against a tire and crawled out on the other side of the truck. The door to the cab was open. The half-empty bag of nuts was on the seat. Without thinking, Yakup snatched it, but then thought of what Grandma Amaya would say, and put it back. He left the sheep and the driver without a goodbye and ventured into the bustling traffic of Kabul.

12

THE KING AND MOHAMMED

It was late afternoon when Yakup stopped in front of a gate with yellow paint peeling off the metal bars. A strip of barbed wire was stretched all around the brown wall. Behind it lurked the crown of a mulberry tree. He knocked on the iron gate and immediately a vicious barking erupted from inside. In between the barking, threatening growls told visitors they had better be careful.

"Quiet," a boy's voice rang out. It resulted in a half-hearted bark and then a submissive yelp. A small door slid open and a boyish face peered out.

"Who are you?" the boy asked. He was a few years younger than Yakup.

"Is this Abdul's house?"

The boy looked Yakup up and down.

"Maybe. Who is asking?"

"My name is Yakup. Abdul is my cousin on my father's side."

"What did you say your name was?"

"Yakup."

"Why have I never seen you before?"

"It's my first time in Kabul."

"If you have never been to Kabul before, how do you know that Abdul lives here?" There was a slight smirk in the voice.

"My grandmother gave me the address. Do you think I would randomly come up to this house and ask for Abdul? Now, does he live here or not?"

"How can you prove that you are who you say you are?"

Yakup did not feel like playing these games, but after all, if they were somehow related, what harm would it do?

77

"My grandmother is the mother of my father, who is the brother of Abdul's father. That makes me the cousin of Abdul. Grandmother Amaya gave me this address. She would have informed him that I was coming."

The face stared at Yakup in disbelief.

"Listen, I travelled all day yesterday from Bamiyan with a flock of sheep and spent the night under a truck. I haven't eaten since this morning, and honestly, I'm getting tired of your questions. If Abdul does not live here, just tell me and I'll be on my way. Got it?"

"I didn't say he didn't live here," the boy said and shut the peephole with a loud clank. There was a noise of someone fiddling with a chain and lock, and the gate opened with a screech.

A big dog jumped toward Yakup—the kind of dog used for fighting. A set of pointy, yellow teeth glinted. Drool leapt from the dog's jaws with each bark. The muscles were tight under the white fur. The animal was stopped short by a chain around its neck that was connected to the mulberry tree in the corner of the small yard. Despite the relative safety afforded him by the constraints, Yakup instinctively took a few steps back. The boy lifted his arm in a threatening gesture and hissed. The dog retreated obediently beneath the tree where it instinctively eyed the newcomer with grave suspicion.

"Don't worry. King is as mild as a lamb. Come in now."

Two rusty chairs flanked the door of a small, red brick house. Two square windows stared into the courtyard from each side of the door. The yard had a tiny square plot where a few tomato plants and withered herbs grew. A tin roof concealed a few meters of ground where, beneath it sat several rusting jerry cans, a shovel, a plastic sheet and some half-empty bags. There was a small latrine to the right of the house.

"Please, sit down," the boy gestured towards the chairs and smiled with his mouth, but not his eyes.

"My name is Mohammed. Abdul is my father. That means we must be family."

The two boys shook hands. Mohammed's hand was moist and the handshake weak.

"I hope you don't mind my questioning you, but these days one shouldn't let a stranger enter through the front gate. There are too many people with dubious motives and too many weapons around."

"No harm done," Yakup said.

"You need a wash?" Mohammed half asked half stated as he scrutinised Yakup, who nodded, sat down and dropped his bag on the ground.

"There's water in the back. I'll bring you some clean clothes."

"Thank you," Yakup said and went to wash.

He returned feeling refreshed, energised. Mohammed sat in front of the house with two cups of chai. He gestured to the chair next to him.

"My dad will be back tonight. He is at work."

King had made peace with the presence of Yakup and was dozing off under the mulberry tree. A muezzin began his call for afternoon prayer from a distant minaret. He was soon joined by colleagues from every direction.

"Are you going to pray?" Mohammed asked.

Yakup shook his head, not knowing if that was an appropriate reply.

"Just remember that it is better if you do pray, especially when Baba is here."

"How come?"

"He takes God very seriously. He wasn't always like that. I think he sees prayer as a time to be meditative. You know, with his second job and all," Mohammed said.

"What does he do?"

"He's a policeman."

"And his second job?"

"Well, a policeman. You see, the police work for the Ministry of Interior. But they also work for others. Baba works for an influential man. Because he is a policeman, he is good with security and that kind of thing, so he helps keep this big guy safe from criminals—and there are many criminals in Kabul."

They drank tea in silence for a while. King was sleeping, his paws moving restlessly.

"Is your mother at work?" Yakup asked.

"I don't have a maman," Mohammed replied in a matter-of-fact way. "She passed away before my memory started to function." He tapped two fingers to his head and pretended to strain his mind. "Poof! Nothing in there."

"I'm sorry. I lost my baba just recently," Yakup said.

"Do you remember him?"

"Yes, he died just last year."

"You're lucky," Mohammed said. He was drumming on his empty cup with his fingers while humming a song. Then an excited smile appeared on his face. "Do you want to see something?"

"Sure," Yakup said.

Mohammed got up and moved towards King.

"Up, King!" He commanded. The dog quickly jumped to his feet and stared at his master in anticipation.

"Sit!"

The dog obeyed.

"Roll."

Again, the dog did as it was directed. Mohammed took a stick and held it up. He pretended to throw it once, twice, three times. Each time the dog eagerly made a move and barked in excitement.

Mohammed laughed. "Look at him." Again, he made to throw the stick but didn't.

The big dog was panicking. The stick meant everything to him now. If King wanted to, he could have easily wrestled the stick from Mohammed, but did not. There was a hint of madness in his eyes as he followed every little movement of the stick.

"Now look at this," Mohammed grinned and tossed the stick to the end of the yard. King stormed towards it, but just before he reached it, the chain caught, sending the animal to the ground by the neck. He pulled at his restraints in a vain attempt to reach his target—tongue hanging out, chain tight at the neck.

Mohammed was laughing hard now. "Stupid dog. Come!" he commanded.

The dog hesitated. The stick was so close.

"Come here," Mohammed said again; this time in a hardened voice. King walked away from the stick with his head and tail lowered. Madness and submission were apparent in his eyes.

"Why did you do that?" Yakup asked.

"It's just a game. Didn't you see how silly he was?" Mohammed said with a childish laugh.

"Couldn't you see that you were hurting him?"

"What do you know about *my* dog?" the younger boy retorted.

"I know that you almost broke his neck," Yakup nearly shouted.

"He is a strong dog. He can take it. And you're welcome to leave if you don't want to stay," Mohammed said with a pretentious tone. He nodded towards the yellow gate.

Even though Yakup felt like getting up and leaving, he knew that there was nowhere else to go. They both knew that.

The two sat in silence for a while. Then Mohammed went into the house without a word and did not come out. Yakup stayed and watched King watching the stick. The muscular dog's mind was still focused on the unreachable object. Yakup got up. The dog looked at him with pained eyes, ears back. The boy walked slowly towards the stick. The path led him within reach of the dog. King lifted his upper lip and revealed his incisors.

Yakup knew that dogs could sense fear, so he kept his slow, unhesitating pace until he could bend down and grab the stick. The moment he lifted it; the dog was up. Madness returned to its eyes. Yakup threw the stick at him. The powerful dog caught it in the air and went into a frenzy of biting and chewing. Soon the stick was nothing but splinters scattered around the now pacified animal. Yakup walked back to his chair and stayed there. King stayed with the remains of the stick.

13

TWO-EYED ABDUL

The wind picked up as evening approached. Small devils of dust flared and disappeared. Tiny dead branches fell from the mulberry tree. The smoke from fireplaces and stoves around Kabul mingled with car fumes and the dust from dried-out open sewers. A fine layer of brown dust covered King's white fur. The wind ruffled Yakup's hair and sand-like particles found their way into his ears, eyes and nose.

A car honked right outside the gate. Mohammed rushed out into the courtyard, the wind catching the apron he was wearing. He tried to keep it in place, squinting to keep the worst of the dust out of his eyes. He glanced at the broken stick next to King, and then at Yakup, before he pushed the iron gate open. An old Russian military jeep sped in. It was one of those with a stick shift and small flashing controls built into the front.

A man was behind the steering wheel. He pulled the jeep to an abrupt halt just under the mulberry tree. The man—small, sturdy, and in a police uniform—stepped out. He was greeted heartily by King, to whom he gave a friendly pat. The dog stayed by the driver's leg. The man scratched the happy dog. Mohammed talked in a hushed voice to the man. Yakup touched the crumpled piece of paper in his pocket with the scribbled address. It was going to be okay he assured himself.

The policeman slammed the door to the jeep and walked towards Yakup—Mohammed and King at his heels. His hair was short and black. It was kept in place under a police cap. He had a thick and well-groomed black beard. A pair of dark sunglasses were pressed tight to his face. Of this face, only a nose and purplish lips were visible. There were stubs of black hair on the very ends of his nose.

He stopped in front of Yakup. They were the same height, but he was clearly a man and Yakup a boy next to him.

"How is Amaya?" he asked in a mild and sincere voice.

"Um… Good!" Yakup fumbled, caught slightly off-guard.

"Ah, the stories my baba used to tell about her. She was a wild one when she was younger." His purple lips twisted into a smile as he continued, "Welcome to Kabul!" He took off his sunglasses to reveal one brown eye and one green eye. The two different coloured eyes unnerved Yakup.

"So, cousin, Amaya told me that you are in a bit of a mess and that we need to see to you getting out of this mess, right?"

Yakup nodded.

"Well, I'm not sure Kabul is less messy than Bamiyan, though, I haven't been up there for ages," the man said. "I would like to apologise in advance for the state of the place. Mohammed and I only have each other now. We could use a woman's hand around here, you agree, Mohammed jan? But with a policeman's salary, it can be difficult to find a good wife these days. Young women are becoming more and more liberated and want to choose husbands for themselves. Heck, I should find a pretty girl in a village and take her as my wife, and well, maybe I'll just go on and do that one day. What do you think, Mohammed jan?"

Cousin Abdul barely glanced at his son as he spoke and never seemed to expect a response from Mohammed.

"Well, cousin, to start, you can sleep on a mattress in the living room since that's where Mohammed is sleeping, but I'm sure you two boys will get along just fine. And it is good for you to get to know some of your more distant family. Mohammed can give you the run-down of the house since he takes care of everything. Before I forget, though, how old are you, cousin? I could use a pair of hands here from time to time since circumstances also demand that I work additional hours when I am not on duty. This supplements the meagre salary I get from the government pays me, and well, I have to really—I have no choice, just simple survival. We all have our paths in life and with two jobs, a man of my age could use the sharpness of a young one like yourself."

He blinked with his green eye and patted Yakup's shoulder. "Now let's get out of this damned wind and dust and get some grub. Come in and feel at home."

Cousin Abdul led the way into the house. An old, dark, wooden chest of drawers sat in one corner of the rectangular living room. On top was a TV that at one time or another had been considered modern. In one of the two windowsills hung an empty birdcage, lined with newspaper. One of the walls had a faded poster of the Kaaba in Mecca surrounded by a sea of white-clad pilgrims. On the right-hand side, wall hung an old cuckoo clock that had stopped at a quarter to ten. Two similarly patterned kilim rugs covered the floor. Pillows and synthetic-fabric blankets were piled against the wall. A red plastic sheet indicated to Yakup where meals were served. Mohammed had set three plates on the plastic sheet alongside tomato slices, naan, rice, beans, yoghurt and greasy chicken.

"Sit down," cousin Abdul said. He had changed into a grey shalwar kameez. The open neckline revealed a patch of black hair, which seemed to grow on cousin Abdul like wild bougainvillea. The back of his hands could almost be combed and the hair on his ears had to be cut regularly by a barber.

"My stomach is an empty pit and it needs some serious filling. Let's eat."

Cousin Abdul stretched out his hands and dug in. The hairy man stuffed his mouth with large chunks of chicken followed by rice and naan used to soak up the remaining grease and fat. He ate a lot and quickly. Then he leaned back and patted his round belly.

"Your father was a good man. Hard-working and cared for his family. My own father, your uncle, always spoke highly of him. I suspect he envied his brother for being Grandma Amaya's favourite."

Air slipped through cousin Abdul's abdomen and found its way out through his purple lips in the shape of a belch.

"My uncle still respected your father despite his choices and helpful nature. He would always say that his mother, your grandmother Amaya, was someone he always missed—right up to his last days.

"She was too far away up there in Bamiyan, which bothered him. But he was the one who chose to give up provincial life and avoid the farming life his father had had.

"Instead, he packed up one day and left in order to pursue life as a city dweller with all the opportunities such a location could offer a rural peasant of sorts. His father, our grandfather, was not happy with this decision. I don't think they talked much during the final few years he was around. That's another reason he envied your dad.

"But as I said, he didn't bear a grudge towards your baba. He knew that it wasn't his fault. But our grandfather was irreconcilable. It sure wasn't your baba's fault that it didn't turn out as my father had hoped it would when he first moved to Kabul.

Heck, even now most of these naive, rural bastards think that they will get a job the moment they arrive in Kabul. However, they soon realise they are one among thousands looking for work, and ultimately, end up displaced and begging in the outskirts of the city or, worse, in the slums and camps wishing they were still back in the villages they left behind. They dream of a simple life when all they had to do was make sure that their tiny plots of sad, dry land yielded enough food for them and their families.

"So, now they come to the cities and rely on do-gooders with political aspirations and the foreigners handing out food, clothes and tents. Some are dressed in green, others in blue. Some mess up, while others clean up after them. I tell you cousin—it is a vicious cycle. The foreign soldiers and the do-gooders use one another in order to achieve their own selfish purposes. Everybody knows this! Bomb a few villages, then build a camp for the displaced to congregate. The soldiers eventually return to the US and Europe and tell the public that they have killed the Taliban and rescued the poor Afghan civilians. It's a load of bullshit.

"No, I tell you, cousin, this isn't an easy place to live. I have seen able-bodied men and women wither into shadows of themselves within weeks after arriving in this city. Kabul will eat you alive. It will already be too late when you realise the city has planted a poisonous seed in you that will infect your provincial mind, draining you of your vitality and seeing you sit, dirty and unwashed, in the gutter with your hand outstretched day in, day out, hoping someone will spare you his charge or left-over kebab. The poor bastard starts scratching his crotch looking for his balls, but he realises that it's too late—the city has sucked, chewed and swallowed them."

Cousin Abdul had to stop talking as he dug his hairy pinky finger deep into his mouth in an effort to dislodge something from between two molars. When his finger re-emerged, he studied the small piece of tomato peel stuck to his nail and flipped it towards the naked chicken bones on his plate.

"What I want to say, cousin is that it is a damn shame about your baba. We thought he made the right choice in staying up there. But now he is dead. What does any of it matter then? I'm sorry about your father. I really am, but I've had a long day. Tomorrow I have to work both the dayshift and nightshift and will be up early to pray, so, get used to it," Abdul said. He got to his feet, stretched, and went outside to wash.

Yakup picked up the remaining cutlery from the red plastic sheet and went over to Mohammed who was washing up in the small hallway between the living room and cousin Abdul's bedroom. The small hallway acted as both a kitchen and a storage room. There was little space, but Mohammed had found a path through the junk and a rhythm to his movements over time.

"Mohammed, can I help you?" Yakup asked.

"I have it under control," he said without looking up from his chores.

"I am not here to create more work for you," Yakup said. "I will help you if you tell me what you need help with."

Still, Mohammed didn't answer.

"I'm not here to take the place of an older brother. I am no threat to you. It probably won't be long before I'm out of here anyway. I just need some time to figure things out." Mohammed looked up from his cleaning ritual. "It's ok. You can take the small mattress from the back there," he pointed behind Yakup where a faded green mattress was shoved between the wall and a broken chair.

"Thank you, Mohammed. It is kind of you," Yakup said and went back into the living room to prepare his bed.

That night, as he lay his head on a pink pillow and the noise of Kabul buzzed in his ears, Yakup realised that this was the first time he had slept in a real house. He fell asleep thinking of his mother, Grandma Amaya, Noor and Zahra at home in the cave and he wished they were all there with him.

14

THE CHEST

The roaring engine of his cousin's Russian jeep woke Yakup. Abdul had slid out of the house as quietly as a cat. Mohammed was outside with his chai.

"Good morning," Yakup said.

"How was your night?" Mohammed asked.

"Fine."

"Dad had to go. Work." Mohammed filled another cup with steaming green tea and handed it to Yakup.

"Thanks," he said and sat down next to Mohammed.

When Yakup's bladder called for release, he went to the latrine behind the house. One step up brought him to a dirty sheet. He pushed it aside and was met by the familiar ammonia stench from piles of urine and excrement that had created a peak that threatened to rise out of the latrine hole. In the small dank shed, flies danced underneath Yakup's buttocks and there were audible living creatures below him that he did not want to think about. He appreciated the darkness of the pit below and hurried with his business.

The sky was grey. A mass without any particular feature, waiting without movement, enveloping Kabul. There was hardly any wind. The frantic braying of sheep cut through the lacklustre morning.

Somewhere someone was using a hammer. It worked rhythmically against iron. A generator buzzed in the background. Vehicles, street vendors, a passing helicopter, a group of school children, a bicycle, a police siren—the sound of a city much different from that which Yakup was accustomed to.

87

"What time is school?" Yakup asked. He was sitting cross-legged and chewing on a piece of naan.

"When I do go, it would be around now. I don't always. I don't have to," Mohammed frowned.

"Don't you want to go?"

"Not really, you see, the thing is that many of the other boys are slow. I get bored with the repetition and the need to simplify already simple points." Mohammed emptied his cup. "But yes, today I'm off to school. If you leave the house, be sure to lock the gate. The key is under the brick next to the tree. I'll be home midday."

The boy picked up a pale blue backpack with a cartoon of two oversized smiling bees and walked out through the gate.

Yakup spent the morning washing his clothes. They still stank of sheep. It took a lot of scrubbing to get the stench out. He hung them up to dry behind the house and then washed himself again. Afterwards, he decided to take a tour of his cousin's house.

He was already familiar with the living room and the hallway, so, he went into the room in the back where there was a small window and a locked door that led to the side of the yard. There was a mattress on the floor and a clothes closet. Up against the wall were two aluminium chests with an ashtray on top. Next to it lay half a pack of cigarettes and the empty wrapper of a biscuit roll.

The chests awoke Yakup's curiosity. There was nothing in the house that indicated any kind of history besides the two chests. There had to be something interesting in them, unless, of course, cousin Abdul had hidden his past somewhere else. Or, maybe he simply didn't have a past. Yet everyone had something to hide. There was always something.

Yakup touched the locked chest. He was itching with curiosity, but the voice of Grandma Amaya made him stop. So, instead, he left the room and returned to the courtyard.

Yakup did not do much over the course of the following weeks. Cousin Abdul told him to stay at home and be prepared. He spent his days reading books and playing with King. Mohammed disappeared to school or somewhere else most days. They had grown closer, but for reasons

Yakup didn't understand, Mohammed had no particular empathy for his new-found first cousin, once removed.

After a few days, Yakup asked cousin Abdul when he might need him to do something so that he could earn money and be on his way. Cousin Abdul answered skirted the question and never brought it up again.

Yakup was getting bored. He even considered going back to Bamiyan and facing the consequences, but the thought of being shot in the back by Rashid or his brothers quelled that idea.

One day, when he was home alone and King lay sleeping under the mulberry tree and the books all seemed too heavy, Yakup decided that it was time to return to the chests in Abdul's room.

He ventured to the gate and stood a moment in order to ensure that he was alone and that no neighbours were not around.

Once satisfied, he returned to the living room, checking that there were no sounds from either side of the courtyard, and finally, stepped into his cousin Abdul's room and towards the two aluminium chests that rested one on top of the other. He took his time looking around and committing to memory where the locations of all the objects before lifting the lid of the first chest.

It contained a few books, including the Quran, some Sufi poetry and a couple of old novels. There were documents with the names and logos of the Ministry of Interior and the European Union's police unit, EUPOL. An empty holster for a gun was on top of some foreign coins and loose nails swam around in the bottom.

Yakup was disappointed. He had violated the trust of cousin Abdul for a pathetic and boring outcome. He lifted the top chest and set it down on the floor in the hopes of discovering something better in the second one.

But a small, black plastic-coated padlock held the lid shut. He pulled at the padlock.

Nothing.

This barrier piqued his curiosity, but the small resistant padlock remained resistant to his efforts. He fished around for one of the loose nails from the other chest and fiddled with the lock.

The padlock's black plastic coating soon became scratched, documenting, one by one, his futile efforts. Carelessly, he had allowed the nail to scratch several fine lines in the plastic. Cousin Abdul merely had to cast a glance at the padlock to know that someone had tried to open it.

Yakup had already come this far and so decided to fetch a hammer and simply destroy the lock in its entirety. He slammed the hammer onto the lock a couple of times and it popped open.

The first thing he saw was a mass of brown pressed flour wrapped in plastic. Yakup lifted it, turned the bulk around and smelled it. It had the vague scent of vinegar. He put it back and lifted a folder with travel documents. They were all for cousin Abdul and Mohammed, but with different names and nationalities. There was a thick stack of US currency in a small envelope. He flipped through a dusty photo album and stopped at one, which featured a younger Abdul and a woman who was holding two babies in her arms. Yakup expected that one of them was Mohammed.

Yakup realised that he had stumbled upon a grave secret in his cousin's home. What exactly the chest contained, or represented, was unclear to him, but the clues all suggested that his cousin was involved in something bigger, and likely, more dangerous. This meant that the knowledge Yakup now possessed a grim burden that could not be erased nor hidden.

Yakup weighted the envelope with the money. There was a lot—enough to take him to Europe. It was tempting and with one of Mohammed's travel documents, it was increasingly tempting. Yakup could simply take these items and walk away. Disappear. He got up, money in hand, and turned toward the door.

It was at that moment that Grandma Amaya appeared, as clearly as if she was right there in front of him. At the thought of her condemnation, Yakup put the money and the documents back into the chest and shut the lid. This was it—there was no way back. Yakup knew he had stepped out of line. He could not hide what he had done. Not knowing how cousin Abdul would react, Yakup realised that his best option, his only option, was to disappear. He could try to reason with Abdul, the policeman on a criminal path, whose treasure box Yakup had broken into. But he did not trust that blood was thicker than the stack of money.

He packed his few belongings with shaking hands. He took a deep breath and went into the courtyard where King lay snoozing under the mulberry tree. Yakup scratched him behind his ears and hugged the big muscular dog that he had grown fond of during his short stay in Kabul. He pushed open the iron gate with the flaking yellow paint and quickly walked away.

15

THE STREETS

It was one of those days where the greyness of the day was refracted in the indifferent faces of people making their way through the streets. It was one of those days that would be forgotten as soon as sleep overtook the people. It was a day, drowned in a sea of thousands of days, where time only existed only as a dragging nuisance. It would prove, however, to be a day Yakup would never forget.

The city grew busier the closer he walked toward the centre of Kabul along Darul Aman Road. The street, crowded with cars, buses and trucks that spewed fat, black smoke choked the many pedestrians. Motorbikes zigzagged between the four-wheeled vehicles and the constant flow of those who dared cross through the traffic.

Yakup walked through a busy roundabout and turned down another street. There were small rectangular clay and brick houses pinned along the hillsides around him. Colourful laundry was hanging from lines swaying in the wind. Fences, walls and gates kept curious eyes from peering into the houses. Small children toddled while their older sisters in veils watched them. Litter was tossed recklessly in piles along the potholed sidewalk or floated in the murky water of open trenches. Women in blue burqas and high heels carried shopping bags in one hand and held children in the other, many squatting near street vendors who displayed their wares on plastic sheeting, walls or stalls along the road.

Young men in western clothing and Bollywood-style haircuts strode with confidence toward universities and office buildings all while donkeys, driven by younger boys in more traditional attire, pulled wooden carts with sacks of potatoes and onions toward markets. Limb men in dirty clothes and turbans, disabled by years of war, rolled about on wheeled boards, venturing into a maelstrom of cars stuck in the heavy traffic in order to beg for handouts. Their efforts under heavy competition from women, shrouded in the burqa, displaying babies in an effort to induce sympathy from passers-by. People hustled their way through the bustling city.

Yakup stopped at a chai stand, washed his hands and face, drank two cups of sugary chai and indulged in a naan to fill his stomach. Grandmother Amaya's roll of notes was growing increasingly smaller. He handed one of them to an outstretched palm.

He passed Kabul Zoo and remembered the story about Marjan the Lion and the Taliban fighter who, in the aftermath of their easy conquest of war-ravaged Kabul, had felt invincible and jumped into the lion's den. The soldier stood no chance and was killed by the lion called Marjan. When his brother, another Taliban fighter, heard what had happened, he was furious and went to the zoo. He threw a grenade at Marjan, who miraculously survived, although with one eye less and his body partially paralysed.

Marjan ultimately outlived the Taliban regime, but upon his passing some years ago, he was commemorated in the form of a statue and a story.

Yakup walked still further into Kabul. He passed street vendors, police checkpoints, mosques and concrete walls en masse. He stopped by the murky waters of the Kabul River, so different from the turquoise of the Band-e-Amir. A group of men were praying at the old blue-domed Pul-e Kishti Mosque while cars, mopeds and bicycles moved in both directions right beside them.

The streets led him deeper and deeper into Kabul. Small boys and girls sold chewing gum, lighters, painkillers and whatever else they could filch and resell as their own.

He passed a supermarket with a high glass façade. Shiny Toyotas were parked out front and a steady flow of foreigners and better-off Afghans made for the doors of the building.

In other streets, butchers and vegetable vendors sold their goods to more average Afghans while just behind them, the destitute surveyed dumpsters in search of leftovers to fill their aching bellies.

Yakup was tempted to fill his stomach with some of the delicious-smelling food from one of the many small vendors near the park, but the small roll of afghanis that Grandma Amaya had given him would not last much longer at this rate. He chose, instead, to venture into the park where a small group of kids were playing football.

As he departed on the other side of the park, he saw a man selling peacocks. They were lined up against the fence. The large birds looked sad in the grey Kabul light and the exhaust from the constant line of passing cars didn't do much for their feathers.

A KFC—Kabul Fried Chicken'—sent another set of tempting smells into Yakup's nostrils. As he passed the restaurant, a group of foreigners came out. One of them looked with pity at Yakup and handed him a plastic bag with the restaurant's logo. The foreigner hurried into his white car and settled in behind tinted windows.

Inside the bag, Yakup found a few pieces of deep-fried chicken and some French fries. The crispy, fat chicken was still warm and full of oil and grease. He retreated to the park where he savoured the salty treat and sucked his fingers clean. He closed his eyes and just before he dozed off on the ground, thought to himself, *maybe life was not so bad after all*.

When he awoke, it was early afternoon. Not knowing what else to do, he picked himself up and walked on. After some time, and having passed so many heavily guarded places, he began to wonder who in their right mind would even consider an attempt at an attack on a house in Kabul; as he knew happened regularly. They would have to be just as heavily equipped and either have insider knowledge of the treasures within—or simply be suicidal.

He recalled the mullah's insistence that there was a better life after death on Earth and could see why some wouldn't mind leaving this place prematurely. He stopped a short distance from a police checkpoint and observed how the cars were pulled over.

A young policeman with a Kalashnikov dangling from his back asked to see the driver's papers. Often, a small bribe changed hands from the driver to the uniformed patrolman. Sometimes the young uniformed men would search a vehicle, open the trunk, look suspiciously at the seats and indicate that heaven would fall if the driver did not do something about a broken light, a missing safety triangle or a hole in the door.

Yakup sat in the shade of a tree, watching the spectacle occur within the busy Massoud Square. The nearby presence of the American Embassy had effectively shut down many of the side streets. The square had seen its share of suicide bombers. The roundabout brought a flow of cars to and from the city—a vein, constantly in peril of being clogged, though never fatally, with slow-moving taxis, bikes, pedestrians, trucks, tanks, diplomatic plates, do-gooders, ambassadors, politicians, journalists, Taliban, mercenaries, prostitutes, drug dealers — all transporting dreams and doom in and out of Kabul.

"Yakup! What are *you* doing here?"

He hadn't noticed the two uniformed officers approaching. Of all people, cousin Abdul was now standing right in front of him.

"This is my young cousin from the province. He is staying with me," cousin Abdul said to his colleague, who glanced at Yakup with little interest.

"Out in the city, are you?" cousin Abdul said, eying Yakup with his brown iris, his beard revealing a smile.

"I thought I'd take the opportunity to look around," Yakup said. His palms were wet with sweat.

"Curiosity killed the cat."

"What?"

"It is a saying. If you look too hard under too many rocks, the city can swallow you and will spit your sucked bones into the dusty streets, where dogs will fight over the scraps."

"I see."

"Why don't you join me for the rest of the day? I'm off duty in a little while and I know a great little place where we can grab some food." He shifted, winking at Yakup with his green eye.

"Um. I wanted to… I wanted to go and see the university."

"The university? What for?"

"Well, I was thinking that I could get an education one day."

"An education? I see. Well, *one day* is quite far away. Today is today. You'll have plenty of time to visit. No more discussion, cousin, you're coming with me. Imagine what people would think if I left my know-nothing cousin alone in this city," he chuckled, his green eye staring at Yakup.

There was clearly no discussion to be had, but Yakup reasoned, so long as Abdul did not leave his side, then he would not be at risk of his cousin's inevitable discovery, and subsequent wrath, of the now breached chest.

16

HETEROCHROMIA

Abdul led Yakup away from the busy main street, past a hospital and onto one of several gravel roads. Discarded paper and plastic trailed them as garbage collectors slung bulging bags of refuse onto their backs or bicycles. Their eyes searched for metal or plastic, weighing its worth in the eyes of the scrap dealers before deciding whether to pick it up or not. There was always the possibility of stumbling upon something that could be of value to them or their families.

"Here we are," cousin Abdul said. He stopped at a small gate near an open square. A few cars were parked under the trees. Cousin Abdul knocked on the gate, which solicited an eye to quickly appear, assess, and ultimately, open the iron-wrought gate with a small creak.

"Give us two of the usual," Abdul said. They sat at a table in the corner of a spacious courtyard. It was empty besides the two of them. "Try to make it edible today. I have a special guest," cousin Abdul said to the sleepy waiter. "I like this place. No nosy people."

He blinked, pulled out a pack of cigarettes from his pocket, took two in his mouth, lit them both and offered one to Yakup. The boy hesitated, then took it. Yakup sucked at the filter and filled his mouth with smoke. His eyes watered as the strong taste rolled over his tongue. He blew out a small cloud of smoke and wondered why people liked this. He feigned smoking for a few more minutes.

"The idea is to inhale the smoke to get the sensation of the nicotine. The filth of the tar makes you aware that you're alive," cousin Abdul said. He dragged on his cigarette and blew a perfect smoke ring in Yakup's direction.

"Of course," Yakup sputtered as he took a drag before coughing. Abdul laughed.

"Smokes are not for everyone. It looks like you haven't started yet. Probably better to keep it that way. For me, it is too late. I wouldn't know what to do without them. We're all going to die one day, and if smoking is the cause in my case, well, I've lived longer than I expected."

The waiter placed two piles of rice and chicken on the table and they dug in.

"You must have wondered what it is I do in my other job?" Cousin Abdul said between mouthfuls.

"A little."

"Have you guessed?"

"I don't think so."

"Try."

Cousin Abdul smiled and looked at Yakup with his green eye, tilting his head like a bird considering how to catch its prey.

"Ok. You're a policeman and also have a business," Yakup tried before returning to his dwindling pile of rice.

"And?" Cousin Abdul kept his stare at Yakup.

"Hmmm… So, a policeman and that's your day job, which means your other job must have some connection to that. I doubt you're teaching evening classes to police cadets."

"Why wouldn't I do that?" cousin Abdul interrupted.

"Well, maybe that is your other job…You do like to talk, as you've said, but would you enjoy teaching a bunch of young Afghan men that see the police force as an escape from something else? Most of them probably believe that serving in the police is only slightly better than working as a day labourer, begging, or vending on the street. They only go through the academy to get into the force so they can augment their pay checks with bribes," Yakup said. "Besides, I don't think you care too much about formal education."

Cousin Abdul was quietly observing his cousin's deduction. "Very clever, cousin, very clever." He lit another cigarette.

"So, I think you put your skills to use in a place that you believe will be of value to you. What exactly that is, I cannot say. You don't seem too distressed about the other job. In fact, you might even enjoy it," Yakup said.

"I like your thinking, cousin. It is clever and cunning." Cousin Abdul smiled. His green eye glimmered. "It's a good thing that we're related. I think you could be useful if you play your cards right. You see, my other job is a bit," he paused before continuing, "murky.

"Now, it is not any different from what is happening all over our country and if it wasn't for the demands made by the foreign moralists, then it probably would be embedded in our legal system and seen as just another job equal to any other trade.

"You see, there is good business in poppy growing. We Afghans supply the world with the drugs they need—both good and bad. Everyone with power is involved. Still, it has to be kept under the radar or we'd have still more problems at the hands of the Americans and their friends. I'm but a small piece in that puzzle. I help with security. That's all. Most of the fat cows are interested in a peaceful and organised trade. But once in a while someone steps on another's foot and shit hits the fan. So, there I am, cleaning up the shit."

Abdul's cell phone rang. He looked at the screen, stood up and excused himself from his explanation.

Yakup hoped that it would not be Mohammed telling his father about the chest. The gate was about ten meters away and cousin Abdul had his back to Yakup. The waiter was absent-mindedly staring at a grainy TV screen. His cousin was still on the phone—back still turned. A gun, holstered, was clinging to Abdul's belt Yakup got up and took a few steps.

"Hey!" Cousin Abdul's voice rang out, having ended his call and turned to face Yakup.

"Where are you going?" he asked. Yakup looked at the gate. He could not reach it without being stopped either by cousin Abdul or a bullet. Even if he did get out of the gate, he would have made for an easy target out on the open street far removed from the hustle and bustle of Kabul

"We have to go," cousin Abdul said. His voice was business-like. Yakup's palm was wet as it gripped his bag.

"I'm sorry," Yakup said as he decided to face the consequences of his earlier actions. The waiter laughed at what was on the TV. Cousin Abdul looked at Yakup with both the green and brown eyes, his head tilting a little to the right. He had put on his police cap. He shook his head.

"I'm not sure I understand you yet, cousin." he said, walking towards Yakup. "There might be a situation at my other job."

He walked over to the counter and slammed his hand down on its surface. "Eh! How much for the pathetic meal?"

Abdul threw a couple of crumpled notes on the counter. The waiter, sensing the urgency hurried to give him his change.

17

LORDS OF WAR

They walked down the dimly lit gravel road in the Wazir Akbar Khan neighbourhood. Cousin Abdul was on the phone explaining something about a situation that needed immediate attention. The streets were heavily guarded. Security personnel stood, waiting for their shifts to end. From time to time the sweet scent of hashish indicated a small cluster of soldiers, teenage boys in uniforms really, were somewhere nearby. Some streets were heavily fortified with high iron gates, concrete blocks and sandbags, no longer accessible to the common Afghan. They had metamorphosed into private fortresses for those who could afford them. Cousin Abdul's employer was someone influential if he lived in this part of town.

"Let me explain a few things to you," Abdul said as he slid his phone into his pocket. He pulled at his thick, shiny beard and licked his purple lips. Yakup nodded his understanding.

"Like many Afghans, my employer has fought in wars. He has made friends and enemies. Sometimes he has done deeds he would rather not have. That has been the way of life in our country for too long, cousin.

"My employer fought with a range of Mujahideen leaders and warlords. Most notably on behalf of the Northern Alliance which managed to keep the Taliban at bay until delivering them a final blow with the help of the Americans. It was conveniently forgotten by the foreigners that the Northern Alliance committed crimes in the conflict, crimes equal to many of those committed by the Taliban. Massoud, the so-called lion of Panjshir, had been assassinated only days before the attack on the two towers in New York. Many of the warlords saw an opportunity to inflict revenge on the Taliban as well as retake power.

"Some of the stories from that period are dark. One was the mass murder of Taliban fighters. In an act cruel even by the standards of this country, two shipping containers were filled with young men who had either been captured or surrendered. The doors were locked behind them. The sun on the metal was relentless and unbearable. The iron cages had no windows and only a little air circulated. The bearded men grow weaker and warmer inside the packed containers. Their tongues stuck to the roofs of their dry mouths, the little piss some of them could produce was thick and orange. The air was heavy with the smell of scared boys and young men who had been fighting for too long had eaten too little and just wanted to go home to their villages. It was not long before the weakest began to pass out. It didn't take long before the first man breathed his last. Others soon followed."

"They were cooked alive?" Yakup asked, appalled.

"You can call it that. The men who opened the containers were met with the horrible stench of death. God only knows how they were able to live with themselves. Those images must haunt them. Impossible to erase."

"And you work for the man that did this?"

"I will get to that. But first, you must understand that these types shift their allegiances as easily as the wind changes direction. In our country, it is not so much about geography so much as to whom, or what, you swear loyalty. We saw this during the siege of Kabul immediately after the Russians surrendered.

"As you probably know, the fragmented Mujahideen fighters paved the way for a renewed Afghanistan, but ultimately, could not decide among their ranks who was the most fit to rule; rather, they started fighting one another and Kabul took centre stage.

"The city was divided into strongholds and while battle lines changed overnight, the civilian population in Kabul paid the price. Shelling became the norm. None of the warlords were strong enough to gain a decisive edge though, and an odd status quo was maintained."

He paused, allowing his words to take effect before asking, "You know Darul Aman Palace at one point had two opposing factions living in two different sections of the great hall, right?"

"That is why it was destroyed then?" Yakup asked.

"Well, yes, partly," Abdul said.

They walked up a dark road. A couple of white Toyota Land Cruisers with United Nations stickers passed them. The heavily armoured cars turned into a corner compound. Before the gate closed, shutting Afghanistan off from the people living inside, Yakup saw armed security guards saluting the foreign men exiting the vehicles.

"Almost there," cousin Abdul said.

"Do you work with security for one of these men?" Yakup asked.

"More or less. Lately, my boss has aired his political ambitions in public. Something that does not sit well with his former friends. The call I got earlier was from one of my contacts informing me that something is afoot. Now, stay in the background and let me handle this."

Abdul greeted a group of stern and armed men who returned his greeting while allowing them to pass.

The curiosity that Yakup had had earlier was wearing off. The effect of his cousin's stories left him feeling ill at ease. It had not been his plan to flee one conflict simply to become entangled in another, and so, he decided that, when the opportunity presented itself, he would disappear. Again.

Besides, as soon as Abdul found out about the broken chest, the trust between the cousins would surely be shattered.

18

THE BEAR

They entered through a tall gate and stepped into a courtyard where men were looking busy, smoking cigarettes, drinking chai and talking. Most of them held AK-47s, guns or other assault rifles. No smiles or laughter resounded from their hushed conversations. Abdul addressed one of them directly.

"Has there been any confirmation that they are on their way?" Abdul asked. The man looked at Yakup and frowned.

"The boy is ok," Abdul said.

This seemed to satisfy the man, who may also have been in charge of the ragtag militia now taking shape in the courtyard. "We heard that *he* has been drinking. You know how unstable that can make him. He wants to put things straight with the boss."

"Hmmm… Do we know, what he has in mind?" Abdul asked.

"We have been unable to obtain information concerning his plans. We're not sure he has any, to be honest. All we have heard from our contacts is that he is drinking and wants to make a show of his power."

The man pulled out a pack of cigarettes, offering one to Abdul before taking one for himself.

"What is the boss saying?" Abdul asked as he flicked the ash from his cigarette butt to the ground.

"He is keeping his calm. He doesn't think anything will happen here in Kabul. Maybe in the north, but not here."

"I'm not too sure about that. That guy has an inflated sense of self and believes he is untouchable. I need to talk to him. Where is the boss?" Abdul asked.

"Inside with the wives and one of his sons," the other said.

Abdul crushed out his cigarette and walked towards the house.

"Yakup," Abdul stopped.

"Yes?"

"Best if you don't come in. The situation is a little tense. I'll find you later."

"That is fine," Yakup said.

Abdul turned on his heel and strode up the stairs to the impressive mansion.

He had not even reached the door before the quiet of the night was broken by the arrival of a motorcade making its way down the gravel road just beyond the walls of the compound. The yard sprang into action with weapons being readied—the nervous air turned into cold fear.

Abdul stood by the steps of the patio. He was fed information by harried men and passed orders to others. He caught Yakup's eye and waved him over. Outside, the road was lit by headlights from pick-up trucks, engines roaring in competition with the noise coming from countless generators throughout the neighbourhood.

"I'm not sure how this will go down. Do you know how to use a gun?" Abdul said.

"Not really," Yakup said.

"It is easy. Take this." Abdul pulled a small gun out from inside his jacket. The iron was warm from the heat of his body.

Yakup looked at the small and surprisingly heavy weapon in his hand.

"Don't use it unless you have to. Now, get into the house and stay there. And *don't* get in the way."

They walked towards the door, but just as Abdul reached for the handle, it opened and the boss stepped out. Dressed in a white shalwar kameez, he seemed more like a family rather than a warlord.

"Is it him?" the boss said, without looking at Abdul.

"No. But he is on his way," Abdul replied.

"How many are out there?"

"It is hard to say. Fifty, maybe sixty well-armed men in pick-ups."

"What is the situation?"

"The men are a bit uneasy. There are reported to be three times as many of them as us and better armed. Many of our men have fought under him and don't want to antagonizse him or see the situation escalate."

Abdul pulled at his beard in a thoughtful manner.

Yelling erupted from just beyond the gate.

"Sir, he is here," someone said.

"We can still get you and your family out the back," Abdul said.

"This is *my* house. If I cannot protect myself here, where then? We stay."

The boss talked into a phone. Abdul was preoccupied with directing men. Yakup moved to one side of the yard and felt himself grow queasy from the scrambling of metal, the fearful eyes of young men, not much older than him, and the empty eyes of the older ones. He wanted to leave and started searching for a way out.

The wall to the neighbouring compound was too tall to climb and too exposed. On the other side of the front gate was a horde of armed men. He seemed to recall that his cousin had mentioned a back door, and so, hurriedly ran around to the other side of the house.

There was a metal door, but it was locked with no key in sight. He returned to the front of the mansion in low spirits. It seemed that the only option was to jump over the wall to the neighbouring compound, which appeared possible if he was able to make his way to the second story and find a suitable balcony. He would have to jump far and risk a painful fall if his gambit proved unsuccessful, but first, he had to get into the house and find the room with the balcony.

The men in the courtyard were preoccupied, but as he opened the door he soon discovered still more inside.

He noted, however, that the hallway was empty. Yakup could see a staircase just past the doorway to another room. He moved in and saw that the door on his left led to a living room where a group of women along with a young man nervously paced. A single shot rang out from outside. The people in the living room crowded the windows.

Yakup used this distraction to dart up the staircase. He took the stairs two at a time, wherein he quickly found the room with the balcony. It was an office or a study of some sort with a large leather chair situated behind a beautifully carved, dark wooden desk. Behind the desk hung an antique Afghan rug of the kind not found in any bazaar. Against a wall stood a towering bookshelf. Emergency communications equipment was situated immediately adjacent to the door that led to the balcony. There were dark brown chairs for visitors. The butt of an almost smoked cigarette lay crumpled in a large glass ashtray.

Yakup pulled at the balcony door handle. It was locked. He looked for the keys, but they were nowhere in sight. He began pillaging through each of the desk drawers only to find papers, pens, clips, stamps, and other detritus, but no key. Yakup tried another drawer. It was stuck, but when he pulled harder the entire drawer gave way and a bundle of keys clattered to the floor. Yakup took the keys, hoping that one of them would fit the balcony door. In his scrambling, he noticed a small envelope with a single photo inside.

It was of Abdul and a group of men in front of a field of poppies and a big pile of opium. Abdul was dressed in a black shalwar kameez and a photographer's vest. He wore a pakol hat over his black hair. A Kalashnikov was slung over his shoulder. Most of them were dressed in a similar fashion. They all had weapons and bandoliers about their torsos. On the back of the photo was written, "Mission accomplished!"

Yakup tried one key after the other in the balcony door. At last, the lock sprang open and he stepped through onto the dark balcony where he could see the spectacle below. The men ran like rats trying to escape a sinking ship. Those who occupied the street outside seemed less confused, but yelling, shouting and general distress emboldened Yakup: he had made the right choice.

It was then that the gate suddenly flew open. The few men that remained inside did not try to fight. A sturdy, grey-haired man walked in. Yakup's heart pumped faster. He looked at the neighbouring wall. Barbed wire strung across the top glinted in the light from the courtyard. He needed something to soften his landing. He hurried back into the office and surveyed the room. His gaze stopped at the wall behind the desk. The rug! He started to pull it off the wall when he heard a brisk voice from down the hallway.

Yakup jumped from the chair and ducked under the desk just in time. The boss, Abdul, the sturdy, and grey-haired man, among others, entered the room. Yakup struggled to control his pounding heart and his breathing. He could see the group from his crouched position under the desk, but they couldn't see him.

"I didn't want it to come to this. But you have been asking for it for some time now. What did you think?" his voice slurred from drinking. He was bigger than anyone else in the room. The size of a bear.

"Times have changed. We have a new democracy now. The Americans and Europeans have changed the rules of the game. We have to play the diplomatic game now," the boss said.

The big man strode up to him and stared him straight in the face with red, swollen eyes.

"You are dumber than I thought. What do you think will happen to your 'new democracy' when the foreigners go home? I can tell you— nothing! Afghanistan has never allowed itself to be ruled by outsiders. This time will be no different."

He turned around and looked at cousin Abdul.

"And these men you have working for you… I hear that you are doing business without me. You disappoint me old friend." He pulled out a gun.

"Please," Abdul said. The man pointed the barrel at him.

"Should I shoot this corrupt policeman in his brown or his green eye?" He aimed at each eye a few times, then lowered the gun.

"Let's solve this as civilised men. We go way back. We fought together. Why this hostility among two brothers?" the boss reasoned.

The big man shifted his gaze to the boss, lifted his gun and pulled the trigger. The bullet entered Abdul's leg. He screamed and fell over in pain. Downstairs, people cried out. Abdul fell on his side and clutched at his leg. Blood seeped through his pants.

"Sometimes an older brother has to educate his younger brother," the big man said

He sent a hard slap to the boss's head.

Another one. And again.

"Why did you have to make me do this, my friend."

Another hard slap. Blood was pouring from the boss's ear. He was on his knees.

"I don't enjoy this." He kicked the kneeling man in the stomach. He doubled over in pain.

"What I'm doing now is a necessity. If I don't, people will think me weak. They will see my silver fur as a sign of age and softness. I cannot allow disobedience." He pulled up the man's white shalwar kameez, exposing his pale and hairy nakedness. Two men held down the broken man. Taking his time, the bear-like man slowly opened his pants and brutally penetrated the boss. The boss's head was mashed into his soft carpet. His eyes were filled with pain, fear and hatred as they slowly met with Yakup who remained hidden beneath the desk. The muscles in his chin moved in spasms with each thrust, but he did not make a sound. The speed increased and the slapping noise of skin against skin echoed in the room. Faster and faster. The bear of a man grunted, groaned and finished, before finally pulling up his pants.

"Trust me, I didn't enjoy this," the -man said. "Take him with you," he gestured to the bleeding and shivering man.

"What about the policeman?" one of the men asked.

"Bring him too," the bear-man said and turned to leave. Cousin Abdul was still lying on his side, clutching his wounded leg, the rug beneath him reddening with blood. One of the men pulled him up. At the same moment, cousin Abdul pulled out a small gun, lifted it towards the Bear-man and fired. The bullet vanished into the ornamental rug behind the desk. The gun was taken from him.

"Finish him off," said the bear-man, as he left the room. One of the men went to cousin Abdul and unceremoniously shot him.

The men pulled the defeated boss through the door and left. Screams erupted as they descended the stairs.

At long last Yakup dared to crawl out from his hiding place. His cousin lay with eyes open; one brown, one green.

Yakup felt a pang for Mohammed who was now an orphan.

He knew that the boss had seen him, and someday would want to eliminate witnesses to his humiliation. He had to leave.

Confused and frightened, Yakup stepped out on the balcony. The big man was dragging the boss by his hair through the gate of his home. Three wailing women tried to reach the unconscious man but were held back. The convoy of Toyota Hilux trucks with armed men sped off into the small hours of the night.

In the confusion, Yakup hurried downstairs and out of the house. He left the compound without looking back and fled into the dark city. Each time a car drove by him he froze and sought cover. He suspected every guard and policeman to be malevolent, and so, hurried in a different direction when he could or avoided crossing their paths altogether.

He got lost, but eventually found his way back to cousin Abdul's house. The events of the night played like a movie on repeat in his mind with pictures and still frames piercing his every thought. He tried to think of Bamiyan, the cave and Grandma Amaya, but these images were replaced by monsters and silver-furred, growling bears revealing steel teeth.

Part II

Iran

19

THE BRIBE

The sun was rising by the time Yakup got to cousin Abdul's house. Mohammed was still asleep in the living room. Yakup gazed at the sleeping boy, fatherless now and left to his own fate. He knew he ought to tell Mohammed that his father was dead, but could simply not. Instead, he slipped into the room and grabbed his small pack of belongings. He put the thick stack of notes he'd earlier discovered in the chest into his pocket and turned to leave the room. Just then, his eyes fell upon the sleeping Mohammed. A pang of guilt hit him. He pulled out the notes and divided them in half. He left them under a note, which read,

Mohammed jan, your baba was a brave man. This is yours. Keep them safe. Good luck.

He left the note and the money on the mattress by the sleeping boy.

In the courtyard, King got up and wagged his tail. Yakup scratched him behind his furry ears.

"I'm sorry, boy," he said. Tears welled up in his eyes. King licked Yakup's hand and pushed at him gently with his snout. The dog looked at the boy with expectation. Yakup turned and walked to the gate. He heard King's chain tighten and the dog moan. Yakup did not look back as he shut the iron gate with the flaking, yellow paint.

Later that day, he found himself on a crowded, ramshackle bus towards Iran. He had decided to leave his native land. Death had come close and he felt the wrath of a fallen warlord coming his way. If he was lucky, the money in his pocket would sustain him all the way to Europe.

It took two days for the bus to reach the border with Iran. There were trucks, donkeys, taxis, carriages, those on horseback and entire families on foot. There were lots and lots of young Afghan men hoping to cross into Iran to work on construction sites, in pistachio orchards, or wherever else the Iranians themselves did not want. These jobs were those the Afghans would gladly take for a pittance. The crowd waited at the border under an already scorching sun.

When Yakup had filled his belly with naan, spicy lamb kebab and chai, he stepped into the line and waited. He had a pile of dollars, which should get him to the other side. He was not stopped on the Afghan side, but he was spotted by an Iranian border guard who already held a woman and a young girl, about Yakup's age, along with a baby in his custody.

"Please, sir, let us pass," the girl said to the guard. "We have been waiting for days. My father is ill and we have to go to Mashhad to visit him before it is too late."

The girl was wearing a veil. Yakup found her courageous for daring to talk to the Iranian man at all. The mere risk of travelling from Afghanistan to Iran without a male companion was dangerous in and of itself. The border guard, for his part, simply ignored the girl.

"You! Come here," the guard said to Yakup.

"Me?"

"Yes, you boy. Come here. What is your business in the Islamic Republic of Iran?"

He had a gun in his belt and held a long, thick wooden stick in his hand. Yakup had noticed other border guards generously dealing out blows with their sticks to young men and boys crossing the border. He did not doubt that this guard would react in much the same way.

"I'm going to a wedding," Yakup lied.

"I see. And where may this wedding be?"

"My sister's wedding is in the city of Mashhad. My father is a businessman and his partner in Mashhad has sealed the business relations through a marriage between one of his sons and my sister," Yakup said. The guard looked him over.

"Why are you travelling alone?"

"I had to sit exams. The wedding party left a few days ago while I stayed behind for my schooling." Yakup hid a smile, feeling pleased with the backstory he had crafted for himself on the bus.

"Why—you should hurry then! You wouldn't want to miss a thing like that now, would you?" The guard gestured towards Iran. Yakup smiled at him. The girl was looking at Yakup with pleading eyes and shaking her head. Her mother was sitting silently with the baby. Yakup took a few steps, then felt the edge of the stick against his throat.

"Nice try, but not very original. I hear hundreds of these stories every day," the guard hissed. "If you want to go to the Islamic Republic of Iran, you should not lie to the first Iranian you meet. Your kind think that we are stupid, but what you fail to realise is that Iranians are far cleverer than you Afghans. You destroy your own country and then want to come to ours—Ha! Now, how badly do you want to get in?"

"What do you mean?" Yakup asked.

"If you don't know, then you should stay in your own country," the guard said with a shrug as he slowly began to lift his baton.

"Wait, wait. I have a little bit," Yakup said and pulled a note from his pocket.

"Not enough," the guard said.

"But I'm just a poor kid. I can bring you more on my way back."

"Don't play me for a fool, boy. Give me the note and get in. I don't want to see your ugly Afghan face again."

Yakup gave him the note and hurried across the border. He was in. He could not believe it. It had been easier than expected. The fact that he had succeeded in crossing into Iran on his first try made him smile.

It was a smile of feeling free from the threat of Kabul, warlords. Death seemed far away. In front of him lay a land of opportunity. But behind him, Yakup heard the girl pleading with the border guard.

"Please, sir. My mother is ill. We need to get to Mashhad and see a doctor."

"Now it's your mother?" the guard stared at her and lifted his stick. The girl looked confused. She realised that she had messed up her story.

"I'm sorry," she said with tears in her eyes. The guard raised the stick to beat her with it.

"Stop!" Yakup cried. The man looked surprised.

"How much for the mother and her children," Yakup asked. The guard stared at him with both shock and disdain, which was just as quickly replaced with a greedy smile.

"What do we have here? Has the ugly Afghan fallen in love?"

"How much?" Yakup repeated, though unnerved now by his

unexpected bravado.

"The mother is cheap and I don't like babies, but the pretty girl is expensive," the guard said, as he took her chin in his hand. She stared at him with contempt.

"Tell me how much," Yakup took a step towards the guard.

"Are you threatening me?" he said.

"I'm not threatening anybody. I want to do business with you, but maybe you're not so interested?" Yakup said and made to leave.

The guard considered this for a moment. He came to the conclusion that there were plenty of Afghans he could be cruel to, but the chance to make a little extra money was too rare an opportunity to pass up.

"I need more of your notes," he said, and nodded toward the pocket from where Yakup had pulled out the dollar bill. Yakup produced a couple of notes more.

"This is all I can give you. Deal?"

The guard looked at the notes, surprised by what this seemingly poor boy had in his pockets.

"Take them," the guard said pocketing the money.

The mother, with the baby shielded on her bag and the girl hurried past the guard who was studying the dollar bills.

"Thank you," the girl said.

"Let's get out of here before he changes his mind," Yakup said, helping her with one of their two bags.

20

MARIAM

Yakup and the women made their way through the crowds at the Islam Qala border point between Afghanistan and Iran. Yakup walked in front, the girl trailing behind with the older woman and the small baby.

"My name is Mariam," the girl said after a while.

"Mine is Yakup."

"This is my mother and my baby sister. We have been stuck at that merciless border for days. We thought we could cross, but then this… that gorilla stopped us and demanded payment. I explained and explained that we had no money, but he was deaf to my pleads, while his eyes were feasting on me in a very dishonourable manner"

Mariam smiled at Yakup, who did not know why he had helped the girl and her family. He was not used to being in a position where he could help others, but now here he was. It made his heart swell.

"Do you have a place to stay?" Yakup asked.

"No," Mariam said. Yakup looked at her again. She was beautiful. Her green veil had slipped to reveal pitch-black hair. Her brown, almond-shaped eyes made Yakup's belly ache with a feeling of pain and pleasure that he was not used to. He felt in his pocket; he still had enough notes.

"It is a dangerous journey to embark on without a man and without money. Why don't we camp together?" Yakup suggested.

"It is sweet of you to offer," she smiled and Yakup's heart thudded. "But how could we possibly spend our night with a strange man without causing suspicion? No, it would be too dangerous," she concluded.

"Mariam, I hope you don't think I would do anything to harm you or your family. It's just that spending the night alone and without a man can have serious consequences around here. We can tell people that I'm your brother. No one will suspect a thing."

Mariam's mother still hadn't said a word. She was present physically, but her mind was elsewhere. She was clad in a black dress. The fine contours of her face hinted at a former beauty now erased by a hard life. Yakup could see Mariam's features in her wrinkled face. Her eyes were different. They did not register any of the commotion around her, whereas Mariam's eyes had overwhelmed Yakup, and without mercy, struck him with a passion.

"What about your mother and the baby?" Yakup said.

Mariam looked at her mother and the baby and for a moment she seemed to forget Yakup was there. She sighed.

"Perhaps you are right, but we cannot have any funny business. We are proud and honourable people. Just because we are not men doesn't mean that we are helpless or that you can take advantage of us. Understood?" she said as she shot Yakup a withering look.

"I never… Of course not," Yakup said, a little hurt.

"Fine then. It's a deal… brother." She smiled and Yakup's heart melted.

A bus brought them to a road skirted with pine trees, turquoise domes covered in fine layers of dust and a series of pointy minarets. Farmers dotted the roadside with pyramids of melons and mountains of mulberries. The blue sky grew white off into the distant horizon and was perforated only by the teeth of an obscured mountain range. The number of dented pastel-coloured cars grew as the bus entered the small town of Taybad.

While Yakup looked for an appropriate place for them to rest, Mariam and her family stayed at the small bus station. He passed groups of men in white turbans and vendors selling pomegranates, butternut squash, onions, garlic and tomatoes from small wagons. Somewhere the call to prayer crackled through speakers from a mosque telling the faithful to turn towards Mecca. Green, white and red flags flapped lazily in the afternoon heat above posters of a stern, white-bearded man, wearing spectacles and a black turban. There was nothing particularly suspicious about the scene, but as with most border towns, trade in illicit drugs and counterfeit products attracted thugs and scoundrels.

The stars made up for a moonless night as the small party settled in for their first night together. Yakup found a place on the outskirts of town where an old couple rented their small shed in the back of a surprisingly lush garden. Brown clay walls sheltered their small property from the outside world.

The couple served them pots of steaming dizi sangi, a stew of naan, lamb, potatoes, chickpeas, tomatoes, herbs and half a raw onion for digestion, all soaked in broth.

Yakup insisted he sleep on the small stone patio, telling the couple that he preferred the fresh air. He winked at the old man as he indicated the noise that the small baby could produce in the night. Mariam, her mother and the baby slept on a rug in the small shed.

Yakup was lying on his back, arms folded beneath his head. He looked forward to a good night's rest in the peaceful garden. The almond eyes of Mariam continued to appear behind his closed lids as did her smile that revealed two perfectly placed dimples.

He still could not return to Bamiyan or to Kabul. The dollar bills had not managed to solve that. He could send money to his family from Europe and maybe even come back for them one day.

"Are you asleep?" Mariam's hushed voice said from behind him. Yakup stopped short in his thoughts and his heart skipped a beat.

"No, no. Just thinking. Couldn't sleep?" Yakup whispered, trying to suppress his increasingly loud heartbeat.

"Thinking about what?" she asked and sat on the patio close to Yakup.

"About everything. About Afghanistan, my family, my future; about why we have to leave our country." He sat up and asked. "What are you running away from?"

"What makes you think I'm running away from something?"

"Aren't we all?"

"If that is true, then what are you running away from?" she asked.

"A lot. But it's a long story. And maybe you're tired and need to rest," Yakup said.

"I'm not tired," she said looking straight through him with her almond-shaped eyes.

It was then that he told her how he always felt that his mother blamed him for his brothers' deaths and how his father had died. He told her the horror of his last night in Kabul, which had driven him to flee to Iran. And he told her how he wanted to go to Europe where there was peace, freedom and security. He admitted that he wanted to study there and work and make a life for himself without being afraid.

When he finished talking, Mariam took his hand and squeezed it, a gesture he had not expected as it was deemed inappropriate between two strangers.

"I will tell you my story now that you have told me yours," she said. The vastness of the darkness above them was intimidating yet had a calming effect. From somewhere within the garden came the chirp of a single cricket and Mariam told her story.

"I am from the northern part of our country. Before I was born, during the Soviet occupation, my mother's father became an opium addict. The opium production in that area enabled the mujahadeen to keep up their fight against the Russians. Many of the inhabitants of those remote parts were addicted.

"My grandfather's addiction soon spread to his wife and their children, including the young girl who became my mother. It is expensive to sustain an entire family's dependence on the drug, which must be satisfied several times a day. Our family was not rich.

"Many families sell a daughter to finance their addictions. That was what happened to my mother. She became an opium bride. She was just a child when her parents sold her like a slave. She became the third wife in a household where she was not welcomed by the older women. They made her work every waking hour of the day. Besides that, she was raped by her husband, a man old enough to be her grandfather.

"The only good thing that she gained from being sold was that she got out of the addiction. She suffered those first days and weeks. Sick as a dog she would scream like she was dying and hope she would.

"It didn't come to pass, of course, and maybe it would have been better for her had she died rather than lived through the hell she was sold into. It didn't take long before she was with child. She gave birth for the first time when she was 11 years old. She lost four children and gave birth eight times. She was lucky, though, as many women die in childbirth.

"With age, the old man lost his reason and grew senile. The stronger wives took advantage of this and managed to excommunicate my mother. She was given a few hours' notice to leave the house and only got to take my older brother and me with her. We walked for days and only ate roots and grass. It made us sick and we all lost weight.

"After days, or maybe weeks, we found a small village in a valley shielded by rugged peaks. The people there had barely enough for themselves, but even so, they allowed us to stay in one of the abandoned houses. It was an odd place, populated by women and children as most of the men had been killed by the Russians.

"After the Russians left Afghanistan, the village went through a time of relative peace. When the Taliban came to power, they easily took the village and left it again. They destroyed all radios, TVs, kites and playing cards. They decreed that all women wear the burqa and forbade them to don makeup. They burned the girls' school, which happened to be the boys' school as well and when the teacher—a woman—tried to stop them, they executed her in front of her students.

"One of the fighters took my mother as his wife. The marriage didn't last long, though, as he died from pneumonia shortly thereafter. My mother later told me that he was a good man who had only joined the Taliban because he had no other choice.

"Soon after, my brother joined the Mujahideen in their fight against the Taliban and just weeks before the Americans bombed them my mother received news that he had been killed. We stayed in the village for a few years after that. We were poor and prayed only to live to the next day. We had a small garden that yielded some vegetables, a goat that provided us with milk, and a couple of chickens. That was all. On most days we ate only one small meal, but we survived with what little we had; not having to rely on others.

"With the fall of the Taliban, the Afghans who had fled the country came back. Our village had its returnees as well. Some of them had lived better lives in Pakistan than in the villages they had come from or returned to.

"One day, a man with a large family returned to our village. He claimed that we were occupying his house. There was nothing we could do but move. Our house and the small garden no longer belonged to us.

The man didn't give us any compensation even though we had repaired his house and kept it and the garden well-groomed.

"We moved to another empty house in the village instead. Our new house needed a lot of repairs and the garden was dry and arid. We struggled, but luckily some of the women in the village helped us and gave us rice and work whenever there was enough to share. The man who had returned from Pakistan anointed himself the mayor of the village. None of the women had the power or guts to stand up to him even though no one felt that he was worthy of such a charge.

"He had left the village with his family when times were tough, but now that he had returned he acted in an arrogant and pretentious manner. He had two wives but felt that a man of his position ought to have at least one more. That was when he came to my mother. He suggested that he could help her by taking me as his next bride.

"She sent him away with a scornful laugh, but he didn't like that and took it as his mission to turn the entire village against us by claiming that we were dishonest women, that my mother had prostituted herself and that was why she had shown up to the town in the first place. We didn't think much of it to begin with, assuming the villagers knew us well enough, but as a powerful man, the others soon began to partake in the gossiping.

"One day when I wasn't home, he came to my mother again and tried to convince her to sell me. Again, she declined. He pushed my mother into the house, threw her on her bed and ripped her clothes off. He raped her and beat her, telling her how he would have his way with me whether she allowed it or not.

"That day when I came home, I found my mother swollen and bruised in her bed, clothing torn. She was silent. Her eyes did not show emotion. We left the village the next morning under the cover of darkness.

"We made our way to Kabul and in the beginning, we lived on the streets among people who, like us, had no money. When it became evident that my mother was pregnant, we were allowed to stay in a safe house for women. We stayed there for a while, but eventually, their funding ran out and they shut the place down."

Mariam stopped talking. This time it was Yakup who took her hand

and gave it a gentle squeeze. The moon had risen and now shone its pale glowing light on the small garden island in the desert of the night.

"The baby—is it his?" he asked. She nodded and rested her head on his shoulder. They sat like that until sleep carried them away.

21

THE RURAL BOY

The crowing of roosters, the tittering of birds and the barking of dogs woke Yakup. On the edge of sleep and reality, he found that Mariam had returned to the shed at some point during the night. He was grateful she had left, as curious minds would become suspicious and the situation could turn ugly.

The old couple brought them chai, naan, salty goat cheese and sweet honey. Mariam, her mother, the baby and Yakup all sat on the patio and took their breakfast. Afterwards, Yakup helped the old man carry firewood. Since last night's sharing of stories and slumber under the stars, it had become clear to Yakup that he had to help Mariam and her family. And maybe not just for their sake.

"I talked to the old man this morning. He told me that his grandson is driving towards Tehran. This grandson has a contact that can help with documents and further transportation towards the Turkish border. From there it is possible to cross into Turkey. Many Afghans are staying in Turkey and we can get help to enter Europe from there. Mariam, I think it would make sense if you, your mother and the baby journeyed with me to Europe. It is a safer place to build a future… and it would make me happy."

Yakup stopped awkwardly. The sun was warming his back and bathing Mariam's face in light.

"Go with you to Europe? But Yakup, it is not possible to go all the way to Europe! It would take months! My mother is ill! And we are travelling with a baby."

She looked even more beautiful this morning, Yakup thought.

"Look, I thought about it. The Iranians deport thousands and thousands of Afghans… What will you do when that happens? Mariam, you know there are stories of Iranians abusing Afghans and treating them with disrespect. Without a man in your household, you will be more prone to danger…"

Mariam interrupted him. "There are many Afghans who work without papers. I met a lady on the border. She told me about it. And besides, we haven't any money for the trip."

"The grandson doesn't charge much… and I have enough for all of us," Yakup said.

"And when we reach Tehran?"

"We worry about that when we get there."

"And how will a rural boy from Afghanistan manage to provide for three more people, one a baby, and ensure them a safe journey to Europe?"

Mariam shook her head. Her black hair fell free of her green veil.

"I just wanted to help," Yakup said, though, he was beginning to feel that this conversation was not going in the right direction.

"It is sweet of you, Yakup, but there are stories of bandits and human traffickers preying on naive Afghan refugees all the way from this windblown border town to the heart of Europe. God only knows how many of our Afghan brothers and sisters try this every day and fail."

The baby started to wail.

"I'm not a boy!" Yakup said.

Mariam looked at him incredulously. She grabbed the child in an effort to comfort him.

"You may not think much of this… this *'rural boy'*, but without me, you would still be with that gorilla at the border. Instead, you are in Iran, in a peaceful garden, drinking chai and enjoying breakfast!"

Mariam turned sharply and disappeared into the shed.

He had felt that there was a connection between him and Mariam last night. She was the only one he had entrusted his story to and had she not also told him her story? No, he did not want her to think of him as just a *boy*.

In truth, he had already dreamed up a future where he and Mariam owned a small house, had jobs, had children and those children would attend university and never have the fear of the constant threat of death or going to bed hungry night after night.

Before Yakup could indulge in more of this fantasy, though, she was in front of him again; this time with a bottle of goat's milk.

"Mariam, listen to me. Afghans are crossing into Europe every day so our chances are good. I admit I don't know exactly how we will do it, but I promise you this: I will do all I can to find a way. When we reach Europe, we will no longer have to be afraid. There will be clean water, food and doctors to care for us. Life in Iran is not easy for Afghans and returning to our own country is suicidal. I know it is a long and perilous journey to get there, but together we stand a better chance. People in Europe have rights… And they care about human rights. They care about us."

Yakup did not know exactly what human rights meant, but he mentioned them in the hopes of persuading Mariam.

Mariam was sitting with the child, who had been pacified with the bottle of rich goat's milk.

"Look, let's say that we did go with you, right? How do we cross the borders? I have heard that it is very difficult to enter Europe. There is also the issue of cost. We cannot accept your charity," Mariam said.

"In life, we must dare greatly, and when we meet an obstacle, we must deal with it. We have already overcome two obstacles on our journey together: crossing the border and getting a ride to Tehran. I'd say that is pretty good in the span of a day. Concerning the cost, we'll call it a loan and figure out a way for you to pay it back when the time comes. Now, what do you say?"

Yakup was feeling a bit more confident with this latest turn of events.

"Can you promise to take care of us?" Mariam asked.

"I promise," Yakup said.

"Good. Then we must appear to be husband and wife. And if you leave me, I will never forgive you," Mariam said. Her almond eyes were deadly serious and Yakup finally felt the gravity of his newfound fate.

"I will never leave you, Mariam," Yakup said. He felt more like a man than a boy. Mariam looked doubtful, but with the baby still on her shoulder and her mother on the rug, she couldn't help but let one of her dimpled smiles dance across her face. Her eyes held his gaze, as she nodded a *yes*.

"Maman! *Maman jan!*" Mariam said in a hushed voice as she gently shook her mother's shoulder. There wasn't much of a reaction as the young girl explained, "Yakup, the boy who helped us cross the border, has promised us safe passage to Europe. We will go with him today. Life is better there."

Mariam's mother blinked and looked into her daughter's eyes as she spoke. Yakup thought he could see a nod and a vague smile on her face. He knew that the journey ahead of them demanded a man and not a boy. For reasons unknown to himself, he had set a heavy load for himself in terms of responsibility, which was made still heavier with the knowledge that cousin Abdul's dollar bills would not last forever.

22

SUSPICIOUS MINDS

A few hours later they found themselves in a car belonging to the old couple's grandson, Ali. They were on their way to the capital city of Tehran. Yakup was sitting in the front seat with Mariam and her mother in the back cradling the baby. The dented blue Mazda wended its way deeper into Iran, rushing by parched bushes, melon fields where fruit pickers stooped, fields of sunflowers as tall as a man, rusty cars in slow disintegration and the turquoise domes of mosques. Green, white and red flags and the wisps of grass on the flat rooftops of the houses blew in the arid wind.

"You're not the first Afghans I have driven to Tehran," Ali said, steering the car around a crater-sized pothole, "So let me be honest with you, if it is ok?"

"Please," Yakup said.

"We Iranians are a proud people. We have housed so many Afghans that no one really knows the number. Maybe those Pakistanis housed more of you, but still, many, many of you came here… Millions. And you enjoy Iranian hospitality." Ali honked the horn to get two goats off the road. "At the same time, Iranians enjoy economic prosperity due to the Afghans. You guys are cheap labour and you take the jobs we don't want ourselves. Many of the buildings in Iran are built by Afghans. Many Iranians are unhappy with you guys and claim you're dirty or that you steal our jobs and abuse our hospitality. So, our government, or whatever they call themselves, has to do something from time to time… instead of just barking, it bites and deports hundreds of thousands of Afghans. But that just doesn't work in the real world."

Ali frowned and shifted his weight. The car made a few abrupt twists and turns, forcing Yakup to hold on to the glove compartment and glance back anxiously at Mariam, who reassured him with a dimpled smile.

"As a consequence, you Afghans are treated poorly by almost everyone: civilians, ministers, politicians, and so on. Let's say that I wanted more of your money. I could easily threaten you by saying that I would stop at the next police station unless you paid up," Ali smiled. Yakup started to worry if he could trust the man next to him and if it came down to it, protect Mariam, her mother, and the baby should the driver really demand still more compensation.

As the car crossed a bridge, saddled camels chewed on grass under the few palm trees while a group of white-clad men drank their afternoon chai. The blue sky was dotted with tufts of white clouds haphazardly tossed onto it.

They stopped to fill the car with petrol at a deserted gas station. Ali took the opportunity to pray in the small prayer room out back while Mariam and her mother visited the bathroom and took care of the baby's needs. There were a couple of burned-out cars, stripped of anything useful and resting in peaceful decay to one side. A dog slept in the dwindling shade of a bench and took no notice of the car or its inhabitants as they roared away from what passed for a gas station and into the fading light of day.

Yakup sat in the passenger seat staring into the twilight as Ali's headlights carved their passage into the unknown. The heavy burden of responsibility that had not existed earlier in the day suddenly fell upon Yakup. It was gnawing at him, painful and troublesome.

They stopped for the night at a small guesthouse. Yakup and Ali settled in the living room. Mariam, her mother and the baby girl had a room for themselves. Ali was snoring next to Yakup, who couldn't sleep, when a faint noise from the living room indicated the presence of what he wanted most, but what he feared could end their journey full stop. He lay still, pretending to sleep. A gentle touch made him shiver. He opened his eyes and saw Mariam leaning over him. Her almond eyes close to his face.

"You're awake," she whispered and sent him a healing smile. The gnawing receded and was substituted with a soft and comfortable feeling.

"I am," Yakup whispered and smiled back at her.

"Are you ok? I was afraid you were feeling upset."

"I'm fine… It was just… I… I was concerned about you."

"Why would you be concerned about me?"

"I got worried about how to protect you… Maybe you are right and I am just a boy," Yakup admitted, looking away.

"If you were just a boy, would I do this?" She placed a soft kiss on his lips, got up and disappeared back to her room.

Yakup was still sleepless, but this time for very different reasons.

23

ENTRY

They drove most of the next day in silence, save the music blasting from the small Chinese 'Soni' radio.

"We'll drive via smaller roads to dodge the police checkpoints," Ali said as they approached Tehran.

"Fine," Yakup replied. The traffic grew thick and the suburbs more frequent.

"We don't want to hassle with those goons," Ali said, wrenching the steering wheel to the right and barely missing a scooter.

"What happens if they stop us?" Yakup asked.

"Best case scenario? They let us go. Worst case? They throw the lot of you in a detention centre and keep you there until they can be bothered to deport you, which you better hope for since prisons in Iran are not places you want to be." Ali paused without elaborating why. He continued, "The most likely outcome is that we will have to grease them a bit and hope the baksheesh will satisfy them."

They drove on for a while. An Iranian pop song was filling the car with synthesisers and a story about illicit love. Both women and the baby were asleep in the backseat.

"What about the man we can get the papers from? How do we find him?" Yakup asked.

"I will tell you the address when I drop you off. He is a friend of a friend, and rumour has it, is the best forger in Tehran."

"Do you know how much he charges?"

"I'm afraid I don't. You know, Yakup, this is not my business. I'm just driving you guys to make a little extra. I don't know the guy, nor do I want to. That is how the business is. Nobody knows anybody." Ali gave a furtive smile.

They stopped at a busy intersection. Men with freshly shaved chins in neatly pressed grey pants and shirts crossed the road through the choking exhaust fumes of the many cars and buses.

"You mentioned a place we could stay," Yakup said.

"Indeed, indeed. Listen, Yakup, I wish I could house you, but the wife wouldn't like it. You understand, right?

"I do. You have already done so much, Ali. My mother and sister really appreciate it."

"Yakup, I don't know what kind of game you guys are running, and it is probably none of my business, but if you want people to think you're related by blood, you'll have to do a better job," Ali said, glancing once more in Yakup's general direction.

"What do you mean?" Yakup replied, feigning offence.

"The way you look at your sister is more passionate than appropriate," Ali said and nudged Yakup with his elbow. The boy reddened.

"She *is* my sister! I have no idea what you're talking about!"

"Just saying, just saying, my friend. You know, like the desert fox, I sleep with one eye open, always aware of the potential enemy or prey… But despair not, my friend—your secret is safe with me." He pantomimed zipping his mouth shut. Yakup gave up the pretence.

"So, you won't tell anyone?"

"Hey, why would I? If I wanted to take your money, I'd have arranged for it long ago." He winked. Yakup knew he was right.

"Thanks, Ali. I'll make sure to make an effort in the future. And sorry for lying, but it was only to protect them."

"I know. That's why I'm telling you. I don't know why, but I kind of like you guys," Ali said. His eyes caught the sleeping Mariam in the mirror.

They had reached a shabby-looking area crammed with apartment complexes and blocks upon blocks of small, cement homes. Ali pulled the car to a halt and pointed to one of them.

"That one. On the 7th floor. Ring the bell and tell them you just arrived." Ali scribbled something on a piece of paper. "Go to this address tomorrow. Tell them that a friend of Majid has sent you. They'll know. Don't forget to bring a credible story. Yakup, be careful and take good care of your family. I hope you'll reach whatever destination you have in mind and that I never see you again."

Ali and Yakup shook hands before Ali drove off. The bell gave a loud buzz when Yakup pressed the button and soon a tired man gave them a tired, but inquisitive look through the door.

"Yes?" he said in a coarse voice.

"Do you have a room? We have just arrived," Yakup said. The door opened and the man turned and walked up the stairs, leaving the door ajar. Yakup shrugged, looked at Mariam, and grabbing their bags, led their party up the steps just behind the man.

24

THE SPARROW

The small flat was situated in a pathetic area of Tehran.

And it stank.

Two other Afghan families were already there, and all shared the same objective—getting to Europe.

They had agreed on a story that claimed they had married a year ago. Mariam's father had died when she was a child, Yakup's father more recently, and Yakup and his family were in danger of being involved in an armed conflict. With the baby and Mariam's sick mother, they had found that the hardship of Afghanistan did not allow them a safe future and they were instead looking for a place with security and access to human rights, education and jobs. They were, in short, fleeing from an impossible future in the hope of finding a possible one. Apart from the marriage, it was the truth.

"I think it is here," Mariam said, looking at the slip of paper and the number of the building in front of them. It was a green apartment block with some shops on the first floor; similar to many they had already passed. One shop with dirty windows was selling used cell phones while another sold fabric. A torn plastic poster on the wall announced a sale on curtains. On the corner was a newsagent, and finally, there was a shop selling office wares.

They entered the latter where a small bell greeted their arrival. A pudgy young man was sitting behind the counter, transfixed by the Bollywood film that blared on the overhead television.

"Do you sell writing notepads?" Yakup asked, raising his voice so as to be heard above the din of a distinguished-looking man denying the love of a young beautiful Indian woman.

"What do you think?" the man retorted, gesturing toward a stand next to Yakup and without looking away from the TV, his face glowing from the sickly green colour of the screen.

Yakup glanced at the stand and then at Mariam.

"Majid sent us," Mariam said.

This caught the attention of the Bollywood fanatic. He looked them over in a nonchalant way, apparently deciding that action was necessary. He picked up a phone and spoke into the receiver in hushed tones, which, only moments later, seemed to summon a chubby lady from the back of the shop. She waved them over.

They followed her into a back room where they ascended a flight of stairs and entered a much larger room. A man was sitting behind a counter, busying himself with paperwork. He was wearing a colourful silk robe with large flowing cuffs, under which one could follow his thin, seemingly translucent arms into the darkness of the sleeve. Light shone through the lone window on the wall behind him, illuminating the man.

The man examined them above round glasses perched atop a crooked nose, which, itself, hovered over a thin, dark moustache.

"Please take a seat." He nodded to the plastic-covered couch in front of him. The plastic squeaked under Yakup and Mariam's combined weight, stretching and moaning in anguish with each little movement they made. A bespectacled man in a black turban and sporting a long, white beard stared out at them from a framed poster on the side wall.

Fifteen minutes passed before the man took off his glasses and leaned back in his chair.

"Now what can I do for you?" he said to Yakup.

"We were recommended to come and see you. A friend of Majid told us about you. He said you could help," Yakup said.

"And who may this friend of Majid be?" The man asked.

"Ehm… he just gave us a lift yesterday and told us you could help," Yakup said and hesitated. "I don't think he gave us his name."

"He didn't give you his name? Yet, here you are in an unknown apartment only because a friend of Majid recommended it? And how exactly is it, you think, I might be of assistance, according to this unnamed acquaintance of yours?"

"We need documents to travel to Europe," Mariam said, leaning forward. The couch complained.

"Dearie me, the little sparrow can talk!" the man chided. "But how on earth can I provide you with documents? I hardly know you and it is a highly illegal undertaking. I don't know any 'Majid' with a no-name friend. I'm afraid I cannot be of any service to you."

He resumed reading his papers. Mariam looked at Yakup and nudged him in the side.

"Sir. His name was Ali. Can you please help us?" Yakup spoke a bit louder than he had intended. The man patiently pushed the paperwork aside and took off his glasses.

"Suddenly this no-name friend of yours has a name? I wonder whether this 'Ali' would be pleased to know how easily the young Afghan boy here reveals his name." The man noted something on a pad. "As it happens, I do know quite a few men named Ali. Can you be more specific about this particular one?"

"We caught a ride with him from the border, where we stayed with his grandparents. He said that you could help us with documents and access to Turkey," Yakup replied.

"If indeed this could be arranged, how would such a sweet young couple on the run be able to pay? There are many Afghans who wish to travel west, but not all have the means."

"We have cash," Yakup said.

"Cash is always good," the man remarked with a concealed smile. "You can call me Majid." He extended his thin arm from its considerable cuff and invited Yakup to shake it. The handshake was weak and dry. "Tea?" he asked and pushed a buzzer. "Before we agree on anything, though, know this: I am not in this business and my name is not Majid— got it?"

Both Yakup and Mariam looked a bit puzzled before nodding their understanding.

"The paperwork will take some days. Then you will have Iranian passports. I will need details about you. I'll find you a nice, small Iranian village where you will have been born and raised. Make sure that you build your cover story and can sell it to the Iranian police. They will not hesitate to toss both of you into a dark pit and let you rot in there forever."

The door opened and the young man entered and placed cups of steaming green tea on the table. He quickly left to return to his Bollywood film.

"Please be so kind as to put names, ages and family status of all concerned on this small paper," Majid said, pushing a pen and paper towards Mariam and Yakup.

"Can we enter Europe with Iranian passports?" Mariam asked.

"My dear little sparrow, I am just a humble forger. Nothing more, nothing less. If you use them wisely, the passports will be a shield against deportation to Afghanistan from Iran and Turkey. Crossing borders is a different and far more complicated matter, some would claim. Those who make such claims have not, though, ever tried to forge a passport," he said, pausing for effect and to sip his tea.

"Sweet sparrow," he continued, "to forge a passport from the Islamic Republic of Iran is not a job for a simple labourer. No, it is the work of an artist. These days most of my so-called colleagues are simply conmen, tricking and cheating. They do not care about their work." Majid looked offended on behalf of his metier. He resumed his soliloquy by stating, "There are only a few of us left who devote ourselves to the art of forgery rather than digitalised monkey work." He slurped his tea with a pinkie raised high in the air and concluded his dialogue simply:

"Come back in three days."

And that was what they did.

The next few days they spent mostly holed up in the smelly apartment. One of the families left and was replaced by another. Yakup and Mariam rehearsed their story. The baby seemed oblivious to the dangerous journey lying ahead of them. Mariam's mother showed little sign of improvement even though the calm of staying in one place seemed to make her smile more often than usual. Once a day, Yakup and Mariam went out to buy food and explore the city to the extent they dared. And so, the days passed until it was time to return to the forger.

"How are Mr and Miss Sparrow doing?" Majid asked when once again they sat on the plastic-covered couch drinking sweet green tea.

"Fine, thank you," Mariam answered.

"I take it that you avoided close encounters with my less civilised countrymen, is that so? And perhaps you followed the procedure of many an Afghan, barricading the Sparrow family in a shabby apartment and missing the opportunity to enjoy the decaying capital of Persia, hm? It would be a pity since who knows how long it will be before an American allows an Israeli to lay the city to waste?"

Majid pushed a folder towards Mariam and Yakup. It contained brand new passports.

"They look real," Yakup said as he studied his new identification papers.

"Well, what did you expect?" Majid looked offended. His moustache quivered as his mouth twitched in feigned hurt.

"No, no, of course not, Mr Majid. It's just that it's the first time I have ever had a passport… and I didn't know what to expect," Yakup said.

"Hrmph! Amateurs! The days when I had professional jobs, ahh…" Majid indulged in the past for a moment.

"Mr Majid, this is excellent work. The details included and the quality of the paper is simply astonishing," Mariam said, nodding in approval.

She looked up and smiled at the forger.

"The Sparrow has insight." Majid smirked and pushed his glasses further up his nose and pulled out a slip of paper. He pushed it towards the Sparrows.

"Now, I believe you need this for the next leg of your journey, but I'm afraid these people are a different kind of breed. Less sophisticated. Very efficient. If I may offer a small word of advice, it would be this: caution and stamina. The mountains are steep and cold. There's no rescue service, so stay close to the head of the snake." He looked from one to the other with a sense of gravity and continued, "When you leave my office, I do not exist any more. Understood?" Majid the forger stared at them over his glasses.

They nodded and quickly fled the narrow back office.

25

WOMAN

They left the sordid apartment early the next morning. Yakup worried a bit about his dwindling wad of cash. He had no idea how much they needed for the journey and had not realised Majid would charge so much for their professional documents.

Yakup reflected on their journey thus far and realised that when he had left Bamiyan he had absolutely no way of knowing what lay ahead of him. One thing was certain, however, and that was the fact that, and never in a million years, would he have expected to be migrating to Europe with Mariam and her family as a presumed husband and father. This thought stayed with Yakup as he looked at Mariam who was sitting on the bus seat across from him holding her baby sister. She was giggling every time Mariam lifted her into the air and smiled her dimpled smile at the baby. *Maybe this* is *my future*, Yakup mused, leaning back in his seat on the other side of the aisle from his new family.

When they first stopped at the police checkpoint just outside Tehran, Yakup had initially panicked at first until it became clear that the men only checked the driver's papers. Throughout the day they passed many more blue and white police stations, and with each one, Yakup worried less and less. The blue sky turned white towards the horizon. It was occasionally penetrated by jagged mountains. Dusty dirt roads, flanked by trees, indicated houses and villages nearby as blood veins indicate main arteries.

These thoughts occupied Yakup's mind until the bus slowed to a stop and dropped them off along a sparsely travelled road near the village indicated on the note given to him just days before. The driver pointed them in the direction of a small gravel road leading towards a series of hills.

They started walking each narrow road, up and down, back and forth, for what seemed like hours.

They were in Iran's backcountry without much else in sight than the mountains hindering access to the adjacent country. It was a natural border in which to keep people from entering or leaving. A perfect setting for smuggling people out of the country.

It was late afternoon when they reached a cluster of isolated brick buildings. The only vegetation consisted of parched yellow grass and brittle stumps of trees. There was a small dried-out well with a broken pump. No people or animals were in sight.

"What is this place," Mariam whispered.

"I don't know," Yakup replied, "But I think we should stay here for the night and continue tomorrow."

"I have a bad feeling," Mariam said.

"Me too."

"What food is left?"

"We have rice and water; some naan, a few beans, nuts and dried fruits. I will try to find a source of water and more fruit, but by the looks of it, I think it is unlikely," Yakup said while looking around the arid area.

"We better ration what we have. I'll start a fire."

Mariam squeezed Yakup's arm and left him to his task.

They picked, at random, one of the abandoned clay structures and used it as a shelter. Yakup was unsuccessful in his mission. When he returned after forging around the nearby hillsides, Mariam had managed to find a dented tin pot and was cooking over a fire she had made with a few dried branches.

"Yakup," Mariam said in a soft voice. He was slowly beginning to recognise her ways. "I know my mother's behaviour is strange and sometimes a bit frightening. She has been through a lot. I told you already. I just don't want you to think it has anything to do with you."

"I know… I know, Mariam. Our country can be cruel," Yakup said. Mariam stirred the beans in the sparse water.

"Especially to my kind," she said.

"What do you mean?"

"Yakup, do you think it was difficult for you to be on your own?" she asked

"I'm not sure I get what you mean. But yes."

"Right. Imagine that I had to do what you did."

"Ok."

"Do you see?" Mariam poured the beans into a small bowl, rinsed the beaten pot and commenced to boil the rice.

"Mariam, I really don't get what you mean," Yakup said.

"Don't you understand that ever since you were born, you have had an immense privilege that I can only dream of? I am a woman. I am not considered to have the same rights and status as you. Half of the Afghan population is discriminated against simply because they were not born male. I never understood why I cannot do the same things as a man. Afghanistan is a country for old men who enslave the youth to fight for them and the women to serve them. It is not a country for me."

And with that Mariam turned around, gently awoke her mother and served her a bowl of rice and beans. The baby came next and then, finally, Yakup.

26

KALASHNIKOV

They were eating in silence inside the abandoned house, the dying glow of the fire, sending Yakup back to his days in Bamiyan. He thought, then, of how his sisters would never be forced to flee as he had. Yakup could not help but envy them, though, and on the other hand, he knew that if Noor or Zahra wanted to go elsewhere, it was simply not an option.

He could not help but think of Zahra being forced into a marriage she did not want and with someone she did not love. She was a strong-willed girl who definitely knew her purpose and who wanted to get an education and become an emancipated human.

"Mariam," Yakup said. She was sitting against the wall, arms resting on her knees. The reflection of the orange glow from the fireplace enhanced her features; she looked sad.

"Yes, Yakup."

"I know you have had a tough time. What you are doing is incredible. With a little luck, we will reach Europe one day. In Europe men and women are treated equally and have the same rights. There you will be as much a man as I." He stood up and looked solemnly at her, his right hand over his heart. "Mariam, I promise life will be better once we make it to Europe."

"Are you sure?"

"I promise."

"How can you promise that, Yakup?" She stood up too and moved close to him so that they almost touched.

"Mariam, I will do all I can, everything in my power, to get you to Europe. How can Europe not be better than what we are leaving behind?"

Mariam took a tiny step closer. Their hands, like magnets, found one another and with lips wet they moved still closer to each other.

Horses were suddenly riding fast through the night, and with a jolt, the door was pushed open by a man with a Kalashnikov.

A young Afghan boy tried to shield a girl he had fallen in love with from a sudden wind, which made the fire start and the tree branch crumble, crack and splinter.

"Who are you?" the Kalashnikov asked, the black iron eye of the weapon training itself on Yakup.

"We are just travellers… We needed shelter for the night," Yakup said. His voice cracked like a choir boy still in the throes of adolescence.

"Don't lie to me, boy," the man with the Kalashnikov said in a hoarse voice.

"I'm… I'm sorry, sir. We needed shelter… for the baby and my wife's mother. She is not well."

The man eyed the baby and Mariam's mother.

"Please, sir, we are just passing through."

"You are Afghans. Where are you going?"

"We have been sent here to cross the mountains. We were told that our contact person would be in a village around here," Yakup said. Mariam had her veil pulled over her hair and face. She could not say anything.

"If you are crossing the mountains, you follow me now."

"Now? Can we not wait until tomorrow? We have travelled since before the sun rose and the women and baby are exhausted."

"You either come with me now or you go back." He turned around and stepped back out through the door.

"We better go with him," Mariam whispered to Yakup and started packing the food. Yakup grabbed his bag and hurried out. "Sorry, sir! We are coming. Just give us a moment to pack up—we are coming with you."

Yakup dumped his bag and went back to help Mariam and her mother When they returned, the man was astride his horse. As soon as he saw them, he gave the animal a small kick and it started walking. They followed, Yakup with two bags, Mariam one and the baby and her mother with a bag over her shoulders.

"Excuse me, sir," Yakup said when he finally caught up with the horse. The man did not react. "Can you tell us how far we are going?"

Still no answer. "Would it be possible for you to carry the two ladies' bags? We have travelled for a long time and have the baby as well." It was a tall black horse with a stride and gait that never saw its rider move up or down more than a few centimetres. Yakup's head was eye level with the saddle and he could only just make out a little of the white in the horse's eye.

"If you choose to travel, you bring what you can. The rest you leave behind," The man said from what seemed like far, far above him. The riffle hung from a strap on the man's back. Yakup turned his head. Mariam's mother was struggling to keep up.

"I know, sir. It is just... my mother-in-law is weak. She hasn't been well and I'm worried." Yakup never saw the boot flying towards his chin. Nor did he have time to realise he was on the ground before the man had leapt off the horse and already hoisted Yakup back onto his feet.

"Listen here, you filthy Afghan. I'm not spending my nights in the mountain to play porter for women and small boys unable to handle a few small bags!"

Yakup could taste warm blood in his mouth. He tried to say something but couldn't. "You do as I tell you. If you do not have the strength to walk in the valley, you will not make it through the mountain pass. If you can't keep up over there, you will be left behind to die. Either the biting cold will get you or you'll fall down from a cliff and be left for animals to eat. Do you understand?"

He finished his tirade by shoving Yakup so that he landed on his back. The man mounted his stallion and moved off. Yakup struggled to get up. Mariam reached him.

"Yakup," she said, "You are bleeding."

"It is nothing," he said, facing away from her. The humiliation stung worse than the pain of the blow.

Yakup pulled himself away from Mariam.

"What do you mean nothing? He kicked you. I saw it. Yakup, let me at least take care of your split lip." She tried to wipe off the blood, but Yakup turned away. He didn't want her to see in case he burst into tears. He was supposed to be a man, and a man does not let himself be humiliated and then cry about it.

"I'm fine. We have to follow him. Come on, hurry! Unless you want to be left behind!" His voice came out harsher than he had intended, and so, he started walking quickly. Mariam stood still, motionless and stunned, for a few seconds. He allowed himself to become distracted by his injuries instead and felt his lip with his tongue. It was numb. Soon enough it would start to ache. He could feel a tear in his flesh. The boot must have opened the lip and let the blood loose. His teeth were still in place. His mouth tasted of iron.

They kept their distance from the rider, taking care never to lose sight of him. It was a moonless night, but the stars painted the swaying silhouette of the horseman, easily distinguishable by the struggling party behind. They did not speak and only after some hours found themselves stopping within the shadow of a barn.

"Wait there until someone comes for you," the horseman said. He kicked his horse in its flanks and set off into the mountains beyond.

27

SHADOW

There were other people inside the dark barn, mostly from foreign countries. Hushed voices in unknown tongues permeated the dark room where most of the speakers were young men. Some had children with them, but it was clear: this was a journey for men with women left at home, wherever that was, to fend for themselves.

There were between 25 to 30 hopeful travellers clustered in small groups; some on blankets, others on hay and still more on the hard ground.

All waiting.

Light started to creep in through the cracks of the wooden walls. Maybe Yakup had slept; maybe he had not. The people in the barn began to grow into humans with faces and bodies. There was a group of Afghan boys in rags who looked like a pack of animals wary of attacks from predators. Then there were people from places with languages Yakup did not understand. His bruised lip hurt with each beat of his pulse.

A boy near the door got up with an excited and anxious look before the others heard the roar of a distant engine.

Someone opened the door to the rising sun and the shadow of a man with a gun, all in silhouette, appeared in its place; blocking the entrance.

"It goes like this: you come out one by one and finalise the business part before you can move on," the shadow said. There were other shadows behind him. He indicated to a nearby boy that he was first. The startled boy looked at his friend with a frustrated and worried face. He could not have been more than 10 years old. One by one, the barn emptied. Yakup's turn came and he gave Mariam as comforting a smile as his pounding lip would allow as he stepped out of the barn and into the glaring light of day.

A truck full of people was parked outside. An armed man guarded it and Yakup recognised him as the rider from the night before. He touched his lip with his tongue. *Were they paying customers or prisoners?* Yakup wondered. Another man sat on a bench next to the barn, weapon leaning against the wall. His eyes were cold, his face weather-beaten and his movements mechanical. He had a list and some documents next to him.

"Come here," he commanded. "How much and who did you pay? Give me your slip," he demanded from Yakup without looking at him.

"We came from Tehran directly without paying. A man told us about the village and the mountain pass," Yakup said.

"What man?" the smuggler asked, cold eyes measuring him up.

"The man with the documents."

Satisfied, the man continued.

"Afghan?" he asked.

"Yes."

"Alone?"

"I have my family with me."

"How many?"

"My wife, her mother and my baby girl."

"We don't refund if some don't make it; we wait for no one," the Shadow said. He was scribbling on a tattered notepad, which featured a smudgy cartoon of a happy, human-like mouse.

"This is the price." he ripped a small slip of paper from the pad, tearing the mouse in two. The price winnowed, still further, Yakup's shrinking pile of dollar bills.

"We'll take you to Turkey. From there, well, it's up to you whether you want to continue or not. Now, gather your family and get in the truck," he said as he deposited the money in a pocket under his army fatigues.

Yakup complied and once Mariam, her mother and the baby were all in the rear, finally hoisted himself into the waiting lorry. It didn't take long before the truck was completely full despite a few young Afghan boys still waiting their turn next to the scribbling man. They were saying something, trying to explain a situation, reasoning where reasoning was pointless.

The man stared at them with the same emotionless expression and said something, which triggered the smaller of the two boys to cry. The older child said something to him and then tried to explain.

The fist of the man moved fast. The boy was in the dust, the man next to him. A thump from a boot landed in the bigger boy's belly, eliciting a grunt alongside more high-pitched screaming from the smaller boy.

The stir among the Afghan men already in the truck came to a halt when a Kalashnikov was cocked, aimed and readied. The man turned towards the truck and the smaller boy picked up a stone and ran towards him in a feeble attempt to harm the brute, which only saw the boy thrown, viciously, to the ground. The butt of the riffle, now high in the air, caught the glimmering morning light just before landing on the face of the small boy. A sound like a hammer against a concrete floor. The small boy fell on his side and lay still. The man turned around once more.

Next to his cold eyes ran a thin red line of blood from behind his ear before settling into his black beard. He stared at the cargo in the back of the truck. A child began crying with a father's palm quickly arresting the sound. The rest stared hard at the bed of the truck.

The engine growled, and as the truck pulled away, the man turned and returned to the two boys on the ground.

The first report of the rifle was all that Yakup needed to hear to know that a second would follow closely thereafter.

28

MOUNTAINS

It was a Nissan in name only. Everything else was Iranian: shaking, bumping, scrambling, jolting. A bucket of bolts. It made it impossible to speak, let alone think. Everything was broken. Desolation flashed past them. Rocks and sparse vegetation. Occasionally, a rodent, disturbed in the course of performing its daily chores, scurrying about as the spectacle passed by. Only those without hope dared navigate this heartless land. The asylum seekers had already seen the brutality shown them by the only people brazen enough to try to earn a quick buck: local smugglers made hard as the rocks around them.

The truck wound its way along the narrow single lane, ascending and descending. The Nissan struggled through each turn. The travellers held on to anything they could, be it an iron bar, a wooden plank or, simply, the person next to them. It was impossible to say how long they drove like that.

Yakup shielded Mariam's mother. The baby girl was fastened close to her body. Only her face was revealed, contorted and displeased, steady wailing drowned out only by the straining engine.

Time passed and the truck came to a halt by a small hut nestled within the canyon walls. Three smugglers appeared from the entrance of the hut next to which stood another group of refugees with canvas bundles, plastic bags and taped rucksacks. They were, like Yakup, Mariam and the others on the truck, at once both fleeing and seeking.

"There are so many of us," Mariam said in a hushed voice to Yakup when they had already leapt from the truck and found a spot to rest near the hut.

"The mountains provide good cover for many as they try to cross the border without getting caught," Yakup said.

The travellers waited by the hut for hours. No one told them anything or asked, *how long? How far? Is there food? Water? Shelter? Bandits? Police?*

Instead, they waited for dusk to arrive so as to cloak them in its darkness.

When it finally arrived, the smugglers yelled at them to get up and get going. One led the way on horseback, his clothes fluttering in the wind. The month of October is not kind to those traversing the mountains. The peaks are preparing for winter, coating themselves in icy layers of frozen water hardened by wind that hammers the solid rock, gravel and ice. Turning slush into concrete.

People walked in a long line; one, two three… forty… more. The narrow path allowed for nothing more than this lone strand of humanity. They kept a brisk pace. Old and young; men, women and children, all walked in silence and tried to keep up. Steep ridges appeared to the left. Then on the right. Rugged teeth threatened to devour them. The darkness grew onto them as a heavy duvet.

No one knew where they were. No one would miss them. The world would continue without noticing their disappearance. Did someone step into the darkness and fall? Sat down to rest and froze into the mountain. Fell behind and got lost.

The moon grew weaker as the sun forced its way through the peaks. They arrived at a shelter. An old couple brought them bread and cheese. The three men left them. The sun warmed their bodies. Maybe they were fewer than the night before, but no one wanted to think those thoughts, and no one talked about it.

The men returned in the evening. The travellers formed a line. There was no visible path. Maybe it was covered in snow and ice. The night was clear, the fat moon rising to assist the travellers with its blue hues. Another night passed into another day; this time there was no old couple with cheese or bread to aid and abet their escape. Small handfuls of dried fruit depleted already low rations. Water that tasted of plastic was gone. The snow and ice tasted of cold iron. Intestines rubbed against each other with nothing to mend them with.

A third night. A shorter line of weaker travellers. Someone was moaning.

It sounded like an animal, but it was a human. Someone without a face. Soon there was no someone.

A baby that couldn't cry. A mother without food or water. No consolation to give.

After some hours, the smugglers suddenly stopped—something had alarmed them. They disappeared into the mountain. The human line rested and began to freeze.

"Yakup," Mariam whispered and reached for his arm.

"Yes, Mariam?"

"Will we make it?"

"We will make it. Don't worry, Mariam, we will make it." He knew he said it once too many.

They descended. At first a reprieve after the long, slow climb, tired legs praised the descent. Soon relief transformed into wary concentration and then fear. Worn shoes lost their footing on the ice. A scream raced by them. The rugged mountain swallowed the scream.

The snow vanished, the path evened out and the night moved on. They arrived at a small river. Clear. Fresh. Alive. Filthy clothes, covered in mountain slush, soiled the creek. A fire burned and cracked, warming bodies and grilling fish. They had crossed the mountain pass. A faint engine grew louder with a taxi growing larger in the distance. It quickly filled with travellers. Another taxi and then another. Finally, Yakup, Mariam, her mother and the girl found themselves in the back seat of yet another taxi. The roads were better on this side of the mountain pass. Here and there a house appeared to grow out of the mountain granite, which soon gave way to tarmacked roads, more houses, shops and a village until finally giving way to a renewed sense of normalcy.

They drove past many small villages and finally reached a city with busy streets. Then came a quiet area. The taxi stopped in front of a dark-brown, two-story wooden house. A man and a woman ushered them hastily inside. They looked nervously up and down the street, but no one seemed to have registered their presence. Yakup was in a room with other boys and men while Mariam, her mother and the baby were whisked away to another room with women and children. This was the city of Van.

This was the country of Turkey.

Part III

Turkey

29

NO MORE GAMES

They stayed indoors so as not to arouse any suspicion in the neighbourhood. A Kurdish family owned the house. They provided food. There were maybe 15 travellers, mostly Afghans, staying there. Yakup shared a room with seven other Afghan men. They spent most of the time in the small room. At night, they shared blankets. There was a TV to pass the time. Hour after hour the flickering box bombarded them with soap operas, reality TV shows, adventure and nature programmes, football, cricket, volleyball, news, cartoons and commercials. Information, repetition, emptiness. They were stuck in the room with the bullying box, and they were glad it was there.

People were biding their time. The baby drew the attention of the women and provided entertainment of a different sort. One infant, the only one in the house who did not feel the burden of being on the run.

In the meantime, Yakup and Mariam spent as much time as possible together. They had found seclusion in a small attic containing old building materials and a small window that let in light through the spider webs and dust.

"How is your mother doing?" Yakup asked one afternoon whilst sitting next to each other in the dim orange glow of the day's fading sun.

"The mountains have taken their toll on her," Mariam said.

They were resting on a small rug and had a view of the sky from the angled window above them. "I think she spent all her energy there. She used up all her reserves and when we finally reached this place, she let go," Mariam said. Mariam's mother had aged those days in the mountains, which led Yakup to ask whether it was for the baby.

"Maybe. Perhaps." Mariam's fingers caressed Yakup's lower arm.

155

They had grown closer. In their papers, they were married, but in their consciences, they were not and any physical contact was indecent and disrespectful, even dangerous, for a young, unmarried couple. But they were married on paper. Holding a hand without movement one day turned into a caress of the same hand the next.

"I think a few days of rest will do her good," Yakup said. Mariam's mother's swift deterioration after their arrival in Van had troubled Yakup. She had grown fragile with a cough she could not shake. Yakup was surprised to see her disappear a little more each day, shrivelling just like a grape to a raisin when kept in the sun. It was as if her sparse fat and muscles had disappeared from under her crumbling skin.

She had barely had any water or food those first few days in the Kurdish house and Yakup began to worry less about her physical state and more about her mental fortitude pondering whether she even wanted to go to Europe

"One of the other ladies is taking good care of her. She used to be a nurse. I'm worried, of course, but my mother is a strong woman. You may not think much of her, Yakup, but she has seen and endured more than many others have."

"I know she is strong. I just don't understand why she is silent all the time."

"She wasn't always like that. After the abuse in the village and our escape, she stopped talking. Not all at once. She still talked about daily trivialities in Kabul. About the neighbour, chai, the weather and so on. But day by day her sentences grew shorter and infrequent until one day she just simply stopped talking.

"I was frightened at first until I realised there was some secret inside of her that kept her distant. I couldn't determine what it was and feared that she had gone mad; she still took care of me and worked hard to ensure that we could eat a little every day, so I let it go. I didn't push or pry.

"I guess I thought that maybe, just maybe, she was afraid of letting something evil from inside of her slip out. Something she could not control. I had heard her scream in the night. She had terrible nightmares, that is, when she was able to sleep. She never told me what they were about, or why she screamed, so I thought that maybe she suppressed them so that they only existed inside of her and wouldn't somehow leach into us. After a while, her screaming stopped altogether and she hasn't spoken since."

Yakup was caressing Mariam's hand. Her nails were short and dyed with henna.

"Maybe she is silent because she is safeguarding something good inside of her. Could it be that she has kept a piece of happiness inside of her that she does not want to lose?"

Mariam turned to look at him. "What do you mean?"

"Maybe she feels that not much good came to her when she spoke and that, instead, she needs to save something, some positive feelings for you and the little girl…"

Mariam interrupted, "Why would she keep her positive thoughts for herself and not share them with me? I am her daughter. If anyone, it is me she should show her goodness to. Do you know how hard it is to be constantly surrounded by silence, indifference, and solitude?"

"Mariam, after the death of my father, when my mother had already lost two sons, she fell silent for long periods. When she spoke, they were not kind words and I was the target of her tirades. I wished for silence rather than verbal chastisement. I believed it was a question of time before my mother's mourning would end and she would accept me as her son again. I'm still waiting for that day to come. Now, though, I'm not sure I will ever see it.

"I'm just hoping that the pain within her has not spilled over into my sisters. Not a day goes by that I do not think about my family and if I made the wrong choice in leaving them behind. Maybe I would have survived the fighting season this year and next year. Maybe I should have stayed and made a plan for my future and the future of my family. But I didn't. I didn't die or survive or even fight. I didn't stay and support my sisters or my grandmother. I left them. I ran away. First to Kabul, then Iran and now in some house in a city and a country, I don't know. I'm still moving, still on the run…"

"Yakup, I know you don't have your family with you and I do," she said, straightening up. "You and I have very little… but now we have each other." The setting sun shone through the murky windowpane. A spider was hanging in its web.

The orange light added a beauty to Mariam that Yakup had not heretofore noticed and he realised what he must do. The sore cut inside of him felt less deep as an indescribable sensation rose in him. He took her hands and pulled her towards him. Their lips met and they buried themselves in the softness of each other. The two secret agents in their secluded hiding place. They knew then that this was no longer a game.

30

BIDING THE TIME

When Yakup was not spending his time with Mariam he tried to escape the triviality of the room with the flickering TV and the other bored travellers. He was helping in the house with chores: cutting vegetables, lighting the fire, cleaning and befriending the Kurdish family that called the building home. In all reality, of course, it was a group of cousins who had seen the opportunity in providing temporary assistance to the many refugees passing through Van on their way to Europe.

The house had belonged to their grandparents, but when they passed away the family decided to use the place as a business. Two male and two female cousins were assigned as the primary caretakers, though, other family members often passed by to check in, assist or provide some of the necessities that running a temporary refugee shelter required. This meant bringing food, clothes, medicine, and in the event of an emergency, a doctor whom they could trust. Sometimes they brought money and documents to ward off traffickers or police who sniffed too close to the house.

Yakup made an effort and was soon accepted by the two male cousins who, in exchange for his assisting with the chores, sometimes gave him crash courses in Turkish. "You don't need much to fool the police donkeys," said Belan, who was in his mid-twenties, and exceedingly strong and cheerful.

"Very true. Just don't let them think you're Kurdish," Serdar, the younger of the two, but equally strong, added. Red-faced from carrying firewood, they had tossed their jackets on a bench in the corner of the kitchen and situated their bulky muscular bodies awkwardly in the wooden chairs. They sipped chai from small cups.

"Just try to avoid them completely, Yakup," said Dilan. Her hair was bundled in a knot, despite this, a small locket kept falling in front of her face. She was cleaning and chopping cabbage at the kitchen table. The cabbage ended up in a steaming pot. Yakup nodded, cleaning and peeling several pounds of potatoes.

"Otherwise, call us, and we'll take care of the donkeys," Serdar said, flexing his right arm.

"Don't listen to my cousins," Dilan, said, blowing a few strands of hair out of her face. "The donkeys may not be very smart, but they do, unfortunately, have much stronger weapons when compared to my cousin's muscles."

Belan got up laughing and lifted Dilan off the floor. She kicked, feigning outrage, but couldn't help but laugh whilst flicking water on Belan.

"Help, Serdar, the donkey is using its waterpower. I am defeated."

He fell into the chair and rested his chin on his chest, eyes closed, dead. Serdar was cracking up with laughter and accidentally spilled his cup of chai, flooding the table.

"Aha! Serdar, who is the donkey now?" Dilan laughed, shaking her head and tossing a cloth towards him. Yakup too was laughing. It felt good.

There were people coming and going in the two-story house. Most were coming from Iran and heading towards Istanbul and Izmir in a bid for Europe. Mariam's mother was doing better while Mariam herself was slowly growing impatient.

"I think we should leave soon," she said to Yakup one day when they were in their attic.

"We will," Yakup said. By now they had grown accustomed to holding each other and no longer felt embarrassed. They were, of course, still cautious not to be followed and surprised in their little hideaway, but at the same time, they took pleasure in seeing a different side to the world: one of freedom and abundance.

"Serdar has told me that there is a truck leaving in a couple of days, and supposedly, the driver is reliable. one of the more reliable drivers. I can try to get us on board... if you really want to leave?"

Yakup traced one of Mariam's eyebrows with his fingertip. He closed his eyes. He was enjoying his stay, but he also had more opportunities than Mariam who was limited to the rooms upstairs and their attic hideaway while he was in the kitchen with the cousins learning Turkish, helping with chores; laughing. The cousins were too worried about curious neighbours to let a strange woman into the kitchen.

The following day he managed to get Serdar alone in the kitchen: "You talked about a truck yesterday. A safe one?"

"They are all dangerous, Yakup, but I know this driver well and he is trustworthy. That is the best I can do. The baby might be an issue, though."

He noticed that the younger cousin looked nervous. It was a reminder that Serdar and his family were running a business and Yakup and his fellow travellers were the commodities in which they dealt.

31

THE TRUCK

They boarded the truck at dawn. A double layer of green plastic tarpaulin was stretched over its human cargo. Yakup, Mariam and her mother were strapped in between the tarpaulin together with young men and boys. Yakup was the last in line, with Mariam sandwiched between him and her mother. The plastic was tight around them. It didn't allow much movement and clung heavily to their bodies. The baby girl was placed in a small box inside the truckload and wrapped in blankets. The plan was that the driver would let Yakup out when they were halfway so he could feed the baby and attend to her immediate needs. It was not ideal, but it was the only way that the driver would allow them to join the group.

Once the driver fixed the tarpaulin tight, Yakup could only see the person next to him—Mariam—who could only see him. Their heads were locked in place, the only movement possible was a fluttering of fingers. They were wrapped as tight as mummies.

The truck's engine coughed and jumped. Then stopped. Another cough and a roar. Exhaust fumes filled Yakup's nostrils, his eyes watered, and the taste of tar, gasoline and soot filled his mouth. The truck started to move, and the rush of air relieved them of the fumes but left them bitterly cold. The green plastic coloured what little Yakup could see of Mariam's face and he imagined that they were in a lush forest.

The travellers could hear the sound of vehicles passing them. The plastic vibrated violently each time a truck or bus overtook them, pulling the passengers back and forth like insects in a spider web. Yakup could see Mariam's lips move, but could hear nothing but the engine, the wheels on the road and the flapping of plastic. They held each other's gaze from time to time, sleep not being an option. Yakup's bladder was full and screamed to be emptied and the soon became an unbearable icy cold, a leg cramp, and a silent scream.

Hours passed until the truck ground to a halt. They could hear voices outside. The back of the truck was opened and someone climbed in.

The policeman moved slowly, opening a box here, knocking a sack there. Yakup knew exactly where the baby was, and he could hear the policeman approaching.

Please don't cry, Yakup pleaded silently. Mariam's and his eyes locked, both of them were thinking the same thing when it started: the vague, unmistakable moaning of a baby. The moaning was only centimetres from Mariam behind the green plastic. It grew louder. They knew it would soon turn into a cry. Mariam started to move her mouth. She was whispering the song she sang for the baby at bedtime. Faint whispers. Yakup closed his eyes and listened. The hushed song, the moaning and the moving policeman took on an orchestral quality, each an instrument of destruction.

The policeman moved closer. Soon he would hear the baby. Mariam kept up the near-silent song. Her eyes were shut as well. The policeman stopped. Listening. He took another step and stopped. Another. Stopped. Another. Yakup could hear him breathe. A shadow moved outside the green tarpaulin.

"Shhhh," Yakup whispered to Mariam. Her singing stopped. The moaning began anew.

"Oi, Demir! We have to go. This truck is clean," someone yelled from the rear of the truck.

"Are you sure?" A deep male voice rang out only an arm's length from Mariam. "I thought I heard something."

"You're hearing ghosts, you fool. We are late for lunch and the driver just bought us a dessert. Let's go."

"What about the sound."

"Forget about it or I'll make sure you're directing traffic for the next two months," the voice threatened; someone laughed.

"Damn!" The man kicked a box, took a couple of long strides and jumped down from the truck. The baby's moaning grew louder and louder. The police were still outside. A high-pitched cry erupted, but only for a split second as it was swallowed by the roar of the truck's engine.

The constant movement of the truck had grown into a familiar rocking for the strapped bodies. Yakup and Mariam had developed a silent connection. After what had felt like hours of wriggling, they finally managed to get a hold of each other's fingers. The contact gave them a feeling of belonging. They were there, together.

They communicated in the roaring silence. Mariam shaped her lips into a sentence that Yakup could only guess at, while Yakup replied and in turn left her guessing. And when the truck shuddered unexpectedly their codes made their facial expressions flicker like broken TVs.

You are mine and I am yours, Yakup imagined Mariam's moving lips saying. He had shut out the roaring of the truck and listened only to Mariam's voice inside his head. He imagined her whispering a Sufi poem from school, something he struggled to remember: *You and I were meant for each other*, he thought. *"This journey is our destiny. The vast forces of the universe cannot function without you and me finding one another. In the giant puzzle for all to make sense, we are but a small one, but without even the smallest piece, the puzzle will never be complete. This is why we have found each other. When the puzzle is in place, wars will end, people will stop killing each other, and when some starve, others will come to them with bread. We, like many others, are part of the last pieces of the grand puzzle that will make everything right. Afghanistan has been shaking. The universe is looking for the pieces. It's trying to place them where they belong. You and I are soon in the place we belong.*

And that was when it happened. The truck leapt, and for a long moment, its human cargo grew airborne. Yakup's hand slipped from Mariam's. Her eyes grew fearful as Yakup started to travel away from her. Above the noise of the engine, he heard her scream his name. Then truck and ground met with an impact that jolted people, iron bars, axles, chassis and tooling. All that could move did. Mariam was gone, blinding daylight in place of the mossy green forest. Yakup tried in vain to catch hold of something with his hands and feet. Then the impact of his landing, dust in his eyes, skin ripping and bones cracking were all he recalled before the darkness.

Yakup eventually woke up, but his breathing was laboured, his mouth tasted of iron and his body screamed every time he attempted to move. His next memory was another awakening, but this time, he was unscathed and fully dressed in a clean shalwar kameez, similar to the one he had left in Bamiyan. He got to his feet on the dark rocky surface and walked towards the light—he was in the Bamiyan valley.

"Yakup," a voice said, "Yakup, my son!"

A man approached him. The sharp light made it impossible to see who it was. There was a woman and two older boys next to him and an old woman held the hands of two girls.

"Baba? Is it you?" Yakup whispered.

"Who else could it be," his father smiled. Yakup could see them all now. Grandma Amaya with Noor and Zahra. His mother, next to his father, with his brothers. Yakup started towards them.

"I'm coming," he yelled. One foot in front of the other. Faster and faster he ran. Then, they were at the Band-e-Amir Lakes and sitting on a large rug eating and laughing, but without Yakup.

Next, he passed Rashid and his brothers. They were bleeding, moaning, their inflamed wounds oozing yellow pus. He could feel his muscles tightening as his speed increased. A roaring bear was copulating with row after row of bearded men in turbans, their shalwar pants lifted to expose their buttocks, while a group of foreign cyborgs stood guard. Yakup did not pay attention. He ran to his father, his mother, Zahra, Noor, Grandma Amaya and his lost brothers. Just as he was getting closer, he slammed into a wall guarded by men. He tried to climb the wall, but young Afghans with hollow cheeks, their clothing ragged and their eyes dead, kept building it higher and higher. He finally reached the top and jumped. He passed clouds and birds hovering above mountain tops. Mariam sent him a dimpled smile as he raced closer to the ground. A man on a horse roared by and snatched his Mariam away. Within seconds, though, they all disappeared.

"Kid," his father said, placing an arm around his shoulders.

"Dad! I missed you so much," Yakup didn't want to cry in front of his father, but could no longer hold back the tears.

"Hush, kiddo, I have you."

And with that, Yakup was returned to the darkness.

32

HEALING

Yakup woke up in a soft bed in an unfamiliar room. Above him was a simple roof with exposed beams, the walls matching the roof. He had a pounding headache and when he tried to get up, pain radiated from deep within his shoulder and his left leg, which felt heavy and appeared to be nearly twice its normal size, left him feeling further immobilised.

It was like waking up from a heavy, restless sleep, only to realise that your body was no longer yours.

The door to the small room opened and in came an old woman carrying a tray with bandages, antibiotics and water. Her grey hair was tied in a knot at the nape of her neck. She wore a turquoise dress made of rough fabric. To Yakup, she looked divine.

"Where am I?" he said and felt pain shoot through his head.

The elderly woman jumped.

"Ahh… awake. Wait, wait just one moment," she said, setting the tray on a chest of drawers next to the bed before leaving the room. There was a window to Yakup's right, and through it he could see a leafless tree stretching towards a wide-open sky. There was movement on the other side of the door and an old man entered. He was wearing a grey shirt, a coarse woollen jacket, a sixpence hat and a friendly face. He slung his coat and hat on a hanger next to the door. He ran a hand through his thin, grey combed-over hair and came up to Yakup.

"We were afraid you'd never wake up," he said with a smile. "Glad you did, though, of course," he hesitantly remarked before asking, "How are you feeling?"

"In pain."

"Mmhh… no wonder, my son. You were in bad shape."

"Where am I?"

"You are in our house. I am Berk. Pleased to meet you, young man."

Berk lifted his hand in a gesture of welcome. In return, Yakup awkwardly tried to lift his right hand, but his shoulder resisted and pain once more shot through his body. His face twisted and Berk put his hand on Yakup's arm and held it down. "Don't worry about formalities, son. We are simple people. Can you tell me your name?"

"Yakup."

"Well, Yakup, we found you the other night lying unconscious in the ditch by the main road. We were on our way home from town. At first, we thought you were dead and as there are no hospitals around here, we decided to bring you to our home. Idil, my wife, has cared for you. I believe you already met her?" He turned and called, "Love! Come and meet Yakup."

Seconds later, Idil appeared at the door.

"I am glad to finally meet you, my child," she said and sat next to Berk. "We were worried you would not make it."

"Thank you!" Yakup said.

"Oh, please stop," Idil said as she gently touched Yakup's arm.

"But son, you need to rest and grow strong again. You can stay as long as you want to or need to, ok?" Berk said.

"We want to help, but we do not have much; we will do our best to make you feel as comfortable as possible as you recuperate," Idil smiled.

Yakup tried to return her smile, but his thoughts weren't on the caring elderly couple. Idil noticed.

"What is troubling you child?"

"Mariam. Where is Mariam?"

Berk and Idil exchanged glances.

"But son, you were alone," Idil said, stroking Yakup's hair.

And with that Yakup fell back into a foggy, coma-like sleep.

Yakup grew stronger as the days passed. It was not long before he started to move and began to help, first, Idil and then Berk with their daily chores. He still felt the fall from the truck deep within his bones but took an almost perverse pleasure in labour and the pain it brought his limbs. It proved to be the perfect distraction from the pain he felt within for having abandoned Mariam.

In the evenings, Yakup tried to learn still more Turkish. Idil, he found, was a good teacher and he discovered he was quick at picking up the words and grammar.

Days grew into weeks, and one evening Berk asked Yakup, who was studying Turkish by the dim light of the living room, what his plans were.

"You know, we are enjoying your company," Berk said. He nodded towards the kitchen, where Idil was busy baking bread. "Especially her," he said, sending a gentle look in his wife's direction.

Yakup was sitting at the rough wooden table in the living room, which was ideal for both meals as well as language learning activities. Berk had built it years before, which was true of almost all their furniture.

"I'm not sure, yet, but maybe I have to accept my fate and return to Afghanistan," Yakup said meekly. "Maybe I was thrown out of the truck for a reason. I miss my family…"

"M-hmm… In the first place, you left because of the conflict that you were volunteered into, right?"

"Yes."

"Then you went to Kabul, where a clash between two warlords almost killed you?"

"Correct."

"If you return, will those threats still be there?"

"I suppose."

"So, correct me if I am wrong, but you fled twice, crossed vast lands, put your life at risk several times and managed to keep yourself alive until you were bounced, at random, out of a truck halfway through Turkey. *That* close to your destination and you want to give up and return…*now!*?" Berk summarised with just the slightest hint of disbelief.

Yakup could not counter any of Berk's statements, and so, let the old man continue.

"You could, of course, choose to stay in Turkey, but it is not easy here for an illegal Afghan."

"What if I stayed with you? You said it yourself, that you like having me around. I can help with the farming," Yakup said.

"What do you see, when you look at me?" he asked.

"What do you mean?" Yakup said.

"Tell me what you see."

"I don't know."

"I'm old. Idil is old. What will you do when we aren't around any more?" Berk rested so that the only sound was that of the wood crackling and crumbling in the fireplace.

"I can stay and work on your farm…"

"Yakup, you are still young. We are old. You must have an idea about what you want to do; what is it? What do you see in your future?"

"I want to repay your kindness… And working for you would be a way to do that," Yakup said.

Berk scratched the grey stubble of his chin.

"We can take care of ourselves, Yakup. We have done that for many years. You need to take care of yourself and the people you care about and if that is you going back to Afghanistan, or you trying your luck in Europe, well, that is not for me to say. Regardless, your fate should *not* be to stay with a couple of old farmers in the middle of nowhere."

"If you want me to leave, just tell me and I will do so," Yakup said. He was getting upset at Berk's persistence. "What I want doesn't matter. It is what you want."

Idil entered the room and sat at the table. "Yakup," she said. "If we were younger, then maybe it could have been an option. Europe will probably not greet you with open arms and a smile, but it does offer opportunities for refugees, especially those from Afghanistan. This girl, Mariam, is somewhere out there. The truck went to Istanbul, right?"

Idil placed her sinewy hand on top of Yakup's.

"You want me to leave. Everyone wants me to leave. I'm an outsider with no home and nowhere to go."

He turned and pulled the door open. He slammed it behind him and stood on the dark porch staring up into the starless night. Then he went back in. Berk was no longer in the living room. Idil was sitting in the same place as before.

"I'm sorry, Idil. I didn't mean to… I know what you did for me. I'm sorry."

Idil was staring into the waning fire. A lone log in the fireplace was now nearly all but ember and ash.

"My child, I do not pretend to understand fully how you feel, nor how fleeing your home and losing loved ones feels, but I understand it rattles you to your core. You realise that you are alone in this world and no matter how much anyone tries, be it your mother, sister or partner, you are alone. Still, you need someone."

Idil was gazing into the fireplace, her hand resting on the table as Yakup had left it. He saw an old woman who looked tired. He could see the end was near for her. Nothing would be left when she and Berk were gone. It was the end of the road for them. Yakup could not change that.

"Come here and sit, my child," Idil said. She looked at him for the first time.

"I'm sorry Idil… I shouldn't have behaved like that."

"I want you to have real happiness. Go and find yourself, your home, your future. Find your happiness, my child. Craft it out of the future. That is what I want."

She smiled. Yakup suddenly felt very tired. He leaned his head on her shoulder. He could feel the bones under her garment and smell her age. She lifted her hand and caressed Yakup's brown hair. He could see a grey membrane over the irises of her eyes. Her wrinkles were deep furrows in her hollow cheeks. Her almost translucent hands were liver-spotted.

33

ISTANBUL

At the beginning of December, when Yakup left Berk and Idil, he suddenly found himself on the outskirts of Istanbul in Zeytinburnu, which was known for its illegal immigrant population, all of whom were hoping to cross into Europe.

It did not take Yakup long before he recognised his mother tongue among a group of travellers, Afghans, who helped him find his way to a house where Afghans stayed. There he could buy a bed in a crowded room with other refugees and migrants. The house crawled with his fellow countrymen and Yakup had a hard time figuring out how many people actually lived there. He estimated around 40 or 50, but it was probably many more.

He shared a room with a group of young men, most of whom had already partly paid organised smugglers for their journey to Greece. Some had paid more than 3,000 dollars for the crossing; for others, the sum was as low as 1,000. The lower the price, the more risk the traveller assume.

Hasan was one of Yakup's roommates. He was boyish looking, of Hazara ethnicity, not from Bamiyan like Yakup, but from the district of Jaghori in Ghazni in the east of Afghanistan. Though Yakup had never been there, he knew there was an enclave of Hazaras who had settled there and who, at some point, found themselves surrounded by non-Hazaras, including Taliban. The day after Yakup's arrival, the two of them stood idly in the street.

"Yes, I have been here for some weeks," Hasan said. He was wearing a cotton shirt underneath a thick cream-coloured sweatshirt, baggy trousers and a skullcap embroidered with a colourful pattern to complete his Hazara look. The skullcap was too small and wobbled on his blonde head every time he turned his head too fast, which was why his movements were cautious and clumsy.

"When will you attempt to go to Europe?" Yakup asked, shifting his weight from one leg to the other. His muscles were still sore from his untimely fall from the truck.

"Hmm… yes, that is a good question. My money is not a lot. I am thinking of other ways."

"Other ways?"

"Yes, other ways. Crossing with the *kaçakçı*, the smugglers; it is expensive. It's dangerous, too. Many die they say. How will you cross?" Hasan asked.

A red cat observed them from a nearby fence post in front of an overgrown building site.

"I'm not sure yet. I haven't made any plans."

"The *kaçakçı* are expensive. I talked to other Afghans, who have spent most of their money or want to save some money for Greece. Some say it is possible to cross without the *kaçakçı*. In a boat that one buys."

"You want to buy a boat?" Yakup frowned.

"*We* want to buy a dinghy; an inflatable rubber boat. It is cheaper."

"And more dangerous?"

"Yes, some believe it is," Hasan said, and adjusted his cap. "Some who make money on smuggling people like us, they say it is more dangerous. They don't want to lose our business."

"So, what are you saying?"

"A boat with five people in it floats easier than a boat with 50 people. In our boat, we will be only five. Yes, five of us. And no one else is in control. No one to take our money for no service and no one to toss us out of the boat and into the sea."

"How will you know your way on the water? It's not like there are roads and you will have to cross at night, right?"

"Easy. One of us has studied the science of sailing, another knows where the boat should launch from and we are a band of Afghan brothers… We could fit one more in the boat," Hasan said.

The cat had redirected its attention to a sparrow in a building site.

An arrow ready to shoot. The bird busily pecking at the ground. Snap! The bird caught. Neck broken. Red cat exploring the weeds, then moving on to lazily reclaim its spot on the fence. Yakup followed the red cat with his eyes. It stared back at him with indifference.

"When are you leaving?"

"Yes, a good question. Depends," Hasan said.

"Depends on what?"

"Weather. Has to be good to sail."

"What do you need for that?" Yakup asked. His only sailing experience was the swan pedal boat on the Band-e-Amir Lake far away in the central highlands of Afghanistan.

"Before I tell more, maybe you tell me if you are interested? You told me you speak some Turkish?"

"I do. How much does it cost?"

"Good, good. Yes, the price. We think around 300 dollars each. I will talk to the others. Ask them if we can fit you into the boat. You have enough to cover the cost?"

"I think so," Yakup said, though, knew he did.

"Good then. I'll go now," Hasan said. He lifted his skull cap either to put it back in place or to bid Yakup goodbye. "I'll let you know tonight," he yelled from down the road.

Getting to Europe wasn't what preoccupied Yakup the most, though. of course, but rather, the search for Mariam. He wandered the streets of Zeytinburnu in the hopes of finding her. He trotted up and down streets and observed anyone with a vague resemblance to Mariam. Every time he approached a look-a-like, though, he ended up disappointed. Once, he even called out Mariam's name and waved only to be met by a pair of angry eyes and a face without dimples.

Back in their room, and after the evening of their talk, Hasan whispered to him, "The others agree: you're in."

"That's good news," Yakup whispered back.

"We'll meet tomorrow and discuss details."

"Sounds good," Yakup mumbled. That night he dreamt about Mariam.

34

BROTHERS

They rose early the next morning and silently sipped two cups of tea. Istanbul's wet streets greeted them along with cars, scooters and pedestrians, who passed each man with studied indifference. Once, when a police car went by, Hasan pulled Yakup aside, but otherwise, it was an uneventful morning walk.

They met the three other boys in the park. One stood with his back to the new arrivals. When they were close enough, Hasan adjusted his cap and yelled with a grin: "Brothers! Meet our latest comrade!"

He gestured to Yakup at his side. The two boys facing Yakup gave him a critical stare. The third boy flicked the butt of a cigarette on the ground and crushed it under his threadbare sneaker. As he turned around, Yakup saw a tall skinny young man with brown hair and piercing blue eyes. It was Dani, the boy from his school back home in Bamiyan, Rashid's crony. His face had been destroyed by acne that had now receded; a few scars had accumulated over time. A smirk revealed a missing tooth. Yakup looked nervously around.

"Well, well, well!" Dani said. "If it isn't my old friend, Yakup."

He hawked and spat on the wet ground before he approached Yakup. He was almost a head taller now.

"Come here!" Dani said. "Is this any way for old friends to greet each other?"

He came all the way up to Yakup, opened his arms and embraced him. After a few moments, Dani pushed himself free of the hug and smiled at Yakup.

"Hah! Who would have believed such a reunion? It is good to see you here. It has been a long time since I saw anyone from back home. You have to tell me everything, Yakup."

He slung his arm around Yakup's shoulder and started walking with him towards the two others. "Brothers! Hasan has found someone from my home. This is Yakup. We went to school together."

Dani proudly showed him to the others as though he were a trophy and then said, "These are 'the Afghan Band of Brothers.'"

"I'm Mir," a short, round-faced boy said in a high-pitched voice. He was of Uzbek ethnicity and came from the northern city of Mazar-i-Sharif.

"Nadir," a strong Pashto boy from Kabul with an adolescent moustache and a tight-fitting, hoodie chimed in. They stood: a mixed group of boys, unlikely to have come together had circumstances been different.

"Yakup."

"You want to be part of 'the Band'?" Dani asked in a delighted voice, "or has Hasan been filling our heads with nonsense?" Dani punched Hasan, causing his cap to fall over his eyes. He immediately pushed it back in place and looked at Dani, hurt.

"I want to go to Europe," Yakup said and paused. "Hasan told me that you're planning to sail there by yourself. Without the smugglers. And cheaper."

"Yes, that was what I told him," Hasan said with his chin held high.

"Hasan also said that you are quite good at the language here," Dani said and pretended to give Hasan another punch. Hasan dodged and his cap slid to the left of his head.

"I have learned a little."

"Good. What about sailing? Any experience?" Dani asked.

"Never tried it before. I can swim though," Yakup said.

"Swimming won't take you far if you fall into the sea."

Mir and Hasan giggled at this, while Nadir looked absent-mindedly into the grey park.

"Do I need to know how to sail?" Yakup asked.

"Not really," Dani said and winked, "Some of us have experience, though, right, Nadir?"

Nadir looked at Dani and nodded.

"He isn't much of a talker, but he has tried to cross before. As you may have gathered, he didn't get there. Nope, the Greek police intercepted their boat not far from the coast. It quickly became clear that they were not going to allow Nadir and the others into their boat. They shouted *malaka*—arsehole—and other swearwords that Nadir and the others didn't understand. The police pulled them, and their inflatable dinghy, aboard their Coast Guard vessel. Nadir, and the other boys on board, pleaded with the Greek police to treat them as humans and to let them apply for asylum. Despite these efforts, though, the police beat them up and threw everything into the water instead—bread, drinking water, mobile phones, flashlights, and everything else from the small dinghy. Gone. Consumed by the murky water.

"The police towed the boys and their dinghy back to Turkey and when they were a couple of kilometres from the Turkish coast, the Greek police forced the boys to jump into the boat. They had made a small hole in the dinghy and sent them adrift with one oar. The dinghy was losing air quickly and the coast was still far away. Few of the boys knew how to swim and the water was cold. They paddled desperately to reach the coast. Nadir was strong and the others gave him the oar while they paddled the best they could with their hands. They were completely exhausted after an hour. It was clear that they would not make it. One of the boys jumped in and tried to swim ashore. He was soon devoured by the dark sea. Nadir was still rowing, though, most of the others had given up. They simply sat still as the air in the dinghy seeped out and small waves slowly filled it with freezing water. It was pure luck that a fishing boat saw them in time and rescued them."

Dani stopped and looked at Nadir, who threw a pebble toward a sign advertising a new tech gadget. A soft clang rang out as the rock made contact with the board.

"What if that happens again?" Yakup asked.

"It won't," Nadir said and threw another rock. It missed and sailed into some shrubs.

"We have a plan," Dani said. "Night sailing."

"Yes, indeed," Hasan piped up, folding his arms and smiling. "If we sail at night, the Coast Guard won't see us."

"How can you find your way in the middle of the night?" Yakup asked and looked from Hasan to Nadir.

"Same way as you find your way during the day: a compass," Nadir said. He was weighing another rock in his hand.

"It doesn't matter when, just depends on the weather."

"How do we know if the weather is right?" Yakup asked. He felt stupid, but he also needed answers. Dani smiled.

"Mir here has a contact in an Internet cafe. He is quite a whiz with computers and the owner benefits from his skills on occasion, right, Mir?" Dani nodded towards Mir, who bowed and smiled in agreement, fiddling with an old Nokia.

"Well, it sounds like you have thought of everything," Yakup said. "Just one more question: where do we get the boat and how do we transport it?"

"That was two questions," Hasan frowned.

"So what?" Dani retorted. "Listen, Yakup. This is where we all come in and you in particular. You speak Turkish, so your job is to be the link between us and the Turks we need to do business with. This includes buying the inflatable dinghy and all the stuff we need. And if we are stopped by officials, or have to bribe someone, you will be the man on the front line. How do you feel about that?"

"I don't know… Fine, I guess. What 'stuff' do we need?" Yakup asked.

"Besides the boat, we need the following: a pump, a repair kit in case of leaks, oars, a compass, flashlights, rope, water and food. Oh, and if we can afford it, some life vests. That should be enough. Then you bring what you need… But as little as possible," Nadir said.

"So, the way forward," Dani began, "is to get the equipment ready and then wait for the right weather conditions. Got it?"

After the group confirmed their understanding, Dani continued, "Now that Yakup is here, we are a real Afghan brotherhood. I have no doubt we'll succeed. Let's get started!"

Giddy with a sense of urgency, they left the park and went about the business of preparing to set sail for Europe like thousands of others before them and after them.

Mir went to check the weather conditions with Hasan while Yakup, Dani and Nadir set off to buy a boat, but not before obtaining the money from the other two, who somewhat hesitantly handed over 300 dollars each. Dani accepted the money ceremoniously as the group's treasurer and pocketed the money with a serious nod. They all knew that it was a considerably lower amount than the *kaçakçı* would charge, and so, didn't even deign to argue or negotiate.

35

DANI

Yakup, Dani and Nadir walked out of the park. Here and there the sun was burning through a dense and dreary carpet of fog.

"I'm starving," Dani said, patting his concave belly. "Why don't we go and get ourselves some good Kabuli pulao? I know this Afghan guy who runs a small place from his kitchen. I tell you, guys, it's a killer."

"Sure," Nadir replied.

"Fine with me," Yakup said, his mind wandering to his grandmother Amaya's juicy pulao of rice, lentils, raisins, carrots, lamb and spices.

They walked through dull-looking areas of Istanbul until they reached a small apartment block. They climbed up three flights of dilapidated stairs and entered a small flat that oozed with the smell of home. The combination of sizzling meat, garlic, onions, masala, cumin oil, ghee and other familiar ingredients made the boys' mouths water. Inside the room, three satiated Afghan men were sitting on a rug, sucking their fingers in order not to waste one drop of flavour from their recently emptied dishes.

"Zamir," Dani greeted a tiny, one-eyed man in a stained apron.

Ten minutes later the boys were sitting with their piles of pulao.

"Zamir left during the Russian occupation," Dani explained. "He returned when the Russians left and got involved with one of the warlord factions. The poor fellow ended up losing his family and his eye to the same grenade. It came in the middle of the night and flew straight into their house in Kabul. After the impact, what remained of his two sons and his daughter were chunks of meat. It was impossible to identify who was who.

"His wife, who had been next to him, was missing a large portion of her skull. He was running around in the inferno looking for his children,

178

yelling at his dead wife, and all this with a bloodied piece of metal sticking out of his eye. He had to fight off the neighbourhood dogs from the lumps of meat that were his children. After that, he left again."

Dani dug his hand into the small mountain of rice, lamb, carrots, onions, nuts and raisins. He scooped a large portion into his greedy mouth. The others followed suit. "He sure knows how to make a good pulao. Mmhmm."

It didn't take them long to finish their meal. The three other men had left. Zamir was in the kitchen. Yakup could see Istanbul's rooftops through the window, minarets reaching for the sky here and there.

"So, Yakup," Dani said and burped.

"So, Dani," Yakup replied and forced a burp. They laughed.

"Man, I haven't seen you for a long time," Dani said, pulling out a sad-looking cigarette butt, lighting it, and puffing on it before dispensing it into the greasy plate in front of him.

"What happened to you?" Yakup asked.

"The same as to all of us. There was no future for us there. We were poor, it was difficult to make ends meet, the political situation was unstable… My father had some sort of debt to a strong family and one day the men came to our house. They demanded my sister in return for the debt my father still owed them. When I heard about it, I picked up a kitchen knife and started towards their house. My father caught up with me and held me down until the rage passed, but then decided to send me to Iran. My sister was, ultimately, cashed in as repayment for the debt."

Dani's eyes were dull. He was scratching his chin, trying to pick something out from within his off-colour skin.

"It was the feeling of hopelessness. There was no way I could alter my fate in Afghanistan. I remember when I was a kid and my dad told me that things would get better now that the Taliban were gone and the foreigners had come. They would help us rebuild our country and secure a prosperous future, but just look at the place! People like us, normal Afghans, are removed from government. We still don't have security or justice and there's not enough food and there are no jobs. If you get sick you better pray for a miracle since medical treatment is too expensive or requires a bribe and even then, is likely to be some back-alley 'cure'. No,

Yakup, the future of Afghanistan is not bright. The people who remain are either disillusioned or in denial," Dani concluded, scratching his cheek so violently that it turned red.

The clouds outside rolled over Istanbul's sky and the Bosporus Strait. Yakup felt drowsy after the meal and blinked a few times too many during the story, but Dani continued seemingly without noticing.

"In Iran, I quickly became part of the pistachio industry. It was run by Iranians, but all the heavy harvesting work was done by Afghans. We accepted the low pay, of course, but my plan was always to make enough money to send for my family to join me in Iran. I even dreamed of making enough for us to go to Europe or the US."

Dani paused, taking took a sip of his chai.

"Was it possible to make that much?" Yakup asked.

"Well, I'm here today without my family… so, I guess not. It wasn't always easy in Iran. Sometimes the local Iranian communities rose against us Afghans and blamed our kind for every type of injustice they themselves encountered; the Iranian Government is clever that way. Every year hundreds of thousands of Afghans are deported. They can deport as many as they want. Cheap labour constantly flows over the border, offering itself to the Iranians. The employers treat us badly since they know we need money and if we don't do as they say, they can easily find another Afghan to fill our shoes. If we don't work hard enough, they curse us or even beat us. Sometimes they withhold our salaries claiming some unexpected rise in taxes from 'the state'.

"Like many others, I was deported back to Afghanistan. The first time I was terrified, but it didn't take me long to return. Unfortunately, the return cost me most of my savings. This time I became a day labourer at a construction site, but it was no different. After a while, I was fed up with the Iranians. They saw us Afghans as lesser humans. So, I decided it was time to leave. After all, what could be worse than returning to Afghanistan?"

The one-eyed Zamir entered the room and cleared the plates. "Good?" he asked.

"Excellent, my friend," Dani said and applauded while nodding his red face in approval.

"Very good. Thank you, Zamir," Nadir said.

"Thank you. The best pulao I've had," Yakup said, thinking that grandmother Amaya's was better, but that she wouldn't mind him not mentioning it to one-eyed Zamir who looked pleased by the flattery.

"More chai?" Zamir asked. They nodded and Zamir disappeared into his small kitchen. Yakup grabbed the pillow behind his back and rearranged it. His leg was feeling stiff and his shoulder ached.

"I only had a little money when I left Iran," Dani continued, "I couldn't ask my family for help. They have nothing and it would be embarrassing and disgraceful. No, I had to find my own way. That was when I met Mir. He had been sent to Europe with smugglers. His parents had paid them some money. His family isn't poor like ours. I got in touch with the smugglers through him. They agreed to take me to Europe. I paid them most of my money, but by the time we were at the border with Turkey, they were demanding that I pay them more.

"I gave them all I had. It wasn't enough, though, and I had to do work for them. I just wanted to get out of Iran, so I didn't care that I had to work under poor conditions."

Dani smirked and shook his head in disgust. He pulled out a crumpled pack of cigarettes and lit one. The hot tea steamed in their cups. Outside the noise of Istanbul on wet concrete was muffled by the closed windows. The dew-layered windowpanes added a misty distance to the city outside of Zamir's small eatery.

"These people don't care about others. They care only about their business. They treat us like animals. Anyway, one day, not too far from Istanbul, I learned later, they start beating Mir, saying that his father hadn't sent them enough money. While beating him, they yelled stuff like, 'You're no one! A non-entity. If you disappear no one will know or care. The police don't even know you exist.' They kept on yelling and beating him. He bleated and pleaded in the beginning, like a goat to slaughter, but after a time, he, too, fell silent.

"Did he accept his fate? That it was the end? I didn't know; I still don't know, but I couldn't just stand there and watch. They were kicking the life out of him. My blood boiled and I jumped the biggest of them. I didn't even get one blow in before they had me cast aside. At least the attention was diverted from Mir to me. But I regretted it moments later. Boy, did I regret it. Well, I'm just glad I passed out.

"When I came to, it was dark. I didn't know where I was. Mir was next to me. He told me that they had locked us in a basement somewhere. It was a place where they kept refugee boys until their families paid the amount they had initially promised to the smugglers… Or simply extra money that the crooks claimed was needed."

Dani leaned forward. He pulled his shirt up and revealed a number of scars, burns and cuts.

"What did they do to you?" Yakup asked, feeling sick and appalled by the sight.

"They chained me to pipes in the basement. Mir and the other boys were not chained. They could move a bit in the locked basement. I think they liked tormenting me, or maybe I was the example. Most of my scars are from that period of confinement."

Dani touched his eyebrow where a purple scar descended down toward his eye. "Mir's father submitted the payment from Afghanistan, but something had gone wrong. Maybe his father had run out of money, maybe he didn't want to pay. I don't know."

Dani stared into the heavy sheet of rain marching over the city just outside the window. "I'm not sure how long we were there. Maybe a month. It was dark, cold and uncomfortable. They fed us one meagre meal per day. Sometimes we were lucky and had something hot, but whatever it was, it was always bland and tasted like rot.

"The darkness and the uncertainty were the worst. From time-to-time new boys were tossed into the basement. One of them kept crying and crying. Even in his sleep. No one was able to handle what we went through and have as the soundtrack a whimpering, broken boy. We tried to comfort him, but we were all scared and weak. In the end, someone put him out of his misery. He was asleep and barely noticed the hands covering his mouth and nose. The smugglers carried his body out of the darkness and soon after that they let the rest of us go."

Dani emptied his cup and got up.

"And so, here we are. Feasting on beautiful food amongst good people. Let's go get that boat, my brothers."

He threw a few notes on the kitchen table and off they went into the wet streets to disappear.

36

FRIENDS

Getting the dinghy was easy. Procuring the rest of the equipment proved just as easy, but to their mounting frustration, the weather refused to cooperate.

Mir and Nadir eagerly monitored the weather conditions. They met every day in the park and debated the situation.

"No need to rush it. The weather will be right when it is right," Mir shrugged.

"You're saying that the wind is blowing in the right direction. Why don't we take advantage of that? We don't even need to use our energy on rowing," Dani said.

"The waves will crush the boat, and we will either drown, because we cannot swim, or because our limbs will succumb to hypothermia," Nadir informed him.

"Arghh… Either the wind is coming from the wrong direction or the waves are too high. Next, you'll tell me that the sea is frozen," Dani groaned, throwing his long arms into the air.

"Yes, we need to leave soon," Hasan said.

"Maybe tomorrow it will be better," Yakup offered.

The days passed but the weather did not improve. Yakup was still trying to find Mariam, but each day his hopes sank further. He asked Dani where newcomers usually went upon arriving in Istanbul.

"Difficult to say, Yakup. All over, but like you, most of the Afghans come to the Zeytinburnu area."

They were sitting in a small square doing nothing as there was nothing to do save wait.

"What about the women?" Yakup asked.

Dani gave him a mischievous smile. "You naughty, naughty boy." He punched Yakup's barely healed shoulder.

"What do you mean?" Yakup said with genuine indignation.

"Well, we all have our needs, right?" Dani said with a grin.

"No, I just… you know it is tough for us men to get here and stay here, but how do Afghan women cope?"

"Ahhh… so, it is all about concern for the poor women. I see, I see," Dani said. He leaned back on the bench and looked at two passing women with long loose hair and enticing eyes. One was wearing a low-necked shirt, revealing ample cleavage. The other was sporting low-cut jeans that barely hid her luscious curves.

"Well, just curious," Yakup shrugged.

"If you're 'just curious,' I suggest you find other women; not Afghans. You can get them all here: Russians, Syrians, Iranians, Turks, light and dark Europeans, Chinese, Bangladeshis and Africans and in all shapes and sizes. They are all here, trapped in this borderland, and well, practising the oldest trade, of course," Dani lifted his scarred eyebrow and sent a huge acne smile at a passing businesswoman in her thirties, who looked at the adolescent with contempt.

"Listen, Dani, I'm really not interested in that. I just wanted to know what our countrywomen do when they arrive here. There was a girl. I often thought about what might have happened to her and her family."

Yakup stood up. He wanted to get away from Dani, but he also wanted answers.

"Easy, old friend, easy. No need to become upset."

"And I'm not your friend," Yakup said into Dani's face.

"What do you mean?"

"We were never friends back home. How can you think that? You were Rashid's friend and he treated people like dirt. And if you were his friend, what does that make you, then? Tell me, Dani, because it sure doesn't make us friends."

Dani did not get up. His face was indifferent and for a moment Yakup wondered if Dani had even heard him.

"I never chose Rashid as my friend," Dani said in a quiet voice. He looked straight at Yakup. "It just happened. I regret it. You see, my family was tied to his. I didn't have an option. I tried to dissuade him from doing ugly things, but most of the time it was like talking to a wall. That family—the one my father owed money to— was Rashid's. And so, as I already told you, I actually hated Rashid; especially his bloody family."

Dani continued looking up at Yakup. His eyes flickered back and forward.

"Maybe we were not friends back then," Dani said, "but *are* friends now, Yakup. We are friends because we have decided it to be so using our free will, right?"

"I guess so," Yakup replied.

"And friends help each other. We are helping each other get to Europe, right?" Dani stood up and smiled.

"True."

"And since you are my friend, I will tell you all I know about the Afghan women. Come, my friend, my brother." Dani put his arm around Yakup's shoulder. Yakup did the same, and in this way, they walked out of the small square and into the bustling city centre.

The rest of that day and all the next, Dani took Yakup to places where Afghan refugees were living. In some houses, they found only families while others only housed women and children. The vast majority were adolescent boys like themselves. All of them hoping to get a better life than the misery they had left behind. On the journey to Istanbul, they had all lost fellow travellers, friends, fathers, mothers, siblings and children to starvation, cold, falls, road accidents, abuse, suicide, murder and prostitution.

The search for Mariam, though, remained futile. Many of the women were reluctant to talk to strangers and those who did talk could tell them nothing about Mariam.

In the end, they gave up, drained of hope and depressed.

"Well, maybe they moved on? You know, thousands of Afghans pass through Istanbul. Maybe they are already in Greece or an even better place…like Sweden!" Dani said as they wandered the streets aimlessly.

"Maybe," Yakup mumbled.

"Don't take it too hard, Yakup. Soon we, too, will be in Europe. Mir told me that the weather forecast is looking good over the next few days," Dani tried.

"Well, we better get home and rest. Maybe this is our last night in Istanbul. Better to be rested and prepared," Dani said.

They parted ways, then, with Yakup trudging through the streets, vaguely hoping to run into Mariam.

He passed shops selling Christmas decorations, candy and ornaments, which reminded him of garish scenes straight out of Bollywood. The shops brimmed with advertisements featuring happy families in front of piles of presents seated in living rooms surrounded by food and other pleasantries. It seemed even happiness could be purchased for some event Yakup failed to comprehend. He thought that if this was what Europe offered, he, too, would soon find happiness. And perhaps, even Mariam. He smiled at the thought and his steps grew lighter in the dark street on this Christmas Eve.

37

THE SEA

The weather did not change the next day or even the day after that. On the third day, and thought it looked better, the band of brothers took the wrong bus, ending up in the wrong part of town, which spooked Hasan who persuaded the others to wait another day. Finally, on December 28, after an early start and a long day on the road, they reached the departure point. By the time they had pumped the dinghy with air and were ready to set sail, however, the sun was still making its way toward the horizon.

"We have to wait," Nadir said.

"Why?" Dani protested.

"Coast Guard. We need a heavy curtain of darkness to conceal us. We can eat first and then set out."

"Hmmm… You might be right," Dani said and looked nervously at the dark sea.

"Yes, I think that is better," Hasan said. He was not wearing his traditional skull cap, but instead an acrylic beanie that sat tight on his blonde head.

Mir nodded in agreement. He wore a thick second-hand jacket that added to his already rotund nature.

They hid the boat and sought shelter under some trees, wherein they filled their bellies with bread, dried fruit and nuts. They were shivering by the time Dani and Nadir decided they could set off. It was a starry, moonless night, the wind was coming from the northeast and the surface of the sea was choppy with a few whitecaps here and there.

"Perfect conditions. It will be difficult for the Coast Guard to spot us without the moon and with all that disturbance on the surface. The wind will push us in the right direction," Nadir said. The coast was clear.

They shoved the dinghy into the waves. The cold water immediately soaked their pants and gave them a sense of what lay ahead. The small boat floated, rocking back and forth on the dark water, causing Yakup to shudder. He would not be able to swim for long in this cold before hypothermia got him.

It took some coordination before they set on a rowing technique that worked. Nadir was sitting at the back as he had more experience and was stronger than the others. To his left sat Mir and Dani with Hasan and Yakup taking up positions on his right. They rowed in silence. The lights from the shoreline grew more distant and soon only darkness surrounded them. They sailed inside a large bubble of darkness dotted with tiny lights from east to west and north to south.

Their arms grew tired as the murky sea stretched on for what seemed like an eternity.

They floated at the will of the deep sea below them, when, suddenly, Hasan yelled at that he could see a boat. The brothers retracted their oars, but the only sound was the water splashing onto the fragile hull of the dinghy, and the squeaking movement of rubber against bodies and oars. They dipped the oars back into the dark water. One, two, one, two. Their progress looked, and felt, negligible. The sea looked the same. The dots in the dome above them changed position with the movement of the earth. The sea seemed less mobile than the universe. Five boys from a landlocked country found themselves in a cold and hostile environment separated from the deep by two layers of rubber and a pillow of air.

The rocking of the dinghy grew more intense. Yakup's body ached. His limbs were suffering. His shoulder screamed, he saw Mariam's face in between the green plastic tarpaulin, lying on a porch in Iran, sitting in a small hideaway in Van. One, two, one, two.

"There!" Nadir yelled, "There's land!"

He pointed into the darkness. The others stared the best they could, squinting, opening eyes wide, peering into the darkness until finally one, then two, and in the end, all could see a dark patch on the horizon.

"We did it!" Hasan yelled. He stood up in jubilation, letting slip his oar. He tried to catch it as it slid into the depths below the brothers, and leaping for it, fell into the Aegean Sea.

Nadir yelled his name. Mir and Dani moved to the side of the dinghy where Hasan was meant to be, causing the dinghy to list, dangerously, on its right side. This gave up still more to the sea: a flashlight, drinking water and heaps of food were gone.

Gone.

Nadir grabbed Yakup and hurled him violently onto the other side of the boat. The bottom of the dinghy slammed against the water and Mir and Dani tumbled into the bottom of the craft with their oars very nearly taking flight as well.

"You fools," Nadir yelled. "If the boat turns over, we're all dead. Take your places and look for Hasan."

"He is gone. He disappeared. It just took him," Mir said in a shaky voice. His soaked jacket hung heavy on his body and his hair was pressed flat against his skull.

"Help! Help Me!!" Hasan's voice spluttered from somewhere in the darkness on Yakup's side of the vessel.

Yakup got up without thinking.

"What are you doing?" Nadir screamed.

"Saving a brother," Yakup shouted back, diving headfirst into the darkness. The cold water shocked him, and for a moment, he feared all his muscles would cease. Somehow, though, he found his old rhythm. Three strokes, breathing, searching. No one there. Another three strokes, breathing searching. Again and again. He couldn't stay in the water much longer. He was shaking violently. Three more strokes. Three more. A feeble voice from far behind Yakup struggled to be heard over the wind, waves and water that constantly assaulted the ears.

"There he is! Yakup… almost… too far… come back… you're…" Yakup couldn't feel his body any more. He had to turn back. Breathe. Search. Return. Wait! There! A body. A sore arm connected to a still injured shoulder locked around a young boy's chest. Strokes with the other arm. Legs thrashing. Waves. Darkness.

Above them the stars of Afghanistan. A strong arm reaching out. Pulling. The screech of rubber beneath numb bodies. A pale blonde boy was unconscious at the bottom of a boat. Boys talking, yelling, caring. Rowing. A cough and violent shudder and the boy gasping. Fear on his face, clinging to the dinghy, and shaking in silence.

It was still dark when they reached the shore an hour or more later. They dragged the dinghy up the beach with what little collective strength remained and hid it in a grove of trees.

They walked in silence, Hasan leaning on Nadir. They reached a small ruin of cottages. It was cold so they lit a small fire with Dani's lighter that still worked. His cigarettes were a mishmash though and he cursed as they disintegrated. Their bodies greedily sucked the heat from the flames. Yakup pulled out the small plastic bag with his fake documents. In the dying light of the fire, he gazed at the photo of the young Grandma Amaya, grandpa and their children in front of the Buddhas. Water had disintegrated part of his family, who stared back at him from the ruined photo. The day Yakup had packed this photo, he and his father had been about the same age, though, now his father seemed younger, less troubled and painlessly oblivious to any world beyond that of the Bamiyan. Grandma Amaya was smiling, too, from somewhere in the past. He missed her. A stab of pain went through his guts but was forgotten as sleep overtook him.

Part IV

Greece

38

BROKEN

The fire had died, the sky was ashen, and the boys had sailed across the sea.

"Let's go," Dani said, getting up.

"Go where?" Hasan asked in a weakened tone. "We don't even know where we are."

"You're welcome to stay," Dani said, shrugging as he stepped through the empty door frame in the nest of cottages and descending down a path. Mir and Nadir followed.

Yakup got up. "Come on, Hasan. You better join us. There's nothing for you here," he said, offering his hand to Hasan who reluctantly took it.

The two of them hurried after the others down the narrow path until they reached a group of houses cloistered by some olive and pine trees.

"OK, let's be strategic here," Dani said, scratching his chin. "Yakup, you go ask them if this is Greece."

"But I don't speak Greek!"

"You speak Turkish, right? If they reply in Turkish, you know we're still in Turkey. If not…. Well, then this is Europe."

Dani smiled, pleased with his logic. Yakup was not too happy with this plan, but accepted his role as interpreter and walked up to one of the houses where a young woman was hanging out the laundry.

"Excuse me, Madame," Yakup said. The woman was busy slinging a large white sheet over the line, whipping drops of water into the air. The sheet hung heavy as a sail. The woman nodded at Yakup.

"Um… Perhaps you could tell me what the name of this place is?"

"No understand Turkish. Greek, here" she said.

"Greece?"

"Greece," the woman said.

Yakup smiled. "Thank you."

"You… alone?"

"Five," he said, showing her the correct number with his fingers. "The others are over there," he said before breaking off, reasoning that he probably ought to be cautious. He bowed and took his leave.

"Wait!" the woman yelled. She went inside the house. Was she calling the police? Should he and the others disappear? Before he could decide, however, she reappeared with a loaf of bread, a bag of olives, a lump of feta cheese and a litre jug of water.

"Take," she said and pressed it on Yakup.

He took it with a smile and thanked her. He walked away, but stopped, turned around and returned.

The lady was still hanging her laundry.

"Excuse me again, but can you tell me where the harbour is?" Yakup asked.

She pointed in one direction and said, "Harbour, ferry, Athens. Attention with police here," she said and shook her head with a grave look. "Detention in Lesbos no good for boys."

"Thank you," Yakup said, finally turning to rejoin his party.

He eagerly reported this latest news to the others who cheered and jumped and embraced. They greedily stuffed their mouths with the heavenly bread, the fat olives and the salty, mushy feta cheese.

With full bellies, they walked for hours until they reached a small hilltop where they could see a town and a harbour. The deep bellowing of a ferry welcomed them.

Let's go to the harbour and board a ferry," Yakup said.

"I'm going to apply for asylum here on this island. It is Greece and they have human rights. Then I will take the ferry to the mainland and meet my cousin," Dani said.

He scratched his acned cheek and looked at the three boys behind him.

"But the woman in the house said we shouldn't go to the police here. Why don't we wait?" Yakup said.

"I have been travelling long enough to do things my way. And I want papers, now. They have to take care of us. It is the law," Dani said with a frown.

"Yes," Hasan said and took a step forward. He was wearing his skull cap again. "Yes, me too. I will go to the police station and get papers as well."

"What if they send you back?" Yakup said. He shook his head in bewilderment. "You have come this far and now you want to risk it all?"

"Yes, but don't worry. There must be a police station somewhere around here where we can apply for asylum, get a place to sleep, some food and maybe some new clothes. We are in Europe," Dani continued with the others nodding.

"Are you guys insane? The woman told me not to contact the police here and that is exactly what you're going to do!?" Yakup practically shouted. Dani looked him straight in the eye.

"Take it easy," Dani said. His eyes narrowed. "We offered you a way. Without us, you wouldn't be here. You'd be rotting in some shabby flat in Istanbul, watching your money disappear with the landlord or some sleazy smugglers."

Dani!" Yakup said.

"Your choice," Dani said and that was that.

Yakup left the Afghan band of brothers behind and walked briskly down the hill towards the town below. He was beyond angry, but he was also inconsolable.

He didn't look back. Mainly because he was angry, but also because he didn't want the others to see the tears in his eyes.

39

ASYLUM

Yakup walked briskly through the narrow streets of the city. A European city. This was Europe. People were supposed to care for one another here. He had fled a country of war and poverty where Greek and European soldiers were fighting. Surely, he reasoned, they would understand the need for him, a boy, to live in their part of the world where he would be protected by those same rights that they preached in Afghanistan.

He walked down a street with shuttered restaurants on either side, serving winter ghosts seated in their empty chairs, hidden behind dark windows. The spire of a church hovered above roofs, presiding over deserted winter streets and a smattering of empty tourist shops. Behind this rose the hill where Yakup and the others had parted. In front of it lay yet another sea that he would have to cross.

It was getting colder and Yakup was tired. Darkness had claimed the harbour and threatened to snuff out the few working streetlamps near the harbour. He walked along the concrete dock towards the ferry. He had to get a ticket. He had barely slept in 36 hours.

The ferry grew in size in front of him. A small container with two frosted windows stood that kept a shadow inside. He stepped up to the white door, took a deep breath and knocked. A giant of a man opened it.

"Hello mister. Is this the ticket office? I would like a ticket to Athens with the ferry boat," Yakup pointed towards the sleeping ferry. He looked up at the giant man in front of him, who looked back at Yakup with a pair of bulging eyes. He gestured Yakup into the office and offered him a chair. The man sat himself in front of a computer screen and picked up a VHF radio. A red button flashed and the radio came to life. He spoke to someone and put down the device in a manner that seemed too gentle for someone his size. He smiled at Yakup, indicating for him to wait before turning his attention back to the flickering computer screen.

It was warmer inside the office and soon Yakup dozed off. He dreamt he was sitting on a chair in the small classroom in Bamiyan. Afternoon sun penetrated the window and lit dust motes that hovered between the rows of boys. There, in the row behind him, sat Rashid and Dani. Both had morphed into rough, metallic machines. Their eyes were shining with hate directed at Yakup. He wanted to get up and leave but could not. Zahra and Noor were sitting next to the metallic boys. They seemed oblivious to the danger. Yakup wanted to warn them, but chains held him fast. He screamed, but his voice was muffled and died long before it reached his two sisters. The metallic boys diverted their attention to Zahra and Noor. Lust oozed from their shiny, robotic faces as they got up and pushed chairs and tables aside. The two girls still didn't know anything was amiss. Zahra laughed and Noor gently stroked her arm. There were only meters between his sisters and the machines. Metal-Rashid lay his rusty hand on Zahra's frail shoulder.

He was transported out of this nightmare by a brutal white noise from the radio and someone knocking on the door. The giant man got up, threw Yakup a look of indifference and opened it. A policeman entered the rectangular white room. He glanced at Yakup before speaking with the giant.

"Come," the policeman gestured. Yakup followed him, uncertain of where they were going. The woman's warning echoed in his mind. It was dark enough for him to slip away, but he was too exhausted and did not know the way.

They walked back into the city and to the police station. The officer briefly talked to a tired-looking colleague behind his desk and then led Yakup down a hallway infused with body odour and half-lit by fluorescent, overhead lamps. An unknown number of eyes stared at the uniformed man and the boy as they passed by as it was impossible to count how many cells there were, or people.

"Mister," Yakup said in Turkish, "I have documents. I just want to go to Athens and visit a friend." The policeman didn't react. He stopped in front of one of the doors and fiddled with a ring of keys. Yakup took out his fake Iranian documents and gently tapped the policeman's arm.

The uniformed man turned around and shoved Yakup's head against the concrete wall. The all-too-familiar taste of iron quickly spread throughout Yakup's mouth. He felt sick. The policeman leaned his face close to Yakup's. At some point, he had donned a mask to protect his mouth and nose. He held Yakup up against the wall, feet above the floor, for a few seconds. He then pulled the cell door open and pushed the boy into the darkness.

He braced himself for the impact with the floor but was caught by a wall of human bodies. The only light came through the bars in a small peephole in the door. He could hear living creatures all around him coughing, whispering, talking, whimpering. The stench was terrible. His stomach churned and it took all he had not to vomit.

After some shuffling and bumping, Yakup found himself sitting on the concrete floor amid the other prisoners. His pants were wet from something in which he had accidentally sat and the stale air in the small cell made his eyes water. To one side of the cell, a group of women clutched themselves, sitting on what seemed to be a mattress. To the other side of the cell were men and boys. Refugees, migrants, criminals. All. A broken sink dripped water next to a hole in the concrete floor and topped with a mount of excrement.

The youngest boys had to sit right next to the slippery hole, shifting as best they could when others came to empty their bowels. Every so often, the swaying and readjustment of human bodies occurred, but most remained inert. The cell was a living puzzle with pieces that never fell into place.

Occasionally guards in surgical masks shoved food into the cell. New people were thrown in and others yanked out, depending on the whims of the guards. No one was told how long they had to stay there or why. Minutes, hours, days. Time melted.

One day, and without warning, Yakup was pulled out. He was handed a document and told to leave the country.

In front of the police station, he looked around in confusion. The last few days already seemed but a fading nightmare. Or had it been weeks? He didn't know what was real any more.

The pale winter sun licked at his face. His eyes were sore and he could barely open them. Despite the fresh air, the ammoniac reek of his own skin still reached his nostrils and made him feel ill.

He was free, yes, but lost and alone.

40

PIRAEUS

The paper from the police allowed Yakup to stay in Greece for thirty days he learned. He endeavoured once more, then, to quickly get to Athens. This time, however, he decided to stay out of the ferry boat office, and instead, have a passer-by purchase him his ticket.

Yakup decided that he would register with the proper authorities and apply for asylum once safely delivered to Athens. He had boarded the ferry without much pretence, holding his new document in one hand and the ticket in the other.

Yakup had managed to clean himself before boarding the vessel. He had also tried to launder his clothes and almost managed to scrub off the damp, rotten stench of faeces and decay that had seeped into his skin during the period of detention. Yakup could, still, from time to time, smell the stench of the cell radiating from his clothes and it made his stomach clench.

He dreaded the thought of having to spend more time in the cramped darkness of that cell as he handed over his ticket to a lazy collections agent, who barely looked at the passengers as he ripped their tickets in two, handing the stub back to the passenger.

The Aegean Sea was quiet. Shrouded in fog, the half-empty ferry slid peacefully towards the Athenian port of Piraeus. Once in a while, a distant ferry horn carved through the mist. Yakup spent hours on the cold ferry deck staring into the water. A tired couple sat at a white plastic table, smoking cigarettes and drinking beer. Occasionally, smokers emerged from within the boat to puff on their cigarettes in doorways. A seagull circled the ferry and then drifted away. The sea parted and shut itself tight in a white twirl of wake.

Yakup wondered where Dani, Mir, Nadir and Hasan were. Maybe

in one of the other cells at the detention centre, or somewhere less unfortunate.

That was in the past now and Yakup was determined to keep floating.

After nine hours, the ferry let loose a deep and long call, signalling its arrival into port and putting in at the quay of mainland Greece. It was dusk when Yakup first placed his tattered sneakers on the steady ground of Athens. *Maybe his first experience of Europe was just bad luck*, he thought, reasoning still further that Athens was the capital of Greece.

Yakup felt reassured by this logic, and so, moved ever deeper into Europe.

The evening was lit by the occasional streetlight, and with confidence and a mile, Yakup walked up to a bus stop. A lady was waiting for the bus. Yakup mustered his courage, and asked her in his best English, "Excuse me, miss, but how do I find the office for asylum?" The lady frowned at him and half-turned away. He tried again.

"I am new to your country and I'm looking for some help. Maybe you know where I can find assistance, food or even a house?" He took a step forward and faced the lady, pleading this time when he said, "I just want to know where I can get some help."

The lady shifted nervously, her eyes flitting from side to side behind her thick glasses. She held her handbag close. He suddenly noticed his own reflection in the glass pane behind the woman—a skinny teenage boy, dark brown hair, ragged clothes. He had grown taller or maybe the loss of weight had made him appear that way. He focused on the woman again. Annoyed with her hostility, he sighed and tried, "Can you at least tell me the direction to the city centre?"

The woman suddenly came to life. "*Malaka!* Arsehole!" she yelled, swinging her handbag. It landed on his shoulder. Yakup covered his face with his arm before the next blow came and grabbed the bag with his other arm.

"Stop it, lady!"

"Thief! Thief!" Her thin voice rang into the darkness.

"Be quiet, please! Just tell me where the city centre is," he begged as they both clutched at the handbag. She was pulling it away while he held on to it without thinking.

"Help!" she shrieked, her spectacles falling to the ground.

"I'll let go, but you have to stop hitting me," Yakup said. The sudden release made the lady fall backwards on the pavement from where she let out another scream. Not knowing what to do, Yakup leaned forward, intending to help the woman to her feet. Then he noticed a slim silhouette of a man on his left.

"Phew! I'm glad that you are here… There has been a misunderstanding and the women fell over," Yakup said.

"Mmhmm."

"Yes, I was just asking directions and she panicked."

"*Malaka!*" the woman spat as she lay on the pavement.

"Typical," the man said. Yakup looked at him. He had a slender face, but the darkness made it difficult to see his features. His straight, black hair was tied in a ponytail with a single lock dangling over his cheek. A small backpack lay on the ground next to him. He seemed to be holding on to something with one hand.

"Can you please just help me get the lady up?" Yakup said and bent towards the now seated woman. She threw her bag against Yakup's outstretched arm, cursing him and struggling to her feet.

"Stay away from the lady," the young man calmly said. He stared hard at Yakup, studying his face with interest. His thin lips were pressed into something resembling a smile.

"I just wanted to help her. She fell…"

"I saw what happened, boy."

"She fell… It was the bag…"

"Your kind like to attack defenceless people. You do not respect women. We don't like that here. People like you have no business coming to our country, violating our laws, stealing from us, taking our jobs, polluting our streets, attacking our women. You even rape your own sisters and daughters."

"I… Listen… I just came… I needed directions. I…"

"You what? Do you think I'm stupid? You're nothing but a filthy dog… And you are far, far away from home." The man's voice was still calm but filled with spite. The woman moved away from the two. She no longer looked scared, but he could sense her loathing towards him.

"I'm sorry," Yakup said, "I'll be on my way." He took a step backwards and half-turned away. Then he saw what the man was holding in his hand — a rope tied into a fist-sized knot on the end. There was a whooshing sound and the knot hit him hard on his left arm. He screamed in pain and tried to fend off the blows. The next swing hit him hard in his kidney.

"Please, stop!" Yakup cried, stumbling away. He stooped over, trying to protect his head with one arm when yet another blow hit his spine and a sickening pain flashed all the way up his spine. He ran, tears streaming down his face. Legs moving. Pain and confusion. A pair of headlights suddenly shone brightly at him. He turned. Jumped over a ditch. Entered a small alley. Running. Not knowing where to or from. Changing direction every time he saw a person or some sign of life. A dog ran next to him for a while, then something caught its interest and it peeled off.

After a while, Yakup stopped when he could no longer run and found himself in an empty parking lot. He looked behind him, panting. Was he being followed? He couldn't be certain, and so, instead, tried to control his breathing.

A streetlamp at one end of the parking lot emitted a hazy glow. A grey-wheeled plastic dumpster lay on its side, offering a sort of refuge. Yakup crawled inside, pulling the lid shut. His arm and body ached. His heart was filled with pain. He kicked some used napkins, old papers, a flat plastic bottle and something smelly from the container. Rain started to tap on his plastic roof. He pulled out the photo of his grandparents and teenage father. The yellowed photo was hazy behind his wet eyes. He trembled in the cold, wet January night. His body was telling him that it needed care and rest. He cuddled up in the cleanest corner of the dumpster, used a moist newspaper as a blanket and slept a disturbed and restless sleep on his first night in Athens.

41

MALCOLM

In his dream, he was falling off a cliff. Mariam was below him on a rock ledge, yelling at him and waving. The wind was pulling at her red robe and veil. He would soon be within reach of her voice.

She was waving.

He was floating.

He could see her dimples as she smiled, and said, "Yakup, we made it to…" but a loud noise extinguished her words. Yakup strained to hear her.

"I cannot hear you," he yelled. Her almond eyes were straining to convey her message.

"We will meet at…" but the noise overpowered her voice yet again. Her eyes caught something behind Yakup. Her face contorted. He turned and saw a large swinging rope with a knot the size of a man fast approaching. He tried to escape, but there was nothing he could do. Not in freefall.

A loud thud pulled Yakup from his slumber. He cried out. The lid opened and morning light poured in. A wrinkled face with searching eyes appeared above the container.

"What the… There's a boy in here! Rosa!" The face yelled, then turned back toward Yakup. "What are you doing, kid?" His interrogator pulled off a cap and scratched a swatch of unruly grey hair. "Let's get you out of there," the man said, offering Yakup a dirty hand. He did not move. The previous evening's experience was still too real in Yakup's mind. The old man sighed and instead grabbed Yakup by the arm, pulling him out of the dumpster.

"Let go of me!" Yakup yelled and jerked himself free from the old man's grip.

"Take it easy, take it easy," the old man said. He had a metal trolley next to him filled with plastic bags. Yakup ran.

After a while, he stopped. He realised how irrational his fear had been. The old man had only wanted to help him, but instead, he had run away. He wanted to go back and apologise, but he had lost his way.

He walked aimlessly up and down the streets of Athens. When he felt he had walked far enough in one direction, he turned in another. Left and right. Looking for someone and no one. He managed to find half a sandwich in a bin. Defying his pride and deferring to his empty stomach, he ate it quickly and without joy. The streets were narrow and busy. Ruins and shops, tourists and hawkers, cats and dogs. Yakup reached a square with a metro station called Monastiraki. He wandered around for a while. Dodging the police whenever he saw them. He was looking for other foreigners, migrants, refugees, someone like him, someone who did not belong and knew how not to belong.

A group of Africans were chatting on a small square, a cardboard box filled with DVDs in front of them. The temple on the large rock hovering above the city was Yakup's guide.

When he was sure that there were no police around, he cautiously approached the group.

"Excuse me," he said. The Africans looked at him lazily, recognizing that this was not a potential buyer.

"I have just arrived. I don't know anybody, nor do I know the city. I thought, maybe you could help me and… and tell me where I can go and get food, a bed and work?"

One of them, in a black leather cap, a ratty brown jacket and a thick cream-coloured scarf frowned and said, "Africans go to Platia Amerikis. Afghans go to the park by Alexander. Food, well, you have to ask for it there. The bed is the grass in the park. Work, there's none of. You have to make it yourself, but don't expect to make any money. Welcome to Athens!" And with that, they all laughed.

"What direction is Alexander Park?" he asked. At this point, a group of tourists entered the square and caught the attention of the DVD sellers. Now the Africans were all politeness and charm as they tried to woo the tourists into buying their merchandise.

In response to a question from one of the potential buyers, the man with the black leather hat said, theatrically and with visible indignation, "Of course they have subtitles! And if you are not satisfied, I will give you back your money and you can choose another DVD free of charge. I promise!" He held one hand over his heart to show his trustworthiness. "You can find me here every day. Ask any of the people in the square and they will tell you," He nodded towards the café and small souvenir shops.

"Hey, you!" A voice rang from behind Yakup. A shiver crawled down his spine and he jumped, but before he could escape, a strong hand clamped down on his left shoulder. He was whirled around and met by a set of white teeth surrounded by a big black smile. It was one of the Africans.

"Sorry about that, Afghan, but I couldn't help it. You should've seen your face, though! Can you forgive me?" He looked at Yakup with a pair of brown puppy-dog eyes. Recovering from his shock and still feeling accosted, Yakup couldn't help but laugh.

"My name is Malcolm. I am from Nigeria," he said, holding out a strong hand and smiling.

"I'm Yakup. From Bamiyan." They shook hands. Malcolm wasn't much older than Yakup, but judging from his strong grip, far more muscular.

"Listen, I hear that you're new here. Do you have any idea where Pedion Areos Park is?" Malcolm said.

"No, but I would like to know where Alexander Park is?"

"They are one and the same. Alexander Park is just easier to remember, or something like that. I'm not really sure since I can't say I understand these people yet," he gestured at a group of random Greeks. Yakup nodded in agreement.

"Listen, my friend, I'm going in that direction either way, so why don't we team up and I'll show you the way? This city has dark secrets that you will learn soon enough. It's better to be careful"

"How do I know that you are not one of these dark secrets?" Yakup asked. The man looked at him and laughed.

"Well played, my friend, well played," Malcolm admitted,

scratching his short dangly dreadlocks. "I leave the choice to trust me up to you, but I am going now if you want in."

He started off and after a moment's consideration so, too, did Yakup.

"Glad you could join," Malcolm smiled.

"My pleasure," Yakup smiled back at him and bowed. They both laughed.

The sun warmed them as they walked through the streets of Athens, passing squares, churches, cafés, sample shops, newsstands, cigarette vendors, narrow side streets and broad avenues, all crawling with yellow cabs, scooters, screeching buses and people. Malcolm talked most of the time. Yakup did not catch all he said, but gleaned that Greece had financial problems and a lot of Greeks blamed foreigners, migrants and refugees for taking their jobs. He also learned that most Greeks didn't like foreigners and that Athens was filled with people from Syria, Afghanistan, Guinea, Senegal, Côte d'Ivoire, Nigeria, Somalia, Sudan and many other countries. Yakup was able to confirm that he ought to be extra careful at night and never walk alone, paying particular attention to young Greek men in black clothes with a sign of some sort.

"Listen, my friend. Life here is not easy. You have to be careful and look out for yourself. Don't trust anyone."

"What about you?" Yakup said, feigning puzzlement.

"Hehe… Me? You can trust, me!" Malcolm winked. "I'm normally not in the DVD business. I am a musician. You can find me in the afternoons and weekends in the square we passed busking for tips. The square is called Monastiraki" Malcolm paused, then pointed out a group of young men in a park. "Those people in there are Afghans, I think. I will leave you here, is that all right?"

He gave Yakup a solicitous look.

"Can I just go up to them?"

"I guess."

" You're at the square every day?"

"Sure."

"Good."

"Don't worry, Yakup. It'll be all right." They shook hands and Malcolm stepped into the busy street where he quickly disappeared from sight.

42

COMPATRIOT

The park was lively and yet peaceful in the fading afternoon sun. Old people sat on weather-beaten benches thinking of times that had been right next to young lovers who held each other and dreamed of times to come. Immigrant kids were selling sunflower seeds to passers-by and stopping to play a game whenever there was a lull in business. Old men from Greece, Africa and the Middle East with hats and thick glasses passed the time playing backgammon or chess. Old women sat in the shade of orange trees wearing old fur coats and head scarves from which locks of grey and purple hair peeped out. They smoked cigarettes and chatted.

Yakup approached the group of Afghan men. Some of them were exercising with rusty iron bars.

"Hi!" Yakup said

"Yeah," one of them replied.

"I am looking for a place to sleep. Would you happen to know where I can find a safe spot?" Yakup asked. The man, in his thirties, looked Yakup up and down, then smiled.

"Lots of people need places to sleep. This park is an overused mattress. Lots and lots of people have slept here," he said while Yakup looked around.

"You may have been here longer than me and know how it works here, but I just arrived after months and months on the road. I don't know your story, but if it is anything similar to mine, you have experienced situations that you thought were only fit for fiction. You have met people filled with distrust, hatred and spite and still more all too willing to place a knife in your back… Maybe I'm naive, but I was just hoping to find

208

some shred of humanity still left in this world. So, if you don't want to help me, fine, whatever, but I don't get it…"

Yakup felt weak. He turned and started walking away.

"Wait!" he heard from behind him. "Perhaps I can help you."

Yakup hesitated, "Really?"

"I'm Michael. Well, Mahmoud, but Michael works better in this place," he said, smiling.

"Yakup."

"Good name! Yakup, Jacob, Jacques. Definitely a name that fits most of the countries around here."

"What do you mean?"

"Well Jacques, if you go to France, it is easier to live under a French name when you are like us. These Europeans only like people like them, got it?"

"So, you're talking to me because you feel comfortable with me being Afghan?" Yakup asked.

"Why yes, Jake! Didn't you yourself use exactly the same approach when you came looking for *your kind* here, in this park?

"I guess I did."

"My guess is that you've already tried the Greek authorities, too, right?" he said with a cheeky tone. "It's just that we've all done that and don't recommend just such an approach. Shame, though, we have to return to the police to get our papers renewed. Anyway. You said you were looking for a place to stay, right?"

"Yes."

"Well, what is your budget?"

"My budget?" Yakup asked.

"Yeah. How much can you pay per night, week, month?"

Yakup scratched his head. The dollars envelope had dwindled to almost nothing.

"I don't really have much. I was hoping I could figure out what to do once I found a place to sleep."

"Normally they charge upfront, but you are lucky since I know exactly the place for you. It is a bit crowded and you'll need to pay in a few days, but it's better than the alternative. Come on," he said and started walking away from the other Afghans who were now kicking an empty plastic bottle towards a two-rock goal.

They walked for ten minutes, crossing streets and turning down narrow alleys until they reached a dilapidated building.

"Mahmoud here. I have a new guest," the man said into the intercom. The door buzzed open and they entered a lift. Mahmoud pushed the button for the top floor. When they reached their destination, he pushed the ground floor button. "Too many people go to the top floor. The neighbours get suspicious and call the police."

"What for?"

"Too many Afghans living here," Mahmoud answered while knocking on the only door. It opened and a tense face appeared.

"Jawad! How are you today?" Mahmoud said, giving the man his cheeky smile.

"Been better," Jawad frowned.

"Meet my new friend, Yakup. He just came in with the boat. He is looking for a place to stay for a while and I could think of no better place than our cosy home."

"Well, come in and see the facilities yourself then."

A dark and moist entranceway revealed itself. They left their shoes by the door as is customary in Afghanistan. Immediately on the left, there was a room, but the door shut before Yakup could see anyone. He thought he heard muffled voices from behind the door. At the end of the hallway was a small kitchen with a few utensils. They passed through it and entered a living room. It was about 20 square meters with a heavy curtain drawn so as to keep out the light. A red-and-brown patterned carpet covered most of the grey linoleum floor. Five men and a small girl sat idle on the carpet and stared at a flickering TV in the corner. The audio from the TV set yelled into their expressionless faces. Jawad turned down the volume. Only then did the viewers seem to notice the newcomer.

"This is… Sorry, what was your name?" Jawad asked.

Yakup made the round of greetings. He and Mahmoud situated themselves along the wall. The girl still stared at the TV screen, but the men took more interest in him.

"Where are you from?" a bearded round-bellied man called

Mohammed Aziz wanted to know.

"Bamiyan," Yakup replied.

"Hazara! I knew it," a short skinny man called Qadir grinned. "I haven't been there for a long time. When did you leave?"

"Last year."

"Only last year! I bet you must feel disappointed. You left the most beautiful place on earth in exchange for this small, squalid flat in an ugly part of a hostile city. What is your story?" Mohammed Aziz asked.

"Don't interrogate him," Mahmoud said.

"It's ok," Yakup said.

He told his story as best as he could, leaving out bits and pieces he thought best not to mention to a group of strangers. When he had finished, the men held a short council and decided that Yakup could stay.

"Most of us stay here indoors, because of the police and fascists," Jawad said. He gestured to the girl. Her father, a toothless elderly man, lived with his younger wife and two daughters in one of the two separate rooms.

"This one is the oldest. The other one is only a few months old. She was born here in the apartment with the assistance of my wife, Alia, who is a nurse… or was back in Afghanistan." The apartment walls were what the girls knew of the world. None of the children went to school, though, they wanted to, but didn't have the requisite permanent address needed to attend.

The other six who lived there were men. They slept on the red carpet in the living room. That made a total of fifteen people in the small space. The Greek owner charged them 800 Euro per month, excluding the water bill. The group had decided that they could afford only one shower per week per person.

Jawad and his family were Pashto and originally from Kabul, having fled when a clan dispute spread from their village to the capital. They spent six years in Iran before finally crossing into Turkey through the mountains. There were more than a hundred refugees at the border crossing between Turkey and Greece. Some from Afghanistan and others from Iraq, Bangladesh, China, Pakistan and many other places. They hid for 48 hours without food. They drank the dirty river water that they shared with the frogs, while mosquitoes assaulted them. They were afraid they would get caught out on the river by the police who fired at them from time to time.

When space became available on a barge, it was quickly filled with hopeful people. Once safely across, they still had to walk over eight hours to the nearest town.

When the police arrived, and they did, the family was put in a camp for one month. Upon release, they travelled to Athens as Yakup had done. In the beginning, they had stayed in Alexander Park and lived day by day. Now, at least, they had an apartment.

Jawad and one of the other men left every morning at 4 a.m. and churned over the city's garbage for scrap metal and discarded electrical chargers, which they sold at the market. If the police saw them, though, then they spray-painted their items to make them unsellable. Jawad earned between four and ten euros per week for his family. Every time he left the apartment, his wife feared that the police would catch him and throw him in jail or, worse, send him back to Afghanistan.

Qadir told a similar story: he had fled due to the civil war and when he reached Athens he was beaten up by a group of fascists. When he went to the police to report the crime, he was thrown in jail because he did not have any documents. It was a year before they let him out. He lived on the streets for a while, selling opium to survive and began using himself, which quickly meant he had to sell more and more simply to fund his own consumption.

One day Jawad found Qadir passed out in the gutter and carried him back to the flat. Since that day, he had sworn off opium, and instead, would busy himself early every morning in search of old discarded food that he might bring back to the apartment.

"I'll tell you what," Qadir said to Yakup one day during a commercial break one late afternoon, "If the authorities gave all migrants in Greece a passport tomorrow, we would every last one of us would be out of here by the end of the week." The break ended and Qadir directed his blank-eyed stare toward the screen. "Even Iran was better than this," he grumbled.

43

MOTHER

Nicos awoke alone in his bed accompanied by the usual indefinable pain in his stomach. The yellow paint on the bedroom ceiling was cracked and flakes had fallen to the floor. The Golden Dawn banner with its black meander hung on the wall.

He knew he should get out of bed before the darkness settled upon him and he returned to the ready escape of sleep. His mind wandered to earlier times when his father had not been so distant and he was not such a bother.

His mother was the love of his life back then. No matter what he said or did, she always stood up for him, made him feel loved and human. His father always questioned him, his ideas.

Perhaps that was when he had stopped loving his father. That love between him and his mother had been enough for both of them.

He knew he should get out from under the warm bedcovers and open himself to the day, but he already felt too heavy.

When he was a little boy, his mother always smiled and took care of him. It was only when his father decided to stop working that her smile faded. He was sure that the first change came when his father stopped teaching at the university and became more involved in politics. His father was at home more often. They had more fights. Almost every day his parents spent time in his father's study, talking among the rows of books and mountains of paper. His parents tried to talk in hushed voices to hide the growing rift between them, but he knew, as children always do.

Some days when he came home from school, they would be in there arguing in loud voices with his mother leaving the study in tears. He had been a light sleeper even as a kid and in the still of the night, the small flat's thin walls hid nothing. He hated his father for making his mother cry.

The alarm clock rang again. This time he reacted promptly, pulling the duvet off, feet hitting the cold stone floor. He turned on the water heater in the hallway and put the coffee on the stove in the kitchen. Nicos stirred dark coffee powder into the water. His thoughts returned to that day when he had run home to tell his mother that the teacher had praised his paper in front of the whole class, his small feet taking the stairs two at a time. Struggling with the key in the lock. Forgetting to kick his shoes off. Calling his mother, who would be napping, as was her wont in the afternoon.

As softly as he could, he opened the door to his parents' bedroom. "Mama?"

No answer. He continued through the small hallway into the living room with its round alabaster table and on into the kitchen. She was not there. He stopped and looked around.

"Mama?" he said again, louder. An eerie silence was the only reply. She was always there when he came home from school. The place felt empty. A deep, worrying sensation enveloped him. He sat in the three-legged chair next to the kitchen window, his toes just touching the floor. Something was not right.

He got up and walked with heavy steps to the hallway. The door to his father's study was slightly ajar. His legs were heavy as if in quicksand. He reached the door. Not wanting to open it, but knowing he had to. The silence was screaming at him. His moist hands touched the cold copper handle. He pushed it open wherein hundreds of books greeted him, but so did his father's old leather chair, which now lay sideways on the wooden floor.

He took a step into the study and then saw the desk. The small green lamp was not where it should have been and the papers, normally in stacks, were strewn all over the table with still more on the floor. His mother's feet hung peacefully just above the messy desk. They were naked and blue. The rest of her hung above her blue feet. A rope was looped through the water pipe in the ceiling and had scratched off some of the paint. His mother's chin rested on her left shoulder. Her eyes were open and unseeing. There were flakes of paint in her long, black hair.

Nicos sipped the last of his coffee and threw his half-eaten piece of toast into the bin. The shower did its best to wash away these images, these memories.

As he dressed and packed his dark blue backpack, he walked his mind through the plan he had come up with. The weekend before he had spent half a day touring the rope dealers down by the Piraeus port. He had finally decided on a dark brown rope, cut to the length of his arm. The thickness and texture gave him a firm grip that ensured he could hold on to it even in a rough situation. He had fashioned one end into a hard knot the size of a tennis ball. He held the rope now. Its weight seemed perfect. He tried it out on his bed, where the knot at the end left a mark the size of a fist on his duvet. He smiled, put the rope in his backpack, swung it onto his back, grabbed the keys and shut the door. His mind focused only on the present and the future as he descended the stairs two at a time and walked into the chilly, busy Athens morning.

44

MICHAEL

Yakup spent a lot of time with Michael. He was older, knew the city and had taken a liking to Yakup, who in return was only too happy to relax and have someone with local insight take the lead. Michael's favourite hangout was Alexander Park since, as he said, "This is a multicultural hub, where we are left alone by the fascists. Sometimes, when I'm in the right spot, and the trees shut out the city, it feels like I'm back in a peaceful version of Afghanistan. Do you follow me?"

"I guess so," Yakup replied.

Michael was an ethnic Tajik from Parwan province in Afghanistan and had been in Athens a little over a year. Over the course of that period, he had been to prison a few times and been beaten by police, attacked by fascists and thieves, lived in six different places and worked for five different employers, most of whom had paid him a lousy salary or no salary at all.

"Yakup, Jacob, Jaques, life here is not easy. Sometimes I wonder if it would have been better never to have left Afghanistan at all, but then I remember the bombs and the shooting and I start to shiver and feel like throwing up. Anything else, even being treated like a second-class citizen, is preferable to that. Nope, I would rather commit suicide than go back," he said only half joking. Despite being only 21 or 22, his black hair was already receding from his forehead, he was too young to be going bald.

"When they first threw me in jail, I began to hate Europe and Europeans," he said, looking around in disgust at the old Greeks across from their backgammon boards, smoking and drinking raki in the sun.

"They didn't tell me why, or how long, I was supposed to stay there. I was in a small cell with criminals from many places. These people had

committed real crimes, I tell you. Dealing drugs and assaulting people—
thieves and robbers—all. I just came here to find a better life."

One of the old men at the backgammon table laughed and revealed
a set of yellowed teeth. He shook the hand of his opponent who nodded
his silvered head, acknowledging his defeat before vacating his seat to
allow another ageing man to challenge the victor.

"No lawyer. No judge. Two sad meals per day. No window; the only
light we had, came through the door leading to the hallway. I didn't
shower for the first two weeks. Neither did any of the others. A few hours
outside was all that was allowed unless someone was fighting, in which
case, we were collectively punished and not allowed out. We were 10 to
a cell."

He regarded Yakup gravely with his deep brown eyes. For a while,
they just sat. Winter in Athens was milder than what Yakup had known
in Bamiyan and the sun warmed their faces and chests. Yakup sat with
his eyes closed enjoying the warmth while a menagerie of colour
shimmered behind his eyelids. Time passed. Maybe a minute. Maybe ten.
Life went on around him.

"The police are bastards," Michael broke in, disturbing his peace.

"I noticed they weren't particularly friendly," Yakup replied.

"They treat us like dirt. And protect those who violate us."

"What do you mean?"

"The fascists, Gaikop. The police look away when the racist attacks
take place. Miraculously they disappear, or someone needs help
somewhere else." He smacked his thigh and said, "Jake, I gotta go—
work. The owner of the pet store has asked me to be there on my day off
to carry feed bags. I don't like him, but at least he pays me," Michael
said.

"I'll see you at the flat then?"

"If he will ever let me go. Adios amigo!" he said, and off he went.

Yakup stayed in the sun, eyes closed, feeling lazy and good. He was
recuperating from the past months of travel and imprisonment. He would
talk to Jawad and Michael about getting a job later today. Maybe
tomorrow. He had to take care of himself first.

The old men had packed up their backgammon games and left the chairs and tables empty. A single red piece had taken cover under a leaf next to the nearby table. Yakup picked it up. It was flat and round; a good fit in his grip. He set it on the table on its side. It rocked halfway round and back again before coming to a standstill. Yakup looked at the piece standing there on the frail rusty table, casting a long shadow. He set off.

45

DESTRUCTION

The park was almost empty as Yakup walked toward one of the exits. The setting sun indicated that he should hurry back to the flat, but he had wanted to climb the Strefi Hill next to the park and see the city from above for some time, and so, caved to this sudden desire to see the sun set over the sea with the city and the Acropolis on its rock, a relic of Athens and Greece's splendour.

The steep ascent towards the hilltop took him no more than half an hour. He reached the top just in time to see the sunset on the port of Piraeus where he had first set foot on continental Europe. The Acropolis stood sternly between Yakup and the Aegean Sea. To his left was the Lykavittos Hill, topped by a white Orthodox monastery. Squeezed in between the Strefi and Lykavittos hills was Athens' anarchistic Exharcheia neighbourhood with graffiti-covered walls, young left-wingers, squats and a thriving café scene. Alexander Park was to the right. The vast suburbs of Athens spread like a long colourful tongue to the edge of the sea and up the hills and far away. Thousands of windows reflected the setting sun. How many hopeful migrants did the city hold? How many migrants were marching at this moment towards the promised land of Europe, crossing mountains, deserts and seas?

Yakup could see someone in the dusk, further down the hill. He decided it was time to leave. He started down the unkempt gravel track. Bushes and trees covered the hill to his right. To his left was a steep drop. He reached the bottom of the path and found himself fenced in along a basketball court. A forgotten basketball sat by the fence. Yakup picked it up. It was soft; some of the air had leaked out. He tried to dribble it anyway, but it would hardly bounce.

"That's mine," a voice said from behind him. He turned and saw a man in a black cotton coat, his hair tied back in a ponytail. He stood on the blacktop of the court. Yakup thought he had heard that voice before.

"Oh! I'm sorry. I thought someone had left it behind," Yakup once more picked up the ball. Dropped it and picked it up again. A dog barked in the distance.

"Didn't you hear me?"

Yakup looked at the man slightly bewildered. "I… I just wanted to throw it to you. Here!"

Yakup tossed the ball towards the man. It landed limply next to him.

"Do I know you?" Yakup said.

Someone was moving outside the fence. Thin, female laughter penetrated the cold evening air. "You ought to. We met before. You, my friend and I."

The man held out his arm. A rope dangled from his fist as from gallows. The thin laughter was closer. The growling of the dog grew louder. The man lowered the rope along his flank. Someone was approaching the iron gate. Yakup knew that this was his chance.

"I'm not sure. I think you've mistaken me for someone else. My friend is coming now. I have to go." He took a few steps away from the man, who did not move. The people outside were approaching the gate. A couple. Yakup made a half circle to avoid the man with the rope, who still didn't move.

"Hey," Yakup yelled to the couple as he passed, keeping a safe distance from the rope. The couple and their dog stood in front of the gate.

"Hey there," a friendly female voice said.

"Good to see you. Can we go together?" Yakup said in a small voice. He walked quickly toward them.

"Good to see you, too," the man said with a smile. He had short blonde hair and a face that bore witness to a rough lifestyle. Yakup looked nervously over his shoulder. The man with the rope had his back to them. He was about five meters away and stood perfectly still.

"You have to help me," Yakup whispered to the couple.

"But what is wrong?" the blonde man asked.

"I think this man was about to attack me. I think it would be better if you came with me. He has a weapon. Let's get out of here."

"Now, now, now. Not so fast," the girl said. She had a piercing through her nose and her hair was also blonde. But it was obviously dyed, dark roots showing around the edges. The makeup around her eyes was black, as was her lipstick. She giggled.

"I'm serious. This guy is dangerous. He wants to harm us," Yakup said, edging his way towards the gate. It was only a few meters away. The dog made a deep growling noise. Its ears lay flat and its front teeth revealed themselves to be a snarl. Yakup stopped short.

"Hey!" The blonde man yelled, "Is this guy telling the truth? Do you want to harm us, man?" A perverse laugh escaped him. There was something savage in his eyes that made Yakup edge further away.

"I believe you have met my friends," the man with the rope said in a calm voice. The blonde couple started laughing. The dog barked. Drool flew from its mouth towards Yakup. He flinched and walked back towards the dark end of the court.

"What do you want?" he whispered.

"He's asking what we want, Nicos." The blonde guy said, kicking at the tall fence. It sent ripples the entire length of the court, the vibrations reaching Yakup where he stood. He kept backing away until he had run out of real estate

Yakup looked around, trying desperately to find an escape route, but the only exit he could see was the gate. To reach it he had to pass the blonde couple with the dog. The fence was no option being about four meters high and wobbly.

"Now I'm not sure you have introduced yourself, boy," Nicos said. The rope hung from his hand. He was moving slowly towards Yakup. The couple flanked him and made escape impossible. "You ran away too quickly the other night. It is not very polite. What do you think, Petros?"

"These monkeys have no manners, Nic," Petros said.

The blonde girl sniggered.

"I believe we should teach you some manners," Nicos said.

"Yeah!" Petros chimed in. The dog growled and snarled. The girl grinned and held its leash tight. Yakup felt like a jellyfish abandoned by the receding tide, slowly frying in the relentless sun. He grabbed the fence and started climbing. It wobbled, swung dangerously from side to side. He pulled himself up with all his strength. Kicked a foot into a tiny hole. Slipped and hung on, heaving himself half a meter higher. His weight pulled the fence back down towards the court. The dog's teeth tore at his pants and shoes. He let go. The asphalt was hard and cold. Yakup could see three pairs of boots and smell the foul breath of the dog.

"Please," he whispered.

"What was that?" Nicos laughed, though he stood there calmly, his voice revealed his mounting excitement. Yakup was on his knees.

"I think the bastard tried to flee," Petros said a boot landing in his ribs. He rolled over on one side.

"Stop! Please!" He tried to get up. The rope whooshed and there was a ringing in his ears replaced at once by a thumping pain. His hair turned wet and sticky. The growling resumed and jaws clamped around Yakup's arm. He screamed and slammed his hand into the face of the dog. It only made the animal fiercer. He found the wet orb that was the dog's eye and pressed his thumb in deep. The animal yelped and let go. The blonde girl pulled the whimpering dog away.

"You hurt him," she shrieked, kicking Yakup in the stomach. All the air left his body and he rolled into the foetal position. Another whoosh and the fist-sized knot slammed into his back. Yakup screamed and writhed. Another kick. The pain was receding along with his consciousness. Soon he was a limp rag doll beneath the blows.

"Stop!" someone said. He could barely open his eyes. He saw a pair of boots. The knot at the end of the rope dangled in front of him. It was stained with his blood.

"Now boy, let this be a lesson to you: we Greeks do not want you here. Take your dirty friends with you and leave our country. Whether you go back to your own shithole of a nation or somewhere else, I do not care. But know that if we ever see you again, and we will if you stay, your time is up." Nicos turned away. From somewhere above him, someone hawked and spat. Something slimy landed on his chin and seeped into his swollen eye and mouth.

"Malaka!" the blonde girl said and sent a final kick into Yakup's crotch. The pain was not immediate and it was only when they had all passed through the gate that Yakup vomited violently onto the concrete. Then he passed out.

When he awoke, the night was silent. His attackers were long gone. His hair stuck to the asphalt in a mix of vomit and blood. His head pounded and his body ached. He rolled over and tried his limbs. Nothing appeared broken. He could hardly see through his left eye. His left hand was in pain as if someone had ground it into the asphalt. He looked at it and noticed something viscid on his fingers—the remains of the dog's eye. He dried his hand on the rough asphalt and slowly tried to get to his feet. When he was upright, he almost fainted again. He leaned against the fence for a while, spitting blood, saliva dribbling from his lips. Then he staggered towards the gate. The soggy basketball lay alone and indifferent where he had thrown it earlier. He stepped out of the court and stumbled down the steep road and into the empty night.

46

NICOS

Nicos' pulsating anger had been tempered. Not that he didn't like the anger. It was one of the only true feelings he could find in him. The other was hate. These feelings seemed to have defeated all else. These feelings seemed to have defeated all else. Happiness was a fleeting emotion that came only when the hate and anger were released.

It was an early Wednesday evening in February. The cold wind was whipping at his slender face and hair. He pulled his black cap further down over his head and pulled the collar of his cotton coat around his neck to keep the wind at bay. He wore black boots and black jeans. He carried a sporty, navy-blue backpack. There was a camera and his rope inside. He smiled his spiteful smile. It made him feel good to know that his rope was resting peacefully in his backpack. It had proven a worthy companion.

He stopped and waited to cross the busy street. He had lived in Athens most of his life and he knew better than to challenge the cars and scooters at this time of the day. Rush hour meant that the roads belonged to the motorised vehicles. The light changed to green on the other side of the street. He quickly stepped onto the striped zebra crossing. A group of Africans were selling DVDs in the glow of a nearby shop window. Athens was filled with Africans. He thought of his rope, but he was alone and they were a group, so, instead, he gave them a malevolent stare.

The Greek Government had let down its people. They had allowed foreigners to buy the country's wealth. They had allowed the foreign-owned banks, investors and their political leaders to impoverish Greece. The worst part, though, was that they had agreed with the other European countries that immigrants could stay in Greece.

He passed the Africans. Body tense. Arms swinging casually by his side, but tense and ready to hit, then run. He knew he was fast and fit, but he also knew that the Africans were faster. They had missed a few that had simply outrun them. The Asians were easier to catch.

They would not attack him. In any event, their punishment would be harsh. He passed them and nothing happened. They didn't know who he was and wouldn't, but that did nothing for his anger, which bubbled and asked why it was he who had to worry about these foreigners in his own country. He hated the fear. This was his country. His city and his streets.

The attack yesterday had been almost perfect. He had planned it and his group had executed it beautifully. Himself, Petros, Eva and her dog, Pericles. The dog had lost an eye, but the veterinary had told Eva that he would survive. It was a battle wound and would make him look even more fierce. The rope had been properly inaugurated. He wasn't sure if it had been a Paki or an Afghan. He thought it was an Afghan and had noted him as such in his records.

He had known Petros since he first started to flirt with political ideas. Back then, Petros had been a shy, skinny kid who was already a staunch right-winger. He had singled out the quiet boy, Nicos, and they immediately become friends. In Petros, Nico had found someone who understood his anger. Nicos had been angry at his dad, other children, his mother's friends and family, in short: everyone. Petros understood his anger and it didn't take long for Nicos to learn where to direct it.

At that time, Nicos thought Petros knew a lot about their society. "The streets used to be safe and there was plenty of work. Now the streets are floating with immigrants. They attack our parents and grandparents and spread diseases from their countries. I tell you, man, all these immigrants are part of a global scheme to control us."

Petros' dad was working as a bricklayer, like his father before him. Petros could not visualise himself doing anything else. Lately, though, it was harder and harder for Petros' dad to find work and he sometimes went for weeks without employment.

"Man, I tell you, these immigrants are taking all the jobs. They don't care about solidarity. They are happy if they can get food, a place to sleep and cigarettes. They steal our jobs and our country." Nicos listened and listened while Petros talked and talked. He repeated what knowledge his father imparted to him at home and only occasionally mentioned how his dad beat him and his mother.

Nicos began to read. He read about the European Union, the international banks and their laws, the migration policy and about Greece. He began to see a pattern: Greece was losing its freedom and self-determination. The EU imposed a number of laws on the weak Greek government, which resulted in the hundreds of thousands of immigrants that came to Greece to stay there. It was left to the Greek people to deal with the immigrants that the rest of Europe did not want. If the immigrants strayed into other countries, the recipient nations were to send the refugees back to Greece. Greece was the weakest kid on the block.

On a hot August afternoon, Nicos and Petros were strolling the city. The heat in Athens was all-encompassing at that time of year. Those who could, often left the city for the cooler weather and soothing sea of the islands. Nicos' father had offered to send him for a few weeks to one of the islands where relatives lived, but Nicos declined. The death of his mother had only deepened the divide and the rift between them.

He and Petros stopped for a rest and a sip of water at Attica Square. A group of four black boys, around their age, talked and laughed with a couple of Greek girls. The girls were smoking cigarettes and didn't seem to mind the attention from the boys.

The two Greek boys were sitting on the rim of some potted plants when Petros claimed, that the girls probably didn't like the attention. Nicos agreed.

"We should do something, man. We always talk about how the Greeks are being stepped on, but we never do anything."

Nicos had looked at the two girls, then the group of boys.

"I'm not sure they mind," he said.

One of the African boys was wearing a baseball cap. He was laughing as a girl tried to play-grab the cap off his head.

"This is our place. These girls are our girls. Born of Greeks. Belonging to Greece. Those fuckers are taking what is not theirs. You're all talk and no action," Petros said, looking at Nicos with contempt. "I thought you believed in this," he said, "But I'm not so sure any more."

They held each other's eyes. A pact materialised between them and Nicos said, "All right, then, let's do it."

Petros grinned. "That's what I wanted to hear."

He reached into the dry flowerpot and found an old iron support for a plant, weighed it in his hand a couple of times and smiled. Before Nicos could stop him, he had reached the group and swung the iron bar at the boy with the baseball cap. The boy screamed in pain. The blow had landed on his shoulder. A crack resounded.

"You motherfucker! Stealing our girls, jobs, country…" Petros yelled at the boy, who lay groaning on the asphalt. Another stroke hit the boy in his ribs. One of his friends tackled Petros. They fell to the ground. That was Nicos' cue.

He went for the second boy—bashing his head in would be as easy as kicking a football. He missed the first kick. The black was struggling to restrain Petros. On his second attempt, Nicos made contact with the side of his head. The boy went limp and fell off Petros. The Greek girls were screaming. He bent down to help Petros up. There was a sharp pain in his back. He turned to see a third boy holding a broken bottle by the neck. Nicos retaliated with a precise blow to the boy's nose. The boy screamed and doubled over, clutching his face. Blood seeped through his fingers. Nicos landed another blow into his unprotected belly. The boy fell over, red bubbles bursting from his nose.

Petros was in a fit. Kicking and stomping on the first boy, whose cap lay limply on the asphalt. Nicos looked around, wondering where the others had gone.

"Petros! *Petros!*" Nicos screamed, redirecting his friend's focus to an approaching army of young blacks, all of whom were rapidly approaching from the far end of the square.

"Let's go," Nicos yelled.

Petros spat on the silent bleeding mass on the ground. "Scum like you don't belong here," he yelled. He picked up the cap and ran. The two girls were sobbing and holding each other. "Whores!" Petros yelled as he ran past them.

They ran through intersections; around corners. Darting in and out of traffic; between pedestrians. They avoided the police and finally stopped in a small back alley.

"I think we lost them," Nicos said, his sides heaving.

Petros had blood smeared in his blonde hair. When he saw Nicos' worried look, he smiled. "Not mine. How's your back?"

"I'll live." They started laughing and felt better than they had for a long time.

"What took us so long!" Petros said.

They went over the fight, praising their bravery and skill, reliving every moment until it was dark.

Soon after the attack on the African boys, Nicos joined Petros at meetings with others like them. A place to belong and where Nicos could flourish and share his sentiments with, and against, society. That was the new dawn.

47

SOUP KITCHEN

Days passed. Yakup did not leave the apartment. He was nursed by Jawad's wife, Alia, and their daughters, Freba and Malalai. The men had decided not to bring Yakup to the hospital, nor to report the incident to the police. Alia had expertly closed the gash at the back of Yakup's head with 11 stitches. There didn't seem to be a fracture in the underlying bone.

"There will be a scar, but when your hair grows back, it will not be visible," Alia had said.

His lip had cleaved on the inside. His left eye was bloated and bloodshot, but eventually, it would all heal.

"Praise God for your luck," Freba had said.

His arm bore the marks of the dog's jaws on his bicep: four holes where the teeth had broken the skin. His back was swollen in a palette of blue, purple, red, yellow and green.

Michael made an effort to bring him the medical items and painkillers he needed. Most of it had been manufactured for animals because Michael could get it from the veterinary office, but Alia was accustomed to improvising as she had done throughout all the campaigns that took place during the war years in Afghanistan. Mohammed Aziz brought new clothes for Yakup, clothes as new as old clothes could be. Qadir collected food and reserved the best of the expired cups of yoghurt for Yakup. The old man's young wife made him a hearty soup. The men in the living room turned the volume a little lower on the TV. There was a feeling of solidarity in the small apartment. The attack could have happened to any of them.

And they all knew it.

Yakup himself was overwhelmed by the kindness he received from the others, but at night he drifted into nightmares of ropes, dogs and the thin pony-tailed man. He woke up sweating. Sometimes a small cry escaped his lips. Once he awoke to find Michael sitting and watching over him in the wee hours, a worried look on his face. Without the care of all the many people in the tiny flat, Yakup didn't know how he would have survived.

But survive he did and on the fifth day following the attack, he got to his feet, put on his new clothes and announced that he could no longer accept the care and kindness they had given him so generously. He promised, then, that he would do everything in his power to repay each and every one of them, no matter how long it might take and that he would not let the attackers scare him off the streets. Several of the men looked at Yakup instead of the TV when he made his announcement. The old man smiled and his wife, holding their baby, rested her head on his shoulder. Their young daughter, sitting with the men by the TV, looked up at Yakup with an adoring smile. Alia, Freba and Malalai all beamed: they had succeeded. They had won; if not the war, then at the very least, the battle. Jawad gave Yakup a handshake and Qadir hugged him and started to cry, but quickly stopped when he noticed that he was the only one doing so.

Fog blanketed the city as Yakup and Michael slowly made their return to the streets, greeting a couple of people as they passed.

"Are you hungry?" Michael asked.

"Yes!"

"Come on then. There is a place we can eat at on Sofokleous Street."

"Will they let us in?" Yakup asked incredulously.

"It's a church. The government doesn't run it."

"Will we have to pretend to be Christians?"

"No, no! Take it easy. These guys don't ask any questions. They give food to those who are hungry. No discrimination. I have been there before. Let the old-timers first in line, but don't end up all the way in the back, in case the food runs out."

They moved quickly through the narrow streets. Rain showers had been coming and going all day. There was no promise of the winter sun's appearance this afternoon and soon the darkness would settle.

They crossed the butchers' market where bulging sausages hung from small stands like red, ripe fruit ready to burst. Colourful intestines from lambs, cows and pigs swam in containers behind the counters while large hunks of pork hung on cold iron hooks next to floating pig heads. There weren't many customers. The butchers, dressed in blood-stained white aprons, worked at the back of the stands, chopping meat with large knives or cleaning cold metal tables. A few sat behind the counters with glum faces. Groups of men quietly conversed. The place smelled of blood, meat and decay.

"Here we are," Michael said. A long line of people stood by the roadside. Perhaps a hundred total; maybe more. Cars sped by, leaving sudsy ruts in the wet pavement. The queue was a mix of Greek mothers, children, junkies, Afghans, Pakistanis, Iranians, Syrians and Africans—anyone who was hungry and willing to swallow their pride.

"Come on, Yakup," Michael said, pulling him by the sleeve to the food line. There was a nauseating odour of sweat, faeces, unwashed clothes and unattended wounds.

"Oi! You! Move on!" a man said, shoving Yakup from behind who stumbled into Michael.

"Hey! No pushing, or none of you will get food today. You know the rules, my friend" someone behind the food stall said. The man behind Yakup mumbled something and held his hands up in an apologetic manner. Yakup thought he might be Eastern European.

"Hey! Afghan boy! Good to see you, my friend."

"Malcolm!" Yakup smiled at the man serving food.

"What happened to you?" Malcolm said, looking at Yakup's still visible bruises.

"Come on! We're hungry!" someone further down the line yelled.

Malcolm scratched his short dreadlocks and lifted his eyebrows. "My friend, I cannot talk now, all right, but why don't you come to Monastiraki Square. I'm playing with the band. Deal?"

"Ok," Yakup nodded, still smiling. Malcolm handed him a plastic plate with food. The pressure of the line was driving him forward and before he knew it, he was next to Michael who had found a spot beneath a tree.

"Can't say it is good, but it fills the belly," Michael mumbled through a mouth full of food.

A young Greek man with thin greasy hair ate next to them. His eyes reminded Yakup of an animal, looking nervously around as it devoured carrion. His teeth were rotten, the nails on his coarse hands black, his shoes ripped and his trousers too big for his scrawny legs. When he had finished, he wiped his mouth with the white bread and tossed it aside.

"Junky," Michael said between bites and to the chorus of heavy raindrops pelting the ground.

48

MUSIC

Days came and went as if nothing out of the ordinary had ever happened. It was some time before Yakup dared to move around on his own again. When he did, he decided to go see Malcolm.

He arrived at Monastiraki Square where Malcolm said he still played. The small souvenir shops in the square, and in the surrounding streets, were run by Greeks. Tourists preferred to buy their souvenirs from a native no matter the cost.

A strong hand landed on his shoulder. He jumped and turned with a smile. Malcolm.

"You are less jumpy than the first time we met, eh? Still, a bit nervous, aren't we?"

He sat himself next to Yakup. A drum hung from a colourful strap across his shoulder. The instrument looked old and used.

"Does it work?" Yakup asked. Malcolm scowled.

"Of course, it does, my friend! Listen, you shouldn't judge a person by his looks. You should know that better than most by now. A drum you should judge by its sound."

He held the drum in front of him and turned it.

"You can see that the skin has been adjusted. I did that myself to get the sound right."

He gave the drum a few gentle taps.

"Listen, my friend. How is it going? Did those other Afghans help you out?"

"They are nice. One of them took me to the house where I'm currently staying at."

"The fellow from the soup kitchen?"

"Mmhmm."

"Are you going to tell me?"

Yakup looked at Malcolm in puzzlement.

"Your lip is a bit swollen, your eye took a punch and you keep your arm at an awkward angle. What happened to you?"

"I'm a bit embarrassed to say."

"Listen, my friend, there's no need to be. Shit happens. If you knew half the silly things I've done in my life, you'd be laughing your scrawny Afghan butt off."

They both laughed. The story of his attack and his convalescence in the flat spilled out.

"Whoa! That is a tough one, my friend," Malcolm shook his head. "It is very sad and it happens all the time. It is a wonder that nothing has happened to me yet. Did you go to the police?"

"No, I don't want to go back to jail."

"But these people almost killed you. They should go to jail for their crimes."

"You told me to come here and hear your music."

Malcolm looked at Yakup, puzzled. No more questions came; instead, he pointed towards the low concrete seating area in the middle of the square.

"That spot is where most people pass," Malcolm said, indicating a spot where a homeless man and his dog were resting on a dirty blanket. "People will hear our music, no matter where on this square we set up. But that spot there, in the middle, is where most people stop and listen. I make most of my money there," he said, laughing and beating a quick rhythm on his drum.

"Do you make good money?" Yakup asked.

"Not enough. Weekends are best. That's when the large crowds gather. I tell you, sometimes we're almost invisible to the outside world because of the crowd surrounding us, especially when there's only a handful of people and it's the off-season."

"What kind of music do you guys play?"

"Mostly African beats. The others should be here any moment," Malcolm said, looking around the busy square. He stretched his muscular arms and yawned, then leaned back on his elbows.

"We usually just sing and play, but when the crowd is large and there's the right atmosphere, we throw in some dance. People like that," he lolled, speaking with his eyes closed, his face to the Acropolis.

Three black men appeared from the flea market street. Two of them were carrying drums similar to Malcolm's.

"Is it them?" Yakup asked.

"Where? Ah, there they are," Malcolm confirmed and in a flash was halfway across the square to greet the others.

As Malcolm and his friends set up their instruments, Yakup's attention moved to four Roma girls in flowered dresses and thick hoodies. Their long hair ranged from deep purple to chestnut to black. They were all carrying flowers. The girls moved like sharks, attacking from the flank, armed with a beautiful flower. The flower would mysteriously appear under the nose of a couple. By mere reflex, the innocent victims would take a hold of the flower. Alternatively, the girls would skilfully plant the flower stem in the belts or waistbands of their victims. Sometimes the girls managed to impose two flowers on the victim before they even knew of it. Then they demanded payment. If the victim had been saddled with two flowers, the girls would demand more money for the second one and snatch the first from their customer. Before the hapless tourist could walk off, leaving the flower on the cobblestones, the girls were done.

Malcolm and his band started to play. A few people stopped and listened. Even fewer tossed a coin into the hat that lay on the ground. Malcolm was fiercely beating his drum.

One of the Africans was singing in a penetrating voice. He moved his hips to the music. It was exotic and enthralling. More people stopped. One man started dancing. The atmosphere was good. It was dusk now and the Pakistani street sellers shot small, flashing hover toys up into the darkening evening sky.

The crowd around Malcolm's band was growing smaller. The bells from the small church on the square began to chime. Then the bearded priest, in a black cloak and small flat hat, came rushing from the church.

"You are disturbing my service with your noise," he yelled and shook his fist at them. "I demand that you stop immediately!"

Surprisingly, Malcolm and the others halted their music as soon as they heard the priest. Maybe the religious leaders here in Europe were feared as much as the mullahs back home, Yakup mused. Then he saw that the priest was not alone, but rather imposingly, flanked by two policemen. Malcolm and Yakup walked quickly away.

"Aren't you worried that they'll arrest you?" Yakup asked.

"The square is safe. The police will not harass us here. Too many tourists and people to take photos. They would oppose a violent arrest of the 'happy African musicians.' Unfortunately, the tourists aren't everywhere."

49

FALLING

They stopped at a small kitchen run by a woman from Senegal. She served them crispy chicken, rice and fried plantains, which Malcolm explained were a large green banana. Their bellies filled and they strolled away, joking about the fat mama in the kitchen, the priest, the police and the fascists. It was the freedom of happiness that made their friendship special.

"You don't have to walk me all the way to my apartment," Yakup said.

"I'm gonna walk you home, my friend. Don't even try to argue," Malcolm put up his fists in a gesture of resistance and cracked a broad smile.

An ambulance and a police van were parked in front of the building. A group of people had gathered. Scanning the crowd, Yakup was able to quickly pick out the toothless man, his wife and their two daughters. The oldest daughter was crying. Yakup leapt towards them but was held back by Malcolm.

"Hold it! Too many police, Yakup. They'll take you into custody."

They waited behind the corner until the police cruiser and ambulance left.

"What happened?" Yakup asked as he ran up to the toothless man. His daughter leapt at Yakup, weeping.

"They… They killed him… They threw him off!" she wailed.

"Who killed who? What happened?"

"They pushed him off the balcony… we were watching TV… they knocked on the door… many of them. They tried to escape. The police beat the ones they could catch… Michael was on the balcony and they pushed him… they killed him, Yakup.”

She was crying too much to continue. Yakup held her and stroked her hair.

The young wife looked at Yakup. Her eyes were dry and strong.

“They took the men, Alia and the children. I don’t know why they didn’t take us as well. You were the only one not at home.”

“Who is *they* and why… why would someone do this?”

“The neighbours… They gave us away. Someone called the police. They kicked in the door and then…” she stopped. Her eyes flickered. “He landed there.” She pointed.

There were small dark stains on the sidewalk where she pointed. Yakup pulled himself free of the girl and walked over to the spot. He knelt on the cold curb. The blood had coagulated and held fast to Yakup’s finger, staining it. The blood of the dead Michael. Yakup wept.

The toothless man and his family left, seeking shelter.

In the early hours, before the first rays of sun hit Athens, a yawning man in overalls, hardhat in hand, left the building. Yakup and Malcolm snuck in just as the door shut.

They tiptoed up to the fifth floor where the door had been broken in and which now revealed an apartment in shambles: the TV lay broken on the floor, a cold portion of rice and beans waited on the kitchen counter, the chairs and table were upturned and the curtain to the balcony door listed gently to the side.

Yakup stepped out onto the balcony and realised Michael must have known that it was the end. What an insult to Michael to have spent years trying to reach a safer port, only to be tossed carelessly from a balcony in a place he so desperately wanted to leave. A vagabond. A transient. This thought made Yakup numb. He went inside, shutting the balcony door behind him and gesturing to Malcolm that it was time to leave.

Back out on the street, Yakup took one last look up at the apartment before he turned the corner.

“Listen, my friend, I know a place where you can stay a couple of nights. I’m staying there myself these days. It isn’t that bad,” Malcolm said, rolling his eyes and retching theatrically. Yakup’s mind raced back to the stain on the concrete. He could not even fake a smile.

50

LOST LOVE

Yakup soon learned that Malcolm was squatting in a building where half the roof was missing and there was a hole between two of the floorboards. Most of the stairs had fallen away and nature seemed to be reclaiming a number of walls as evidenced by numerous flora and fauna. One of the walls was black with mould. Still, it was a sort of shelter.

Malcolm was busking and working as a dishwasher, but the pay was poor and just better than nothing. Yakup collected food in the early hours of the day and whatever else he could find in the trash that might generate some income. Regardless, food was always a point of concern.

There were days when they had plenty and could sleep with full bellies, but those were offset by others when their bellies ran empty. Those days were hazy and at night their dreams were foul. Yakup tried not to think about juicy Afghan pomegranates, savoury Iranian broth in hot clay pots with spicy meat chunks, delicious humus served with newly baked bread or the crisp pieces of tomato, cucumber and onion covered in a layer of feta cheese soaked in olive oil that he had tasted in Athens. On lean days, it could happen that an apple disappeared from a vegetable stand or a bag of nuts vanished from a small shop. Life was like that.

"We were joined by a couple of local guys at the square," Malcolm said one afternoon in Alexander Park.

"I thought you were an 'African rhythm band'," Yakup replied, with a crooked smile.

"My friend, these two brothers were half Greek and half British. I can't say that they are the most talented musicians I've ever played with, but they do a killer mixed lingua rap and the crowd went wild when they saw us and two of their own rocking the square."

Malcolm stood up from the bench and imitated the awkward, rhythmless movements. He burst out laughing, which was contagious and got Yakup chuckling, shuffling and sliding around the squat.

"Move that skinny Afghan butt, my friend," Malcolm laughed.

Yakup moved to music that didn't exist. He hurled himself around and barely noticed Malcolm.

"My friend, I have no idea what you're doing, but I love it!" he yelled.

It was liberating to be dancing away all the pain and sadness. Yakup felt the blood pulsating through his veins—every movement a cathartic release.

He blinked, then, and realised that Malcolm had stopped dancing and was looking at him in surprise. Tears poured from Yakup's eyes. He felt embarrassed and stopped his madman's dance. The momentary escape that the dance had afforded him was over. He lost his balance, hit his arm on the bench and started sobbing uncontrollably.

"Easy, Yakup," Malcolm said in a calm voice.

"Why? Why should I take it easy? I was never meant to be anything. This is my fate! To be forced to fight in Bamiyan or to watch my uncle murdered; in Iran where the smugglers treated me like garbage; in Turkey where I lost my love. I was almost killed on the crossing from Turkey to Greece where I was abandoned by people I had come to look upon as friends..." Yakup stopped the narration of his miseries only because he had to cry some more.

"My friend, you have had a short and tough life, but you have to keep on fighting," Malcolm said. Yakup could do nothing but look at him with swollen eyes and wet cheeks.

"I hope it was not my silly dance that made you cry."

Yakup attempted to respond to Malcolm's efforts to cheer him up, but his mouth twisted instead and he wept some more.

"Sorry! I didn't mean to make you cry. Let me tell you a story. I have been here for a while. In fact, much longer than I intended to and I really didn't want to come here at all," Malcolm said. He fiddled with a tassel on his drum. "You know, how many Africans dream of going to Europe to make money and come back to their families and villages as big men with new clothes and lots of money, right? Well, that was not, and is not, why I am here.

"Love made me leave. She was tall, slender, dark and more beautiful than you could ever imagine. She and I were from neighbouring villages. I keep her alive in here," he said, pounding his fist softly over his chest. "I left for love, but now I'm stuck in this place, where there is no life.

"Where I am from, if you want something, then you must be willing to give something in return. I grew up in a small village in Nigeria. One of the places where the wind always blows the dust in your eyes, ears and mouth. I was an ignorant and happy child who spent my time playing with the other kids in the village. One day I went to collect water from the well and I met this girl from the neighbouring village. I was completely smitten from the moment I saw her. I couldn't speak and dropped half a bucket of water. My heart was heavy yet filled with an unfamiliar excitement as I walked home. I went to the well at the same time every day, although it wasn't too manly, in the hope of seeing her again and exactly a week later I was rewarded. She was with two other girls. I had prepared a speech to introduce myself but was at a loss as soon as I saw her. The beauty, she looked at me without scorn or irony, while her friends giggled.

"Her name was Karen. Her family had been farmers for generations. Still, they struggled and were at the mercy of the weather like any other subsistence farmer in my part of the world. I offered to walk her home and what should have taken one hour we did in three.

"From then on we often met at the well. It didn't take long before a meeting was set up between my parents and Karen's. That was when I learned of an entirely different plan.

"Karen's beauty had not gone unnoticed in other parts of our region. One day a man and his son came to Karen's village in a jeep. They were from the city. He was a businessman and his son was destined to succeed him one day. He had money and status. They would provide an extremely generous dowry for Karen, which my family could not. When my parents came back from the meeting, they told me the truth and something inside of me shattered.

"I ran out of our hut, through the yellow grass, across small fields of sorghum, over the dry bush, and finally, along the cracked path that led to Karen's village. I had to hear the words for myself.

"As I approached her home, I saw her sitting by the side of her family's clay hut. Her eyes were bright in the moonlight. I walked up to her, and for the first time, could see a sadness in her. We embraced and cried in silence. That night we went into the bush and talked about the unfairness of it and how we might be able to reason with her parents and how we would raise a family together. We made love that night under the stars.

"I woke up the next morning to screams. Karen's father was beating me with a stick, yelling at me to get out of there and never to return. Karen was screaming and trying to hold him back, but he struck her as well telling her that she was bringing shame to him and the family. He was flanked by men from the village. I had no choice but to flee. I ran and stopped once to look back. I yelled with the full force of my lungs to Karen, to her father, to the men from her village, to anyone who would listen, that I loved Karen, that she was destined to be mine, that I would return and take her as my wife and that I would make sure her family would be compensated better than the businessman and his son could ever dream of doing. But still, they chased me away."

Malcolm sighed. "That was the last time I saw her. I left the village the following day. I was determined to get to Europe and make enough money to win Karen back. I saw other travellers like me perish in the desert and when we thought we had made it upon reaching the sea we were soon sorely disappointed We were too many people in a tiny boat and I don't know how long we spent on the sea, but I do remember the man who fell overboard. He couldn't swim. There were no life vests. He screamed and screamed until the sea filled his lungs and took him. We ended up in Greece and I've been here ever since."

"What did they do to her?" Yakup asked, but Malcolm offered no answer.

51

DYSFUNCTIONAL

Time passed and life in Athens went on. One day a group of men wandered about their derelict building as though looking for something. Malcolm was sure they were civilian police. After that, they slept under bridges, in squats, in parks and under whatever shelter they could find. Yakup worked when he could, but finding steady employment in Athens was next to impossible, and so, he took to collecting and selling scrap metal.

The competition was fierce and days could pass without him making any money. The friendship between the two young men grew, though, even when they did not stay in the same place. Some days Yakup was invited to sleep in a flat with other Afghans; at other times one of the men in Malcolm's band offered him a space. But within a few days of being on their own, they always found each other. Often, they shared shelter with other foreigners.

Yakup met people from far away. The newcomers seeped determinedly through porous land and sea borders that the government could not seal. Most were stuck with little access to papers or asylum processing opportunities once in Greece. Rules of law imposed by the other countries in Europe meant they could not leave the country, and so, no one really knew how many Afghans, Syrians, Pakistanis, Iraqis, Bangladeshis, Senegalese, Guineans, Nigerians, Libyans, Albanians, Russians, Georgians, Ukrainians, Roma and other migrants and refugees lived illegally in Greece.

Yakup and Malcolm were sitting on the lip of an empty fountain in Eleftherias Square, surrounded by white-washed buildings and a park of grey concrete that was dotted here and there by dark green-orange trees laden with fruit. A group of homeless people had set up camp in an empty flowerbed nearby but had abandoned their cardboard shelter.

"Did you hear about the guy from Guinea who died last night?" Malcolm asked.

"What happened?"

"It is a sad story, my friend. The police are doing one of their checks. The Guinean is straight, but he doesn't have his papers on him. Apparently, he had been at the police station to renew them many times but had had no luck. You know how it is: a mob of foreigners waving their documents in the hopes some administrator will take pity on them. Anyhow, this dude doesn't have his papers. He runs. The police chase him. Suddenly he finds himself on a bridge. Police coming from both sides. He is healthy and could outrun the police, but there's no escape. He looks left, then right. He knows that there's a fair risk of getting a beating. He starts to panic. Looks down. Maybe five meters. He can do it. He knows he can. The police are closing in. He steps over the rail. Maybe six meters. Police are almost there. He jumps. The police grab his jacket, but they are too late. His landing is awkward, and he dies on impact."

"Bastards! Why can't they leave us alone? Or let us leave?" Yakup said, shaking his head before landing it in his hands, which were nearly in his lap. That's when he asked, "Why don't we just leave?"

"Trust me, I want to, but if I go anywhere, I need a job or else I'll have no choice but to go back. But I can't go back without any money otherwise Karen's parents will not let me have her," Malcolm lamented, looking at his once-red sneakers upon the blue tiles of the fountain.

"How long since you talked to her?" Yakup said.

Malcolm lifted his head. "What do you mean?"

"Well, I'm wondering if you know anything about her situation. It wasn't like you left on good terms with her parents. What about this other guy? The one who was rich? I'm all for dreams and hopes, but maybe keep it real. Maybe Karen is no longer there for you."

As soon as Yakup had said it, he knew he had made a mistake, but there was no taking it back. The words ignited something Malcolm had clearly already contemplated, which caused his friend to stare even harder at the ground.

A group of four or five men entered the square at the far end and spread out.

"Yakup, you don't know Karen. How can you know what you're talking about?" Malcolm said, glaring at him. "I hope… and I believe. In love. What do I, *we*, have without it?" Yakup looked at Malcolm with eyes pleading for forgiveness but found surprise and outrage in the face of his friend.

The men were moving closer. Two of them had black helmets in their hands.

"Malcolm, look!" Yakup cried, pointing behind him. A slim man jumped down the small set of stairs some 30 meters away, his black boots hitting the cement with a thud. Malcolm finally turned around.

"Holy… Let's go."

They ran. Behind them, boots pounded the cement. They ran faster than either had ever done before, dodging cars, people and motorbikes; dashing through arcades and into parking lots; past gates. Panting. Then, into a park. They jumped a hedge and collapsed on the other side. When he could speak again, Yakup said, "It was him… The man with the rope."

52

OLD GREECE

They lay panting for a while behind the bushes. Adrenalin had pushed them beyond the limits of their physical capability and they were drained.

A few minutes later Yakup tried to apologise once more, saying, "Malcolm… I didn't mean to…"

"It is fine," his friend said. "I believe that hope is not an anchor… it is a sail. One day the wind will take me… to where I belong."

Yakup knew he would never talk about Karen again.

Something moved in the bushes nearby. They both sat up. Alert and ready for another flight. Then movement from the other side. Suddenly from all around them. From the bushes came people. Old people. Some had canes, others held sticks. They had Yakup and Malcolm surrounded.

"Come here," a brusque voice commanded. An old man with a wrinkled face stood before them. He had wispy grey hair. Between his knuckled nose and upper lip was a large, and surprisingly well-groomed, moustache. The two young men hesitated, but seeing no conceivable way out of their new quandary, simply decided to obey the old man. They looked at each other, then, puzzled.

Malcolm shrugged and moved towards the old man. Yakup followed. He led them to a small elevated pitch surrounded by a few sad-looking bushes and shadowed by a small tree from whose branches hung a ripped and tattered sheet of green tarpaulin. The ground was covered by an old, dirty rug with sun-bleached plastic bags, containing still more plastic bags and old clothes, scattered about. A big, furry dog lay peacefully on the ground. At first, Yakup mistook it for a fluffy toy animal until it rose and walked up to the old man.

"This is Mr Know-it-all," the old man said, patting the dog. "He doesn't look like much, and he probably isn't worth a lot these days, but he and I go way back and we're sticking together until the end."

The dog's thick fur was black, though, greying, which could have been age or dirt, or, most likely, some combination thereof.

"That must be the sorriest dog alive," Malcolm burst out, rolling his eyes and letting out a small laugh.

Mr Know-it-all swung his head towards Malcolm and Yakup, making a swift move towards Malcolm. He bared his teeth and growled. Malcolm let out a surprised yelp of his own, and stepping backwards, stumbled over a piece of plastic bag and landed on the ground.

"Mister! Get your Mr. Dog away from me. He is vicious," Malcolm yelled. The dog was looming over him now.

"His name is Mr Know-it-all," the old man corrected. "And he is his own creature."

He snapped his fingers and mumbled something to the dog who returned to the rug.

"Don't worry, Mr Know-it-all," the old man said calmly "these two are not dangerous."

Mr. Know-it-all regarded Yakup with a pair of brown eyes and wagged his tail.

"Can I offer you two skinny youngsters a cup of tea? You look like you could use it," the old man said. "And then maybe you can explain to me why you came running into our camp in such a rush." Before either could answer, he had handed them a couple of dented metal cups with thin brown liquid steaming inside. The heat hurt Yakup's hands, but he held on to his cup politely.

"You, Asian boy, you can sit there on the chair since your friend has already decided to settle in my bed."

Though the darkness made it hard to see, Yakup swore he saw a faint blush dance over Malcolm's dark skin. Malcolm shifted his weight but refused to give up the bed. In all actuality, the bed was just a thin mattress, two synthetic blankets and a flat pillow. Elsewhere, there were stacks of tattered books, two small green plants in clay pots next to one of the bushes, and conveniently, a small opening where a fire smouldered. This was where the old man had retrieved the burning hot metal cups. Yakup could see someone using the fireplace on the other side of the opening and realised that a similar 'home' was adjacent to the one they currently occupied. The narrowness of the space made Yakup's thoughts shoot back to the caves of Bamiyan. There was a homey feel to the place.

He felt the old man's eyes on him. The man nodded towards Yakup and sipped from his uneven metal cup. "What happened to you?" he asked.

Not knowing exactly what he meant, Yakup started from the beginning.

"I grew up in a cave in Afghanistan…" Yakup paused as maybe this wasn't what the old man had meant, but that was the story Yakup told him. When Yakup finally reached the part about the man with the rope, he realised that he had been talking for a long time. Malcolm and Mr Know-it-all were asleep next to each other, yet, the old man sat raptly. Yakup kept quiet and waited in the semi-darkness.

"Can you describe the men who chased you?" the old man finally said.

"There were four or five of them. At least two of them had attacked me before. I recognised them… Then there are the beating patrols. That is something we call them because they usually beat up people without asking questions."

"But by people, you mean foreigners," corrected the old man. He was poking the embers with a stick to keep the fire alive.

"Yes, foreigners. They usually attack when we walk alone or in twos. They drive two or three scooters and cut your escape options off. There are usually two aboard each one. The one riding pillion has the club. He jumps off the scooter and the beating starts." The old man stopped moving his stick, staring absently into the glow of the fire. "Of the two who attacked me, one of them is blond. He is very agitated and yells stuff like *'You're a plague on Greek soil'* and *'Leave this country or die' and* many other vicious things. He smiles when he beats victims. At one point, you just don't hear him any more. His voice becomes a buzz among the blows and the kicks."

Yakup took a sip of his tea. It was thin and tasted mildly of anise. Malcolm, he noticed, had drained his cup. He slept cuddled up next to Mr Know-it-all.

"The other one is the leader, I think. He scares me the most," Yakup continued, draining the last of his cold anise tea. "He is thin and has dark hair in a ponytail. For some reason he… he carries a rope with a hard knot dangling from the end. He uses it as his weapon. I know it only too well, I'm afraid…" The old man was still staring into the fading glow of the fire. The shadows flickered on his wrinkled face. His large nose cast a long shadow on one side of his face and Yakup could see his eyes were misting over but didn't know if this was from the fire or the story. Maybe he was just tired, being an old man and all.

"Sometimes they attack girls and women, too," Yakup added and sighed. The old man turned and looked at Yakup.

"This is not my country any more. These are not my people," he said in a low, but intense voice full of sorrow.

"Greece! The so-called 'cradle of democracy and civilization.' It has long had a democratic deficit. We praise ourselves for a glorious past, but we cannot seem to build a future as bright." He took a pouch of tobacco from among his things, opened it and then seemed to forget it in his hands. Instead, he nodded towards the dark city.

"There!" He pointed into the dark duvet of night that floated above the shimmering lights of Athens. "There is our famous Acropolis. That was where the people of Athens gathered and discussed and voted on their living standards. Back then only men could vote— not women, not children, not slaves."

His fingers found a lump of tobacco and molded it into the shape of a cigarette. He placed it on a thin piece of paper and started to roll.

"Today, citizens are sitting in the parliament discussing and voting on their living standards," he said, pausing to wet the edge of the paper with his tongue. "Today, people are sleeping on the marble steps of Syntagma Square just below the Greek parliament. Both citizens of Greece and people who came here to find a better life. Who are the slaves now? In the land of the blind, the one-eyed man is king. We are not blind, but some believe we are. We can see that they are naked."

The old man pulled out a small bottle from one of his many plastic bags. "I once fondly hoped that those in power would work for the people. Instead, they reap the benefits and hide their crimes," He lamented, lifting the bottle and sipping from it generously. He stuck the rolled cigarette between his lower lip and grey moustache and lit it. The match briefly illuminated his battered face.

"We once proudly said, *'Greece is the beginning of Europe'*, but maybe it is the end," he concluded, taking a long drag and blinking. "It is time to sleep. I have had a long day, and so have you, it seems.

You can sleep next to your friend and Mr Know-it-all on the mattress. Just for the night."

"No, no, I will wake Malcolm and we'll sleep on the ground."

But the old man firmly insisted and after a few minutes Yakup was next to Mr Know-it-all on the mattress and had, himself, dozed off, warm and almost safe next to his friend and the peacefully sleeping mutt.

53

THE CAMP

Yakup woke up the next morning to find Malcolm and Mr Know-it-all playing with a stick. Yakup knew that Malcolm was strong, but he was struggling to pull the stick from Mr Know-it-all's firmly shut jaws. Instead, it was the dog who had the upper hand, wrestling the stick from Malcolm, who, again, fell backwards on his bum laughing. Yakup laughed, too. Mr Know-it-all registered that he was awake and greeted him with a big wet lick on his face. Malcolm was laughing so hard that tears were running down his cheeks. Yakup laughed too as he wiped the drool off his cheek. He felt a drowsy happiness inside and wished that he, Malcolm, the old man and the dog could go away together, take care of each other and live a normal life.

"Listen, the old man left before sunrise. I'm not sure where or why, but maybe we should move on?" Malcolm suggested.

Before Yakup could answer, however, they were interrupted by an elderly woman with her hair festooned with grey and purple curls. She entered the old man's hideaway through bushes, which doubled as a doorway.

"I heard we had guests," she said and looked sternly at both of them. They exchanged worried glances.

"I also heard that you have behaved and that you had an unfortunate experience yesterday. My name is Rosa," she said, smiling and holding out a wrinkled hand.

"Welcome to the Elders Camp," she said and spread her arms out to indicate the trees, bushes, trolleys and scattered plastic bags. Malcolm frowned in puzzlement.

Rosa sat down with some difficulty on the small stool. "I'll tell you in a minute, but first I want to ask young Yakup here why he seems so familiar. I have a feeling that we have met before."

"Um… I don't recall."

"Hmm. I could be wrong of course. My memory isn't what it used to be," she said, smiling and clasping hands together in her lap. "Well, then let me tell you who we are. Most of us used to have decent jobs. We were teachers, nurses, clerks, carpenters and so on. We could support ourselves and our families. We grew old and were supposed to live off of the state pension once we retired and could no longer work. Then the economy took a turn for the worse. People lost their jobs and homes; some of us lost our families as well."

She shook her head pensively. "Greek family ties have always been strong, and many rely on a son or a daughter to send them small amounts to add to their pensions. But some simply cannot afford to care for their elders nowadays."

She gazed at Yakup, unseeing, and continued, "The worst part is that those who cut us off from society are the same ones benefitting from the crisis. That is why you see this."

She opened her arms to indicate their squalor and got up with a bit more energy. "At first there were only a few of us, but soon we realised that there were many in similar situations. Your friend, old man Elias, we like to see him as the founder of our camp. He takes care of us. He is a real politician. We are fighting to keep a semblance of normality as well as to keep our dignity intact and to avoid the depression that is enveloping our country.

"Homes in villages are sold far below their value, but people are glad to sell and survive for a few more months. Others are forced to live in their cars. They park them in a different spot every night. I guess that lifestyle can be appealing to adventurous, freedom-seeking adolescents like you, but when you are retired, being forced to sell off your family home and have no economic options, well, it feels like selling a piece of yourself. Having to rely on others is, of course, a threat, but to us, the real danger is succumbing to the deep, dark swamp of depression that many Greeks are already mired in. We struggle to get up and fight on. The alternative is too dark for us to consider. I would be happy to start over, but where and how?"

She smiled at Malcolm, who nodded in agreement. "When we go to bed, we know we have made it through another day. Six more and that's a full week. And so it goes."

Abruptly Rosa said she had business to attend to and trudged away.

The two young men sat in silence, thinking.

"Listen, my friend, the longer I stay in this country, the less surprised I am about its inefficiency," Malcolm said at last. "How can a society leave its elders to themselves? What kind of humanity is that? Where I come from, it is a violation to leave your elders to themselves. You come from the womb of your mother, she nurses you, your father ensures that there is food in your belly; family is there for you. Without them you would not even be alive," Malcolm said, rising to stand. Mr Know-it-all observed the agitation of his new friend with interest.

"Maybe we just don't understand their culture," Yakup ventured.

Malcolm shook his head in dismay and patted Mr Know-it-all's broad head. The dog wagged its tail and dug his snout into Malcolm's thigh. A trail of dog drool stained his pants. He drew his leg back, but Mr Know-it-all followed him with tail wagging faster and eyes that begged for a scratch behind his ear. Malcolm laughed and ended up on the ground in a friendly tussle with the large dog.

Voices carried through a commotion from the other side of the bushes. Yakup peeked through the branches.

"What's going on?" said Malcolm.

"It's the old man, Elias!"

He stood in the middle of a circle of old men and women. Some leaned on canes, a few sat or supported each other's frail bodies. Elias had his cart with him. It was filled with leftover food that he distributed to the circle of furrowed skin and toothless jaws. It seemed to be a regular ritual. Each waited for his or her turn and soon everyone had found a spot in the clearing to eat their rations.

"Come! Have some food," Elias said and handed them a package of yoghurt and a slice of brown bread.

"But we don't want to take your food. You have already been so kind to us …"

"Nonsense! Don't be silly! Do you really want to argue with an old man? Do you not respect his wishes?" he chided, winking.

Yakup blushed a bit, accepted the food and thanked him.

"How did you get all this food?" Malcolm asked. There was a white yoghurt moustache on his dark upper lip. It made Yakup smile. Elias dipped some bread into his yoghurt and gave it to Mr Know-it-all. The dog licked the yoghurt off the bread.

"As you may have noticed the yoghurt is past the due date and the bread is stale. No one wants to buy it any more, so the shops throw it away," he sipped from the yoghurt. "That is good for us. We eat the supermarket's leftovers and go to soup kitchens for the rest." He threw another slice of dry bread to Mr Know-it-all, who caught it mid-air and immediately began chewing.

"A society should take care of its people. This is what we are trying to do here. We have different skills, different levels of energy, different contacts and different needs. We try to combine this to make a small functioning micro-society."

"But why doesn't the government help you?" Yakup asked. "But why doesn't the government help you?" Yakup asked. Elias looked at him with a sad smile and raised his bushy eyebrows.

"I told you a bit about it last night. The Greek pride has been hurt badly by the realization that our society did not live up to the standards it set for modern democracy. Greece is a debt-ravaged country walking a tightrope between young men armed with assault rifles and the rise of a phenomenon that bears strong similarities to that of the 1930s. Those men you ran away from yesterday are the outcome of the latter. As you know from your own country, Yakup, it does not take much before the situation descends into an abyss of violence and self-destruction. Both sides have an appetite for destruction and they feed off of each other's hunger," he quieted, lighting a cigarette and leaning back while blowing a heavy cloud of smoke into the crisp morning air.

"It is a vicious cycle that has to be dealt with at all levels of society. A new narrative is necessary. It is an illusion that this society can continue without compromising humanity more than is already apparent. The current system ought to be a metamorphosis but is, unfortunately, a continuation of the past."

He dragged on the cigarette and coughed violently. Yakup handed him a bottle of water. Elias waved him off but took the water bottle anyway.

"Don't worry," he said in a rusty voice. "There are plenty of other things that will kill me before the smoke gets to me," he said, smiling and sipping generously from the bottle. "So, to answer your question would be complicated. First, the government and the politicians would need to help themselves and for that to happen they first need to transform the political system as well as the civil society and the normative thinking in modern Greece. There is the middle of the political spectrum with most of the old actors, but there are increasingly dangerous ideological factions pulling the middle towards them. Populism is an easy win in our societies of today, I'm afraid. There is of course much more to it, but I won't bore you with those details," Elias looked at his cigarette and decided it had come to an end. He threw it into a small clay pot next to him filled with cigarette butts.

"I'm not bored," Yakup replied.

"Well, I still have to send you on your way. You are both welcome to pass by again, but now I need a nap. I would like to hear more about your experience in Greece and I'm glad to tell you more about our situation… if you are interested of course," Elias said.

"I would be happy to pay you a visit later," Yakup said.

Malcolm declined, "I have to make a living. I'm playing with the guys this afternoon and have work tonight. Another time, though," he promised.

Thanking him profusely, they shook hands with Elias and patted Mr Know-it-all. Then they headed back into the busy Athens streets with all its monsters.

54

REBETIKO

Yakup spent his day in the vicinity of old-man Elias' camp. He tried his luck with a few dumpsters and found the soggy end of a sandwich and a slightly bruised banana. He decided against the sandwich, and so, sat down on a bench to eat the banana and let his mind wander off to Mariam. He had taken up a habit of shutting his eyes to let his mind escape into a world where he and Mariam were together even though it saddened him to open his eyes again and only Athens but no trace of Mariam.

After a few hours, he decided that it was late enough in the afternoon to go and visit Elias again. He was drawn by the thought of more stories and insights about Greece.

"Hello," he said out loud as he entered the small clearing to which Mr Know-it-all responded with a resounding bark. The dog was pleased to see Yakup and the feeling was mutual. Elias was nowhere to be found, however, and so, Yakup sat down on a stool and looked around. One of the plastic bags languished next to him and he couldn't help peering inside. There was a plastic folder with a photo of a young boy and a woman. The woman was beautiful. The boy was skinny. He let his finger slide over the plastic surface.

"How are you, Yakup," Elias said, appearing without warning.

"I'm sorry. I didn't mean to…" Yakup stuttered.

"It's fine," Elias assured him. "The photo is of my son and wife."

He moved over next to Yakup, who handed him the photo not a little ashamed. Elias stared at it before tucking it into his shirt.

"I'm sorry. I didn't mean to go snooping," Yakup said.

"Don't worry about it."

"Where are they now? Your son and wife?"

"My wife passed away years ago. My son and I had a falling out some time back. I haven't had much contact with him since."

"Does he know how you are living?"

"Yes, he does. Now we ought to go before it is too late."

"Go where?"

"To dinner," Elias said and winked at Yakup.

They walked out of the park where the old people camped and deeper into the city until they reached a district of bars and restaurants where people drank and smoked on benches.

"A teenager was killed by the police right here," Elias said, nodding towards a graffiti-covered wall. "Do you see the little signboard?" he asked. Then Yakup noticed that along one wall was a plaque with a photo of a young boy stuck to the wall. The facade of this building was heavy with graffiti, like those around it, and the memorial seemed to blend in.

"Who is that?" Yakup asked.

"The kid was shot dead by the police some years back," Elias said in a low voice. "They shot him down in cold blood, claiming that he was throwing stones and bottles towards them. Everyone around here knows that the boy was an innocent victim of brutal police violence and exploitation of power. Even if he had been throwing stones or bottles, it does not justify death by firing squad."

"Was he a migrant?" Yakup asked. Elias looked at Yakup and put a hand on his shoulder.

"I know that migrants are killed and nothing happens, but it tears me up inside that some of my countrymen have such an ugly view of immigrants and think nothing of crimes against humanity just because of their place of birth and ethnicity. He was a Greek boy. Alexandros Grigoropoulos. This area, Exarcheia, has a history of revolution in Greece. The killing of Alexis in 2008 sparked protests nationwide, but before that, in 1973, there was an uprising at the Athens Polytechnic. A military junta tank crashed through the campus gates and more than 20 civilians were killed. The uprising ended the junta's power."

Elias patted Yakup's shoulder and turned away, leaving the latter to look at the flotsam of the wall: graffiti and still frames of angry demonstrators, their faces covered, carrying sticks and hurling Molotov cocktails. Black city, burning sky. Yakup ran after Elias and caught up with him. They walked in silence. The walls of the buildings were a mosaic of opposition —protesting the abuse of power by the government, discrimination, fascism. The art varied from large drawings to small political slogans. Art mixed with politics. A place to speak. Street democracy. A multifaceted message telling the established political system and its institutions that resistance was real, just as it had been in 1973.

Elias stopped in front of a small restaurant. Through the hazy windows, they could see crowded tables and the hurried movement of waiters.

"I know them in there. They always find me a seat," Elias said. He patted Yakup reassuringly on the back and swung the heavy wooden door open. They were immediately surrounded by the sound of glass, cutlery, dishware, laughter and conversation amongst the various groups of people seated around the small, one-room restaurant.

The air was thick with the aroma of veal, pork, fried vegetables, stews and undefined local dishes. Yakup could see into the kitchen where bulky sweating men in stained aprons moved large black pots and pans back and forth on a massive old stove. The kitchen was small, but the men moved gracefully around each other's hefty bodies, manoeuvring the pots with strong arms. They were each a member of a well-oiled machine, knowing each other's exact position and purpose and without having to utter a word.

Elias pulled Yakup along. They zigzagged through chairs, tables and waiters until he was greeted by a smiling, sturdy man with black hair and gentle, though, bulging eyes. Like the cooks, he wore a stained apron. He gave Elias a big hug with his enormous hairy arms.

"Meet my friend Yakup," Elias said and pushed Yakup closer to the spotted apron towering in front of him.

"Yakup, this is my old friend Costas. He is the owner of the best place to eat in this city."

A glass shattered somewhere in the back. Costas briefly glanced in the direction of the noise, but with some effort, redirected his attention towards Yakup.

"A pleasure to meet you Yakup," Costas said, snatching up his hand

and shaking it before Yakup had time to return his greeting.

"Look at this scrawny kid you're bringing, Elias! We need to feed him, or my customers will think I serve too small portions. Come with me and I will treat you to all the wonders of 'Costas' Kitchen'," he said, laughing, and leading them to a small table near the corner of the room. Two musicians were playing guitar and tamboura lute while singing Greek folk songs. A steady flow of waiters ensured that the wine jugs on their table were never empty. The older of the two musicians was sturdy and wore a white suit. His hair was crisp and white as was his beard. He had on a pair of square dark glasses. The younger of the two had a serious look on his long face; he was skinny with sinewy fingers that moved graciously up and down the frets and strings of his guitar. He had a ponytail and a day-old beard. Any time the music afforded him the opportunity, he reached for a rolled cigarette on the edge of a table, puffed, and nodded with a smile at Elias and Yakup, and turned to his instrument.

"This is a beautiful song from the Port of Piraeus—a rebetiko. Such tradition. Such beauty," Costas said, singing along, swaying into the kitchen.

There were about twenty tables in the restaurant covered with braided breadbaskets, salads hidden under chunks of feta and glistening in olive oil. Tables shared dishes of meat, vegetables, pasta and fries. There were water carafes and small tin jars filled with local wines, small crooked glass bottles with raki, Greek coffee and small sweet deserts. The clientele was a melange of couples, families and men getting drunk on wine and high on folk music.

Elias ate and so did Yakup. A symphony of tastes known and unknown filled him. He ate like he hadn't for a long time. As the food on the platters dwindled, he grew drowsy and soon dozed off to the music.

He woke up, not knowing how long he had been out. His head was resting on Elias' arm.

"Welcome back," Elias said. Yakup looked up into his friendly wrinkled face. His moustache crawled into a smile.

"Meet Andreas," he said and gestured towards the young musician. "This talented young man is the nephew of Costas and an avid critic of our society. He used to study political science, but found our system too corrupt and inadequate to bother with; now, he pursues his real passion: music. Correct?"

Andreas smiled and shook Yakup's hand.

"I hear you met some of the guys of my generation, but from the other side," he said, frowning. "Those ignorant fools do not properly represent my generation nor this country."

He began to roll a cigarette. A table of inebriated men had taken over the music. They were singing and barking poetry from Crete. They drove the rhythm by slamming empty raki glasses onto the table.

"Many Greeks have lost their jobs, homes and dignity in these lean years and there is little hope left. You could refer to it as a Greek tragedy or a collective depression," he explained, rearranging himself on the wooden chair. "We have long had a so-called democratic government, but in reality, many of the politicians have been in power for generations and have spent that time reaping the benefits of long periods of economic prosperity. They did not follow the rules of the game even though they, themselves, had set the rules. Instead, they became greedy and arrogant. That often comes with power." he said, pausing.

He then took a sip of his beer, Elias of his raki and Yakup of his soda. He continued:

"They thought that they were above reproach. They were elected as representatives of the people but acted as if they were above them. Above us," he said, gesturing at the people in the restaurant. "Money went in, but never came out, and in the end, they stuck us, the people, with the bill."

Andreas took a draught from his wine jar, nodded towards it and gestured for Yakup to have a sip. The boy shook his head.

"This situation benefits some. They see opportunities in others' misfortune. They feed on insecurity and ignorance, which allows them to sell their ugly ideas. The fascists have to be fought, but they have grown strong because of the economic crisis and the suffering it has brought for so many, such as our dysfunctional asylum system, as you probably know better than me, right?"

Yakup nodded.

The restaurant was almost entirely empty at this point. The white-clad musician had packed his gear and poked Andreas on the shoulder.

"Let's go," he said.

"I was just having a talk with our new friend Yakup," Andreas replied.

"Fine, but I need your help to get to my place," the other man said. He was still wearing his shades.

"Ok, ok," Andreas replied. The white-clad man turned around and moved towards the door.

"He can't see," Andreas murmured, moving his hand back and forth in front of his own eyes to demonstrate his point. He got up and swayed a bit. "Why don't you join us? He lives just by the VOX bar at Exarcheia Square. VOX is occupied by squatters. Nice guys, but they are often getting into trouble."

"I think I should stay here," Yakup said and looked at the still-sleeping old man.

"Don't worry about him. He sleeps better here than in the streets. Anyway, we'll be back before you know it. A few hundred meters each way. Would you deny a blind man and a drunk a little assistance?" Andreas gave him a shrug and a slow, but obvious wink.

Yakup was reluctant to leave Elias, which Andreas noticed immediately.

"Costas! Yakup here will pop out for ten minutes. Tell Elias that I'll bring his friend back. He is helping us with the instruments," Andreas said. Costas nodded from behind the counter. Yakup got up. These people had fed him, talked to him and treated him as a fellow human. He cast one last glance towards the sleeping old man as the heavy wooden door shut behind him.

55

EXARCHIA

The cool wind in the street cleansed the odours of food and smoke from their bodies. The two musicians and Yakup walked towards the crowded Exarcheia Square.

"Did they give you papers?" Andreas asked.

"Ehm… Papers?" Yakup asked.

"When you entered this country, did they provide you with documents to legally stay here?"

"Well, I have a paper, but I have to renew it," Yakup said.

"The situation is bad," Andreas said. He stopped in front of a street vendor to buy two beers and a soda. "Legally the asylum seekers cannot go anywhere other than Greece since the regulations require them to apply for asylum in the first EU country they enter. It is clear that the regulation is failing to protect the rights of the asylum seekers because it is based on the false assumption that all EU countries provide an adequate level of protection. At the same time, it fails those countries on the border of the EU like the already-weak Greek system," Andreas explained, rolling a cigarette and lighting it. The grey smoke rose in front of his face as he continued.

"In 2011, a judgment by the European Court of Human Rights recognised that other EU countries cannot send asylum seekers back to Greece as they are faced with inhuman treatment and degrading conditions. At the same time, those already in Greece cannot leave and are living under conditions that the Court defined as inhuman and degrading. It is absurd! What's more, Turkey can open and close the gates and let people flow into Europe to put pressure on the EU. Chaos and disregard for humans!" Andreas shouted, spilling a bit of beer on his friend's white jacket. The older musician didn't notice, but simply 'stared' straight ahead.

"But what about human rights then? Will they only give them to me in another European country?" Yakup asked.

"I can't say that I know the situation in other EU countries very well, but I find it hard to believe that it is worse than here. The Greek state is faceless and confused. The police and the fascists work together to get to people like me and you. Both of us are in danger of being attacked by right-wing groups, while the police stand idly by. If the police are inactive, it is because of the government's inaction. The police are an institution under the government after all.

"You see, Yakup, it is not just you, who are deprived of your rights in this country, but all of us without jobs, without hope for the future, and so, we choose sides. I believe in humanity, but others believe that the foreigners are the root cause of the problem. Just ask Elias; he knows better than any. His own son is a fascist, a violent type. It is difficult to accept if you know good ol' Elias. He used to work for the university while being active in the left-wing protest movement," Andreas said, slurring a bit at this point, but continuing on nevertheless.

"When his wife took her own life, he stopped with the politics. His son blamed him for the death of his mother. Maybe that was why the boy chose the other side. In any case, Elias went through a period of heavy drinking and depression. When he returned from the depths, he found that he had lost not just his wife, but also his son and job. He couldn't pay the rent and was kicked out of his house. He had some sort of awakening and decided to help himself and other old people in a similar situation, which was why he established the camp away from institutions and the state…self-sufficient survival on a budget."

Andreas got up. "Let's go," he said, burping.

"But what about Elias' son?" Yakup wanted to know everything. They were walking across Exarcheia Square, a fire was burning inside an old oil drum in the middle of the square and surrounded by people drinking canned beer, smoking weed, talking, playing guitar. The cafés and restaurants around the square were packed. Under the trees and just beyond blocks upon blocks of flats, the square served as a communal gathering place for students, civil servants, anarchists, drifters, unemployed Greeks, migrants and people who simply wanted a good time on a Saturday night.

A group of people ran towards Yakup, Andreas and the blind man.

"The police," someone yelled. And then the blinding headlights wielded by speeding motorbikes swarmed the square like sinister bees.

The motorbikes headed for the crowd and deposited themselves into the surprised mass of bodies. They were two aboard each bike. The policeman riding the pillion had a club that randomly hit the nearest targets. A man yelled. A woman screamed. The bikes left confusion, fear and anger behind. They disappeared as fast as they had appeared. Yakup lost Andreas and desperately sought escape from the crowd.

"Bastards!" someone yelled.

"*Malaka*, arseholes!" another roared. Fists raised, bottles broken, bins kicked over and tossed in the dark. Green-clad riot police moved in with shields, helmets, gas masks, teargas canisters and sticks. The people had had time to organise themselves by now. Bottles and stones flew towards the police. This was not their home turf and the riot squad knew it. The wall of people pushed against them. A smoking canister landed next to Yakup. He clapped his hand over his mouth. Someone kicked the canister away, though it was too late for Yakup who began coughing as his nose ran and eyes watered.

"Stand still," someone said. Blinded, Yakup obeyed.

"Help me," he said in a thick voice. Someone poured liquid into Yakup's eyes. It soothed the pain, but his eyes were so swollen it took some time for him to open them.

"Stop!" Yakup pushed the person's arm away.

"Can you see again, Yakup?"

"Andreas?"

"Yes."

"I thought I lost you," he gasped, still choking.

"Likewise. I saw you when the canister landed. Let's get out of here," Andreas said and pulled Yakup by one arm and the blind man by the other through the tense crowd.

Elias was sitting against the heavy wooden door of Costas restaurant when the three stumbled through the entrance.

"What happened?" he asked.

"The police. They attacked VOX."

"Are you all right?" Elias asked.

"Yakup was unlucky. He got some tear gas in his face. If you have some milk or lemon juice, it should soothe it."

"Why don't you come back with me to the camp, Yakup? The restaurant is closed, but I have remedies that can help you and you can get a good night's rest. You will be safer with me than by yourself," Elias said.

Yakup nodded. His head was pounding and his eyes were two swollen slits.

"I'm sorry about this," Andreas said. Though he swayed on his feet, his concern was genuine. "I am sorry… I'm really sorry about how you were treated… I have to go home now. I worked all night, drank lots of vino and then this… this 'action' has drained me."

Andreas fished a ready-rolled cigarette from his pocket and lit it. "It was good to meet you Yakup. All the best. My advice, though? Get out of this country. The sooner the better."

He turned around, guitar and ponytail swinging and left the old man with the wrinkled face and the boy with battle scars. He almost stumbled over a scooter that lay on its side in the street, like a testimony to the faceless attackers from the faceless state.

56

HASAN

Yakup woke up next to Mr Know-it-all. It was early morning and Elias was snoring under a plastic sheet, which doubled as a blanket. Yakup touched his face gingerly. It was still a bit numb from the teargas. His lungs felt battered. He decided to get up and go for a walk in the crisp morning air. A stack of newspapers lay unpacked in front of a newsstand. Two homeless people lay on collapsed packing boxes, cocooned in sleeping bags. A man with a trolley was looking for something in a dumpster and a dog was sniffing garbage. A blonde girl was sleeping on a bench, head pillowed on her shoulder. Her jacket lay on the ground. A deep red needle mark was visible on her outstretched arm. Below her lay a used syringe. Yakup took the jacket and gently placed it on top of her.

Back home in Bamiyan, the routine of the day had been so simple. He missed it now. The tea, chores, school, home tasks, stories and sleep. Why did other people have to decide how he should live his life? That was how it had come that he had to leave Afghanistan, but it was no different in Iran or Turkey. Now, and here in Europe, he still had to rely on the mercy of others. Was it an inherent need in people that those with power had to control those without?

Yakup missed his sisters, Grandma Amaya and his mother. He would give anything to see them again. One day he would. He knew it. He knew that he had to leave Greece. It was not a place to stay if he wanted a better future. The homeless with the trolley was pushing his cart in Yakup's direction, stopping at each bin and searching it for scrapped valuables. This, too, was a routine Yakup knew only too well.

He hadn't lost all hope of finding Mariam, though, he was painfully aware of the fact that the more time that passed, the less likely he would be of ever reuniting with her. He imagined that Mariam was waiting for him somewhere, while he was wasting his time, trapped in a place where he was not welcome. And for this reason, he knew that he had to continue his journey. Maybe if he stayed with Elias he could be safe and make a little money to buy his way out. He got up, smiling into the pale winter sky that he knew he shared with Mariam wherever she was as well as his family back home. He felt relieved having hatched a new plan.

He took two steps and then stopped. The homeless with the trolley stopped as well. It was a boy, not a man. They stared at each other for a moment or two.

"Hasan?" the homeless turned and started pushing his belongings away from Yakup, but one of the trolley's wheels became stuck between two slabs of concrete.

Yakup moved towards him and asked again, "Hasan?"

The homeless turned around and confirmed that it was, indeed, Hasan. "What? Yes, I know, I know. I bet you're pleased to see me like this," Hasan hissed.

His light hair had grown long and unkempt. He had a dirty baseball cap on his head instead of the ill-fitting skullcap and his clothes were rags.

"No... No," Yakup assured him.

"Yea, sure... You're probably laughing at poor Hasan for ending up like this," he said.

"Hasan, I'm not..."

"Stop messing with me. You always thought you were better than me, us. You should have left me to drown in the sea."

"What is wrong? What happened to..."

"Stop that. At least have the balls to admit it," Hasan said, spitting on the ground.

"Listen, Hasan, our parting was not good, I admit that, but I have no idea what you're talking about. Please tell me what happened," Yakup said.

Hasan's eyes flickered. "You can see what happened, yes? I lost."

"I don't know what you're talking about... Tell me what happened to the others!"

Hasan appeared confused, then said, "Well, since you ask, yes, I will tell you." Hasan held his hands in front of him in a gesture of deep consideration.

"Nadir quickly went away and tried to get to Italy. The last I heard was that they caught him when they cleared one of the shanty towns where the illegal migrants stay. Maybe he was sent back, but maybe not. Who knows?"

Hasan continued, "Mir's parents came for him at last. They sent him money and he went north with the smugglers. Dani was furious. He thought he and Mir were in it together. You should have seen his rage."

Hasan smiled bitterly, adding, "Yes, furious. He didn't stay long. No. He left Athens to go north. I hope he found Mir eventually."

"What happened to you, Hasan? Why are you like this? They were your friends… I was your friend!"

"I have no friends. No need. Now I have myself."

Hasan turned and pushed his trolley away from Yakup.

57

PROGENY

It was afternoon when he returned to the camp. Rosa was cooking something over a small fireplace.

"There you are. He was worried about you," she said, sending Yakup a relieved smile. "He is in there," she said, pointing towards Elias' living area complete with his dirty mattress, the trolley and the plastic bags scattered around the clearing and all neatly tucked under the plastic tarpaulin of the tree.

Yakup was greeted by Mr Know-it-all who yelped with happiness. Elias was reading and looked up at Yakup.

"How are you feeling?" he asked.

"My eyes are still a bit sore and my throat itches, but I'll survive," Yakup added drily.

"Good; let Rosa have a look at you. She's good at that."

After Rosa had confirmed that the previous night's tear gas exposure had left no lasting damage, he recounted to Elias what he remembered of the night, leaving out Andreas' revelation about Elias' family.

"I want to tell you a story," Elias finally said. Yakup nodded in approval. Mr Know-it-all had placed himself next to Yakup, resting his snout on Yakup's thigh. "As you know, I have a son. Or I used to have a son. Before I was who I am today. I also used to work at the university. I was a professor of philosophy; a job I loved. I was also involved in politics. It took much of my time. I felt responsible for our society. I had to help cure it.

"You know, better than most, than none of us is born truly equal. We are all born into this world alike; tiny, wrinkled and innocent, but if you are born to the upper echelons, things are just easier. There are exemptions, of course, but I wanted to change the status quo.

"As you can see, however, nothing has really changed, especially the social contract between the politicians and the people who chose them to represent their, our, country." The wind rattled the branches above the man, the boy and the dog. Haze from the Aegean Sea blurred the sky. Elias stroked the stubble on his chin. His fingers were callused and cracked.

"I spent most of my time at the university and at political meetings. When I first met my wife, she was a student of mine. She worked part-time for social justice and she was the one who encouraged me to enter politics. She suffered from depression. It was not a new condition and something she battled her entire life. You wouldn't have noticed, though, she appeared happy… She was happy.

"We had decided not to have children. My wife feared that her condition would somehow, genetically or otherwise, paint the world black for any children. I was fine with that…in the beginning. Maybe I thought she would change her mind with age or maybe I would slowly accept it. Time passed, we grew older and I grew impatient. So, I started to pressure her. She wouldn't have it. Always using the same argument: that she would not dare risk imposing such sadness onto an innocent child. But I pleaded and pleaded. I wanted a child. I wanted to be a father. The ultimate responsibility is the creation of life and the responsibility for it. In the end, she gave in.

"We had a son. She adored him. She gave him her all and for a long time, she showed no sign of depression. We were happy, but of course, it didn't last. It was then that I decided to take time away from the university and only focus on politics and family. I spent more time at home. We went to doctors and discussed treatments. She was in an institution for a while. When she came back, she was better, but only for a few months. She was able to hide it from our son. He was only a boy then and she didn't want him to suffer because of her illness. I admired her for her strength, but it was just a mask for what was happening within her. She let it out on me and I tried to take it… I wanted to take it, but sometimes I couldn't.

"The only safe haven for her was our son who, soon enough, proved himself to be her undoing. Her greatest fear was to hurt him with her illness… And when she could no longer take it, life, me, him, everything well, it was he who found her body," Elias concluded, depleted. Yakup fiddled with his fingers. "A chasm opened, then, between my son and me. He blamed me and for some reason I blamed him. Of course, I knew he was just a boy and it was she who did this cowardly act to herself.

"My son and I lived separately, though, in close proximity to one another for years. We learned to live in silence. I quit politics and got my old job at the university back. My son spent most of his time on the streets. I tried to talk to him, but it didn't have any effect. Instead, we fought. It was our only way to communicate. I could see his hate. I could see the contempt in his eyes… and maybe he could see it in mine… We differed in values and political ideas. I believe… hope that he did it to spite me. He came into my study one day with his bags packed and told me goodbye. I didn't try to stop him. I feel ashamed to say that I felt relieved… But I did.

"He came to our home from time to time, always when I was out. I never saw him, but I noticed some items or others would be missing or the drawers disturbed. I buried myself in my work during this period, but in the end, I escaped into the bottle. Then the economic downturn took hold and I lost my job. There were others; younger and stronger. Soon, of course, I couldn't pay my bills.

"One day I was evicted from my own home. I stood there on the street. Everything I had ever had in my life was gone. Days turned into weeks turned into months all out on the streets. I ended up in the gutter with a bottle as my companion. One day I woke up and there was this kind and concerned face staring at me. It was Rosa. She took care of me and I woke up from my nightmare. We soon realised that we weren't the only ones in this situation, and so, decided to help each other to make the most of what time we have left, which is why we are where we are today."

He attempted a smile. The aroma from what Rosa was cooking wafted through the air, whetting their appetites. Mr Know-it-all cosied up to Rosa in the hopes of receiving a reward. Elias and Yakup soon joined Rosa for the meal. It was a vegetable stew of potatoes, carrots, tomatoes and leek on top of steamed rice. When they had eaten and darkness had fallen, Yakup, Elias and Mr Know-it-all sat beneath the tree watching the city lights sparkle and dance. In the distance, the light shone on the Acropolis. Elias rolled a cigarette and coughed.

"What about Mr Know-it-all?" Yakup asked

"My old buddy here? He has been by my side for a long time. He was by my side in the gutter and we'll stick together to the end. Isn't that right, buddy?"

Mr Know-it-all looked at him with devotion and leaned his furry head into Elias.

"And what about your son? Do you know where he is?"

"My son has chosen a different path in life. A dangerous path that he doesn't understand. He believes he can cure the malaise of the system through violence and persecution of the people he does not understand. What he doesn't grasp is that if he and his friends manage to eradicate all foreigners, homosexuals, eccentrics, queers, disabled, deviators and others who in their opinion do not fit in, in the end, it will be their turn. There is always a last carriage of the train… I am afraid that the attacker you have described could be…" Elias' hand stopped scratching Mr Know-it-all's head.

"Andreas told me something, but I refused to believe it… Is your son the man with the rope?" Yakup said.

Elias sighed. "I honestly don't know, but from your description, it could be him… I'm sorry Yakup."

A car screeched in the distance. A dog barked. Mr Know-it-all swung his head in the direction of the new sound. Yakup thought of the man with the rope. The boy who had lost his mother. The fascist who took pleasure in beating another human being for no other reason than his being different.

"Why?" Yakup shook his head in disbelief. "He doesn't even know how similar his story is to mine. Do you think he would treat me differently if he knew my story? Would it matter to him?"

They thought this over while Mr Know-it-all ran off to look for an old bone to chew on. "I don't know Yakup. I cannot tell you how much I loathe his behaviour… their behaviour… I want you to stay here. If you want to, you can stay with us here. Mr Know-it-all adores you… Rosa, too. What do you say?"

"But how and where? I barely make any money and you only have one spot in which to sleep," Yakup said.

"Rosa and I can sleep together," Elias explained. "And you could sleep here with Mr Know-it-all guarding you. You will be safe with us. Instead of bringing money, you bring your youth and energy. We are a bit low on those qualities."

Elias smiled and stuttered, "I don't know what to say."

"Just say 'yes'," Elias said, returning the smile

58

REMINISCENCE

The whole of that spring Yakup stayed with Elias, Rosa and Mr Know-it-all. He helped around the camp, collected food with Elias, assisted Rosa in cooking, played with Mr Know-it-all and slept under the stars and the plastic tarpaulin, dreaming of Mariam. He started reading Elias' books. Slowly in the beginning, but faster and faster as spring turned to summer. First the English ones and then the Greek ones with the help of Elias and Rosa. When Yakup had finished *Oedipus* by Sophocles, Elias fished out the *Iliad* by Homer and so it went. The books were an escape.

Malcolm visited during the summer months when many Athenians departed for the lesser-known islands, lending a hand and staying for days at a time. As the days became cooler, the same people returned to the city and their jobs, or lack thereof. Despite the events that had led Yakup to the camp, those days with Elias, Rosa, Mr Know-it-all and the others were almost carefree.

One morning, Yakup pushed the trolley alone, searching through dumpsters and garbage bins, while Elias slept late. More often than not, or so it seemed to Yakup, Elias seemed to need more and more sleep. Returning with the catch of the day, Yakup quickly distributed the bread and vegetables to the elderly people, each of whom he knew by now. But Elias was not there.

"Good morning. I saved some for you," Yakup said, placing a loaf of bread, some spotty tomatoes and a soggy cucumber on the wobbly milk crate next to Elias, who nodded in approval but did not touch the food.

"Yakup, there's something we need to talk about," he said, sitting up.

"What is it?"

"Greece is old and tired. It is feeble and shaking. It is like an old man returning to infancy, losing his memory and reason. While Greece will last and hopefully rise to be a reasonable country once again, there's not much hope for me," he said, coughing.

Yakup began to make his bed for him. "What do you mean?"

"You are not stupid. This life isn't easy. I may be tough on the outside, but I'm worn on the inside." Elias looked at Yakup, then, and said, "I'm dying, son."

Yakup didn't say anything for a while.

"But what about Mr Know-it-all? You cannot leave him alone. What about the camp, Rosa and the others?"

Yakup's voice was more condemning than he would have wanted. Old man Elias' liver-spotted hands shook a little. He was looking particularly fragile this morning.

"I am not the reason they survive. We are not indispensable. Someone else will take my place and life will go on. That's how it is," he said. His hand rested on his dog's back. "But can't we get you some help? Some medicine and a doctor? There must be someone who can help?" Yakup felt himself panicking.

Elias scratched Mr Know-it-all, who yawned and stretched lazily. Elias' gaze remained on his dog. He sighed.

"There's no one, who can help me. I have had my time, though, it may not have played out as I had expected," he conceded with faraway eyes.

"I can get some medicine. I think there's a doctor in my…"

Elias cut him off, "Yakup, there's no need. I cannot be fixed any more. Look around you. There is no use in remaining alive in this place if I cannot function."

"I can take care of …"

"Enough now," Elias interrupted, his voice rising. Elias continued smoking his cigarette, coughing occasionally.

"I would like your help with something, though," Elias said after a while.

"Of course—anything!"

Elias got up. It was only then that Yakup realised the stiffness with which he carried himself, how it had been a struggle for him to stand up, his use of the tree as a makeshift cane, the coughing that made him short of breath, which were all facets of Elias and dying.

They walked slowly away from the camp and through narrow streets that turned into broader boulevards until they reached a residential area.

"Where are we going?" Yakup asked. Elias didn't say anything but stopped in front of an apartment block in decay.

"What are we doing here?"

Elias started towards the iron gate and tried to push it open, but to no avail.

"A little help here," he said.

Yakup looked around. He could see no one. He stepped up to the gate and pushed it open. A space large enough for a man to pass through materialised. Mr Know-it-all found his own way in and was sniffing around. Elias pushed himself in and stepped over the tall grass and the trash that had collected throughout the small front yard. The door and the windows were shuttered with boards. Despite all this, Elias walked around to the back where the boards nailed to the door were easily pushed aside.

Elias entered. Despite his reservations, Yakup followed. The hallway was dark and damp. Yakup could hear Elias scrabbling somewhere deep within the building.

"Hey! Where are you? I can't see a thing," Yakup whispered.

A beam of light penetrated the darkness. Elias held a torch and said, "This way." He gestured towards the stairs. Some of the steps had rotted away. They entered the remains of a corridor on the second floor. The hinges of a door creaked, but budged with Elias' urging, granting them access to an apartment that had once been beautiful, complete with wooden floors and panels and a high stucco ceiling. The remnants of a chandelier lay cracked where a dining-room table had once stood. The heavy curtains were torn or altogether gone; the windows boarded up. The house had been sealed off for years.

"Come with me," Elias said. He led them into a room with dust-covered books and sat in a leather chair by the desk. "Sit down," he gestured towards an armchair.

"Was this your office?" Yakup asked.

"This was my *life*. This room and these books. The hallway we came through. The rooms we passed. The people who lived here. Now it is nothing, the people, gone. I am here to say goodbye."

There was a framed photo on the desk of a woman with thick, black hair. She was wearing a red dress. Her eyes and smile were directed not at the lens, but at the photographer behind it. A cross was placed next to it. Yakup could not take his eyes away from the woman staring back at him.

"That's my wife," Elias said.

"She is beautiful. I mean she was…"

"She left me right here, in this room." He opened his arms. "But I never left her. She is a coward for what she did, but she, her disease, they are both, also, a reflection of my cowardice."

He held the frame, opened it and took out the photo. He then ran his thick, callused fingers across the surface, barely touching it as if afraid to break it. "She also left my son, and like me, he, too, could never leave her. Somewhere inside of him, she exists. I know it."

"It's time to go," Elias said. He clutched Yakup's shoulder.

Exiting the apartment was like surfacing from a tomb. He was happy to have helped Elias but even happier to leave the decaying crypt behind. The two of them walked in slow silence, accompanied by the dog. The noise from the streets freed Yakup's mind as they made slow, but steady progress back to camp.

They found their site deserted, so, Yakup helped Elias to sit under the tree. He made him a cup of tea and sat with him until he regained his breath.

"I want to see my son one last time. I want him and me to part in peace," he said between fits of coughing. "I want him to understand that what he has become is wrong. I want him to repent. I want the two of you to meet and make peace. I want to do this today. Tomorrow could be too late."

"You want me to speak with the man who attacked me twice? The same one who threatened to kill me if he ever saw me again?"

"Yakup, I am the only one who can remove this threat from you… he is my son after all."

Yakup looked at him, not knowing how to respond, but finally saying, "I don't know if I can do this."

"No matter what my son has become, he will not harm you in front of me."

"You don't understand. You haven't felt his anger. You didn't see me after the attack…" The thought of that dreadful night made Yakup shudder. The rope, the cold pain, the laughing blonde the snarling dog, the whoosh of the rope before impact and the smell of tar stuck to skin.

"You're right, I don't know his physical anger, but I know his psyche. I am his father," Elias said.

Yakup thought of his own father and how he would never disobey him. It would bring shameto the family. In Afghanistan, you had to respect your father and your family. Yakup was not sure if it was the same here. Most of what he thought he knew about Europe had been completely turned upside down.

"I will help you," Yakup finally said. "How do we find him?"

"We go to him. When he left his childhood home, he left a note with an address. I never brought it with me, but I took it from my desk today," Elias said, struggling to get up. Yakup offered him an arm. He took it, shaking. The effort caused a coughing fit that lasted for minutes. His energy was leaving him; he was turning pale, almost green.

"Maybe it is better if we wait," Yakup said.

"My son… I have to see my, uh, son," he said as he tried to rise again.

"You need rest. We can do this tomorrow," Yakup said.

"Tomorrow is too late. We must go, now," Elias whispered feebly. He tried again. Yakup could see that he could not reason with him.

"Can your son not come to you?" he asked.

"How?"

"Well, we can ring him."

"I don't have a phone number. We must go there."

"You cannot go. You need to rest. I will not risk your life for this. I can get him for you. Where is he?" As soon as the words were out of his mouth, he realised the stupidity of what he had offered.

"Would you do that?" Elias regarded him with watery eyes.

"I… I guess so."

"Then you must take this," he pulled out a folded slip of paper with an address, a pen and the photo of his wife that had, until recently, rested, undisturbed, on his desk. Elias sat leaning against the tree with his eyes closed. Mr Know-it-all lay by his side. Yakup stared at the paper. He knew the place, but he didn't know if his feet would carry him there. Elias lowered his head and breathed heavily. He was asleep.

59

VISITOR

It didn't take Yakup long to find the building where Nicos lived, but it did take him some time to figure out what to do. He could not just go in and ring the doorbell. That was too dangerous. He could wait for him to enter or exit the building, but that could take ages.

He finally decided that he had to meet him on the street, in public, in order to convey the message to him about his father.

As soon as he had made up his mind, he could hear his heart drumming blood through his veins, and momentarily considered returning to camp and lying to Elias that his son was not home. He decided against it. He salvaged a piece of paper from a bin and wrote a message. He went to the front door of the apartment block and pressed a doorbell at random.

"Yes?" a voice scratched through the intercom.

"Newspapers," Yakup said in a matter-of-fact voice. The door buzzed open. He pushed it hard and stepped into the narrow hallway. Nicos lived on the fourth floor. Yakup slowly ascended the stairs. He pulled the note and the photo from his pocket, and once on the third floor, tiptoed up the final flight of stairs. The door on the left was the entrance to the lion's den. Yakup felt nauseated as he approached the brown wooden door. Silent as a cat. Ears trying to catch any sound that might escape from inside the flat. He moved closer to the door. One step. Another. He just had to lift his hand to knock on the door. Was the man in there? Was the rope? And the blond-haired man and woman? Yakup moved his head closer to the door. He tried to look in through the peephole, but couldn't see anything. He laid an ear against the brown wood and listened. He thought he heard a noise, but wasn't sure. He closed his eyes and felt the life behind the door.

The noise of a door opening on the ground floor startled him. He quickly put the note and the photo on the doormat and knocked. Yakup bolted down the steps, moving quickly. The plan was to meet Nicos outside. He reached the third floor. Nothing happened. On the second floor, he stopped again. Still nothing. Someone was climbing the stairs. Yakup restrained his breathing with difficulty. The person was at the second-floor landing now. It was the blond man. Yakup realised the danger he was in, but it was too late. There was nowhere to go but back up. Yakup turned for the third floor, taking the stairs two at a time and kept moving. A door opened. A slim dark-haired man stepped out in front of Yakup. First with a surprised look. Then a vicious smile. A strong pair of hands grabbed him. He pushed, struggled and kicked, but to no avail.

"What is this? Are you paying home visits?" Petros said and laughed. "Or did you invite him home, mate?"

"What are you doing here?" Nicos said.

"Your father…" Yakup ventured.

"The creep has a voice," the blond interrupted and shoved Yakup against the wall.

"Easy now, Petros. I want to know what he's doing here."

"Hell yeah! Maybe he wants to rob us. Revenge. Is that why you're here, you son of a whore dog?" Petros pushed Yakup again. His eyes glimmered with hate.

"Stop, eh? Let him talk."

"It's your father," Yakup stuttered.

"If you say anything about my father, I'll kill you after a long prelude of pain, do you understand?" Nicos said in a calm voice.

"Your father is dying!"

"My father is already dead."

"How would you even know his father? Why would his father even take note of someone like you?" Petros asked.

"I'm telling the truth. He is ill. He sent me here… to get you. We went to his old home… He said goodbye to the house and his wife… your mother." Yakup said.

"Now I know that you are lying. My mother is dead."

"I know," Yakup said. "He told me." Only then did he remember the photo. "There." He pointed towards the grey mat. Nicos looked down cautiously, then bent to pick up the photograph. He examined it for a few moments.

"What's wrong, mate?" Petros said.

"I'll take it from here," Nicos said.

"What?"

"Just leave, Petros."

"You can't be serious. Do you honestly believe this Paki?"

"What is it you don't understand?" Nicos shot Petros a dangerous look. "Now go."

"You're making a mistake, mate,"

"I don't care what you think."

Petros let go of Yakup and started down the stairs. Nicos waited until the ground floor door had opened and closed.

"If you are trying to play me, you will regret it. I am sure you understand that. Now, tell me what you know." He stood in front of Yakup, tall and with his black hair hanging loose.

"Your father sent me here to get you. He is ill. He said he has to talk to you before… before it's too late.

Nicos stepped back into the apartment, took his jacket, slammed the door shut, and pushed Yakup in front of him down the stairs.

60

TWO SONS

They walked in silence, crisscrossing streets and squares. Nicos, a few steps behind Yakup.

The camp grew visible from a distance. Yakup hoped that Rosa and the others were home by now, but to his dismay, there was no such luck. Instead, he heard the barking of Mr Know-it-all and relaxed a bit. At least he was not alone any more.

"This way," he said, pushing through the bushes.

Elias was in the same position Yakup had left him in: eyes closed, back against the tree. Mr Know-it-all was sitting next to him. Elias seemed small compared to the large, black dog. Yakup knelt by him and took his hand.

"Can you hear me?" he whispered.

Elias opened his eyes and forced a vague smile on his dry lips. "Don't worry about me," he said.

"He is here," Yakup told him.

Nicos was standing just inside the thicket, watching them.

"Son!"

Nicos did not move.

"Dad."

"Good to see you, son. Come here."

Nicos stepped forward. He stopped. Took another step. Stopped again.

"Sit down," Elias said.

Nicos knelt next to his father.

Mr Know-it-all started to growl.

"Easy, old pal, easy."

The dog went silent.

"Nicos, my child," Elias, began looking at his son through hazy eyes. Nicos stared at his father, through years of what living on the streets does to a person. A man.

"How long has it been… three years?" Elias said.

"Four."

"Four then. How are you?"

"How I am? Why do you want to know?"

"Can a father not ask this of his son while teetering on the edge of death?"

"What do you mean?"

"I'm dying."

Elias opened his frail hand and reached out to Nicos.

"Yakup here has been a great help these past few months. I met him one day when he came crashing into my home. Someone was chasing him. He didn't know why. He just knew that if they caught him, they would hurt him. They had done that before. He left his home and travelled a long way to find security. I wish he could, but you and your friends beat him up. For no reason, Nicos. You must…"

Elias stopped and coughed violently. Nicos patted his father's back. The coughing stopped but left the old man with tears in his eyes, which traversed the maze on his face.

"We should bring you to a hospital," Nicos said.

"No hospital can help me, not any longer."

"They can try. I will make them."

"No," Elias gasped, looking into the dark eyes of his son.

"There is something, I want you to know. I didn't know what to do after your mother died. I know I didn't always do the right thing. I wasn't the father you needed. I was devastated when she took her life. We both were. There was nothing we could do to stop it. It was her choice."

"You drove her to that point," Nicos' voice rang out, cold with rage. He wiped a tear from the corner of his eye. "Walls are thin, *dad*. I heard you fighting. You caused her so much pain."

"Oh, my son! You were young. There's so much you don't, know.

"I know what I heard and what I saw. That's enough for me."

"Fragments taken out of context, blended with the vivid imagination of a child. It can distort the truth and shape it into monsters. No, my son, your mother suffered from depression; ever since she was a girl. There were times before you came into this world when I was on the verge of leaving her. I never could though; I loved her too much…" he paused to cough. Leaves tumbled from the branches above, leaving the tree to shiver in its nudity with its bony branches stretching for the sky.

"Her sadness stopped for a while when you were born, but it never disappeared. In the role of mother, she managed to bury it deep inside her. She controlled it. But it was there. Always waiting and when it resurfaced, it had gathered strength. Your mother and I worked together to make her better. We didn't want to involve you. You were a child. I tried to help her, but it was not enough. And in the end, the pain was too much for her."

"No, that was not how it happened. You terrorised her. You were jealous of me—you wanted her for yourself."

"Son, I'm telling you the truth. Think!"

Nicos' confused mind went back to his childhood. Days in short pants, bruised knees and untied laces, running home on summer afternoons and playing in the garden with the neighbours' kids; jumping the stairs to get to his mother and entering the apartment filled with happiness, but only to see his mother red-eyed in the kitchen, staring out the window; remembering the doctor talking to his father; hearing the arguments muffled from the other side of the wall and distorting the truth in the darkness of the night. Blinded by love for his mother.

"It can't be…" Nicos said. He started to sob.

"I'm so sorry, son. We should have told you, but then it happened and it was too late. I'm sorry. I was drowning in my own selfish sorrow and forgot my responsibility. Can you forgive me?" Elias asked, tears running down his cheeks.

"Dad… I always thought, it was… I never… I'm sorry…"

For a while, the two, father and son, held each other. Light was slanting through the trees by now and the evening cold was beginning to settle.

"Yakup, come here," Elias said.

"Why do you want him here?" Nicos flared.

"He is my son, too," Elias said, taking Yakup's hand and pulling him closer. "I do not want my two sons to fight. Now, please promise me that the fighting ends here."

"I cannot promise…"

"Do you want to deprive a dying father of his last wish? Promise me. Please, my son. Promise me…" Elias coughed violently.

A wheezing noise rattled with each breath. He pulled their hands together and rested them on his chest. Nicos' fingers were cold under Yakup's touch. Faintly, Elias' heartbeat within its frail ribcage. For a while, they sat like that until the pounding faded away and the wheezing stopped.

61

FEAR

The yellow leaves rattled and danced in the small clearing.

"What should we do?" Yakup eventually asked. Their hands still rested on top of each other. Nicos looked up as if he had just been startled by a bad dream.

"What?"

"I said,' what are we going to do now?'" He looked at Elias between them.

"Oh!" Nicos blinked and slid his hand away from Yakup's. He stared into the wrinkled face of his father for a moment.

"What *you* should do is to get up and get away. This has nothing to do with you," Nicos said, glaring at Yakup. The tears had dried and the old Nicos was back.

"But your father wanted us to make peace. You heard him."

"You and I are not friends and never will be. You used an old, confused man to your benefit and now that he is gone you should be, too."

"I didn't use him. You can ask Rosa. He wanted me here and you weren't there for him… What kind of son does that to his father? You blamed him for the death of your mother, but he did all he could to keep his family together. You turned against your father. That is disrespectful," Yakup said. Sudden fury and courage had come over him.

"You heard what he said: *I* am his son. That means *I* will stay by his side."

Nicos swung at Yakup, but he dodged the blow. "You promised your father peace, let us respect his wishes," Yakup continued invigorated. They were standing in front of each other now. Yakup could feel every muscle tense in his body as adrenalin infused him.

"I gave you a chance, *boy*. I want to keep my word, but how can I when you broke your promise by being present? If you had listened to me, we would not be in this situation, would we?" Nicos towered half a head over Yakup. Yakup's fighting experience was limited to the playground in Bamiyan and TV wrestling shows. Nicos had probably fought more fights than he could count.

"I do not want to fight you. It's disrespectful," Yakup said.

"You don't have to fight. Let's call it a punishment," Nicos said, and with that, he was flying at Yakup. The boy moved quickly to the side and avoided the attack. Nicos stumbled over his father's stiff legs and fell to the ground, but was up in an instant.

"Nicos, your father is lying dead next to us. He deserves better. He deserves that we bury him in peace."

"Shut up you pathetic parasite. This is your last chance. Get out of my sight!"

It was at that moment when Yakup felt something within him shift on its axis. Sometimes one is exposed to something so extreme that it is impossible to ignore it. An action that stirs and rattles you; it pulls your entire universe out of place. An action that demands a reaction. For Yakup that moment was now.

"No!" Yakup said. "I live here. If you don't want to look at me, you go."

"What? Ha… Are you completely mad?" Nicos said, scowling

"Either you respect Elias' last wish, or you leave."

Nicos' thin, white lips were pressed together. The vein in his temple throbbed. He took a step towards Yakup who held his ground. Nicos stopped. There was a deep growling noise. It was Mr Know-it-all. Nicos glared at him. The black dog growled, baring his teeth at Nicos.

"Get your dog out of here or he will suffer the same destiny as you," Nicos said, in a high and thin voice.

"Mr Know-it-all is *not* mine. He is his *own*. What he does is *his* business," Yakup said.

Nicos drew a deep breath, gathered himself and appeared to weigh the situation. He knew it was a risk to take on both the dog and the Afghan boy. Both dog and boy were determined to stand their ground.

"Fine. I'll leave then," Nicos said. Yakup was surprised and relieved, but he did not let his guard down so easily nor did Mr Know-it-all. Nicos' chin sank to his chest as he stared at his father's body.

"Let me say goodbye to him," he said. Yakup looked from Nicos to Elias. He nodded his assent. Nicos bent over his father and rested for a few seconds with his knee on the ground.

Things happened very fast after that. Nicos picked up a rock. It struck Mr Know-it-all, who yelped in pain. Blood trickled from his soft black snout. Confused with the sudden pain, he looked up at Yakup looking for an explanation. Then a hard kick slammed into his neck and he fell over. Yelping. Panting. Not understanding the sudden pain or the attack. He whimpered and looked at Yakup, who leaned over the injured dog. Mr Know-it-all tried to get up but failed.

"Easy, my friend," Yakup whispered to him.

"Didn't I tell you to leave my country? Why don't you listen?" Nicos drove his boot into Yakup's stomach. The air left him. He struggled to breathe and stumbled to his feet. His lungs pulled in air as he coughed and looked up at Nicos. What he saw was a savage with hair hanging lank from his scalp, eyes blazing with hate.

"You parasite," Nicos said through clenched teeth. He hurled himself at Yakup. Instinctively, the boy doubled up, arms up to protect his head, but the attack did not come. Instead, there was a scream. Yakup looked up and saw Mr Know-it-all atop the screaming man, his jaws locked silently on Nicos' face.

"Help… help me!" Nicos pleaded. Yakup made eye contact with the man. The dog growled and tore at Nicos' flesh. Seconds that felt like an eternity passed. Then Yakup acted.

"Mr Know-it-all! Stop! Enough!" he yelled. The dog turned to look at Yakup. Blood was everywhere.

Nicos' fingers landed on a rock, which connected Mr Know-it-all's skull, just above the ear. The dog let go, dragging himself away and yelping in agony. Dark, thick blood spread over the fur of his throat.

Nicos got to his feet with some effort. The dog had left deep, ugly gashes on his chin and cheek. Nicos' mouth hung open; his hair was wet with blood. He looked at Yakup, swaying back and forth. Yakup had found a thick stick and held it threateningly in front of him. Nicos brought a hand up over his face, feeling his injuries with horror.

Yakup knew he could end the matter once and for all by raising the stick and following through, seeking vengeance for Michael and so many others, but that was not him; he was not like the man in front of him. He let the stick fall to the ground, where it landed with a thud on the yellow leaves. He stared at Nicos who stared back, registering that the fight was over. Slowly he turned and staggered away from his dead father and the Afghan boy.

Yakup turned to Mr Know-it-all. He was lying on his side, half-hidden under a bush.

"Mr Know-it-all… I'm so, so sorry," Yakup said, tears filling his eyes. The dog's tail moved up and down and he licked Yakup's hand. "I'm here, old pal," he said what he thought Elias might have said. He found an uninjured spot on the dog's body that he could pat and did so. Yakup sat there for a while, weeping until a shudder went through the animal, his mouth fell open and his tail went limp. The yellow leaves turned rust-coloured red.

62

LEARNING TO SWIM

The plastic tarpaulin whipped and snapped in the evening wind. Yakup had lost Elias and Mr Know-it-all. He had lost his family, Mariam, the Afghan band of brothers, Michael and now this. Yakup wrapped Mr Know-it-all in the blanket and pulled Elias' body onto his mattress covering him with a blanket. He knew that he had to leave.

Yakup walked without purpose through the darkening city streets. He was in a part of town he didn't recognise, but he didn't care. He barely registered his surroundings; the sleeping bags and blankets that cocooned the homeless, who slept on top of ripped cardboard boxes, layered in all their clothes. He wished for oblivion but couldn't find it.

When he was a child and had felt hurt or slighted, he had sulked, cried or screamed the feeling away. The hurt would go away and he would soon feel happy again. Maybe the memories of his childhood were altered. The brain is an extraordinary organ that can choose to keep certain memories and leave others blissfully behind. He wished that his brain could suppress the events of his journey.

He crossed a small bridge. A train rushed under him screaming into the night. He knew of others like him who had ended their journeys when the trauma and despair had become too much to bear. He walked next to the railway under the bridge. His stomach hurt and his mouth was dry. Grandma Amaya, his mother and the girls were far away, and seemingly, from a different time. Had they even existed? He loved Mariam, but had she loved him back?

A rat crossed the wet rails and disappeared into the bushes. He picked up a rock and threw it aimlessly in the direction of the rat.

Elias had been good to him and Mr Know-it-all had saved his life, but Yakup had let Mr Know-it-all down. He had let his family down; left them without a man in a male-dominated world. Maybe they thought he was dead, and maybe that was the best. Then the darkness inside of him would go away for good.

The night didn't bother Yakup. He was shivering without sensing it. The railway was in front of him. An iron snake twisting its way first into the Balkans and then throughout the remainder of Europe. *Would he be more welcomed there?* he wondered.

He breathed in the wet, moist air of the Athens night in an attempt to vanquish the pain in his gut. He could hear a distant train approaching.

Yakup blinked. He could feel the cold now. The soft rain was doing its best to soak him. His ears registered a faint shrieking of heavy steel wheels. His eyes and face were wet. He didn't know if it was tears or the faint rain, but it did not matter. Nothing mattered. He was tired. Was this what he had expected? What any of them had expected? He could end the journey here. The gravel around the rails shook faintly. The shriek of steel grew louder. A dim light was getting brighter.

He was invisible next to the rails in the darkness of night. He could see the lights from Acropolis, the city of Gods, towering above Athens in whose streets he was invisible except for those who saw him not as a boy, but as an aberration. A couple of steps could liberate him; set him free and release him from the pain. The hissing and screeching grew louder and louder. The light grew brighter. Just a few more seconds and it would all be over. His hair and skin were soaked.

The bright light of the train was a fireball hurtling towards him. He thought of the sun over Bamiyan and remembered a sunny day by the turquoise Bande-e-Amir lakes. A scrawny boy on his father's naked shoulder, a rope tied about his waist. The sun warm, the water cold.

"Don't worry," his father tells him soothingly. "This is where my brothers and I learned to swim, where your grandfather and his father before him learned to swim."

He hangs inches above the cold water.

"When I set you free in the water you must not panic," his father says. "The lake is our family. It is your friend. You must get to know each other," his father says, smiling and tugging at the thick rope. "This is the same rope that held me when my father taught me how to swim. It ties the family together. The first time I tried to swim, I didn't know how. It takes courage and practice, remember that."

The boy screams and tries to hold onto his father's shoulder. The man throws him in. The cold water engulfs him. He loses all sense of direction, gulps water, not air. Panic takes hold of him. Then he feels the tug of the rope and suddenly he is on the surface. He coughs and splutters saliva and lake water. His eyes are red.

"Now move your legs up and down. Hold your arms in front of you. Just as we practiced at home," his father's voice cuts through the water in his ears. He tries to remember the movements they practiced on the dry plateau in front of the cave. His mind turns to the creatures lurking in the depths beneath him

"That's good. Now move your arms," he instructs. The boy can only see water and wonders if the voice could be praising someone else.

"That's it, good job!" his father's voice trills with pride. The boy turns his head and swallows a big gulp of water. He coughs violently and almost panics again, but a tug on the rope reminds him that he is still safely moored to the father he adores.

All that summer they went to the lake almost every weekend. Each time Yakup improved his swimming and by the end of the summer, he felt safe.

One sunny afternoon, when the summer was nearing its end, he sat with his father by the shore of the lake. They had both been swimming and their bodies were aching from the effort.

"You have done well, my son. Each time we have been here you have improved. The training has made you a good swimmer. You will never forget this," his father said.

The boy nodded and smiled.

"What did you learn?" his father asked.

"I learned how to swim," the boy replied, head lifting proudly.

"You learned how to swim, yes. What else?"

"What do you mean, Baba?"

His father looked at him and repeated his question. The boy thought for a while and tried to answer.

"Well, at the beginning of the summer, I feared the water. Now, at the end of the summer, I like the water."

His father smiled at him.

"Good. Anything else?"

"Hmm. I learned how to swim… and to understand the way water behaves. When I'm in the water, I feel free… so… maybe… I should not fear what I don't understand, but instead try to understand it, because when I understood what the water was I learned how to handle it," the boy said.

"Mmhmm", his father said and put his arm around his son. Two teenage boys were racing the last of many swan pedal boats towards the shore. The shadow of the mountain was falling on the mosque on the other side of the lake and women were packing up for the day.

The train screamed past Yakup in the wet Athens night. The screeching wheels shot fireworks at him. Gravel danced. The train was gone. He was alive.

Yakup turned around and stared into the darkness, away from the tracks. He ran through the bushes and back into the dimly lit streets.

63

LAST WORDS

The sun was rising in a haze over Athens. The lazy streets glittered from the overnight rain. Kind souls followed a daily routine of setting down food for stray cats and dogs in their usual spots. Workers poured hot coffee into mugs, preparing for the day ahead.

Yakup had passed out on a bench at some point in the early hours, impervious to danger, not even knowing where he was exactly. His mind had been too busy trying to figure out the best way to leave Athens. In the daylight, however, he recognised that he was in *Junkie Alley* near the old university. A couple of strung-out kids slept haphazardly on a bench next to him. One of the two sleeping men had a brown beard and red scratches across his face. The other one was completely covered by a blanket. Yakup could smell them. The remains of a souvlaki kebab roll and some sour milk sat next to the bearded junkie. Yakup's stomach ached from hunger. He quietly lifted the milk and sniffed it. His belly churned and he put it back. He picked up the souvlaki. The bread was soft and moist, the little meat that was left was dry and there were hardly any tomatoes or onions left. His belly screamed for a bite. With his eyes shut tight, he chewed, albeit only after removing a strand of wiry brown hair.

He finished the sad souvlaki and got up. He wanted to leave Greece as soon as possible, but there were a few things he had to do first. He walked doggedly back towards the camp all the while worried that Rosa and the others might suspect him of wrongdoing. He hesitated as he closed in on the camp. He could see movement beyond the bushes and hear the murmur of voices. He looked from side to side but saw no one. He quietly walked into Rosa's small shelter, but she was not there. He continued to Elias' shelter. Rosa sat in his chair; eyes closed. She looked fragile and smaller than usual in her big jacket, her wispy hair an unnatural purple in the grey morning light.

"I was so worried about you," Rosa said, her eyes still closed.

"I… I'm sorry," Yakup said.

Rosa regarded him gravely, then gestured to the mattress that Yakup had slept on more nights than he could remember. He sat down and told her what had happened. When he finished the old woman had tears in her eyes.

"We buried Mr Know-it-all last night. We had a short ceremony in memory of our friend earlier this morning. People paid their respects," she said and wept some more.

"Rosa there's more I have to tell…"

"Before you start, I want to tell you something," Rosa interrupted him. "We have discussed among ourselves and we all know how dear you were to… to him. So, we decided that you should have the option of moving into his place. You can stay as long as you like," she said rather ceremoniously, but her smile was sweet.

"I don't know…" he stuttered.

Rosa looked at him in surprise. Then she lowered her eyes and nodded. "I see… This is probably not a place for someone your age anyway."

The camp was quiet without Mr Know-it-all to liven things up. Yakup could see a fresh pile of earth behind one of the bushes.

"It is not that I don't want to stay with you, but I must leave Athens," Yakup said, staring at the ground. "I am not destined to be here."

He looked up at Rosa. She held Elias' grey sixpence hat in her lap. She worried the edges with her bony fingers.

"Where will you go?" she asked.

"I will go to England. One of my father's brothers lives there. I should have left earlier, but I found it was easier to stay here, among my friends, Elias and Mr Know-it-all… all of you made it easier to stay here, but this isn't my final destination. It never was. I know that now."

Rosa pushed herself up. She went over to Yakup and embraced him. She was remarkably strong for her fragile appearance.

"He left something for you," Rosa said, pulling out an envelope from one of Elias' many plastic bags and handing it to Yakup who sat back down on the bed and ripped the envelope open.

Dear Yakup,

When you read this, I will no longer exist as a physical presence on this earth.

Whether I exist as another entity is only for me to know. What we do know is that you still exist, and I hope, will continue to do so for many years to come. I have won and lost the most important people in my life. Towards the end, I almost gave up. My departure from the world was not, because I gave up, but because I got up and continued to live. I left with a clear mind. Maybe not with a clean conscience. I tried to seek repentance for my mistakes. By now you know, if it was granted to me. I hope it was. These final words to you, my friend, I write, to urge you to choose life.

You have told me your story. I will never fully understand the life you have lived so far, nor the loss and pain you have suffered, but I feel I know you well. Evil exists in mankind. You know this better than I. You also know that good people exist. I choose to believe that most of us are the latter. You are a good person, Yakup. Never forget that and never be someone else. You have conquered more challenges in your short life than most of us will face in an entire lifetime. Yet you can still smile, you still treat others with respect, you still have retained your sense of dignity and you have an appetite for life that drives you further than most others I have met. There are few I admire, but you, Yakup, are chief among them.

I foresee a better future for you. A future with your uncle, who you must go and find. In the hope that you will listen to the last scribbles from this old man, I have left you a small token that can facilitate the next part of your journey. The end of Europa has no room for you, Yakup. I am afraid that my blood is cold. Go north and find what you are searching for.

Your friend, always,
*   Elias.*

There was something else in the envelope. It was a stack of Euro notes. He stared at them for a while and then slipped them into his pocket.

64

BEING CHINESE

He had often walked by the small shop but had never stepped inside. Not that he didn't want to, but simply because the opportunity hadn't presented itself. It was a small shop that sold electrical appliances. It was nondescript, anonymous. No one really knew how long it had existed nor did they care, but the little shop had something more to it than met the eye. The owner, a bespectacled man from Afghanistan, who always wore the same white shirt and grey trousers, had made it his business to provide hopeful refugees and migrants with the means to exit Greece. He worked meticulously from the adjacent room. His shop was thick with the smell of food during lunch and dinner. It was brought to him by his wife. Out in the street, young Afghan men kept watch from the nearby shops. As soon as anyone suspicious approached, someone would ring the owner and that was how the small shop stayed below the radar.

Yakup did not excite the young men's suspicion. He simply went into the shop where he gave, in the form of payment, most of Elias' gift to the bespectacled man in the white shirt and grey trousers. A week later Yakup's identity had changed to that of one Jin Tian: a Chinese tourist who had dated entry stamps from when he arrived in Greece in his 'new' passport.

Yakup didn't have enough of Elias' notes to both pay for the fake documents and buy a plane ticket, though, which led him to travel to Brindisi in Italy via Ferry out of Patras.

While he waited for his new passport, Yakup, or Jin as was now his official name, spent hours near the Acropolis observing Chinese tourists. He spent a long time in the many Chinese shops on Sofokleous Street, near the soup kitchen, until one of the shop owners had to ask him to get out unless he actually wanted to buy something. Befuddled, he bought a

Chinese children's book and left the shop.

On the day of his departure, there was still one more thing he had to do: say goodbye to Malcolm. He had looked for him at all his usual spots: Monastiraki Square where he used to play music, the soup kitchen in Sofokleous Street, Plateia Amerikis where many Africans lingered, the squats and the bridges where the two of them had regularly slept before Yakup had moved to the elder's camp. He greeted those he knew without explaining why he needed to find his friend, but Malcolm was nowhere to be found. It was with a heavy heart that Yakup boarded the bus with his small sport bag, having left a note with Rosa that she was to give to Malcolm should he ever return to the camp.

He had made sure that he was well-groomed and looked as respectable as he could despite his limited resources. He had bought new second-hand clothes as he had outgrown his pants and shoes, and so, it was about time he got new clothes. He entered the bus and saw others waving goodbye to friends and family. He looked through the window hoping to see Malcolm. With a pang of sadness, he returned his gaze to the frayed blue material on the seat just in front of him. Athens rushed by the dusty windowpane and was soon replaced by a rural landscape. He was again embarking on a journey and leaving Athens as but another stain on history.

Part V

Calais

65

NORTH

Whether it was luck or simply that Yakup made a good Chinese tourist, he could not say, but his arrival to Italy was unceremonious and free of hassle, especially from the border patrol officer.

And so, he suddenly found himself in yet another country. He could stay in Italy, but there had been stories among the migrants in Greece that Italy did not offer people like him a better life and he would have to start from scratch again. He didn't speak the language nor did he have any contacts. No, Yakup's mind was set on one country: England. The country he and Mariam had talked about. The place where they had imagined a future together.

He boarded a train in the Italian port city of Brindisi and from there saw landscape racing past him as the train sped farther and farther north. He put his hand over the passport that lay in a zipped inner pocket of his jacket. He had made it a habit, every so often, to tap his chest lightly to ensure that his Chinese identity was still with him.

The train reached the French border after a long ride, and again, nothing happened. In fact, he wasn't even sure when they crossed it. They reached Paris in the early hours of the morning. Yakup spent a few cold hours in the City of Light, warming himself by a cylindrical heater in Gare du Nord train station, which stood opposite a couple of scruffy men. One of them offered Yakup some food. Workers cleaned the station in the early hours, preparing it for another busy day. Soon, the place echoed with people streaming on and off trains. Yakup already had his ticket for Calais and boarded the morning train. They soon slipped through the suburbs of Paris and into the flat scenic fields of the northern country.

The steel wheels screeched to a halt around midday. The cold air in Calais was moist and the smell of the sea caught Yakup's attention—a fresh infusion of hope. It was hard for him to believe that it had been so easy to get to the north coast of France. Yakup walked in the direction of the water and smiled to himself. He passed the city hall with its fairy-tale turrets and well-kept garden and continued through almost empty streets; the shops and restaurants closed. He passed a square ripped open by road construction. It was colder than in Athens and Yakup's clothes couldn't keep the damp chill at bay.

He crossed a cobblestone pier riddled with small hills of fishing nets. Small skiffs lay swaying below on a mud-covered bottom. The tides had to be the culprit. There was a fortress, and behind that, two blue iron cranes standing idle next to a large blue and white ferry. That would be Yakup's access to England.

The sea was covered in fog. From somewhere deep inside the grey soup, ferries bellowed like whales in a vast sea trying to locate each other's positions. The sandy coast was dotted with small colourful huts used by summer guests. Rows of wooden groynes protected the beach from erosion. Screaming seagulls took off as Yakup approached and landed again once he had passed. He walked for some time, not knowing where to or why. The row of beach huts ended. He passed a concrete bunker. On the dunes, dry grass swayed back and forth. Yakup climbed one of the dunes and stared into the distance. Somewhere out there, buried in the heavy, grey carpet, was England, his uncle, Mariam and his future. It was impossible to see where the water ended and the sky began. He suddenly felt a strong urge to swim. The only swimming he had done since leaving Bamiyan was on the crossing to Greece. He tightened his muscles, closed his eyes and imagined himself in the soft water. He could almost feel the comfortable repetitiveness of the strokes, his mind focusing only on the simple task of swimming.

The contour of the horizon was growing darker and dusk enveloped Yakup with a chilly breath. He started back along the beach. A ferry was leaving the port in the distance. Small waves lapped against the sand. He came to a road with a large apartment complex. A recent fire had tainted the facade of one of the blocks. A distant memory of war-torn buildings in Kabul flashed past Yakup's eyes. Lights in the windows bore witness to lives lived within the blackened concrete.

He had expected to bump into Afghans or other refugees upon his arrival. But with darkness upon him and no such luck, he found himself without a place to sleep. He decided to walk back along the beach and look for shelter, He noticed that one of the beach huts had a broken window. He looked around and could see nothing but the dark sea, the curves of the dunes and the apartment blocks. He didn't want to break into someone's place, but it was getting too cold for a moral argument.

He climbed in through the broken window. The small hut was used for storage. There was a deck chair, an umbrella and a stack of fishing nets. In the closet, he found a can of oats, some canned tuna and a bottle of a sweet-tasting liquid. He gulped down a few sips. After his simple meal, he felt warmer, a bit dizzy and more at ease with the situation. Yakup laid himself on the fishing net, pleased with his now mounting victories, which, after all, had seen him travel, alone, from Afghanistan to the northern coast of France. He was so close to his goal. It was impossible to miss. All he had to do was to aim at the right spot and put the ball in the back of the net. Easy.

66

SHATTER

Yakup woke up with an aching head and a sticky mouth. He grabbed the bottle next to him but decided against drinking from it as he caught the scent of the sweet liquid. Instead, he climbed out of the beach hut where he was greeted by a cold wind. He walked in the direction of town, searching for something to drink or eat. He happened upon two fellow countrymen who offered him water and pointed him in the direction of the parking lot where daily food distribution by private organisations took place. Calais wasn't a big city, so it didn't take Yakup long to find the place. The parking lot was surrounded by warehouses, silos, cranes and a few flat-roofed houses. It was empty save for a group of seagulls.

It was too early for lunch and Yakup knew that the nagging of his belly would wear off soon enough, so, he waited for his next meal, electing to, instead, explore the adjacent port. He needed a boat to cross the sea and the obvious choice was one of the large steel ferries that moved in and out of the port one after the other. Maybe his streak of luck would continue and he could board a ferry immediately. He smiled to himself as he walked out of the parking lot.

He didn't get far before his heart skipped a beat. There was a group of six people sitting around a small fire on the other side of the road. They were Afghan-looking boys and men. Except for one of them—a girl. Mariam.

He blinked and rubbed his eyes. Mariam's hair was hidden under a beanie. Her almond eyes looked bored. *She looks like a boy*, Yakup thought. But there was no doubt in his mind—it was Mariam.

She lifted her eyes and caught Yakup's eyes. For a moment she looked at him without recognition, but only for a moment and then she saw Yakup. Her bored eyes grew soft for a second. Those stubborn and fierce almond eyes that Yakup had missed so terribly much, but the look he saw in her eyes now was of fear, of defeat. She held his gaze for only a second longer, then she lowered her eyes and glanced at the boys and men around her. She whispered something to one of them. He nodded and she got up. Mariam didn't walk up to Yakup, but instead, turned the corner of a building. Yakup followed.

"Mariam. Is it really you?" he asked as he came around the corner and saw her.

She stood there. They stared at each other. It had been almost a year.

"I looked for you," Yakup said. Mariam nodded.

"Where were you?" he asked. A gust of wind pulled Mariam's jacket open. She quickly pulled it tight as if to hide something.

"I…I thought you were dead," she said. Her eyes flickered. "I had hoped you were not, but I thought…"

He took a step towards her. She withdrew and looked over her shoulder.

"I'm not dead, Mariam. I was looking for you in Istanbul. What happened to you?"

"I managed, Yakup. Without you."

"What do you mean?"

"Please, Yakup. Be careful. He is dangerous…"

She looked beyond Yakup's shoulder and her face regained its numb and bored expression. Yakup turned and saw someone approaching. A familiar character. Someone he had never expected to see again. Rashid. The same Rashid that was once just a chubby kid he knew a whole other lifetime ago; the same one who let his pain turn into anger and poison other boys. Rashid, the child of a family wounded by war. Rashid, the son of Afghanistan.

Despite their closeness in age, Rashid had shed most of his puppy fat, grown thicker facial hair than most and now had a body that was more mass and muscle than fat. His eyelids were still heavy, and his mouth hung open.

"Rashid?" Yakup said. He was still not sure that the man in front of him was the boy from Bamiyan. He moved a step closer to Yakup who was painfully aware of how small he was compared to the man in front of him.

"So, this is where you're hiding, eh? How long have you been here?" Rashid asked.

"I arrived yesterday," Yakup replied.

"Hmm. Going to England?"

"That's the plan."

"The plan," Rashid repeated and nodded in a cool manner.

"Yeah! I want to buy a ticket for the ferry and cross to England."

"Ha! You want to buy a ticket and cross to England," Rashid repeated.

"Yes," Yakup said in a low voice.

"You are a fool. There is no way that they'll let you aboard the ferries crossing the channel. The English are controlling the port on this side to keep us away from their side."

Rashid's brown leather jacket creaked as he dropped his arms and laughed at Yakup.

"But I have a passport. That was how I got out of Greece, through Italy and am now here, in France. I simply used my Chinese identity," Yakup said and proudly patted his breast pocket, where his fake passport was safely stowed. Rashid lifted his eyebrows and stared in interest at the place where Yakup's hand had just been.

"Let me see," Rashid said. Yakup hesitated and glanced at Mariam, who was still behind him.

"I don't think it is necessary…"

"Show it to me," Rashid interrupted and stepped closer. Yakup's heart pounded faster. He didn't want Rashid to see his fear.

"Another day," Yakup said and took a step back. Rashid moved fast. He grabbed Yakup, ripped his jacket open and pulled out the document. Then he pushed him away and looked at the passport with a smug smile.

"This will never take you to England. No point in keeping it in fact. Why, maybe I'll just help you out here, Yakup. You know, if they catch you with fake documents, they might punish you severely. Better to avoid that."

He pulled out a knife and stabbed the document a few times before tossing it at his feet.

Yakup watched his hopes of going to England flutter on the pavement. He bent down and reached for his torn identity papers. There was no chance of fixing the passport. Rashid's blade had gone through Yakup's Chinese face and cut several of the pages.

Yakup turned towards Mariam.

"Let's go," he said, suppressing tears.

She shook her head and took a step backwards.

"What is wrong, Mariam?" Yakup asked, reaching out to her.

He felt a hand on his shoulder. It was Rashid. He grabbed Yakup by his nape. A familiar scent of sweat clung to Rashid. Maybe it should have incited fear in Yakup, but the sudden rush of memories in Yakup's mind made him smile.

"You haven't learned to fear the predator, have you Yakup?" Rashid hissed in his ear. He shoved Yakup away.

"Thought you could get away with that trick of yours, did you? What kind of man leaves his sisters and mother alone, not to mention that old hag of a grandmother? A household of women in Afghanistan… And here you are, eh? Thinking that you can stroll up and take Rashid's property."

He nodded towards Mariam. Yakup turned and looked at the girl.

"How do you know each other?" Yakup asked. Desperation was growing within him. All his hopes and dreams were evaporating on a cold and grey day in the north of France with an audience that consisted of the very last person he ever wanted to see alive again and the very person he wanted most to have in his life.

"Didn't she tell you that we are together?" Rashid asked, moving closer to Mariam. He put his arm around her shoulder. She withdrew a bit. Rashid gazed at her with dead eyes. Yakup worried that he would harm her, but then Rashid's gaze turned gentle. She had a certain leverage over the brute.

"Just go," Mariam said to Yakup. Her eyes were pleading. "There's nothing for you here," she said.

"Better follow the woman's advice," Rashid said smugly.

For a moment Yakup stood still. He searched in Mariam's face for a sign, anything that might give him hope, but there was nothing.

"Last warning boy," Rashid hissed. He was only centimetres from

Yakup. "Or you'll end up like your father."

The shattered hope of a dreamt-up future brought Yakup back to life. He glared at Rashid and drove his foot into his testicles. Rashid was too slow to dodge the impact. He bent over and moaned. Yakup glanced at Mariam as he turned and ran off. He thought he saw her almond eyes fill with fear and pain.

He kept on running. He knew that the predator was only paralyzed for a short while. He ran back the way he had come, past the fortress, the scorched apartment block and the small wooden beach huts until he finally stopped in the dunes. In the lee of one of them, he sat with his knees tucked against his chest, resting his pounding head on his arms. He didn't care about Rashid or why he, of all people, should suddenly enter his life again, but the words about his family stung.

He cared about his sisters and Grandma Amaya and his mother. Of course, he did. It was Grandma Amaya who had arranged for his escape. It was her plan he was following by going to his uncle in England. Still, the fact remained that it was he, Yakup, who had left them. He cared about Mariam. It was not his fault that he had fallen off the truck and almost died. Nor that Mariam was nowhere to be found in Istanbul. Still, it was Yakup who had invited Mariam and her family on the journey to Europe and left them.

Somewhere a ferry bellowed in the thick mist with a hollow and mocking cry. On its deck were people who could cross the channel without a worry. People who had access to countries around them without having to fear the consequences of being caught or the consequences of staying put. People who did not know what it meant to live in constant fear of losing your life and of those around you being taken from you unjustly. People who did not know how it was to flee war and persecution. People who were ignorant of the danger of being an illegal human in a repressive state. People who did not have empathy for Yakup and others like him who lived as shadows just beneath the radar, in constant fear of being sent home, kept in detention or attacked. A lack of empathy that stemmed from ignorance, not evil. These people simply could not comprehend a life on the edge where one neither belongs nor feels welcomed enough to try. Politicians in these countries make decisions that cause people in foreign lands to flee and seek refuge. The people on the ferry were a different kind. They had rights, he didn't. Human rights weren't meant for ghosts.

67

INTERTWINED

If the ferries would not take Yakup to England, he would take himself. He got up and walked towards the sea. The pale sun glared at him, the wind had fallen quiet and the sea was lying lazy in front of him. He stretched his arms as he had done so many times before on the shore of the Band-e-Amir lakes just ahead of a swim. He kicked off his worn sneakers and tore off his pants, jacket and sweater. His bare feet slid into the cold sand. His uncle and England were somewhere on the other side. There was nothing more for him here.

The water cooled his legs. He shivered when it reached his crotch. He stepped up on his toes as it tickled the soft skin of his belly. Goose pimples popped up along his flesh. Yakup braced himself for the swim ahead. The water enveloped him. For a moment he thought of abandoning his plan, but soon his head, body and limbs had adjusted to the cold water. He moved his arms and legs. At first, he was rusty as an old engine—spluttering and kicking, but soon enough the old engine found its rhythm. Three strokes and breath in. Three strokes and breath in. Eyes opening with each breath of air.

On his right, Yakup could see the distant harbour where a ferry was about to land. On his left, he could see the beach that continued into the pale sky. Beneath him, he could see Afghanistan, Iran, Turkey, Greece, Italy, France and England. He could see the people there. His family in Bamiyan, smiling and happy. The bear-man in Kabul, vicious and growling. His cousin's lifeless eyes in two colours. A bearded border guard laughing. Mariam. An old couple in a green garden. Mariam. A forger of documents. Mariam. A shadow riding on a horse of fire. Mariam. A wooden house with Kurdish cousins and a secret attic. Mariam. Idil and Berk. The Afghan Band of Brothers. A smelly, crowded

311

cell. Malcolm, old man Elias, Mr Know-it-all and a vicious rope swinging. Boats, cars, trains and buses. Everything intertwined and divided with only one constant noise—Yakup! Yakup! Yakup! He caught the sound of yelling at every third stroke. It confused him and he lost his rhythm. He stopped and looked towards the shore. It was only 50–60 meters behind him. He felt tired already. Someone was on the beach yelling and waving. It was Mariam.

He returned to the shore tired and cold.

"What were you thinking?" Mariam yelled at him as he stumbled to the beach in fits of shaking.

"I… England… Swim…" Yakup's teeth were chattering.

"This may well be the most inconsiderate and stupid plan you have ever had. Do you know, how far it is? At best, 35 kilometres if you keep to the right path and if the current doesn't take you. Or if you're not torpedoed by one of the many ferries. Can you even swim?"

Mariam scolded him while he gathered himself and pulled on his moist clothes. When he was dressed again and his shaking was less violent, he looked at Mariam who was quiet by then.

"Why did you do that?" Yakup asked in an agitated voice.

"What?"

"Why did you stop me?"

"Do you want to kill yourself?"

"Why not? There's nothing for me here, right?"

"Don't be stupid, Yakup."

"You said it yourself," Yakup said, hurt and cold.

"Please. I expected more from you. Do you think I want to be with someone like that… that brute?" The look of disappointment she sent Yakup sliced through his heart. He was still shaking. His shoes were wet and filled with sand. He knew he must've looked pathetic to her in that moment.

"I know him…" Yakup said. "We went to school together. He was a bully. It was because of people like him that I left. Now he is here… and you are with him."

He turned away. He was trying his best to control the shivering, but it was an unfair fight.

"I left him to see you. He doesn't know where I am… but we have to go somewhere to warm you up, but also where he will not find us. Please, come with me. I want to hear your story. I have been so worried."

The compassion in her voice partly mended Yakup's wounded heart. He walked next to her, wet sand in his shoes and salt sticking to his damp and wrinkled fingers. They passed the rows of wooden groynes where a yellow dog was sniffing around one of them while the seagulls moved up and down the shore in their usual pattern. They reached the beach hut where Yakup had spent the previous night and crept inside.

As soon as his teeth stopped chattering, he told her his story. He wanted to tell her that she, Mariam, had been part of his journey. That he hadn't been alone that time at sea, or in jail, or when he was most depressed in Athens. She was always present in his mind, but now that she was here, physically, he felt more alone than when she was but an imaginary friend. He knew he missed the Mariam from the attic in Van but was unsure if he had missed the Mariam that was here with him now.

"I searched for you," he said instead, looking into her almond eyes. She smiled.

"I am happy to see you again Yakup. When I tell you my story, could you please not ask any questions?" Mariam said. Yakup nodded.

The wind was picking up again and the sun was setting outside the small hut. The sound of the sea and wind surrounded them in their small wooden cave.

"The day I lost you I also lost a piece of myself. It happened so fast. I have cursed myself many times for not holding on to your hand. Instead, I yelled and yelled until my voice disappeared. The driver never heard me. I couldn't move under the tight plastic sheet. Mother didn't know what had happened until we were hurried out late at night near Istanbul. They didn't care, the driver and the other passengers. No one cared!" Mariam had tears in her eyes. The sea sent gusts of wind and salt across the beach.

"Where are your mother and the girl?"

"I… I cannot… not now Yakup," Mariam said with tears in her eyes.

"I didn't know what to do after we lost you. We barely had any money and our documents were no longer being accepted. I told myself that you would come the next day. When you weren't there I told myself you would be there the following. I kept on like that for months. I never lost hope. I thought maybe, just maybe, you had continued. That you had crossed the border and were looking for us in Europe. I never dared to imagine that you were… gone… So, I made a decision to go and find you. My mother and the girl were helped by a charity organization and I spent my days in the streets of Istanbul searching for you when I knew my mother could, and would, devote all her energy to the baby, which she did."

Mariam took another sip of the drink. A ferry roared from somewhere in the distance.

"In the end, I couldn't find you. Time passed. And with Mother and the baby in a safe place, I made up my mind to go to England. This was the place we had talked about, Yakup. I thought that maybe I could find your uncle there and he could tell me where you were… or if you were… So, I started preparing for the journey. I knew it would be difficult, if not impossible as a girl, which is why I got myself some boy's clothes. I cut my hair short and tucked the rest under a beanie. But I still looked like a girl.

"I was walking on the street one day when I came along a group of Afghan boys. I kept my distance and observed them as they played a trick on people passing by. One pretended to be a cripple begging for money. When someone was about to donate a coin or two, one of the boys came up and pushed the 'cripple' over. At that moment a couple of the other boys would come up and tell the harassing boy off. He would run away, leaving the 'cripple' with the coins, while one of the other boys ran away with their victim's wallet. Ideally, the pickpockets would get the wallet, empty it for the cash and return it to the oblivious victim who would find his cash missing the next time he had to pay for a coffee or something.

"Their leader was brutal and stronger than any of the others. A savage. Rumour had it that he killed people in Afghanistan, and frankly, I have no doubt that he did. He never told me, but the way he behaves… If one of the other boys in the group made a mistake while executing their scam, he punished them. He would walk up to the unlucky boy and grab the skin of his chest and twist it until tears appeared in the boy's eyes. Sometimes the skin cracked open and blood seeped through the victim's clothes. And the worst part? He grinned while he was doing it. Yakup, Rashid enjoys hurting other people. That is what makes him so dangerous."

"So why are you with him then? Has he hurt you? Mariam, you would tell me, wouldn't you?" Yakup's voice rose.

"If I wanted to continue my journey, if I wanted to find you, I needed company. So, I went up to Rashid and started talking. I was scared, yes, but I needed him. He was rude to me at first, but after a while, it was clear that I could manipulate him. He isn't too clever and he quickly fell for me, I think. He told me that they were 'earning' their money to go to northern Europe. He wanted to go to Sweden. I didn't like what they were doing, but I needed them. I stole a wallet and handed the contents over to Rashid. It turned out that I have a hidden talent and am a very good pickpocket. I told Rashid that I wanted to work with them and travel with them. He agreed. Soon I was his prime thief. I was smaller than the others and the victims never suspected me. I looked too innocent," Mariam admitted.

"I managed to convince Rashid that it was better to go to England because the opportunities were better there. Whether he believed me or not doesn't matter and one day we up and left, travelling through Bulgaria. There we had a bad encounter with the police. They beat us up and told us to never come back. One of the boys had a bone broken in his arm. Another had his skull smashed open. It was ugly, but we all managed to move further into Europe. We lost a few of the boys on the way. One had a cousin in Austria and another a brother in Germany. Then there was one who disappeared as soon as we reached France. Along the way, two more joined us. That's how it goes, I guess... So, here we are today."

She smiled. But he couldn't. His heart was in conflict. His mind raced through stories of their future together and stories of Mariam and Rashid together.

They sat across from one other on the fishing nets. Yakup had found the remaining oats and tuna. They shared it and sipped the sweet liqueur. He knew he should be happy that he had found her again, but what really worried him was how far Mariam had gone with Rashid to achieve her goal. How many nights had they stayed together?

Maybe she could sense his unease, or maybe she herself needed to have clarity, but in either case, she said, "Yakup, I know what you are thinking, but it is not like that. I knew I had to get him on my side if I wanted him to help me reach England and so I charmed him. Fortunately, he fell for it. I think he thinks we will marry one day, but it is you who I want. Ever since the day I met you."

"Did he touch you…? Did you let him…?" Yakup's jaws tightened and his eyes narrowed. Mariam looked down.

"He tried, but I manage to hold him off. I told him that we should wait, follow the tradition and wait for marriage to consummate our… our affection."

"How can I trust you?" Yakup asked. A moment of silence followed. The wind howled through the wooden planks.

"I can only give you my word. If the things I did in my struggle to find you are now coming between us, I can do nothing about it. I can only believe that you are who I thought you once were; the same Yakup that helped a lost family on the border of Iran, the Yakup who took them under his wing and showed them his good heart and compassion. The Yakup whom I love and who I think still loves me. The Yakup that I want to make my future with. If you do not believe that, then there is nothing left," Mariam said, looking at Yakup and waiting a bit.

Then she got up and moved to leave the small cottage for the darkening beach.

"Mariam," Yakup said, gripping her shoulder. She turned with tears in her eyes.

"I trust you. You are mine and I am yours," he confessed, pulling her into him and together they spent the night in the windblown hut on the edge of their future. They mumbled stories of what would be and kept each other warm under the wooden roof covered by the same star-speckled night sky that they had first slept under long ago in a small green garden in Persia.

68

AN OPENING

Yakup woke up with a smile on his face for the first time in a long time. Mariam was breathing deeply next to him. Her skin looked almost translucent in the morning light. Her complexion had been darker when he first met her long ago on the border between Afghanistan and Iran and where the sun had been relentless. Her eyebrows were thick and a tiny bridge of hair stretched between them. Her breasts had grown. Two ferries brayed at each other somewhere at sea. A dog barked nearby. Yakup and Mariam had arranged the fishing nets to form a mattress and a cover. It felt like a bed fit for royals. Everything else was outside and far away.

Mariam stretched, yawned and opened her eyes. She blinked and after a moment, smiled.

"My Agent," she said and snuggled closer to Yakup. His heart dissolved with love once again.

They were eating from the stockpile and sipping water when Mariam asked Yakup what their plans were.

"I'm not sure," he said somewhat sheepishly with a mouth that had gone dry from the oats. "I guess it is to catch a ferry, go to England and find my uncle."

Mariam nodded, but it was clear that she was not convinced. "Do you have any suggestions?" he asked. She took a sip of water, turning over options in her mind.

"Swimming is out of the question. Others have tried and failed. There was an Asian woman some time back. She wore a wetsuit and had food and water with her. They found her body on the beach."

Mariam gave Yakup a concerned look that stung him. He knew he was a good swimmer, but he conceded with a smile that he was not *that* good.

"And the ferry?"

"I have been here for a few weeks now and it is clear that crossing on a ferry is very difficult. Some try to jump aboard the trucks, others pay the drivers, but most of them are caught even before they leave the port," she said.

"What if they catch you?"

"I'm not sure… Some are thrown in jail. Others are sent back to their countries."

Yakup handed Mariam the can of tuna. She sniffed it and left it untouched.

"What about your uncle? Can't he send you some money?"

"I don't know. I cannot contact him. I lost his phone number in Turkey. I kept it with my belongings I had back then and when England and my uncle still seemed so far away." Yakup said. "Maybe I lost it when I fell off the truck," he said, taking the tuna and stuffing a bit in his mouth.

"Was it the grey cloth bag you had in the truck?" she asked.

"Yeah… It was probably destroyed when I hit the ground," he said, trying to swallow the canned fish.

"But I know where that is!" she blurted out, grabbing Yakup's hand.

"What do you mean?"

"I know where it is," she said, standing.

"Come!" She tugged at Yakup's hand and started for the window.

"Where are we going? What's going on Mariam?"

Yakup was trying to keep up with her fast strides along the beach.

"When mother and I reached Istanbul we saw your bag was still there. We took it with us."

"Do you have it here?"

"No. Not here. It is in Turkey."

"In Turkey," Yakup repeated, jogging just to keep up with Mariam. "How on earth are we going to get to it if it is in Turkey?"

"If we're lucky, Mother still has it at the shelter. We'll call her," Mariam said, smiling at Yakup as she took off running. A ray of sun shone in between the white clouds that hung like chunks of woollen tufts in the sky. Yakup and Mariam were also elevated with a sense of achieving a future they had never really dared to believe in, but which was now, suddenly, within reach.

They passed the fortress and the skiffs in the small harbour. Mariam led the way and only stopped in front of a building where a group of Syrians were gathered.

"Wait here," she said to Yakup and pushed her way through the group into a small office. Yakup could see through the window Mariam speaking with someone inside. Then she stepped into a phone booth and rang a number. She stole glances at Yakup as the phone rang. The words tumbled from her lips. After a few minutes, she beamed at the receiver, made a couple of small leaps in the air, thanked the well-groomed man in the office and rushed out to Yakup, brandishing a scribbled piece of paper triumphantly.

"She was happy to hear that I found you and the phone number was there!"

They hugged and danced in a circle ignoring the people around them.

"I have an idea about how we can cross the channel," Yakup suddenly said.

"What is it?"

"You know how I told you that I crossed from Turkey to Greece in a small boat? When we passed the small harbour I thought that maybe we could somehow get our hands on one of those skiffs. There are plenty of them. Someone must have surely crossed the channel in one at some point, right?" Yakup said.

"I don't know… They are arresting those who help us. They charge them with people-smuggling," Mariam said.

"What are the other options? Strap ourselves under a truck?"

"People die doing that and most are not even getting all the way to England. I heard of some Sudanese men who clung to the hull of one of the ferries. It was sheer luck that they didn't die. They hung onto the side for an hour and a half and just as the ferry was about to dock at Dover port they were found and brought aboard. They thought they had made it, but the ferry was French and they were sent back."

They passed a line of garbage bins. Instinctively, Yakup peered into several to see whether there was anything that could be salvaged.

"Mariam, you and I have conquered challenges before. You remember, we crossed through Iran and then endured the tough walk across the mountains to Turkey. From what you've told me, your journey before we met and after we lost each other was filled with danger. This is the last step. Just over there, on the other side, is our future… When we have settled, we'll bring your mother and the girl… Maybe we can find someone who can help us cross… a freight ship maybe. Or a truck. Or a smaller boat. Something must be possible. Where there is a will there is a way," he said, giving Mariam a clever look.

"More like—where there are humans in despair, there are others ready to take advantage of their misery," Mariam frowned.

"Whichever… The point is that surely there must be someone willing to take the risk of assisting us in crossing if we pay them. I mean, what is there for us here?" Yakup asked. Mariam stopped and looked into the distance. They found themselves on higher ground and could see the ferries at port. The floating fortress lay, hulking, on the grey-green mass of water.

"We have to leave soon," Mariam said. Yakup took her hand and squeezed it gently.

"And we will," he assured her.

"Yakup… You don't understand. If he finds us, there's no telling what he will do to you… and me…"

"I will not let him touch you ever again. Never!"

"Then we must leave. Calais is too small. He will find us here," Mariam sighed.

69

FAMILY

They returned and made another call. This time Yakup joined Mariam in the small booth where they were forced to make physical contact. Mariam smiled and waved the small note with the green-penned number of the unknown uncle Amir in England.

Yakup started to worry. What did he know about this man, his father's brother? Nothing. Grandma Amaya had given him the note with uncle Amir's number and told him to contact him. All he knew was that he was his father's brother. Amir had moved to Kabul as a child due to an illness that could only be treated at the hospital in Kabul and had stayed with distant relatives who treated him poorly. In some stories, abuse was mentioned while in others he was treated as a servant. Regardless, when they decided to leave one day for Europe during the Russian occupation, they decided to take him with them. They just hadn't the opportunity to tell Grandma Amaya and it broke her heart when she learned he was gone.

Uncle Amir eventually parted ways with his relatives, scrambled around Europe for some years and ended up in England. The story was that he had brought shame to his relatives by falling in love with a local girl. In one of the stories, he had decided to leave them. In another, he had been told to leave. Whatever the case, Uncle Amir was his only relative in Europe and his only bastion of hope.

He held the receiver with a clammy hand while the phone rang on the other side of the channel. Five times it rang. Then someone in a hurried, coarse voice spoke into the speaker.

"Ello, Falstaff's."

Yakup could not speak.

"Ello? Who is it?"

"Amir?"

"Yeah! What d'you want?"

"Eh…" Yakup's mouth was dry and he was struggling to make sense of the coarse, fast-speaking voice on the other end.

"You wanna talk to Amir? Hold on…." The voice called to someone, somewhere, and then the phone clanked against something hard. Yakup could hear the blurred hiss of machines through the receiver. Then footsteps approached and someone picked up the telephone. He felt weak and worried that his voice would fail.

"Hello," a tired voice said.

"Amir?"

"Who's asking?"

Yakup struggled to reply but was suddenly overcome with anxiety.

"I'm gonna hang up," the man threatened.

"Amir khan!"

There was a brief silence. Then, "Who is this?"

"I am Yakup. Your nephew on your mother's side. I am the grandson of Amaya jan and the son of Ali Khan, your brother."

Yakup felt immense pressure mounting. He realised that he had no Plan B if his uncle Amir couldn't help him.

"Yakup? Is it really you? They've been so worried. Well, me too… of course," Amir said.

"They?" He didn't understand who 'they' could possibly be. Yakup did not know anyone in England. "You are one missed boy! Did you know that?" Amir said. His tone had changed from exasperated to comforting. "Where are you?"

"On the coast of France. In the town of Calais."

After that followed a stream of words from Uncle Amir, praising him for his bravery and resourcefulness. They talked for no more than 15 minutes, but in that time Uncle Amir managed to tell Yakup how Grandma Amaya had called him several times to tell him about Yakup and what had happened to her and the others in Bamiyan. Yakup listened in disbelief to the story that uncle Amir told him.

The lives of Grandma Amaya, his mother and his two sisters, Noor and Zahra, had taken a twist shortly after Yakup had fled. In the period after Yakup's disappearance, life in the cave had grown worse. His mother was more sullen and grumpier than ever, Noor, too, grew edgy, Zahra buried her sorrow in books and Grandma Amaya unconvincingly tried to keep up the little family's routine. It was not long after Yakup's disappearance, however, that a young boy knocked on the door to the cave. It was cousin Abdul's son, Mohammed. He was immediately invited in by Grandma Amaya and eventually broke down crying in her arms as he told her that his father had died. The boy had nowhere else to go and could only think of his relatives in Bamiyan whom he had never met. Grandma Amaya was relieved to have her great-grandson with her.

The arrival of Mohammed changed their lives for the better. It was as if the arrival of the boy reignited the family. For once they had not lost a family member, but instead, had gained one. Yakup's mother changed too. She became emotionally protective towards Mohammed and took him as her own.

Not long after Mohammed joined the family, he revealed a rather large inheritance from his father. It was an explanation that was rapidly accepted by the family. Only Zahra was suspicious. It didn't take long though before she too accepted Mohammed's simple explanation. The family's newly acquired wealth soon proved beneficial. Mohammed was pleased to have a caring family around him and therefore granted Grandma Amaya regency over the money. They soon moved from the cave further down into the valley to a brick-and-clay house with two rooms and a small kitchen. Not long after, Noor met a young man from a decent family in the valley. He was only a few years older than her. They fell in love and the wedding was practically a foregone conclusion. Zahra was still in school and number one in her class - a fact that had not gone unnoticed by the teacher. He had contacted an international organization that aided gifted children and youth with educational grants. They had agreed to provide Zahra just that if she kept up the good work. With Noor's wedding in the making and Mohammed's arrival, their mother had agreed, to both Zahra and Grandma Amaya's satisfaction, that Zahra could go on studying. Grandma Amaya still told stories in the evening, although she tired faster and sometimes drifted away in her thoughts. They all missed Yakup immensely and worried about him. Uncle Amir concluded by adding, "They will be thrilled to hear that you are alive and well."

70

PHILIPPE

They woke up before sunrise and walked down the abandoned beach. The horizon was just beginning to glimmer through the darkness and the morning mist. A jogger crossed their path. Her dog ran up to them with a wagging tail before it got distracted by a seagull and sauntered off. Yakup and Mariam held hands and walked in silence. This was it. The last leg of their long journey. A final push before they would achieve their goal. The deep roar of a ferry mumbled through the thick fog. Mariam stopped and turned to the sea.

"What is wrong?" Yakup asked, staring at the dark waters.

"You have to promise me that we will make it?" she said, eyes pleading.

"We will make it. There is a reason we met. We started together and now we'll end it together," he said.

"I can't wait to begin our future," she said. They continued walking towards the meeting point. The air was heavy with humidity and the morning fog blinded them. The eerie atmosphere would be an advantage in the upcoming crossing. They had arranged to meet Philippe further down the beach, beyond the bunker and then a couple of kilometres beyond where the dunes would shield their departure.

Philippe was a broad-shouldered local Frenchman with long tangled hair and a sailor's furrowed face. He wore a crude jacket and loose pants. The importance of Philippe was that he had a skiff and was willing to help them. They had paid him the remainder of their combined cash. It was not a lot and not enough for Philippe, but he had agreed to take the rest of the money from uncle Amir once they reached the British coast. Amir had bargained with Philippe by cell phone and an agreement was reached. Yakup was pleased with this development as it gave Philippe an incentive to deliver them to uncle Amir unharmed even though Philippe seemed like a nice enough guy and told them that he felt it was his humanitarian duty to help people in need. Still, Yakup knew from experience that trusting people could be dangerous, especially when Philippe's humanitarian duty needed money to be activated or what he called 'helping himself before he could help others'.

A man's figure materialised in front of them. The fog made it hard to see who it was, but they thought they recognised the broad-shouldered silhouette of the Frenchman. Mariam squeezed Yakup's hand and he felt a pang of excitement. He turned to her and smiled. They did find it a bit odd that four more silhouettes appeared behind Philippe, but by then it was too late.

71

REVENGE

Maybe it was fate. Maybe they should have been more cautious. Maybe they should have thought about the consequences of their actions. Maybe it was just sheer coincidence. Or, maybe if one of them had reacted just moments sooner they would have noticed that the silhouette was not that of Philippe, but instead a group of young Afghan men.

"Now who do we have here?" Rashid smirked. His leather jacket creaking.

"Did you really think that I would let this pass? That I would simply stand by and watch this… this *boy* sneak off with my property?"

Behind him stood four boys as dark as ghosts in the night.

"I'm no one's 'property'," Mariam hissed. Yakup held her hand tight. Rashid smiled viciously. He barely glanced at her, staring, instead, at Yakup who felt small and weak in front of his old classmate. The fog seemed heavier, the sea more hostile and the sand thicker.

According to Rashid, Yakup had stolen his woman, his 'property'. Nothing in Rashid's mind could change that perception, which meant that Yakup had dishonoured Rashid. For this crime, there had to be a punishment and in a tough world, an even tougher punishment was necessary. Yakup knew this and so did Rashid.

"You disappointed me," Rashid said. He almost looked as he assessed the situation in front of him. "But I have to give it to you girl— you played it well," he said, staring at Mariam. "A pity, though."

"Rashid…" Mariam began, taking a cautious step towards him. Yakup noticed Rashid's heavy fists opening and closing. The air oozed with tension. A cold shiver slid down Yakup's spine. He knew he had to do something. If not for himself, then for Mariam, but it was as if the fog made him react in slow motion as though in a dream where one's legs are leaden or trapped in cement. His throat was clamped shut with fear. He simply stood there, one foot behind Mariam, silent and weak.

"Come," Rashid said, gesturing to Mariam. She took a step back and her hand brushed Yakup's.

"No!" she said in a low voice, holding his stare. Rashid's eyes flickered. For a moment it seemed that he accepted her choice; just for a moment. Then he blinked with his heavy eyelids and hardened again. They were the eyes of someone who could pound a man to death, bashing the head into a mass of blood, brains and bone fragments.

"You have no choice… neither of you," Rashid said, beckoning to his group. They moved closer. It was then Yakup saw the tall, skinny Dani. His skin looked sick in the fog and he stared blankly at Yakup.

"Dani! What are you doing?" Yakup said. Another motion from Rashid and Dani reached for Mariam without looking at Yakup. Yakup looked at him in bewilderment for a second. Finally, Yakup's feet did as they should. He leapt at Dani.

"No, Yakup…" he heard Mariam yell, but it was too late. Rashid had grabbed him by the throat. His strength surprised Yakup. His Adam's apple was painfully squeezed under Rashid's firm grip.

"I will enjoy this," Rashid said with a sneer. Yakup could feel his sour breath on his face. He struggled with both hands on the strong arm that held him.

"Let him go," Mariam said from far away. He could feel his eyes bulging and his lungs screaming for oxygen. In a desperate attempt, he swung at Rashid and manage to scratch his cheek. It did the trick and a moment later he found himself panting on the wet sand.

"Pathetic," Rashid said. "You are a coward. Just like your weak old man, but at least he died fighting like a man. You fight like a girl."

Yakup pushed himself to his feet and panted heavily. He spat a mixture of saliva and sand, straightened himself and mustered his will.

"Do you remember that day by the lake, Rashid? That day when your older brother and his friends made fun of you? They tormented you. I know. I saw you… I understand how that must have felt. You were just a boy then. Rather than hurting each other, we ought to help each other."

Yakup was surprised at the growing strength in his voice, which was no longer croaking so much as bold and confident. He stared straight ahead into Rashid's eyes. It felt good. A couple of the other boys looked at each other not knowing what to think of this new development. Yakup continued, "We are here not as individuals, but as one. Why do you want to hurt me, Rashid? We have all lost… You know better than most how we struggle and fight our way through life. We see people all around us who have grown up on this continent with all these benefits and who have been fighting wars in *our* country. You and I came here for the same reason. Why do you want to hold me down? Let us work together, Rashid!"

Yakup could see the frightened, chubby boy in the eyes of the muscular man Rashid had tried to become. He could see that hurt boy on the shore of the lake long ago. He could see how the man Rashid had shielded himself from the pain his heritage had forced upon him, Yakup, Mariam and so many other Afghans. Yakup understood why Rashid was evil, why he had thrown stones at the innocent donkey a lifetime ago, and he understood why he treated Yakup as an enemy. Rashid was a victim. That sudden knowledge made Yakup realise that there was still hope. Hope for Rashid; hope for himself and Mariam.

"Yakup…" Mariam said in a low voice. Rashid shot her a look of malice. The suffering child was gone.

"Shut up… both of you. Shut up! I'm in charge here. When I'm done with you, I'll deal with your dishonest girlfriend here. Did you know how she led me on? The slut begged me to take her, but I told her that we must honour our heritage and…"

"You lying bastard!" Mariam interrupted in a rage. She tried to free herself from Dani's grip but to no avail. Her face was red. She looked like she was on fire with the vapour of fog whirling around her.

"At night she snuck up to me and tried to seduce me. I had to wrestle the whore off me," Rashid said, shaking his head mockingly.

"It's not true…" Mariam muttered. Yakup tried not to look at Mariam. He knew that Rashid was lying. He was almost certain of that. Rashid grinned and winked at her.

"You have to wait, darling. Tonight, you can enjoy all of us," Rashid said, gesturing to his group. "And you can be the guest of honour, old friend." He nodded at Yakup with vicious eyes and his mouth ajar.

Two of the boys pushed Yakup in front of them through the fog. They led them to the bunker Yakup had passed just days before. They entered the small, dank concrete room. Dim light came from the door and an aperture in the cement. There was a broken chair in one corner. It was tangled with a thick rope attached to a broken orange buoy stained with green algae laying in one corner. Yellowing newspapers, broken bottles and trash were strewn across the bunker. A dirty old mattress lay haphazardly across the floor. Yakup and Mariam were pushed onto it. The smaller of Rashid's boys didn't look well. His eyes flickered from side to side in a nervous manner. He looked like he was about to be sick. Dani was silent. The two others tense with excitement.

Rashid slowly strode back and forth on the dirty concrete floor. Each step seemed to reverberate through the dank walls covered in green growth. It reminded Yakup of the algae that he had long ago feared in the Bande-e-Amir lakes. From the shore, he peered at the green, treacherous-looking strands of plants just visible beneath the surface of the lake. They frightened him and he feared that they would pull him down as soon as they touched his thin legs. His father had carried him out into the water at first. It had seemed easy; the plants lazily swept aside as his father strode through them. There was a rope around Yakup's waist and he clung to the strong, sinewy body of his smiling father. The water beneath him. His toes occasionally touched the surface. Yakup retracted his feet with a jerk, but there was no avoiding the inevitable. His father dropped him in the water. He forgot the plants in spite of himself and at the shock of the cold, mountain water. He never gave the plants a second thought after that.

Rashid was with his back to them. He was staring out into the fog surrounding the bunker. It was impossible for anyone from the outside to see them. The damp from the mattress seeped through their pants and Mariam shifted uncomfortably.

"I bet you didn't see this coming," Rashid said turning. He held the rope in one hand. The orange buoy lay motionless on the floor by the end of it.

"Now, who should we start with?" He looked from one to the other. "Yakup! What do you think? You or the whore?" he asked, frowning and trying to sound like an interrogator. There was no answer. Rashid stepped forward and the buoy followed him with a hollow bounce.

"Rashid, we would have told you that this is not about you. Yakup is family. He helped my mother flee from Afghanistan and cross into Turkey. I had to talk to him. He had to know what had happened to her. I'm sorry if you misunderstood. This morning was our last walk. I told Yakup that I had to… that I wanted to come back to you. Isn't that right Yakup?" Mariam said.

Yakup nodded.

Rashid squinted.

"What is that? Did you hear something?" he asked, turning left, then right and theatrically gesturing to the other boys who were pretending to look around the dark bunker in an effort to find the source of the 'noise'. Only Dani did not seem amused with the playacting.

"Rashid, please," Mariam said, starting to get up. It took less than a second for the rope to hit her ribcage. She fell, screaming in pain. The buoy scuttled back to its owner across the cement.

"Stop it!" Yakup yelled and got up. His voice reverberated in the room.

Rashid stood still. The dark space went silent.

"All I asked was that you decided who came first. But you didn't, Donkey. You probably should have. It may well be the last decision you make."

"It doesn't have to be like this," Yakup's voice trembled.

"Decide."

"I… I don't want to. Just let us go, please Rashid."

"Last chance."

"But…" Rashid pushed Yakup to the ground. "Hold him tight. If he moves, make sure that he feels sorry he did. You two—help me with the whore," he said, gesturing towards the mattress where Mariam lay in the grey strip of light from the door. Rashid and two of the boys tied Mariam up with the rope while Dani and another held Yakup down. In the beginning, she struggled, but it was an unfair battle. Her hands were tied behind her back and she lay helpless on the wet mattress. Yakup caught her eyes. He could see fear in them, but no tears. Rashid noticed their contact.

"Now, donkey, I'll show you how to treat a whore" he said, grinning and moving closer to Mariam. She struggled to get up, but to no avail. Rashid stood tall in front of her. His fists opened and closed. Without warning, he bent down and lifted Mariam by the hair. A scream of pain and anger tore through the bunker. He kissed her violently. Yakup thought of the warm sour breath Rashid had exhaled on his face earlier.

"Argh!" Rashid yelped, pulling his head away and touching his lip to reveal blood. He spat and slapped Mariam hard. Mariam's mouth was bloodied, but there was a trace of defiance in the smile she now wore. He motioned to the boys. One for each leg. He ripped her jacket open. Pulled out a knife and slit her T-shirt open. The knife moved to her jeans. He slit them open. They were soon at her ankles. Rashid looked at his victim. The bleak light shone on the side of his face and Yakup could see his jaws tightening and loosening.

"Please… Rashid…" Mariam murmured through red, clenched teeth. Her lower lip shook. Her eyes were wet. Rashid's boys stared hungrily at her exposed body. He turned to Yakup with a vicious smile.

"Bring him here," Rashid said, and with that, they lifted Yakup to his feet.

"Dani, don't do this," Yakup whispered, "you're better than this. Please help us. We are brothers, you and I. Please, Dani."

"Shut up," Dani hissed and pulled his 'brother' towards Rashid.

"There's no need for this," Yakup's voice trembled as Rashid brought his knife to his chin. The metal blade rested just below his eye. He could feel the blade on his skin. "Pull his clothes off," Rashid said. Dani hesitated. Rashid noticed. "Now," he said in a low voice without breaking eye contact.

"But you never said anything about him…"

"You are as pathetic as you are stupid. Do as I say!" Rashid turned the knife in his hand. The blade shone vaguely in the dull light. Yakup stood naked in the dim light a moment later, ashamed and trembling. Rashid looked his nakedness over with a smile.

"Just a little boy," Rashid said, shaking his head slowly from side to side. "Well, I cannot see why she would choose you," Rashid said, laughing with a couple of the boys making a similar effort. The dank bunker resounded with their strained mirth.

"So, you want my 'property', eh? Then take it!" he said, gesturing to the naked Mariam whose hands remained tied behind her back, legs held open by the two boys. Blood was smudged on her cheek. She had stopped fighting. A tremble went through her body from time to time.

"Come now. I know you want it," Rashid, said, pulling Yakup in front of Mariam.

"Look at that!" Rashid whispered into Yakup's ear. "All you have to do is bend over her and stick it into her. It is easy. Don't you want to? Or maybe you can't? Doesn't your manhood work?" A smug smile spread on Rashid's face. His hand with the knife moved towards Yakup's scrotum. When the cold blade touched Yakup's skin a shiver went through him.

"So, what is it? Will you claim your prize or should I claim your pride," Rashid said, pressing the blade harder against Yakup's loins.

"Please, Rashid. You and I know each other. We grew up in the same place. We both played by the feet of the Buddhas, we sat in the same school, our fathers knew each other and before them, their fathers. You and I are the same," Yakup heard himself say.

"If we are the same, then why am I the one in control and not you? You and I are not the same," Rashid hissed into Yakup's ear. "You cannot even protect yourself. What makes you think you can protect someone else? You're weak and have been since the day you were born. And my father was nothing like yours, nor was…"

"STOP this madness, Rashid. I warn you. It will be worse for you," Yakup's voice rang hollow in the bunker as he interrupted Rashid. The small boy holding Mariam flinched at his sudden outburst. Rashid took a slow step backwards. He stared at Yakup. He nodded.

"Hold him down," he ordered Dani and the other boy. But they didn't react. "Hold him down, damn you. Or do you want me to slit you open?"

"Maybe it is enough Rashid," Dani said in a low voice. Rashid stared at him again.

"Have you forgotten where your loyalties lie? Or should I remind you who your family owes gratitude to?" Rashid threatened, moving the knife menacingly.

This galvanised Dani and the boy into action. They shoved Yakup to the concrete and held him down. Yakup cried out as his unprotected shoulder slammed into the floor.

They had been so close to reaching their goal, but instead, they were at the mercy of a traumatised psychopath, a sadist who bore a grudge against them. A ghost from the past that had reappeared. Yakup wanted to scream and cry his anger out, but he couldn't. He left his body and suddenly saw the clarity of the situation. One despotic leader, four weak followers; all victims looking for a way out of their internal misery. Abused by the world and now themselves abusive.

Rashid's voice pulled Yakup back to the stark reality of the situation. Both he and Mariam were naked in the cement bunker, vulnerable as subordinate animals waiting for their master's command.

"Now, donkey, this is what happens to those that disobey me. Watch and learn," he said, unzipping his pants and bending over to caress Mariam's naked skin. She shuddered in revulsion.

"Don't do this!" Yakup yelled. He struggled, but a knee was driven into his back and the pain paralyzed him.

Rashid laughed and bent over Mariam. Yakup closed his eyes tight. Opened them again. His head was twisted and held down with an arm. He could see Rashid bent over Mariam. Behind them the diagonal light passed through the door. The fog was lifting, the sun burning hot now, the grey blanket retreating and escaping from the madness within the bunker. Suddenly a shadow in the doorway. An animal. A yellow dog. Barking reverberated in the closed space.

The boys let go of Mariam. Rashid leapt up. Dani and the other boy loosened their grip on Yakup. Mariam drew a leg up to hide her nakedness.

"Shut up!" Rashid said, throwing a stone at the barking dog. He missed.

The dog barked again. Its tail wagged nonchalantly, waiting for what would happen next.

The fragments of glass from a broken bottle shimmered in the advancing sunlight. Rashid hurled another stone at the dog. This time it hit its target. The dog yelped and ran back out of the entrance to the bunker.

"Let her go!" Yakup screamed. He was standing up, naked and

furious.

"Dani! Why the hell did you let him go?" Rashid yelled. He looked around to find Dani in the bunker. He stood behind his master, silent and pale.

"Dani! Goddammit! What is wrong with you?" Rashid asked, turning towards him.

"It's enough," Dani said in a flat voice. He held the broken bottle in his hand. Rashid looked from the bottle to Dani's eyes. He tried a smile.

"Dani! My friend!" Dani moved rapidly towards Rashid. Rashid moved and stumbled on his pants and fell into Dani. A shard of glass pierced his throat. He managed to get on his legs again. His leather jacket grew wet and sticky. The small boy vomited in the corner. The other two looked at one another perplexed. Yakup grabbed Mariam and held her.

"Dani," Rashid gurgled. Dani and Rashid made eye contact for a moment.

"This is for my family, for me and everyone else you have tried to destroy," Dani said. Rashid touched his throat, but a bottle stopped his fingers. The impact made him scream, legs shaking. Rashid fell onto the mattress. Yakup pulled Mariam away. They quickly gathered their clothes. Dani stared at the dying Rashid on the dirty mattress. Rashid leaned back and fell into a ray of sunlight. The fog had lifted. The sun shimmered on the bloody glass. A gurgling followed bubbles of blood and something yellow and black. Dani was still standing in front of the mattress with Rashid lying prone. The other boys ran out of the bunker and into the sun. Yakup led Mariam out of the door before stopping and turning back.

"Dani…" he said.

"The donkey in Bamiyan, the band of brothers…. this. I'm sorry Yakup," Dani said, not looking at Yakup.

"What will you do?"

"I'll find my way. You two get out of here. Go!" Yakup turned away from Dani and Rashid who lay limp on his back with a broken bottle in his throat. Mariam had pulled her ripped clothes on and Yakup did the same.

"Let's get out of here," he said as they stepped into the sun.

72

SWIMMING

They are walking on the beach. Slowly moving forward. Mariam is leaning her head on Yakup's shoulder. He is holding an arm around her. He has blood on his hand. The cold saltwater won't wash it all off. They are dressed. She is wearing his jacket. He is in a T-shirt. Her pants are torn. A rope holds them up. The fog has almost cleared. Gone to sea. The sun is warming their still-shivering bodies.

"He didn't…he didn't do it," Mariam murmurs.

"I know."

He comforts her.

"Do you think he's…"

"It's over."

The dunes meander to their right, the sea licks the sandy surf to their left.

"So much blood… He must be dead," Mariam says. "I hope he is."

Seagulls take off and land.

"It is over, Mariam. We don't have to be afraid any more." Further up the beach is a skiff. A man sits on the railing. It is Philippe. He looks them over with a puzzled stare.

"You're late," he says, his thin, curly hair shifting in the breeze. "What happened to you?" he asks, scratching his chin.

"Just a delay," Mariam finally answers.

"Sorry, Philippe. We had to take care of something first… say goodbye," Yakup says and frowns. He hides his bloodstained hand in his pocket. An image: Rashid, Dani, the bottle. It flickers through Yakup's mind. It was surprising how easily the bottle perforated the skin. His heavy fall was only stopped by the sharp glass from the bottle. It was a clean cut that ripped the skin open and continued into the jugular.

"Hmm..." Philippe looks them over again. Hesitates, but nods. "Fine. We better move."

They pull the skiff into the water. First Philippe jumps in. It rocks under his weight. He stretches over the railing and pulls Mariam up. She stumbles and sits awkwardly on the bench. Yakup pushes the small skiff free of the sandy bottom. His legs are wet. He pulls himself up. Philippe lowers the small engine into the water and pulls the string. Smoke, a spluttering; once, twice; then the engine bursts to life. The dunes grow smaller behind them, a seagull flies next to them and screams for a moment before turning back to shore. Somewhere in the mist, a ferry lets fly a deep baritone belch. They sit together in the front. Philippe is in the back by the outboard controlling the skiff. Yakup looks at his hand. The blood is gone.

"Do you think, he'll be there? Your uncle Amir?" Mariam asks. Yakup nods and squeezes her arm. In the last phone call with uncle Amir, Yakup had learned that he had no children of his own. Not that he didn't want any, it just hadn't happened he had said with a forced laugh. Yakup sensed a sadness in his uncle's voice but didn't ask any more questions. Amir had instead started to talk about how much he was looking forward to welcoming them. Amir lives with his wife and he has told Yakup that he and Mariam can stay with them for as long as they like; they are family.

They agree that Philippe will set them ashore on the beach near Dover. Uncle Amir will meet them there and pay the remaining fee to Philippe. No one knows what exactly will happen after that.

A wave unsteadies the skiff. Mariam cries out and Yakup holds her tight. The waves are bigger out in the channel.

When Yakup first left Bamiyan, he didn't expect that the world would be so big. He had travelled across the world through Grandma Amaya's stories, but nothing had prepared him for the journey ahead.

His mind wanders to that early morning when he left the cave in Bamiyan and followed the path down the valley, taking his first steps into a new world on a journey that brought him farther away from home than he had ever thought, or wished, to go. He had left like a thief in the night. Maybe one day he would return. He had resented his mother for her behaviour. He had feared that he wasn't good enough for her to love him. That all seemed long ago. There was still a pang of guilt inside of him, thinking of her, but now he understands her better. She had lived a life of happiness and joyful expectation of the future to only lose two children and her husband. He had not understood her bitterness in the beginning; now he could see that she had not dared to experience anything else. Those she had loved had left her. If she allowed her love to shine on Yakup, or anyone else, they might leave her, too. Deep inside her, she had shielded her love for Yakup, Noor and Zahra. She could not, would not, allow whatever it was that snatched her other loved ones to take the ones she loved most of all.

The French coast is gone. Around them is only a grey sky. There is no wind. The engine is beating rhythmically. Yakup looks behind him. Philippe nods at him and indicates the direction they are travelling with another nod. He is holding a pipe that he occasionally puffs on. The rising smoke has the same shade of grey as the mist around them. It reminds Yakup of the mornings in front of the cave within the cliff near the empty spaces where the giant Buddhas once stood. Two of them. Both gone. Like his brothers. He had blamed them for taking his mother's love with them to the grave and blamed them for leaving him alone, but his brothers have grown inside of him since he left home. He feels that with each challenge that arose on his journey their legacy grew stronger. The blame he once felt is gone. A brotherly love that he has not felt before. The farther he has travelled from home, the more vivid his brothers are in his mind.

Mariam pulls his arm. She points to the left and into the greyness. A giant shadow is hovering behind them in the mist. It moves faster than their small skiff. Soon it is in front of them and disappears. It generates waves that makes the skiff bounce and bob. It reminds Yakup of the swan pedal boats on the Band-e-Amir lakes and how a similar sound escaped them when the pedals ploughed through the water and propelled the boats forward. They had frightened him a bit in those first summer days, but as his talent for swimming developed, he soon learned that they were easy to outmanoeuvre and easy to outrace. His father had taught him to overcome his fear of the water. He had taught him how to swim. He missed his father, but he no longer needed him to stay afloat. The man that Yakup had grown into could swim by himself.

Philippe turns the skiff. There, in the distance, is the coast. They look at each other, smiling. Their eyes have seen so much, but now they only see each other and their future together.

AFTERWORD

It was a crisp and cold January in 2008 when I first arrived in Kabul, Afghanistan, in order to take up my inaugural position within the United Nations Refugee Agency. At night the temperatures dropped to well below freezing and I struggled to keep warm. This despite having donned layer upon layer of clothing taking up a position just beside the Bukhari oven in the UN guesthouse in Wazir Akbar Khan—the diplomatic area of Kabul.

A few days later I visited, for the first time, an urban dwelling of displaced Afghans. They were among the more than five million refugees that had returned to Afghanistan following the fall of the Taliban only to find their land and homes inhospitable. With no clear access to jobs or income, they were forced to find an urban setting in which to look for work in a land that was no longer recognizable to them. I realised, then and there, that whatever cold I had felt that first night paled in comparison to what these men, women, and children were now faced with.

Children, in particular, were dressed lightly and in ill-fitting clothing with many wearing flip-flops without socks or other protection against the hard, icy mud surface that my sturdy winter boots easily traversed. Large families were crowded in tents and makeshift shelters where their belongings threatened to burst through the tenting. While there, a local truck arrived with food aid, and in an instant, everything turned to sheer pandemonium and chaos. Once the truck was emptied, however, calm resumed. Our mandate at that visit was to speak to different groups of people so as to understand their situation and conditions.

Once we had assessed the situation we returned to the warmth of our Toyota Landcruiser and deliberated on the assistance we should, and could, provide. It was clear to me that no matter what aid we could offer within a realistic frame, it would never be enough to sustain the many people in need. It was also at this point that I came to fully understand why so many Afghans continue to risk their lives in an effort to start over again in other countries.

A few years later on a hot and dry August in 2015, I found myself among thousands of people who were chaotically occupying a train station in the once sleepy border town of Gevgelija just on the southern edge of North Macedonia. Here were mothers, fathers, grandparents, and children as well as lots of others who had embarked on a perilous journey. They were refugees and migrants who had travelled from far away, across mountains, deserts, and the open sea. Refugees forced to flee their homes in Syria, Afghanistan, Eritrea, and Iraq, among others, washed ashore here hoping to be protected by the writ of human rights laws in Europe, and in so doing, live a life of dignity.

I was in the midst of all this and knew, only too well, that a few days before, the choked Greek border had collapsed and a crush of people moved into North Macedonia. They were met by jittery border guards and police who tried to contain the large crowd, by at first, their presence and commands, which eventually gave way to blows from batons and the firing of teargas. Those few tragic days could have been avoided and we all knew it.

This was just one mere incident in the so-called European Refugee crisis. Thousands of refugees and migrants chose this Western Balkan route as the most optimal way toward entry into the European Union where they hoped to get protection and apply for asylum under the 1951 Refugee Convention and its 1967 Protocol.

Regardless, the Greek asylum system was overwhelmed and incapable of processing such a high number of refugees and migrants entering their country via Turkey. With Greece becoming yet another barrier to entry, the route took many of them toward North Macedonia and into Serbia, from where they could enter the European Union via Hungary. Most continued through Austria and into Germany, where many stayed with others travelling still further north into Sweden in particular. It was not just North Macedonia that was ill-prepared, it was also the EU. Blatant violations of human rights towards the refugees and migrants took place along the routes from their countries of origin. Many lost what was most precious to them as well as the only thing they had left: Their life.

Each human being carries his or her own story, but the reasons for flight remain similar: the rule of law in their home country breaks down and they are exposed to violence, discrimination and other human rights violations, while others are seeking economic and educational opportunities in their quest to escape poverty.

The rise of nationalistic political parties and movements that are anti-immigrant and anti-refugee across Europe and the United States only makes it more difficult to garner support for refugees and migrants in developing countries; rather, vast resources are funnelled into preventive measures at the borders of Europe. NGOs in the Mediterranean region who are dedicated to saving lives at sea are penalised when they attempt to do so. Sadly, such policies lead to severe violations of human rights for those en route to the EU, with loss of lives at sea, and in Libya, a primary transit country for refugees and migrants, but also a country with a dysfunctional and fragmented state, where the rule of law is dramatically reduced if not broken down completely.

Somehow the shift of violations from inside the EU to outside its external borders seems to be more easily digestible for the Union. From a legal perspective that may make sense, but from a moral perspective it is highly questionable.

They are strong, the human beings who have the willpower to cross continents, and in so doing, do battle with a clandestine industry of smugglers who treat people as though they are nothing more than goods and not human beings as they. Refugees and migrants open themselves up to the mercy of legal systems they may not understand and try to re-establish themselves as human beings in countries where many locals consider them non-state persons at best and intruders at worst.

Imagine who these people are. They may be desperate, yes, but they are brave, courageous, and strong. They are a group of people who are willing to work hard in order to support a life free from peril. They are a group that should not be seen as a burden, but rather as a power supply to support an ailing Europe that has been struggling with an economic crisis for years and an ageing population.

Why is it that we leave this power hub of people in legal limbo? Why are they subject to a set of laws that they do not understand and which, sadly sees them return to a life with little dignity? We praise ourselves for the human rights standards that we have been fighting for so long, but we easily cast them aside when it suits us. Go to Afghanistan and see what the billions of dollars spent every year has done to these people, continue to neighbouring Iran and ask the Afghan refugees how their lives are. Next, cross the border into Turkey alongside your brutal smuggler and test your own stamina in the mountains before entering a small rubber boat near Istanbul in order to cross the frigid sea in the dark night and see if you can find Europe. Stay in an overcrowded detention centre for months, if not years, not knowing what will happen to you, all the while fighting to sustain your hopes and dreams, then move into a small shabby flat with 15 other refugees who all make their income by collecting scrap metal. Go on and prepare your meals from thrown-away vegetables and bread while looking over your shoulder every time you're in the streets to check for hostile locals. Then wait. And wait. Wait for years to get legal status and hope that you still have your dignity and esprit de corps. Welcome to Europe!

There are around 100 million forcibly displaced people in the world today. That is more than one percent of the entire world's population! The staggering figures constantly erase records on a scale never before seen. This is not fiction—this is fact. Almost 40 million of the displaced are children who are the most easily exploitable. They are increasingly exposed to violence and abuse given how frequently they are separated from their parents or family. It is estimated that on average one child dies each day on the Mediterranean Sea.

The refugee crisis is real. It is an explosive political topic in all countries around the world. Every day the media is ripe with stories about refugees, their struggle, and the perceived threat they pose to host nations. Dead children washing ashore in Greece, trucks filled with bodies in Austria and border police firing teargas along the border of North Macedonia and Greece are only a handful of the stories news outlets cover. What of those refugee camps forcibly emptied in Bosnia ahead of winter? What about the systematic beatings of refugees in Croatia by Government officials? That is the shrewd reality for many refugees with a legal as well as moral claim to life in an overtly connected world.

No, it is certainly not easy being displaced in today's world. The UN Refugee Agency reports an increase in displaced people every year followed by a decrease in the resettlement of the displaced by those countries that are supposedly the world's richest. These are cold, hard facts. These same pieces of evidence point toward a continuous increase in refugees and migrants moving into Europe from Syria, Afghanistan, Iraq, Libya, Sudan, and Somalia, among others. Despite mounting public debate and more media exposure, a real political change looks far off despite the growing number of refugees in need of assistance. The global forced displacement is dwarfing anything the world has ever seen before.

Behind each figure of displacement is a story of loss balanced by hope; shattered dreams buoyed by human resilience and the will to live. And so it is with the novel *The Boy Who Could Swim*. I have lived in Afghanistan, travelled to Iran, seen Turkey, faced Greece, and been to France, where I spoke with refugees and collected their stories. I learned about their dreams, their sufferings, their comradeship, and their loneliness. They told me who they used to be, why they had to leave, what happened to them on their journey, and who they became once they arrived. *The Boy Who Could Swim* is their collective story, as told through the main protagonist, Yakup, who is forced to leave the people he loves and the place he calls home: Afghanistan.

And remember: it may be you and I who end up in need of assistance next.

www.ingramcontent.com/pod-product-compliance
Lightning Source LLC
Chambersburg PA
CBHW061922220726
48287CB00018B/292